Lilly

Dave Pomfret

Dave Pomfret

Copyright © 2024

All Rights Reserved.

Lilly

iii

To Brier and Sarah (and Wee Ollie), and to Tierney Rae.

I love you. Thank you for your patience with me.

I'm just trying to get it right.

This book is an accident. The delivery system for creative works clearly malfunctioned, dropping a near-wholly complete novel into the scattered mind of a songwriter.

With the support and encouragement of these kind and generous folks, I managed to fill in the blanks, as best I could.

To my Michelle Morra: thank you so much for your love and encouragement. Writing our stories together has been the most magical experience of my life. I love you.

To my family: thank you for shaping the stories that formed this novel, even when they came from moments of heartbreak. To Larry, Laurie, Rick, Mom and Wimpy, Dad and Jean—you continue to influence me, no matter where you are.

To my son Brier: thank you for being the steady, unwavering presence in my life that Brad mirrors on the page.

To my daughter Tierney: thank you for never giving up on me, and for being the coolest huMan ever.

To Sarah, my daughter-in-law: thank you for complementing and completing my boy. You are an inspiration, and the best Mommy a Gramps could hope for, for his Grand Dude.

To Ollie, my Grandson: you are everything. I believe you sent this story to me. Thank you. I love you.

Lilly

To my Niecey Meg: you are my biggest fan, and I am yours. Thank you. I love you.

To my siblings Gary, Jan, and Ken: You know what the Old Boy was like. I hope you find some joy in these pages.

To my nephew Jayson: thank you so much for painting a perfect picture of what life is like as a student at Queens. You rock.

To Daniel Miller, Dave Kenney, Brian Miller, and the staff at Miller Shoes: Thank you for saving my ass time and time again. And thank you for your understanding while my focus was split between footwear and writing this book.

To my Fry Truck bandmates, Dan, Chris, Matt, Carrie, and Robin: thank you for your awesomeness, and all the music we have shared together.

A very special thank you to the poor souls who were forced to read early versions of the Manuscript: Brandon General, Jamie Tennant, Brennagh Burns, Mike Trebilcock, Chad Gupta, Luke Daniel, Colby Rawn, Amber Hamilton, Christine Edworthy, Kevin Land, Marc Cote. I can't thank you enough for your input.

To Martin Verrall: thank you for all the chats, the support, and for being the coolest guy I know.

To Joan KrygsMan: when I was about ready to throw my laptop (and this story) off a bridge, you stepped in with an editor's eye and saved the whole damned thing. Without your help, there would be no Lilly. Thank you.

To those who've battled addiction, mental illness, or loss: this book is for you. May it remind you that even in the chaos, connection and love endure.

And finally, to Lilly, who came to me almost fully formed: thank you for helping me tell this story.

Contents

Chapter 1: The Shrink 1

Chapter 2: Shackin' Up 6

Chapter 3: Light Bulb on a Train 15

Chapter 4: Fa la la la 20

Chapter 5: Fa la la la WTF? 41

Chapter 6: The Book Of Luke 46

Chapter 7: Water Wings 57

Chapter 8: Five Star 67

Chapter 9: The Blur 85

Chapter 10: This Won't Hurt a Bit 103

Chapter 11: Road Trip 136

Chapter 12: She's Come Undone..166

Chapter 13: The Great Gig in the Mind 183

Chapter 14: While You Were Singing 223

Chapter 15: The Messenger Came Today....................................244

Chapter 16: Through the Eyes of a Flower 265

Chapter 17: The Aftermath 278

Chapter 18: The Hardest Thing..293

Chapter 19: Celebration Time, Come on 320

Chapter 20: The Deepest of Cover..333

Chapter 21: Shrink Wrap 347

Chapter 22: Mama, I'm Comin' Home..370

Chapter 23: Do Not go Gentle 386

Chapter 1:

The Shrink

The morning grey began to peek through the blinds, just bright enough to startle my eyes from slumber. I felt groggy – still exhausted, really. I was fairly certain I had been dreaming, though I hadn't remembered a dream in decades.

Blinking at the intruding light, I scanned my now familiar surroundings. Room B116, Willow Grove Unit 1, Juravinski Psychiatric Hospital, my new home since the incident. It was utterly sterile, with walls the kind of grey you only saw on the saddest of days. One lonely light fixture (with a tone dulled to the hue of cold pea soup) tried – and failed – to brighten the surroundings. The furniture was… minimalist. A bed, a small dresser, and a desk with a chair. All the same grey as the walls.

The little ensuite was on the fritz, so I was sharing the communal loo down the hall with all the other inmates. I was in no position to complain. Not that I would have. Here, I felt safe – mostly from myself. At least I wasn't in jail, and I very well could have been.

This morning was to be my first session with Dr. Redwood. I had no idea what this young shrink was going to ask, and the last thing I needed was another "expert" trying to explain what was wrong with my brain. But I was willing to talk, regardless of the outcome.

I was getting dressed when there was a knock at the door.

"Mr. Isaac. Breakfast."

The door opened and the same young fellow who showed up every morning stood there again, with his stainless-steel tray of flavourless offerings in plastic containers. Herman was a nice kid. He didn't seem at all fazed by anyone in this place.

"I'll come back in about 15 minutes to walk you down to Dr. Redwood's office, ok?"

"Thanks, Herman. I'll try to scarf as much of this stuff down as I can."

I was nervous. How much could I say? Fuck it, I was already in here, and not likely to leave anytime soon. I would just go with it, embarrassing as it was.

Herman came back exactly fifteen minutes later. I had eaten all of the cardboard pancakes, and most of the plastic orange.

"You ready, Mr. Isaac?"

"I don't think I could be any more ready, Herman."

He wasn't listening. But then, it wasn't his job to listen. He wasn't a doctor. And besides, his attention was sharply trained on the very pretty young lady working behind the desk outside my room. Watching him, it was a relief to see people behaving normally, considering the shitstorm from which I'd only recently emerged.

Herman walked with me through two sets of doors, and down a long corridor. Everything was the same sad grey, but these walls were adorned with messages of love and hope from families of people who had killed themselves.

The office of Dr. Sarah Redwood was the last in a long line of name-plated doors. Her name plate looked as though it had just been installed that morning. Herman gestured toward a chair.

"Dr. Redwood will be right with you, Mr. Isaac. Good luck today, Sir."

"Thanks, Herman."

The entire floor was on lockdown. There was no chance of me – or any of the other lunatics – making a break for it. But really, I didn't want to escape. For the past week, they'd kept me so drugged up that I slept nearly all the time. My brain felt like it might be turning to mush, but at least I couldn't hurt anyone in here.

I'd been waiting no more than five minutes when the Doctor entered the room.

God, she is a child. How is she supposed to help me?

"Hello, Allan."

"Hi Dr. Redwood"

"You can call me Sarah. If you like."

"Ok, Sarah. How long have you been doing this?" She knew exactly what I was insinuating. There was no way in hell she'd had enough experience to help someone in my situation.

"Longer than you might think. Are you settling in okay?" She was dancing around my question.

"I think I'm okay. A little skeptical."

"Understandable. Are you comfortable in that chair? There is a couch, if you'd rather."

"I'm good here. Thanks, Doc."

"Okay. So, Allan, you know why you're here, correct?"

"Yes, I killed a Man. A young Man." It still felt like the words had to be pushed out, like garlic through a press.

"If that were all, you would be in prison. Why are you here at Juravinski?"

"I guess... uh, I guess I've been having trouble discerning reality from... well, not reality."

What an understatement.

"What does that look like for you? Can you explain?"

"If I could explain it, I wouldn't be here. It's nuts. It just doesn't make any sense."

"I have all the time in the world. You can take as long as you need, if you'd like to try."

"Can I ask you a question?"

"Absolutely"

"Are these sessions confidential? I mean, can I get in any more trouble? Can I get anyone else in any trouble?"

"You're safe here. Our only goal is to help you get better. No one will be in any trouble, I can promise you that."

"Ok. That's comforting. I'll be as honest as I can – but I'm still so confused."

"I understand. I've had a look at your file. How did all this confusion start?"

Boy, did I have a story for her…

Chapter 2:

Shackin' Up

In my mind, the entire ordeal had begun a few months before I found myself at Juravinski. About a year earlier, I had started dating Bridget Reynolds, an old flame, from a thousand years ago in college. She was tiny, forever searching for something to stand on to level the playing field. Her shoulder length, mousey brown hair – now just starting to show the years of blow dryers and dye jobs – framed sultry brown eyes that looked as though liner had been perManently tattooed around them. Her nose was a button. She was incredibly fit, with a devastating smile, and a laugh that could melt the polar ice caps.

I'd been married, with children – my son Bradley was now 18 and my daughter Tessa was 15. From her previous marriage, Bridget also had a 19-year-old son, Aiden, and a 17-year-old daughter, Pamela.

My family situation growing up was, well… fucked. Since my early teens, all I'd ever wanted was a "normal family." My parents divorced when I was 13. My brother Will and I grew up with our Dad, Reg, and Stepmother, Liz.

Dad was a drinker. Scratch that. Dad was a drunk. He would think nothing of downing a forty ouncer of vodka and heading out on a road trip. Every three or four years, that would start to weigh on his conscience. He would drive until he found a ditch as deep as his shame and park his car at the very bottom of it. He was a wonderful guy – just maybe not the best role model.

Our mother, Maureen, had also remarried. Her husband Carl lived with the goofy nickname "Siss" for his entire life. I liked him, but I never got used to calling him that – and we didn't see them much. Dad kept us busy with hockey and baseball. Plus, Mama Liz had installed a pool. Their house was just... more fun.

Will and I were a product of each of our parents' second marriages. We had three half siblings from Dad's first marriage – Garth, Fran, and Keith. They were all significantly older than us, all grown up and married with kids by the time my first memories began to stick. From our Mom's side, we had two half siblings, Rick and Lana. They were closer to us in age, so when I was little, they lived with us. To clear up any confusion, I have provided a diagram.

What it actually looked like:

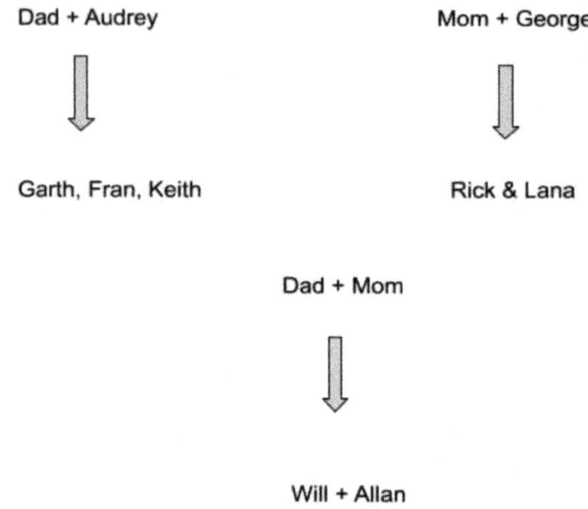

Then Dad married Mama Liz, who had no children of her own. BUT… Mom married Siss, who had three kids. Just to add to the mess. Their names were Dennis, Lisa, and Mickey.

What it FELT like:

Rick had given me my first guitar, so he has always held a very special place in my heart. The poor guy never quite seemed to find his way in this world, always after a quick buck, or a quicker high. He died at 37, with a stranger in his bed and a needle in his arm.

Lana was another story. She had the sweetest heart, but when she was 17 or so, she started having in-depth, three-way conversations with herself, and swatting at demons only she could see. My parents assumed she was "into the marijuana." By the age of 18, she was diagnosed with Schizophrenia. So much for "normal".

By the time I reconnected with Bridget, all of my parents were gone. Siss died of a massive heart attack right in front of Mom, less than two months after retiring. A few years later, right after Tessa was born, Dad's body finally gave way to the decades of boozing. Mama Liz lasted a little longer, a cigarette dangling from her face until the day the cancer took her. Mom was the last to go, the summer before I met Bridget and again, after a decade of living with Alzheimer's. Watching her, incapable of feeling anything but fear – afraid of anything from her own hands to the light in the room – was pure hell.

Bridget's family life had been far more stable. Her parents were deep into their 80s, but healthy. She had two siblings, Matt and Robin – both with solid marriages and well-adjusted kids. Bridget's marriage was the first broken one her family had known. That kind of stability was sexy as hell to me. With one fell swoop, I could have myself a completely normal life – or so I thought. I would come to learn that the only thing keeping me from that was my own crazy brain.

Two months into our new romance, Bridget and I moved in together. Our kids didn't love the idea as much as we did, but we did it anyway. She owned a nice house in Oakville. I did not own a nice house anywhere. The obvious choice was for me to move in with her.

Our joined-up family wasn't perfect. You could hardly even say we were a family. My kids didn't talk to her kids. Her kids barely talked to me, let alone my kids. My kids only visited every other weekend, and only if it suited them. When they were there, they holed themselves up in the basement.

Bridget's ex-husband had constructed a rec room down there, crudely tucked away in the far corner. To get to the finished part of the basement, you had to first navigate your way through the very unfinished part of the basement. There were beds set up down in that little room, so that is where my kids slept when they visited. It felt like they were on another planet. Bridget's kids were similarly absent. I assumed they were always in their rooms – or maybe they were in Russia. Impossible to know.

At the time, I was 47. Bridget was a couple years older. We were hopeful that the situation with the kids would soften, but we weren't counting on it happening any time soon. Part of the problem was me. This was not the first time I had jumped too quickly into a cohabitation situation. I could see that my kids were growing tired of the same old story. *"Hey, meet so-and-so. She is your new stepmom, and the love of my life!"* I could also see that they were growing tired of the whole idea of stepparents in general.

Step-parenting 101. Lesson 1. How to alienate your step kids.

Parent them.

There is nothing worse for a teenage step kid than a stepparent who tries to be a PARENT- parent. With very few exceptions, teenagers already kind of hate their parents, at least on some level. I had been a stepchild, and I knew all too well what it felt like to have some stranger look down her nose at me to remind me which colour toothbrush was mine, to Not Forget. Ugh. I tried to tread gently around Bridget's kids, because I knew how much they likely hated me.

Bridget, on the other hand, had zero idea that my kids would not be all warm and fuzzy with her. (Thus, the toothbrush talk. Seriously.) Their little basement cocoon seemed to drift even further away. I missed my kids. I missed being cool to them. Now, I was just the eye-rollingly weird old Man who shacked up with Mrs. Toothbrush.

I wasn't quite sure if her kids hated me, or if they had always been a little antisocial. I suspected it was a bit of both, mostly the former.

Bridget and I wound up spending most of our time in our bedroom. She was working on her Masters. Apparently, that was a necessity, for reasons that I never quite understood. Something to do with work and career and advancement to non-existent positions. Whatever the reason, it kept her very busy. Which left me very bored. I would lie on my side of the bed – reading, or sleeping, or daydreaming. Bridget would be off in study land, beside me on the bed, but in deeply intimate relations with her laptop.

Despite our middle-age, we were still so new. The whole thing felt like it was sinking into the same mundane void of shit that most marriages do. Was it me? Did I require "newness"? I really didn't think so – I was still excited. I still wanted all of us to be a big ol' happy family, playing Trivial Pursuit and Pictionary, laughing and drinking eggnog in ugly Christmas sweaters.

Trump had just been elected as the President of the United States. There was a general feeling that the bottom of the world had fallen out. The sense of doom seemed to make everyone in our little household want to cocoon even more.

Christmas was approaching and I wanted to coax Bridget out of her laptop, and the kids out of their respective caves. I needed to find a way to bring us all together, to somehow lighten the malaise – because I do not swim well in mundane shit voids. I knew that if we couldn't find some spark, some commonality, I would slowly drift into myself. And I would leave. I had a history of leaving. I did not want it to come to that. Again.

One evening, Bridget yawned and folded up her laptop a little earlier than I expected. I had been reading, but was more than willing to toss the book aside if shenanigans were a possibility. Alas, shenanigans were not a possibility.

"Wow, I'm tired tonight."

That statement shot down any hope.

"Maybe early to sleep tonight?" I asked.

"Yeah. I think so. Sweetie, I'm still into you. You know that, right?"

"I know, Babe. But thank you. I needed to hear it."

We took turns in the bathroom, and crawled into bed. After sharing a goodnight kiss, we pulled the covers up. But before I could close my eyes, Bridget reached over and touched my shoulder.

"Al! Wouldn't it be nice if the kids hung out more?"

"Yeah. It would. Maybe in time?"

"Maybe. I don't know. Maybe we should have a baby? You and me! You know, to bring everybody together!"

We both laughed out loud; we were too old, I had been snipped a decade earlier, and the idea of having a little person around made me cringe.

"I wonder what our kid would look like? Would you want a girl or a boy?"

Now she was just fantasizing. I'd been in several relationships well past my fathering days, and this particular conversation seemed to be inevitable. I offered the same answer I always did.

"I think we'd have a girl. And I think she'd be beautiful, just like her Mamma!"

"Ahhh. Thanks, Hun. Goodnight."

“Goodnight, B. Sweet dreams.”

We kissed again, closed our eyes… and that was that.

Chapter 3:
Light Bulb on a Train

There was one problem with moving into Bridget's house in Oakville – I didn't own a car at the time. I still had my job at Miller Shoes in Hamilton, and the walk from Bridget's to work would have been... a long one. Thankfully, the provincial commuter train ran frequently from Oakville to Hamilton.

Still, to get from Bridget's house to Miller Shoes was a 4-step process. First, Bridget would drive me the three kilometers to the Bronte GO station. She had to get to work too, so that meant I was a little early every day. Almost every other passenger was travelling the other way (toward Toronto), so I generally had an entire car to myself. The ride would last about 25 minutes, coming to a stop at the Aldershot station. I'd disembark, and then walk through a long underground tunnel to where the bus was waiting. The bus ride was another 20 minutes, to City Hall in downtown Hamilton. From there it was a ten-minute walk to Miller Shoes. Getting home was the same trip in reverse. Every day.

I'd never been a commuter before. I hadn't known there was a magical place where, for a few minutes every day, I could be alone with my book, or my thoughts, without a soul to distract me. Had I known, I might have found a reason to ride trains much earlier in life. The quiet was heavenly, a rare time when I could explore corners of my mind I'd never visited. And I loved reading. During those few months, I was ploughing through at least a book a week, losing myself in dysfunctional family dramas like The Corrections by Jonathan Franzen, and journeying through father-son dynamics in Cormac McCarthy's The Road. I even felt a strange affinity for ColeMan Silk in The HuMan Stain.

I had a few other indulgences for my soul. Although I was not enough of a rockstar for my kids (or step kids) to find me cool, I was in the midst of recording my second record. I could listen to early mixes, over and over again. There was no one around to be offended by the noise escaping from my shitty earbuds. The record was sounding great. I was reading amazing books. Life on the train was… glorious.

Then there was my newly discovered pseudo-talent: sketching. A few years earlier, I had replaced my very stupid phone with a slightly smarter one and discovered I could draw pictures with my finger on the screen. With the indispensable help of the eraser function, I could make squiggly lines and curves look like the faces of Instagram friends. I would post sketches and ask Insta-Land to guess who I had drawn; it was a fun little game. My sketches were no more than digital stick figures at first, but I was getting better.

One mid-November morning on the train to work, I realized I'd forgotten my book. And my ears needed a break from listening to my still-unfinished record. After scrolling for a while… an idea! A REALLY cool idea! I would sketch what a child might look like if it was fathered by me, and mothered by Bridget. I was tickled with myself. For reference, I could use pictures of my daughter, Tessa, and Bridget's daughter, Pamela. If Bridget and I had a daughter together, I thought she might look a little like both of our girls. Brilliant.

With most of my sketches, it was still difficult to tell if I was trying
to draw a face or a shoe. I really wasn't all that good. But lightning struck
in that moment, and I nailed it. In five minutes, I managed a surprisingly
believable rendering of what our girl might look like. I gave her red hair,
and green eyes. She looked smart, and confident. She had Tessa's longer
face and nose, and Pam's eyes, angled slightly downward at the corners.
Almost sad – but still, they seemed to dance off the screen. Lilly looked...
alive. I texted the image to Bridget.

-Hey, Babe, meet Lilly!!

Her response was decidedly… meh.

-Cool. Who is that?

-Ha! Try to guess, B.

-Busy right now. I will in a bit. Xo.

Well, shit. Here I thought I'd created a masterpiece, and Bridget
was about as excited as she would have been if I had drawn a shoe. And
speaking of shoes, I climbed off the bus and walked the ten minutes to
Miller's to try to sell some. My dream of being the next Van Gogh
evaporated.

With the store very slow that day, there was more time for my
brain to spiral into the tornado of all things Lilly. Maybe this little sketch
could bring the family together? Maybe Lilly was the missing ingredient?
The common thing? She could become something more than just a sketch.
I could create an identity for this kid. She could have an email address – a

backstory. This could be so much fun. How could I introduce her to the kids? Would they think I was nuts?

CHRISTMAS! That was it. Perfect.

Everyone would get a gift from their big sis, Lilly, along with an email. I would have to keep it light, so everyone would know it was all tongue-in-cheek. And just like that, Lilly was born!

There was finally a text from Bridget, just before I hopped back on the bus.

-Great sketch. New co-worker? She's very pretty.

Damn. I was hoping it would be more obvious. I'd have to explain when I got home.

That night, I took an Uber home from the GO Station because Bridget was already brain-deep into her laptop, and didn't want to take a break to pick me up. When I walked in, she peered up, just long enough to notice me.

"Hi, Sweetie! How was your day?" she asked.

"Not bad. Pretty slow. I was really hoping you would be able to guess who the sketch was supposed to be."

"Oh, yeah. That was cool. Not a co-worker?"

"Nope. No other guesses?"

She thought for a second, then shook her head.

"I got nothin'."

"Really? Nothing familiar?"

She continued to shake her head.

"Lilly is… the daughter we never had! I used Tessa and Pam as reference, kinda. Can you see it?" I shoved the sketch in her face again.

"Ohhhh… wow, that is sweet. Yeah. I can see some similarities. Very cool. We should frame that."

Not exactly a ringing endorsement, but it was at least positive. She thought it was sweet. The wheels were in motion. Lilly would be a part of our first family Christmas.

It would be upon us before we knew it.

Chapter 4:
Fa la la la

I had three weeks to create Lilly's backstory, buy gifts for each of the kids, and put the emails together. I felt like this was the best idea I had ever had – the best idea ANYONE had ever had. I let the idea marinate for a few days. Having decided to use up some holiday time, I would be off from the 20th until the 27th of December. There would be a couple of days before Christmas to put everything in place.

I decided that Lilly was a student at Queen's University in Kingston. She was in her fourth year, studying medical science. She was vegan. She and her boyfriend, Nick, had spent the previous Christmas with Bridget, so this year they were with Nick's folks in Montreal. She knew that there was a tentative unease in the family, now that it was all under one roof. And she wanted to be the one to break down the walls. Other details were coming to me, but I had the basics – everything I needed to make her plausible.

And the gifts. For Bridget, I planned to frame the sketch I had done, and include a letter from Lilly wishing she could be with us for our first Family Christmas together. For the kids, my hope was to get each of them one thing – something that would combine with all the other kids' gifts, making something they could all share. But what could it be? I spent a few days wandering through craft stores, witchy stores, hobby stores, but nothing jumped out at me. Until a trip to the grocery store to pick up a few appetizers.

It hit me in aisle six. WHAM. BOOM. I had it!

Each kid would receive a mason jar with an ingredient in it. Brad would get a jar of cocoa powder, Tessa would get sugar, Aiden would get oat milk (that lid would have to be screwed on super tight), and Pam would get a mixture of cinnamon, cayenne, and crushed candy canes. Heat that stuff up in a pot and VOILA! The tastiest Mexican Christmas Cocoa in the History of Holidays!

But... WRAPPING! Shit. It would have to look like a talented girl did it – not like the work of an eye-rollingly weird old Man. AH-HA! Nadene was a friend who put together really cool gift baskets – and I was willing to pay her a fortune to make this stuff look believable. I bought all the jars and ingredients and headed to her shop.

When I walked in, I could see that Nadene was absolutely overwhelmed with work. Piles of flowers, wicker baskets, and so much cellophane it felt like a magic house of mirrors.

"Hey Al! Merry Fucking Christmas!" Her voice full of the wonders of the season.

"Deeny, you're going to kill me."

"Ah, no I won't, Buddy. I'll just say NO! Absofuckinglutely NOT!"

"I haven't even asked yet." I was certain I could charm her.

"NO! Get the fuck out! Merry Merry!"

"How about I just tell you a wee story whilst you work away? You know, keep you company for a bit."

"You're an asshole, Isaac!"

"Ah, that is sweet of you, my friend. Let me tell you about Lilly! But you have to promise not to tell anyone, ok?"

"Fuck off." She seemed to mean it.

"Alright ol' Buddy. Have a wonderful Christmas."

Shot down in flames, I headed for the door, resigned to wrapping the stuff myself. But before I even touched the handle, Nadene barked from behind a bouquet of Teddy Bears.

"Who the fuck is Lilly? Are you having an affair?"

I had her! That was all I needed. Explaining my idea – how I wanted to bring our family together – I could feel her mood soften as I detailed how Lilly came to be.

"Damnit, Al! You are a sweet asshole, but you are still an asshole. Just leave all the stuff there. I'll have something put together for tomorrow."

"Deeny, you are a fucking ANGEL! Thank you soooooo much!"

Chuffed, I left everything with Angel Nadene, and headed home. I knew she would come up with something spectacular.

December 21st and I still had a couple days to write the tear-jerker email. I let the whole thing float around in my mind, like a kid on an inner tube. Lilly was forming in my brain all on her own, it seemed, and I was letting her come to me.

I propped up my laptop, opened G-mail, and clicked on "Add another account". I wondered if there was anyone else out there in this great big world who spelled LiLLy with three L's. I had known a few LiLy's in my life, and I knew the flower only had the two L's – but when she came to me, LiLLy was LiLLy, and that would be her name. I typed in my first hope, lillyisaac@gmail.com. No luck. There were others out there. The suggestions that were generated were the typical invert-names-add-numbers options. I did some mental mathematics to determine how old Lilly would be, and came up with a birthday for her. July 16, 1993. Happy Birthday Kid! I typed in lillyisaac93@gmail.com. Success. Lilly was coming to life. She had an actual email address, and a date of birth to prove it.

I decided I would send one email, the same one to all four kids. I needed to do it right. It had to be fun. It had to be cool. And (most importantly) it couldn't make me look too crazy. I hovered my hands over my laptop keyboard, all Ouija-like, and waited for divine inspiration.

It came – an email for the ages. The kids would all receive the message at the same time. There would be a little note included with each gift, "Merry Christmas! Check your email." We planned to exchange gifts on Christmas Eve, and my kids would arrive around lunchtime. My secret hope was that the family would all hang out and do the Trivial Pursuit/Pictionary thing, but I wasn't counting my chickens. Sometime after dinner, we would all gather around the tree, and for the first time, I would play the Santa guy, doling out the presents.

Bridget's house was practically devoid of decoration. The walls were naked. The only pieces of art were on the floor, leaning against the wall, underneath the spots ON the wall where they might one day hang. She was terrified of putting holes in her freshly painted walls. And apparently paint is considered fresh for at least five years. With no curtains or blinds, the windows were like giant telescope lenses. Onlookers the world over had a clear view of our desolate domestic landscape.

But, this Christmas, there it was – the tree. An oasis of joy in an otherwise lifeless space. And I believed that once Lilly was introduced to the family, that joy would fill the room. It would bring our home to life.

On the 23rd, I got a call from Nadene. The gifts were ready to be picked up. That was the last thing I had to do before the big reveal. I told Bridget I had some last-minute shopping to do.

"Ha. Men!" She shook her head and snickered. "Last minute much?"

"I know, B. I just had an idea. I think it's pretty cool."

"Ok babe. Can you stop at the liquor store too? We could use some wine. Maybe some rum too."

I hadn't had a drink in six years, but I didn't mind. I knew she would be busy getting everything ready at the house.

"Alright, love. No problem. I won't be long."

I gave her a peck on the top of her head and was on my way. I stopped at the LCBO first. The parking lot didn't seem too nuts yet, and I thought I could beat the rush.

I had been a very drunk guy for a lot of years, but six years earlier, in April of 2010, I had managed to get my ass sober, and I stayed that way. Temptation was not an issue – it just didn't happen to me. Once you realize that booze is a big, fat, nasty liar, you don't want anything to do with it – ever again.

There was no line-up in the store. I grabbed a bottle of white, a bottle of red, and a 20oz bottle of rum. Bridget had already bought the eggnog, so we were all set for bevies.

My phone was buzzing when I got back to the car. It was Nadene.

"Hey, Deeny."

"Hey. Are you on your way? I have to take off super soon. Bit of an emergency going on."

"Ok Buddy. Everything ok?"

"Ya. It's just Mario being Mario. A Mario emergency."

"Ahhh, fair. I'll see you in ten."

"Thanks, Al."

Nadene and Mario had been married for a long time. Once in a while, Mario would get himself all tied up in knots over why he couldn't find his pants, or remember what colour toothbrush was his. Nadene had more patience than anyone I knew, in perfect contrast to her profanity-laced bluster. When I got to her store, she was waiting at the door with a giant bag in her hand – and looked exhausted.

"Hey, Deeny. Thanks, so freakin' much. Seriously. I owe you, Buddy."

"Yes, you do!"

I knew it; she'd done me a gigantic favour.

"Merry Christmas to you and Mario and the kids."

"Thanks Al. Same to you and B, and all the kids. Including this Lilly brat. Oh, you're not allowed to peek. I want you to be surprised too."

"Ok, Buddy. I promise I won't peek."

We shared a quick Christmas hug, and I headed home.

Bridget had the place looking cozy – or at least, as cozy as she could. She had decked the halls with boughs of holly. Well okay... she'd lit some candles and tossed some garland around. A line of stockings dangled from the fireplace mantle. Cozy enough.

"Did you get the wine? I could use a glass."

"Yup! I can pour you one? White or red?"

"Red. For Christmas!"

I poured her a glass of red and brought it to her on the couch. Sitting down next to her, I could see the other gifts were already under the tree. With the gas fire glowing and the tree all lit up... it felt like Christmas.

My plan was to wait until everyone went to bed, and then tuck the giant bag with Lilly's gifts behind the tree. I wanted it to feel as though Lilly had dropped the bag off in the middle of the night.

The hour was getting late, and we were both too tired to cook, so we had pizza delivered, and Bridget finished off another glass of wine with her two slices.

"I'm heading to bed. You coming?" she asked.

"I won't be long. I just have a couple things to do. Right behind you."

"Okay, Babe."

I couldn't tell if she'd given me a come-hither look, or if she had something in her eye. The way things had been going, I suspected the latter.

Once she was in bed, I snuck out to the car to grab the bag. There was a perfect spot right behind the tree, where the cat must have been snoozing earlier when Bridget put the gifts out. Lilly's bag of presents had a home.

By the time I got to bed, my lady was already snoring – must have taken care of that speck in her eye.

I barely slept that night. I was as excited as I ever had been for Christmas. When the day broke on Christmas Eve, I was already up. Bridget and I made breakfast. Her kids poked their heads out of their bedroom doors, and did not see their shadows – so even they joined us at the table. My kids would be arriving in the early afternoon, and Aiden and Pam seemed excited, which was a first. I was surprised they even remembered I had kids. Pam ate like she hadn't eaten since the last time she left her room (which may have been the case). She finished before anyone else, and excused herself.

"I'll be right back; I just have some wrapping to do."

Aiden jumped up. "Shoot. Me too. Totally forgot." He swallowed roughly five waffles whole, and headed back to his room.

Bridget looked agitated. "Maybe not so much weed all the freakin' time, guys?"

Both Aiden and Pam practiced the ancient art of tokery. They were experts, and Bridget didn't mind. They did it at home more often than not, so at least she knew where they were. But it did mean that they lacked focus.

"It's no big deal, B. We have lots of time. Zero hurry," I reassured.

She was always anxious when my kids were visiting. She so desperately wanted them to like her, but it was an uphill climb. I had a feeling that this Christmas would turn things around, maybe flatten the grade of that climb a little. There were still a couple of hours before my kids were scheduled to arrive. Beyond showers and donning our gay apparel, we were ready.

Pam and Aiden put their freshly wrapped presents under the tree, and we all got ourselves gussied up. Tessa sent me a text saying they were on their way. Brad and Sierra had just picked her up. They had a half hour drive from Hamilton, which gave Bridget time for a nerve-calming rum and eggnog, and her kids time for a quick puff. I was bursting at the seams to reveal our new family member. It felt like forever before the doorbell rang, but when it finally did, I opened the front door to my favourite sight. Brad stood behind Tessa and Sierra. Three gigantic smiles. They clearly had rehearsed a greeting; Brad counted in.

"Feliz Navidad," they sang in unison – one of my favourite Christmas songs.

"Merry Christmas guys! C'mon in. Let me take your coats. Brad, you can just put the gifts by the tree."

It felt so strange to me that my kids still felt the need to knock – and that I took their coats – like they were guests. We had never been a huggy bunch – not since they were little, at least. I was shocked that they all gave me, and Bridget an almost-enthusiastic Christmas squeeze. They even acknowledged Pam and Aiden with a genuine smile-and-nod "Merry Christmas" and were acknowledged back in kind! It already felt like the best Christmas ever.

Now, I was feeling some trepidation. I really hoped they wouldn't think I had gone off my rocker with this Lilly stuff, but they were all smart kids; they would know that I was just trying to bring us all a little closer together. I hoped.

We were inching closer to Lilly's big reveal. The plan was to have Christmas dinner, then gather around the tree to exchange gifts. I was anxious. Bridget had the turkey in the oven. The air in the house (for once) did not have even a hint of weed stink – it smelled like Christmas. I laid out the appetizers: shrimp, crackers and cheese, veggies and dip – the usual suspects – then went back to help Bridget in the kitchen.

Brad instinctively grabbed my guitar and started to noodle. He was a very large dude, and my guitar always looked like a toy in his hands.

"You play too?" Aiden asked.

Wow. Brad played just about every instrument known to man, and Bridget's kids had no idea. He nodded, and noodled away. Tessa, Sierra, and Pam took turns complimenting each other on how pretty they looked – and they did look pretty. Tessa was model-gorgeous. Blonde hair in rolling waves. Huge blue eyes. And a wonderful softness that made her instantly likeable. Sierra had been Brad's girlfriend for three years already. She was a lovely girl with long brunette hair, big brown eyes, and a confident smile. They seemed like an old married couple, and I was certain that's what they would be one day. Pam was cool. She acted like she didn't care what anyone thought, and worked very hard to maintain that appearance. She changed her hair colour almost hourly. At the moment, it was stark black, with a patch of purple hanging over her right eye. A nose ring had recently been added to the ensemble. I hadn't noticed it until just now.

"Would anyone like a wee drinky?" I offered the brats.

At this time of year, I wasn't too concerned about legal drinking ages. Tessa and Sierra asked for Cokes. Brad, Sprite. B's kids were all over the rum.

"Pam, you girls can set the table, ok?" Bridget instructed from the kitchen.

Tessa and Sierra had no clue where the dishes might be, and I was fairly certain Pam didn't either. Bridget was on the Mother train again.

"I've got it Babe – let the kids chat for a bit."

Al to the rescue. Disaster averted.

Once I had the table set, everyone took a seat. We were about to dig in.

"I'll say grace," Brad offered.

God. Please don't make us hold hands. Please do NOT make us hold hands.

"Dear Lord, we thank you for your abundance. We ask that you bless this food which we are about to devour, because it smells absolutely delicious. We thank you for delicious smells. We thank you for family, and for extended and new family. In Jesus's name, Amen. Pass the rolls."

Phew. No hand holding. Brad's sense of humour belied his tender years. He was already in Dad joke territory, but it worked. He made us laugh – all of us – even Pam and Aiden.

Damn, maybe this crew doesn't need any help at all. Is the Lilly thing even necessary?

The doubt was growing stronger, but I was in too deep. My investment of heart and soul, too great. The show must go on!

This meal was beyond decadent. With Bridget as the main chef and me as her sous, it was... magnificent. All the usual fixings, with an added dash of *"I'll show them how awesome I am!"* tossed in for good measure. Everyone had seconds, Brad had thirds. And he was the one insisting we have dessert immediately. I was stuffed, and super-excited about introducing Lilly, so I made the executive decision to postpone the dessert, much to the relief of all but Big Brad. I knew we had the Mexican Christmas Cocoa coming up. He would not have to wait long to satisfy his sweet tooth.

"Let's do the gifts. Dessert can wait a bit."

I took my place on the floor by the tree and Bridget pulled her chair from the table to sit beside me. Aiden settled into the La-Z-Boy chair right next to her. Brad and Sierra cozied up on the loveseat against the wall, while Pam and Tessa claimed the couch that divided the living room from the weird space by the window. I think it was supposed to be an office of some kind, but it had become a no man's land where art and curtains could be stored.

It was time. I reached under the tree and grabbed the first present.

"To Brad and Sierra, from Dad and Bridget."

I passed the envelope to Brad. He opened it.

"Ah, cool. A night at the movies and a gift card for the Keg! Thanks so much, guys."

"These will definitely be put to good use. Yay. Date night!" Sierra added.

For Tessa and Pam, there were gift cards for their favourite fashion stores, and for Aiden a car maintenance kit. He needed it; he had just purchased a barely roadworthy jalopy. Brad and Sierra gave us each a very ugly Christmas sweater, and Tessa gave candles. Pam and Aiden teamed up to buy the whole family – all six of us – a day in an escape room.

Well, shit. That would be a much simpler family-building activity.

"Okay, what's next? Here we go! To Bridget, Love Al. Merry Christmas, Babe."

Bridget opened the box to find a beautiful set of pearls, with earrings to match.

"These are beautiful, Al. Wow. This is too much. Thank you, Hun." She was almost tearing up, and gave me a big smacker, right on the lips and everything. She put the earrings on – stunning. I had done good.

The only gift remaining that wasn't from Lilly was a tiny box for me.

"To Al, Love B."

An initial ring. Simple, 14k yellow gold, with AFI (F for Frederick, my middle name) diagonally engraved on the flat surface on the top.

"I love this, B. Thank you. Thank you so much." I *was* tearing up. Not at all sure why, but this seemed to be the most precious thing anyone had ever done for me. I hugged Bridget for a long time, nearly sobbing. I had to pull it together. My emotions were getting the better of me.

"Hey, what's this other stuff?" Aiden broke the awkward moment.

"Oh yeah, that stuff. I almost forgot!" I replied, like it was no big thing.

"Babe, this is for you."

I handed Bridget the first ever gift from Lilly Isaac.

She read the tag. "To Mom, From Lilly, Love you so much, Merry Christmas'. Huh? Ohhh. Right. Lilly. Cool."

For a moment, I thought she'd forgotten about the whole sketch thing, but she smiled as she peeled back the wrapping paper and opened the box. I had folded the letter and placed it over the framed sketch.

"Wait a minute. Who is Lilly? What's happening?" Pam was confused.

Bridget pulled the sketch from under the letter and held it up for the kids to see.

"Al drew this. She is supposed to be your Big Sister. Well, what she would look like, if we had her when we dated back in college. He named her Lilly."

"Oh. Hi Lilly!"

The kids all waved at the sketch and said "Hi, Lilly," laughing.

"Yeah, She's kind of half Tessa, half Pam… I tried, anyway."

They seemed to think my little idea was cute. Phew.

Bridget started reading the letter. Out loud.

Mommy Dearest,

I am so very sorry that I can't be there this year. It is soooo freakin' exciting that you guys are all together this Christmas. I have honestly dreamed of this day since all the other guys were born. I always knew that you and Daddio were meant to be together, and now you are!!

YAYYYYYYY!

Nick and his family all say Merry Christmas.

(Don't tell anyone, but I think he might be popping the big question on this trip.)

I asked Dad to sketch me so you could finally hang SOMETHING on the wall.

Don't be afraid, Mother! One tiny hole won't harm anything, and you'll be able to look at my beautiful face anytime you want!

I love you so much. You are the very best Mom on the planet.

Merry Christmas, Lady B! You deserve to be happy!

Love, Lilly. (and Nick)

"Holy shit. You went to a lot of trouble, Al." Aiden was irked.

"Oh, there's more, Buddy. All in good fun."

I was trying to keep the mood light. All the other kids looked a little confused but were taking the idea in stride. I pulled the bag of presents from behind the tree.

"Hey, look guys! I think Lilly got something for you too."

That got Aiden back on side. When I reached into the bag, I could feel that Nadene had pulled out all the stops. Each gift was in its own spectacular bag. The kids' names were hand painted on wooden tags. *"To Tessa, Love Lilly," "Merry Christmas Big Brad, Love your Big Sis, Lilly," "Merry Merry Aiden, Love Lilly," "Pammy, Merry Christmas, Little Sis. Love Lilly."*

I handed them out.

"Brad, Tessa – here you go. Aiden, here's yours. Pam. Now, you all have to open them at the same time, ok?"

They were already pulling the tissue out of the bags. Aiden was the first to find his jar. He held it up. Nadene had hand painted a lily on the jar.

"What am I supposed to do with a jar of milk?? What the fuck?" But he was laughing.

The other kids had their jars out by now, each with a different coloured lily painted on it.

Pam figured the ingredients out. "I think we are supposed to make something. This is fun!"

"Wow, Al. This is beautiful." Bridget was all in.

Tessa was the first to see the note.

"Hey, it says to open my email. Did you guys get that?"

"Oh, yeah. I did."

"Me too."

"Yeah!"

"Yep."

The kids all had their phones with them. They opened their emails.

Hey Guys! All four of you are getting the exact same message.

One of you should read it out loud.

Ever the spokesman, Brad volunteered.

First, I love you guys. I have ALWAYS wanted you to know each other, and now you do! I am so excited! I know things feel kind of strange right now, but they don't have to. You are all so cool in your own ways. All of us have our own personalities. I think we have way more in common than you realize. SO, here is your first bonding exercise. I want you all to take your jars, and dump them into the same pot. Heat on medium for 5 or ten minutes and stir stir stir! Trust me on this. You will LOVE me even more!

(Aiden and Pam, put a splash of rum in your cups!)

Here's some stuff you need to know.

Tessa and Brad, I know my Mom is not your Mom, but she is freakin' cool.

And she loves you. And she REALLY wants you to like her. So, for me, please try? I appreciate it.

Aiden and Pam. I know my goofy Dad is not your Dad, but he is freakin' cool. And he seriously loves you. I think you can already tell. He is not trying to replace your Dad, but he wants you to like him. So, for me, please try? I appreciate it.

I so wish I could be there with you, but Nick and I were there with Mom and Pam and Aiden last year, so Nick's parents insisted we be with them in Montreal for this Christmas.

(Don't tell anyone, but I think he is going to propose! EEEEEE!)

Sierra, you are part of this too! Mom and Dad both love you and are so happy you and Brad found each other.

I promise we will all be together soon. Let's plan on doing something for my birthday, which, in case you forgot, is July 16th.

I LOVE YOU. LOVE EACH OTHER. I JUST KNOW WE ARE GOING TO BE THE COOLEST FAMILY EVER.

Now, go make some cocoa. And have a big ol' group hug for me.

Merry Christmas to the Isaac/Reynolds Crew.

Love, your grateful Big Sis,

Lilly

It worked. All the kids were laughing along. They got the idea. The sense of family, of being open to each other, was palpable. They all went to the kitchen together, where Brad grabbed a pot from the ceiling rack, and put it on the stove. They emptied the contents of their jars into the pot. Tessa was ready with a giant wooden spoon for stirring.

"We gotta keep these jars. They are so cool. Who painted the flowers?" Pam asked.

"Well, Lilly did, of course!" I said, knowing full well that I would need to empty my bank account for Nadene.

It got a decent laugh from everyone. Bridget and I stood watching, my arm around her shoulders, her arm around my waist. It was a moment to take in. There wasn't a grumpy face among the bunch of them.

"Merry Christmas Everyone!" I blurted out, with tears welling up in my eyes.

There was enough Mexican Christmas Cocoa for everyone. It was unlike anything any of us had ever tasted – spicy, sweet, chocolatey, and delicious. Lucky guess. I'm sure I didn't invent it, but I'd come up with the recipe on my own. Bridget and her guys added a splash of rum to their drinks, and they loved it.

I couldn't remember a happier Christmas. Even going back to my childhood, there wasn't one I could think of that had filled my heart this much. My little idea had worked. The kids knew what I was trying to do, and it seemed like they'd all been ready for that push. We all wanted the same thing – I just hoped it would have some legs, a lasting effect.

As it turned out, Bridget and I would be left alone that night. My kids were heading home to spend Christmas morning with their Mom. Her kids were being picked up by their Dad to spend the morning with him. The goodbye hugs felt a little more genuine than they ever had before.

"Hey, I'm gonna email Lilly back to thank her!" Tessa joked.

That brought a chuckle from all of us.

With that, they were gone, and Bridget and I were alone. It had been a long, happy day. She was a little tipsy, and I was buzzing from my plan having come together. We got ready for bed.

"Thanks so much for being a good sport about Lilly, Babe," I said.

"Oh, Sweetie, Lilly was great. I just wish she really could have been here. That would have been even more special."

"Yeah. Me too, B. Me too."

We kissed a long goodnight kiss, but we were both way too tired to take advantage of the empty house. I think I fell asleep first, but I'm sure she wasn't far behind.

And visions of sugar plums danced in our heads.

Chapter 5:

Fa la la la WTF?

BANG! CRASH! OUCH!

At some point in the middle of the night, I was jolted out of peaceful sleep, certain that Santa's sleigh had crash-landed on my head.

"Holy fuck, B! What the hell was that?"

"Huh? I think you're dreaming Babe. Go back to sleep."

"You didn't see the flash? Hear an insane jackhammer sound??"

She had not heard the sound, nor had she seen the light. Maybe I was dreaming, but my heart was pounding, my chest heaving, and I had a crushing headache. It really hurts when someone crashes a sleigh into your head.

"Wow. Some dream. Holy shit! I'm sorry I woke you, Babe. I think I need some water."

I stumbled to the kitchen, feeling woozy and disoriented. Something was definitely… off. Popped a couple of aspirin with a glass of water, then made my way back to bed, and managed to fall asleep again without much trouble. When I woke in the morning, Bridget was already up.

"Wow, how're you feeling, Sleepy Head? You slept late on Christmas morning!"

"What time is it?" I asked.

"It's 10:30. Late for you."

She poured a cup of coffee and handed it to me. I felt hungover – something I hadn't experienced in a very long time. The coffee was a Godsend.

"Thanks Babe. I'm so sorry about waking you like that."

"Huh? I don't remember anything. I guess I was out?"

"Yeah. Well, sorry anyway."

We took our usual seats in the living room, sipping our coffees. Part way through a discussion on the benefits of leftovers for breakfast, Bridget spotted something under the tree.

"Hey, what's that? Looks like we missed one."

She crawled under the tree to retrieve a single present. I would have bet anything I owned that box hadn't been under the tree the night before.

"Ahhh. We missed your present from Lilly! Here you go, Hun."

Bridget handed me a gift about the size of a paperback, with a wooden tag, hand-painted in a pretty scroll.

Merry Christmas Daddio

Welcome Home.

Your Lilly Doll

Bridget's face had not even a hint of an impish grin, but she looked mildly curious.

"Wh… what's going on?? When did you have time?" I was stuttering and confused.

"What do you mean?" Her head was tilted doggy-like, as though I was speaking a different language.

"I mean, did Nadene do this? How did it get here?"

"What? Nadene?? We probably just missed it – it's from Lilly."

Alright. I'll play along.

The wrapping was professional, way beyond anything Bridget could have done herself. Nadene MUST have had something to do with this. She probably reached out to Bridget after my visit and arranged this. Bridget must have slipped the little box under the tree before I woke up. I had their little game all figured out. As I started unwrapping, I glanced at Bridget. She looked so… genuine. Damn good actor, I had to admit.

I ripped the corner of the paper, revealing the bottom of a shiny, black picture frame. Maybe Bridget had framed a copy of my sketch for me? The silver letters at the base read: BEST DAD EVER!

"Cute touch guys!" I said.

Bridget looked at me, as confused as I was. "What do you mean?"

She leaned over my shoulder to see what I was looking at. I peeled the rest of the paper away to reveal the image. My heart went to my throat.

"What the fuck?? What… how did you guys… what the fuck?"

The picture fell from my hands, landing face-down on the floor.

"What kind of game are you playing?"

"Al, Baby! Are you ok??"

I picked up the picture again, my hands shaking. I rubbed my eyes so I could be certain of what I was seeing. This was no sketch. It was a photograph of me, arm in arm with a young redheaded girl – a girl who looked almost exactly like the one I had drawn.

"How the hell did you guys do this?? What's going on here? B?? Please don't fuck with me." I was pleading now.

"Babe. Relax. For god's sake! It's a picture of you and our daughter."

"Our daughter? Bridget, I sketched her. I made her up. What in the actual fuck is going on here?"

"Jesus, Al. You're joking, right? What do you mean you made her up? What are you even talking about?"

"Bridget. Stop. This isn't funny at all."

"You're scaring me. Are you ok? How many fingers am I holding up?"

"Three, for fuck's sake. What's going on? Who is that? How did you do that? You had no time!"

"Oh My God, Al. You really need to lie down. Do you want me to call the doctor?"

"What? I don't need a doctor; I need someone to tell me what the fuck is going on?"

"You got a present from Lilly, and you are losing your mind over it. That's what's going on. And you're scaring me."

"Bridget, I am asking who that girl is. I'm asking how you and Nadene pulled this off."

"Nadene? Jesus Christ, Al. What are you talking about? That's our daughter, Lilly. Our baby girl. The one who brought everyone together last night? Our pride and joy?"

"Bridget. Come on. Don't."

"Al, please lie down. I'll get you some aspirin. Okay? Please, for me?"

I could feel all the blood rushing from my face. My hands were shaking, and I was drenched in a cold sweat. Feverish.

Maybe I'm still dreaming. Yes, I am asleep, and I am fucking dreaming.

"Okay. I'll go lie down. Maybe you can tell me what the fuck is going on, when I actually wake up?"

Dream-Bridget gave dream-me some dream-aspirin, and a dream glass of water. I dream swallowed the pills, and dream returned to bed (where I probably still was) to dream myself back to sleep.

"Please, don't wake me up until the world makes some sense."

I dream closed my eyes, hoping that this little nightmare would end soon.

My nightmare was just beginning.

Chapter 6:
The Book of Luke

I did fall asleep, and managed to stay asleep for some time. But my brain was spinning, and there was no relief from the incessant headache – the aspirin must indeed have been dream aspirin. What I had just seen was flat out impossible. I opened my eyes to a warm, bright Christmas day. Maybe this time I was actually awake, and everything would be as it should be.

Reaching for my phone to check the time, I found it was 12:45PM – still lots of day left. Still, I was surprised that I'd slept that long. There was a text notification on my phone, probably a Merry Christmas from my brother. Will lived in Barrie, about an hour and a half Northeast of us. We did not see each other often, but when we did, it felt like we still lived together – we were very close, despite the distance.

God, my head was killing me. I had to do something to fix that. I was searching in the washroom for something stronger than dream aspirin when I heard Bridget through the door.

"Sweetie? Are you feeling better? Did you sleep?"

Did this mean I wasn't dreaming?

"I did – but my head is still killing me. Do we have anything stronger than aspirin?"

"Maybe in the cabinet. There should be some extra strength Tylenol. Did you get the text?"

"What text?

"I'll let you see for yourself. Exciting news!"

I found the Tylenol and swallowed four, dry. I wanted more, but it didn't feel like a good idea. Back in the bedroom, I lowered myself onto the edge of the bed. I could see my phone face-down on the bedside table, but I was afraid to pick it up. Finally, I did – I mean… I had to. On the screen there was a text notification from a name I'd never seen, but was clearly already in my contacts.

Lilly Doll

-Daddiooooo!! He DID it! We are ENGAGED! EEEEEEEEEEEEEE!

Below the text, there was a picture – a photograph – of the same young redheaded girl I'd seen in the frame earlier. This time she was accompanied by a handsome, dark-haired fellow, and she was holding up her left hand to show off a sparkling diamond ring.

I started shaking again. I was not dreaming. I am not a praying man, but I looked to the heavens and pleaded for help. How could this be possible? What had gone wrong with my brain? Was it something to do with this headache? I was terrified.

"Al? Did you see the news? Isn't this exciting? I'm so happy for them." Bridget called from the living room.

I didn't respond. Instead, I began scrolling through the text conversation with "Lilly Doll". It was substantial – an endless trail of messages from her, and responses from me.

Scroll back.

June 10, 2015. *-welcome home baby doll! I'll see you on the weekend.* From me.

May 11, 2015. *-Daddio, super awesome marks! I'm a freakin' genius. Proud?? Lol.* From Lilly Doll.

It went back YEARS. All the way back to when I'd first bought the Smartphone. I couldn't wrap my head around it. So, I punched myself – right in the face – to see if I was dreaming.

I was not dreaming. Ouch.

I had absolutely no recollection of any of this, but here it was in front of me. Something was very wrong. I had to figure it all out – but how? I needed to speak with someone outside the family. So, rubbing my rapidly blackening eye, I texted Nadene.

-Hey Deeny, can I call?

-Sure Buddy. Give me 10 minutes. Is everything ok?

-Yeah. I just have to ask you something.

-Kk. I will call you in 10. Xo

Shit, I still hadn't responded to Bridget.

"Uh, yeah! Wonderful news."

"I can't wait to see them." I could hear the excitement in her voice.

See them? What the FUCK? They didn't even EXIST.

"Yeah. Uh… Right. Me too. You know – I think I'll take a short walk. Maybe some fresh air will help my head?"

I stopped by the door to tie my shoes.

"Are you ok? Do you want me to come with you?" Bridget looked concerned.

"Nah, that's okay. I won't be too long. Love you."

I was out the door before she could answer.

Less than fifty yards from the house my phone rang. It was Nadene.

"Hey Deeney."

"Hey Al. Merry Christmas! What's up?"

"Yeah. Merry fucking Christmas. My brain is malfunctioning, that's what's up."

"Yikes. You okay? Did Lilly's stuff go over alright?"

"Yeah. Maybe a little too well. Thanks again for all your work on that – it was really beautiful."

"Seriously, Buddy. Happy to help. So, what do you need to ask?"

"Well… It's about the Lilly stuff. My memory is a little shifty today. Can you help me remember how that all came together? What exactly did I ask you to do?"

"Jesus, Al. That doesn't sound good. It was just a few days ago."

"Yeah, I know. Please – just tell me what happened?"

"What happened? What happened is you came to me with a bunch of shit to wrap up, last fucking minute! I wrapped it. Pretty nicely too, if you ask me."

"Ha. Yeah. You did. But what did I say?"

"What the fuck, Al? You said Lilly couldn't make it home, but she wanted to do something special for the other kids. Does that ring a bell?"

I couldn't answer. I couldn't move. Nadene was over on the dark side, with the rest of the world. And I was either insane or dead. Neither option felt particularly good.

"Al?? Are you there?"

"Uh… yeah Deeney. I'm here. Thanks. I've gotta go."

"But, what…"

I hung up on my friend. I was spinning out of control, and I needed to grab hold of something.

I was only a ten-minute walk from Lake Ontario – some time by the water might do me good. It would look pretty in the Christmas sunshine, and might bring me some peace. I made my way south on Third Line toward the shore. Still felt like a basket case, but the outside air was calming my nerves. My phone rang again just as I approached the water. My old buddy, Luke Daniel. Luke had been my friend for 25 years, and my doctor for 24 of them.

"Hey, Luke. Merry Christmas."

"Hey, Buddy! Merry Christmas. How're you doing?"

"Not so good, Buddy."

"Yeah. Bridget just called me. Did you want to stop by?"

I wasn't surprised she had called the Doc; I would probably have done the same thing.

"On Christmas day? Are you sure, Brother?"

"Absolutely, my friend. The door is open."

"Okay. Thanks. See you in 15."

Luke lived only a few blocks from Bridget's house. It would be an easy walk. It was starting to get darker, so I checked my phone for the time. I'd been gone longer than I realized – it was nearly 4:30. I texted Luke to make sure a visit would be ok this late in the day.

-Hey, it's super close to dinner time. You sure it's ok for me to come by?

-No problem at all, Man. We aren't eating until later.

-K

When I called Bridget to let her know, the call went straight to her voicemail.

"Hey B. Thanks for calling Luke. I'm going to go see him now, but I shouldn't be too long."

Luke's office was in the addition at the back of the L-shaped bungalow he owned with his wife, Hannah. I made my way up the driveway, and finding the office door open, I walked in. Luke hollered from the bowels of the house.

"Be there in just a sec, Al."

I'd been in this office thousands of times. Luke had his degrees displayed on the back wall – he'd gone to Queen's. Also, several photographs of himself and Hannah, and their two boys, Colby and Oscar. Colby must have been in his early 20s by now, Oscar a couple years younger. A few other pictures – I even found myself in two of them. Golf stuff – Luke and I had been in the same foursome at several charity tournaments.

"Hey, Big Guy!" He entered through the door that connected his office to the sunroom.

"Hey, Buddy. Thanks so much for seeing me."

"Absolutely any time, my brother. What the hell is going on?"

"I have this headache. It's the worst. Fucking ever."

"Yeah, Bridget mentioned that. When did it start – and what happened to your eye?"

"I punched myself last night. For real. Right in the face. Anyway, In the middle of the fucking night, I heard a loud noise – and I thought I saw some sort of bright flash. But Bridget didn't hear or see anything. I'm starting to think my brain just... broke."

"Ha! Yeah. Something like that. You don't have a history of migraines, right? Did the headache start after you punched yourself?" He smiled.

"No… before. And no, not that I'm aware of. There's something else, too. Did Bridget tell you?"

"Yes – she mentioned some confusion. Is everything okay with the kids? Some big changes this year. How's Lilly doing at Queen's?"

"Jesus Fuck. Brother. Seriously?"

"Talk to me, Man?"

"Dude. Either all you fuckers are playing the nastiest joke ever on me... or I'm certifiable."

"No jokes, Al. What exactly is going on?"

"You are going to want to check me into the fucking nuthouse."

"Not likely. But... let's hear it?"

"Right. So, here it is. I woke up this morning to a completely different reality than the one my memory tells me exists. My memory from fucking yesterday. How is that even POSSIBLE?"

"Wait – what do you mean? What's different?"

"Lilly. Lilly is fucking different."

"Right. Bridget mentioned she and Nick got engaged. You okay with that?"

I broke down. My head sagged to my lap, and I started sobbing. Shaking.

"Jesus, Brother. Nick isn't a bad kid." The poor Doc was as confused as I was.

"My God. What the fuck is happening, Luke? What is wrong with me?" I was spiralling.

"You gotta talk to me, Al. It's me. You are safe here."

"I am NOT FUCKING SAFE!!"

I was barely able to speak. Ugly crying – a drooling mess.

"Take a deep breath, Man. Come on. Breathe. I'll go get you a glass of water."

He passed through the door to the sunroom into the kitchen just beyond. I tried to take deep breaths.

"Here you go, Buddy."

"Thanks, Luke."

I had a few sips of the water. It did help calm me down a little.

"Dude. Lilly. Isn't. Fucking. Real." Somehow, I managed to get those words out, with involuntary heaves punctuating my speech.

"Lilly isn't real? In what way?

"I made her up, Man. From a fucking sketch. I drew a picture, and I made up a backstory. And I wake up today, and that sketch is now a real person, and the backstory is a real person's fucking story!"

"I'm... still not sure I get it."

I tried once more to explain.

"Luke. Bridget and I talked about what our kid might have looked like, if we had had a fucking kid. We have NOT had a fucking kid. I drew this sketch, and I made up a story to bring the family together. Now Bridget, Nadene, even you, for fuck sakes. You are all acting like Lilly is an actual fucking person?? I have her in my phone contacts? There are actual photographs of me with this kid? What the actual fuck, Man. This is... INSANE."

"Al, I can assure you Lilly is your daughter. I delivered her, for Chrissakes. She and Colby have been best friends their entire lives. They're even at Queen's together. I think we need to take a look at your brain, Brother."

"No shit." I was in tears again.

"I'm going to get you in for a scan, ASAP. Holidays might get in the way, but I will do my absolute best to get you to the front of the line. I'm also going to talk to my Psych buddy. He should be able to see you in the next few days."

"Okay brother. I appreciate it."

"In the meantime…"

"Yeah. I was going to ask."

"In the meantime, I want to give you something for that headache, and something to calm your nerves. Do you think you'll be okay to go home?"

"I mean, yeah. Where else would I go?"

"Yeah. I know. So for now, take these, as often as you need. Go home and hug your lady. And I don't think you should talk about this with anyone, including Bridget. No need to scare the shit out of people before we can take a closer look."

"Okay. I agree. But... I can't bring myself to respond to this though." I held up the picture Lilly Doll had sent me in her text. "I just… can't."

"I get it. But you might want to consider trying to re-familiarize yourself with her. Maybe look through some old pictures. Anything to trigger your memory."

"I don't think it's my memory, brother. I haven't forgotten anything – I just have a completely different memory."

"I understand. We'll figure it out, Al. I promise you that."

"Ha! Don't make promises you can't keep, Doc!"

That was advice Luke had given me many times before, and he was dead right. Never make a promise you can't keep.

I had very serious doubts that my good friend could keep this promise.

Chapter 7:
Water Wings

I left Luke's office, downing four of the pills without water as I walked. Too many, I knew, but I just wanted to pass out. The phone had been buzzing non-stop while I was with the Doc, and when I finally checked, there were seven texts and two voice messages.

Bridget Reynolds

-Sorry I missed your call Babe. I hope Luke can help. See you soon?

Bradley Boy

-Hey Dad. Bridget said you aren't feeling well. Anything I can do?

And five messages from:

Lilly Doll

-Daddio? No words? Nothing? I thought you would be super excited?

-Hey, Mom says you aren't feeling well?

-Dad, please don't ghost me. Just let me know you are ok. Mom is freaking.

-Okay. She told me you went to Doc. Good call. I am worried about my Daddio.

-Nick sends his love too. Xo. Please call when you can?

Okay. This was too much. My immediate temptation was to swallow the rest of the pills and go to sleep forever. I could not respond. I needed to get back to normal, somehow. I needed to own my brain again. There were only three or four blocks between Luke's house and Bridget's. I pointed myself in the direction of home and started walking, one step at a time.

By the time I arrived, I was thoroughly stoned. Four was clearly way too many pills at once. Bridget greeted me at the door – actually, three Bridgets greeted me at three doors. Fortunately, one of the Bridgets grabbed me (so I didn't have to choose). I remembered Luke told me to hug her, so I squeezed her, with all my might. There was such a desperation to feel something... normal.

"Wow, that is a tight hug. You okay Babe?"

I couldn't answer. I just squeezed.

"Come on Al, let's get you to bed. You've had a really hard day."

She was literally holding me upright by this point. The hallway to the bedroom seemed a hundred feet long, but my Bridget had hold of me. She half-carried me to the bed, where I collapsed and passed out cold.

When I finally came to, the sun was shining – I knew I had slept through at least one night. I was still clinging to a faint hope that everything had been a dream. But this new "reality" had its boot heel on my throat.

I had watched my father fade away into dementia, and then my mother's life fragment into a fine dust with Alzheimer's. My sister still lived a life tormented by voices and hallucinations. I knew better than most, that a firm grasp on reality was a precious possession. How could my brain have mixed things up so badly?

My love, my friend, and now my doctor, were all confirming that my perception of reality had been violently shaken. I was carrying 45 years of clear memories, but suddenly half of them were wrong? Overnight, I had somehow replaced the life of a beautiful daughter with... a void. A black hole. I could not accept that. There was some evil force at work here.

Bridget heard me moving and brought me a coffee.

"What a Christmas, eh Sweetie? How are you feeling?"

"A little better, I guess? The headache has finally eased up, at least."

"And Lilly? Is everything coming back now?"

Poor B, she was so concerned. I didn't have the heart to tell her, but I was not about to accept that I was nuts.

"I want to look at some pictures, if there are any. Is that okay?" I asked.

"Oh Babe. What happened? This is breaking my heart."

"I wish I knew, B. I wish I knew. Do we have any pictures around?"

She was obviously holding back tears, as best she could.

"I'll see if I can find some." She left the bedroom.

I could hear her walking down the stairs, but I only followed her as far as the dining room table. In the vast chaos of the unfinished portion of the basement, Bridget had stored all manner of heirlooms, memories, and souvenirs… and photo albums. She eventually emerged from the stairway with two of them. I was still groggy from Dr. Luke's pills, but I braced myself. I was still trying to steady my eyes as she opened the first album.

"Here she is, Day One! She was so beautiful. And my God, I was a baby too. Wow."

There she was. The Bridget that I had loved so deeply in college. Completely exhausted and holding a precious baby girl. The love in her eyes was that unmistakable first-time parent kind.

"Where was I? Was I there for the birth?"

She looked at me, amazed, and curious. "Al, you took the picture."

"Oh my God. Oh, my fucking God."

"Well – you were hammered. Not all that surprising you don't remember."

"Babe, I remember everything from when I was drinking. I swear to God, this did NOT happen."

"This? No bells ringing?"

She showed me the same beautiful baby girl, in my arms. MY ARMS. I was looking at a picture of myself. I was wearing clothes I remembered owning, but I was holding a baby I knew I'd never held.

"Jesus Christ Babe. I'm sorry. This is too much," I said.

"Please keep looking, Babe. Maybe something will click. It has to."

I kept flipping through the pages. This kid was adorable. There was a slight sense of familiarity, but I chalked that up to having invented her... IN A SKETCH.

I opened the second album. Clearly, this one was mine. The first few pages were of me and my ex-wife, Donna. About five pages in I found a photograph of a little girl. She was sitting at the edge of a dock, on a lake, with a rowboat tied up to her left. The sun setting over the water beyond her.

"This! This looks familiar!" I said, practically rejoicing.

"Oh, good sweetie. Something's clicking."

I felt some hope that maybe I was scratching the surface, but then I remembered why the photo looked so familiar. I grabbed my phone and started looking back through all my sketches... and there it was. Before Bridget and I had rekindled our relationship, I had sketched that image. Right down to the stupid rowboat. Right down to the little girl's pink bathing suit and water wings. I had never ever seen these photographs before. But I'd sketched this one, like I'd copied it. I held the phone up to Bridget.

"Well, yeah. You sketched that from the photo, right?"

"Babe, I have never seen this album, let alone this picture. Never."

She shook her head. "This is serious mind fuck shit, Al."

"Tell me about it. I need a drink." I was only half joking.

"You'd better not!"

"I'm kidding. But this is seriously messing with me."

I continued to flip through the pages. There were so many pictures of this little doll. With me in a snow fort. With Donna on a toboggan. The picture that struck the deepest chord was of "Lilly" sitting in an orange chair, in a hospital room, with a deliriously excited grin on her face. She was holding a baby, and I recognized the little fella. It was Brad.

I have distinct, vivid memories of that day. I wasn't even drunk. Donna and I had visitors in the hospital, but no children. Her parents were there. My Mom was there. Will came at some point too, but that was it. No kids. This image made absolutely no sense.

The pull to get back to my normal was overwhelming. Like there was some mammoth underground beast, reaching up from Hell with a thousand tentacles, ensnaring my limbs, trying to drag me home.

"I can't do this, B. I just... can't," I said.

"Babe, can't do what? What are you saying?"

"I don't even know. But this can't be. This is not my life."

"Oh my God, Al. What did Luke say?? We have to get you back!"

Jesus Christ. Of course we did, damn it. We had to get me back to my life. Wherever I was, wherever we were, I knew this was not real. And yet, here I was. Protesting seemed to do no good. As Luke had said, I didn't want to scare the shit out of everyone else. I was fucking terrified – but hey, that was ok, right? As long as no one else was scared.

"You know what, B? You're right. Luke said to just do what we're doing. Look at some pictures, try to find a connection. It'll come." I was lying. Inside, I was dying.

"Something has to click, baby." The panic in her eyes made her confidence less than convincing.

It was Boxing Day. Two days ago, I'd been having the time of my life. Since then, nothing but a waking nightmare. I was due back to work the following day. That would at least (hopefully) offer some relief – some sense of normalcy. There wouldn't be so much pressure to accept this unreal reality. So, I painted on my very best shit-eating grin, and pretended I was excited to come to grips with being the new me.

For most of the day, I didn't say much. Just grinned. Bridget's kids came home in the late afternoon. Aiden seemed to take particular joy in my predicament.

"Hey, Big Al! I hear you've been having some issues. Did you maybe dip into my stash?" He was laughing.

More shit-eating grin from me. Clearly Bridget had let the cat out of the bag. I was nuts. I was certifiable. Go Team Al. Yay. Pam actually gave me a hug.

"You okay?" She asked. She meant it.

"I'll be fine. Thanks, kiddo." I didn't mean it.

The kids retreated to their respective caves and fired up their fatties. This was a bit of a relief – it was normal. It was my life. I even considered sparking up myself. It couldn't have made things any worse.

I could not wait to get out of that house; morning couldn't possibly come soon enough. I had never been more excited to get to my stupid job. I found a book and climbed into bed, but the letters were jumbled on the page. I looked for something with pictures, but nothing. By 5 PM, the afternoon sun was fading to darkness. I was still staring at the jumbled up letters when Bridget called me for supper.

"Food is ready, Sweetie!"

"Sorry Babe. I don't think I can eat." I knew whatever I tried to choke down would come straight back up.

"Okay… I can bring you something later if you want?"

I had no desire for food. My appetite had forsaken me entirely. I must have nodded off for a bit, because the next time I heard anything, it was Bridget getting ready for bed, and maybe something else.

"Sweetie, maybe we can refresh your memory this way. Do you remember when we conceived her?" She was now naked, and God she was beautiful. She pulled the covers down, and took me in her mouth, but my body wouldn't respond.

"I'm sorry Babe. I don't think this is going to happen. Too much stress. Maybe those pills that Luke gave me? I don't know. I'm just not feeling it."

That was literal. I could barely feel what she was doing – it felt like I was becoming a Zombie.

Bridget would not take no for an answer. She kept trying… and it started to hurt.

"For fucks' sakes, Bridget. I said NO. I just can't."

I was loud enough that the kids probably heard me, but they were probably too stoned to notice. Bridget finally took the hint and gave up.

"I'm so sorry, Sweetie. I just thought..."

"I know B. I get it. I'm really sorry. Let's just try to get some sleep."

We rolled over, back to back, and tried to sleep. But she was crying – the bed was shaking with her sobs. I was terrified of what might be waiting for me on the other side of sleep. I needed pills. I grabbed the bottle Luke had given me and swallowed three more. That should have been enough to numb me to her crying. I felt bad, for the few seconds that passed before I passed out.

The pills knocked me out, but I still woke before Bridget did, and before daylight. She was off work until the New Year, and I didn't want to bother her. There was plenty of time, so I decided I would walk to the train. I tiptoed around the peaceful house, getting ready. The glow of streetlights flowed into the living room through the massive, uncovered window. On the coffee table I could clearly see both the sketch I had done of Lilly, and the Best Dad Ever photograph from Christmas morning. It was like a divine light illuminating the evidence of my insanity. I left a note for Bridget between the two frames, to let her know I'd left for work and didn't want to disturb her.

It was a much colder morning than the previous two had been. Snow was falling lightly as I walked to the GO Station. On foot, this was about a half hour walk, and the walking felt good. I was starting to relax. My headache was virtually gone. Only my appetite was still nowhere to be found. Stopping into the Tim Horton's at the gas station, I ordered a gigantic coffee – and, just in case, a blueberry muffin. Anything more felt like an impossible digestive task. I hadn't yet checked the time, but the sun was just beginning to inch over the horizon. My phone indicated it was 6:45 AM, so I was still early. No book, no headphones – and certainly no desire to sketch. I planned to enjoy the scenery and just try to clear my head.

My head had other plans.

Chapter 8:

Five Star

From the moment I boarded the train, my mind was racing. Going back over the events leading up to Christmas, I could smell the memories. Every molecule in my body knew these events to be true. I did sketch a make-believe daughter. I did create an email address for her. I did get Nadene to wrap everything up at the last minute.

But now everyone, including Nadene, was telling me that none of this ever happened. That my mind somehow obliterated an entire swath of the last 23 years and replaced it with a strange, made up story. It did not compute; the numbers didn't math. Someone had obviously slipped some kind of wacky mushroom into my cocoa. I knew what was what, and this was not what.

"Next stop, Appleby." The train announcement sounded perfectly normal. There was one other person in the car with me, and only the top of their head was visible. I had no idea if it was a man, woman, or child. Watching the trees whiz by, my mind desperately went back to searching for some kind of explanation.

And WHUMP! The stranger plopped herself into the seat directly across from mine. She was a kid – maybe? Dressed in cool, raggedy stuff, with a mustard yellow toque pulled down over her hair. Fingerless gloves and shiny Doc Martens. She extracted a cigarette from somewhere under her toque.

"Got a light, Mister?"

"I don't smoke. Sorry."

"You're not sorry. That's okay – I shouldn't smoke in here anyway. Where you headed?"

"Work. In Hamilton."

"Ew. It's still Christmas. Who wants to work?" She scrunched up her nose, like the thought of work smelled like ass.

"Believe it or not. I do. I've had a brutal few days."

"It doesn't take a genius to see that, Mister."

"What do you mean?"

"You're all screwed up. Your aura's eating itself."

"Ah. The old aura. Right."

"Seriously, Mister. You're a mess. I don't think you should go to work. And anyway, I don't think that's where you're going."

"I am. I'm going to work. Miller Shoes."

"Whatever. Do you sell Docs?"

 I wasn't surprised she asked.

"No. We used to, but not anymore."

"Too bad. I love Docs. What's your name, Mister?"

"Al."

"Call MEee Al, call me A-A-A-AL." She was singing a bit of the Paul Simon tune.

"Yeah. That… Al. What's your name?"

"Well, Mister Al, I definitely don't think you are going to work today. I'm Ally, oddly!"

"Hello Ally Oddly."

"You're funny, Mister Al. Mister Al with the fucked up aura."

"Where are you going? And you shouldn't smoke." I suddenly felt entitled to offer fatherly advice.

"I know, I know. And yet, I do – strange, isn't it? My Dad is picking me up at Aldershot. I think I probably do it to piss him off."

"Why would you want to piss your Dad off?"

"He only sees me when it's convenient for him – sometimes it feels like he doesn't remember I even exist. He's all in love with his new lady."

"Oh. Wow." Her words were a knife in my brain.

"Hey – your aura just went all funny."

"I guess I'm not all that different from your Dad."

"You're a dude. Dudes are messed."

"That may be very true, Ally Oddly."

"Summerville. Ally Summerville. Pleased to meet you Mr. Al."

"Allan Isaac. Same to you Ally."

"Allan Isaac? You're a musician, right? My mom talks about you sometimes."

"Yeah. I am. Do I know her?" It felt good to be a tiny bit famous.

"I doubt it. She's very quiet. Her name is Tricia."

"I don't think I know a Tricia." I went through my memory banks – untrustworthy as they were – and could not picture a Tricia at any of our shows.

"Yeah. She's quiet."

"Next Stop, Aldershot." The train conductor's voice was loud over the intercom.

"You gettin' on the bus now, Al?" Ally asked.

"I am. Be nice to your Dad."

"Whatever. See you later, Mister Al. Don't go to work!"

"Don't smoke!"

She seemed to be in a hurry, but she did have time to pull that smoke out again as she ran through the tunnel. She stopped for a second to light it.

I made my way slowly through the mostly empty tunnel. There had been something comforting about meeting Ally Oddly. I was glad she had appeared in front of me. I normally would pay no mind to any talk of auras, but I was intrigued by what she thought she had seen. I knew I was messed up, and curious that it was that obvious.

Regardless. I was on my way to work, and I was looking forward to it. I boarded the bus.

And then all of a sudden, I was not looking forward to work. Instead, I was starting to panic.

What are they going to say? They are going to ask me about my Christmas! Are they part of this giant shit show conspiracy too?

I was beside myself. I would not be able to handle questions from my work colleagues about Lilly. I couldn't face it. I had no idea what to do.

The bus ride seemed to take no time at all. I stepped off in front of City Hall and headed toward James Street North. The anti-abortion assholes were set up as usual, at the corner of King and James. Pictures of bloody babies were held up on placards, brightening the mornings of the passersby. This morning it felt like they were directing their vitriol right at me. I made eye contact with one very enthusiastic placard-waving fellow, who gave me a knowing wink. *What the fuck was that?* I ignored him, and lowered my eyes.

I made it past the throng without looking back up, until a homeless gentleman approached me. He looked familiar, but I couldn't place him. There was some loose change in my pocket, which I offered to him.

"Thank you, brother. God Bless."

I didn't answer. My insides were shaking. I was still on the west side of James Street, and Miller Shoes was on the east. "Don't go to work today". Ally Oddly's words were ringing through my head. I was now approaching York Boulevard, where I would normally cross over to the east side of James.

I did not cross. I kept walking. I passed Vine Street and then walked on, straight north, past Miller Shoes. Coming up on Cannon Street, the lights turned in my favour. I crossed, still heading north. Apparently, that was it – I was NOT going into work today. But where would I go? The Mulberry Street Coffee House? No, I knew too many people there. Down to the lake? The underground beast was pulling me, somewhere. I glanced across James Street and spotted Ola Cafe. Brilliant! I waited for a break in the traffic, and then stepped onto the crosswalk.

And then I stopped. This was not a job for coffee and cannoli. I turned around. The Five Star Cafe was right there. Perhaps the only cafe on the planet where not a single drop of coffee had ever been served, it was fondly nicknamed "The Dive Bar Cafe" by its regulars. And that is where I was being pulled. The entire face of the bar was a window, part of an old store front. Sidewalk folk could look in and see exactly who was there, and what they were drinking.

"Am I actually doing this?" I asked myself, out loud.

I hadn't had a drink in six years. But as angry as I had been with booze, it had never done what sobriety was doing to me now. Sure, there had been some pretty serious drunken delusions, but I had never been this fucked up, back when I was drinking. Ever. I made up my mind on the spot; I was going to drown this motherfucker. I wasn't even surprised at myself.

This was not a drastic-times-call-for-drastic-measures kind of thing. This was a shoot-me-in-the-face-or-at-least-make-me-numb situation. And I opted for numb.

Except it wasn't open yet. Damn it. But I could detect movement inside – the lights weren't on, but someone was definitely in there preparing to open. I tapped on the door, and a friendly face came to let me in. My old buddy, Daxy. This gal had poured several thousand pints for me, back in my drunky days. I no longer frequented the drinking establishments unless I was performing. Five Star was not the kind of place that would have live music, so I hadn't seen my friend in some time.

"Hey, Al! How the fuck are ya?" She opened the door and invited me in.

"Been a rough few days, Dax, gotta say."

"Over Christmas? That sucks! What's up, Man?

We made our way over to the bar, where I pulled up a stool, and Daxy took her usual spot behind the taps. She looked good. She kicked booze a few years before I did – there had been a couple of relapses, but she looked healthy enough now. The tough years had left her with some scars of course, but also a look of wisdom.

"I can't even say. Seriously, I'm worried that I am going full-on nuts. Everything is... fucked."

"Doesn't sound good, Al. What brings you in here? You still at the shoe shop?"

"Yeah. But I just walked clean on by this morning. I don't think I can handle working today."

"Well. I'd offer you a pint, but I know you don't..."

"I think today I do, Buddy," I interrupted her.

"Fuck. Are you sure, Man?" She was concerned. And she was right to be.

"I really think I am. And if you say, 'This too shall pass,' I might have to fucking kill you."

"Ha. Okay, understood. What'll you have?"

"Keith's." Right back where I'd left off six years earlier. Alexander Keith's India Pale Ale. Breakfast of Champions.

Daxy had a grin on her face, but I could see she was still tentative.

"Trust me. Just this once. If I have enough, I'll tell you what the fuck is going on. Then you'll get it."

"I trust you, Al. Here you go."

She poured me a pint – my first in an eternity.

"Hello darkness, my old friend," I sang to a beer, in keeping with the Paul Simon theme of the morning.

Some things are like riding a bike. Drinking is not one of those things. It's far easier to fire up a good bender than it is to get back up on two wheels. There was a time in my life that the mere sight of a full pint glass would get me tingling. I wasn't quite tingling now, but I was looking forward to the possibility of numbness.

And I did not hesitate. I gulped the entire pint down without once coming up for air. My old life came flooding back. For the last six years beer had been a pathetic, toothless crack whore – and now here she was, suddenly, the sultry temptress once more. I could feel the first gulp straight through to my fingertips.

"Damn. That's Good."

It tasted like friendship. It had been my sworn enemy for so long, but today I welcomed what it offered with wide open arms.

Daxy pulled me another, and another. I was four pints in when she opened the bar for business. The sun was rising, turning the giant window of the bar into a mirror. Passersby were now more likely to see their own reflections. Not me and my beer. The place began filling up with regulars – I recognized some familiar faces, but not a friend among them.

"Shit! I have to let work know," I said out loud, to no one. "Better just text."

It was the first time I'd checked my phone all morning. Even with my glasses on, the screen was blurry. There were indeed messages, but I wasn't going to mess up a perfectly good morning buzz by reading them. I found Dennis Miller's number in my contacts.

-Boss, really sorry but I am under the weather. Crazy few days.

I knew they would have preferred a call, but there was too much background noise, and I was probably slurring a bit by now. And that would not have gone over too well. In that moment, I really didn't care if my boss got the text. The phone went back into my pocket.

"Hey Sister, I'm dry." I beckoned Daxy to pour another.

"Dude, you're half in the bag. Maybe slow down a little?"

"Oh, I'm all the way in the bag. Cheap drunk, it would seem. Do you even have coffee here?"

"Ha. Maybe some instant shit in the back?" She really had no idea.

"Fugg it. Just give me a beer. I'll drink it all slow-like."

She pulled me another pint. Disappointment was burning in her eyes.

"Are you fuggin' dishapoined in me, Dax?"

"I'm not disappointed, Al. All good, Buddy. So, are you wasted enough to tell me what's been going on?"

"I might be. Lemme zhip on this one for a bit, K?"

"Alright, Brother."

I was thinking if I had much more, I might pass out on the stool. I wasn't much interested in sharing the story. But, maybe one of these barstool prophet types would have something to tell me that made sense.

Before I could open my mouth, my old friend Marvin Carol pushed in through the front door. Marvin (also a singer/songwriter, local celebrity), was a talented fellow. I'd known him for some time, but this morning he looked different somehow. He must've had a haircut, and maybe a beard trim. He looked like he'd lost some weight, too.

"Hey, Marvin. You clead ub real good, brother. Good to shee you, Man."

"Hey, Al. You too. What the fuck are you doing here?" He gave me a firm, confident handshake.

"I know, Man. I know. Just a fugged up few days."

With our hands still clasped, he pulled me closer and looked into my eyes with an almost hypnotic stare. It was creepy.

"Al. You don't belong here, Man."

"I know, Marvin. It's been sigs years, Man. Six years! Fugg, Man."

"Al. You do NOT belong here," he repeated himself.

My foggy brain could sense that there was something important in what he was saying.

"Well, I AM here. And I'm having another pint. Daxy!" I called for the barkeep again. "One more, and one for Marvin."

"Hey, Marv. The usual?"

Marvin nodded. Daxy pulled a pint of Keith's for me, and an Ex for him.

"Al tells me he has quite a story to share." Daxy was goading me to get on with it.

"I bet he does."

Marvin's stare was unrelenting.

"Are you tryna hymnodize me. Whad the fugg, Man?" I slurred.

"Tell us your story, Mate." Marvin wanted in on the secret too.

I had no issue with telling Marvin. Like my sister, he lived with Schizophrenia and might have some insight into my current state of mind fuckery.

"Ahright, you bazdurds. If you insist."

So, Daxy did her best to keep track, whilst serving the other patrons. Marvin leaned in closer to decipher my mumbling. I told the whole story. From the day I first reconnected with Bridget, straight through to Christmas day, when everything went to shit.

"And that's how I ended up here. Now, you fuggers are gonna tell me that everyone is right. Thad my memory is fugged. I forgot my own daughter?? Bullzhit!" I was sob-slurring now.

"That is some seriously fucked up shit, Brother. I didn't know you had any kids at all," Daxy said.

That was almost a relief for me. But Marvin didn't say anything; he just kept staring at me.

"Say something. Tell me I'm nuts, Buddy." I was hoping for any kind of insight.

"Al. You do not belong here," he said again.

"You keep saying that, Man, But here I am. And I'm already pished, so… Whatever."

"Brother. I hear what you are saying. I can see the fear. I can see it, Man. You don't belong here."

"Whad the fugg are you tawgin' about?"

"I am saying I get it. I have been there. Fuck, Man. I have been there. And I don't belong there any more than you belong here."

"Marv! Dude, what the hell is that supposed to even mean?"

He pulled me by the arm to a table in the corner. There were only half a dozen other drunks in the place, but Marvin seemed to want a little more privacy.

"Al, my friend. That shit has happened to me – I know the feeling. They tell me I'm nuts, but I am not nuts. Maybe I am somewhere, but I am not nuts here."

"Dude. I am already dizzy. You're making it way worse."

"You've gotta get back, Man. You don't belong here."

"Get back to where?"

"Back to where you created a sketch, and an identity for this kid. Back to your reality. This is a different one."

That sounded completely insane, but somehow it was starting to make sense to my drunken brain.

"Yeah. I would love to, but this seems to be reality. And here, I'm nuts." I was beginning to feel resigned to it.

"You do not have to stay. Most people never move. You have moved. I have too. So, now I know. And now you know," he explained.

"Moved? What the fugg?" I had no idea what he was talking about.

"Al, there is more than one reality – all kinds of them, actually. They're flying around the multiverse, all at the same time. From what I can see, a few lucky people can trigger a jump from one reality to another. You triggered something, Man. YOU fucking triggered it."

"I think maybe you're off your meds, Brother."

"Ha. yeah, I thought you might say that. Maybe I am, and maybe I'm not. But, you aren't on anything at all, and you can see clearly that you were in one place on Christmas Eve, and an entirely different place on Christmas day. You take meds, they blind you to both of those places, and then you are just in limbo, Man. Fucking LIMBO."

"I don't know, Man. What if my brain just had a meltdown?" I asked.

"And created two completely different sets of situations? Think about that. That makes way less sense than what I am saying. Doesn't it?"

He had a point.

"Nothing makes any fuggin' sense. Nothing! This is just... crazy."

"Dude. Where do you think you got the idea to sketch Lilly? How'd you know what she would look like? You know how when you write a song, it sometimes just falls right out of the sky?"

"It does! Thas juz the way it is."

"What if you have a foot in more than one reality? And in Lilly's reality, you know what she looks like. What if you hear a song in Lilly's reality, it is shared with Al in HIS reality? It would totally feel like it fell from the sky, right? If you are not completely, consciously aware of the connection to Lilly's reality." Marvin was on a roll.

"I need another pint. Dax!"

Daxy had not heard any of our conversation.

"You get this shit all straightened away, fellas?" She was laughing as she approached our table.

"We are shining a light on it, my friend. Shining a light," Marvin answered.

"Glory Hallefugginluja." I was not as enthusiastic. "Let the fuggin light shine on two more beers."

Daxy laughed again, shook her head, and went back to the bar.

"Are you following me, Brother?" Marvin was apparently concerned that I was too drunk to keep up. By now, his face was floating, superimposed over a swirling void.

"I hear what you are saying. And it is FUGGED UP. So's whadever's happening ta me. I don't know what the fuck is what. This is brutal."

"I am tellin' you, Man. You triggered the jump. You're here now. And even if you can make it back there you are going to remember being fully conscious here. You gotta know that, Al," he explained.

"So, I am going to remember being fuggin nuts. Not knowing my ass from third base. Yay, me."

"Dude, you are going to remember there is more than one you. Simple as that."

"In what world is more than one me SIMPLE? Jesush."

"Exactly." Marvin sat back and folded his arms. Like he had just solved the mystery.

"K. So… Whad the fugg am I spoza do, Man? If all this is true, I am fugged," I said, feeling desperate.

"You wanna know what you have to do? I will tell you. But it depends on what you want. Now you are consciously aware of two realities. You are going to feel a little bit crazy – whether you stay here, or go back there."

"I want to feel sane. I want to have a firm grasp on reality." That was my only concern. It was the Beast, pulling at me.

"Well, Buddy, now you have a grasp on two realities. Maybe not as firm as you'd like, but you've got a grasp."

"Whad the fugg."

Daxy returned with two pints. This motherfucker was proving harder to drown than I had anticipated.

"Here ya go fellas. Maybe no more after this one, Al?"

"Whadever."

Marvin gave me that hypnotic stare again. He leaned in, put his elbows on the table, and clasped his hands under his chin, deep into the thick of his grey beard.

"Al. This isn't your place. At least you know that now. You could stay if you wanted to, but you would never feel settled, and your actions would cause… ripples here. And I think you're here for a reason. Find out what you need to find out. Hear the song you're supposed to hear. Untrigger the jump. Whatever got you here, you've gotta just undo it. Trigger the jump back."

"I don't even know what the fugg that means, Man."

"Just be careful, brother. Ripples. You will make ripples."

"Yeah. I gotta do that right now. Breaking the seal. Be right back."

I managed to get up and stagger to the men's room, a little surprised that I had guzzled that many pints without having to go sooner. The room was much cleaner than I'd expected. Leaning my forehead against the wall above the urinal to steady myself, I peed for a solid eight minutes.

When I finally finished, I stumbled toward the sink. And for the first time in days, I saw my reflection in the mirror. I was still me. I was still the same might-have-been-handsome-at-some-point, balding, bearded dude. Maybe a little blurrier than I remembered, but… beer. I washed my hands and splashed my face. It didn't help. I was still hammered.

Marvin had left by the time I found my way back to the table. That was disappointing; his ramblings had started making sense to my drunken brain. If I could retain some of it, maybe it could help. I still had half a pint left, so I sat back down to drink it.

Daxy joined me at the table.

"Hey, Buddy. Marvin got the tab. He said to give you this." She handed me a note, folded up, four times over.

"Well, that was mighty kind of him. You cuddin' me off, Sister?"

"Yeah. You're done for today, Man. How're you getting home?"

"Home? Fugg, yeah. I gotta get home. Gotta untrigger something… or something."

She looked confused. "Can I call you a cab?"

"Nah. I'm good to walk, for now. I'll figure it out. Hey – thanks Dax. I don't understand why, but I needed this."

"I trust you that it's just this once, okay? If you're diving back in, I don't want to be the gal pouring. Fair?"

"I don't think I'm diving, Buddy. But if I do, I promise I'll go elsewhere."

We shared a quick, familiar hug, and I headed out the door. I couldn't remember if I finished the pint, but it didn't seem to matter.

Chapter 9:

The Blur

The rest of that day still lives in a thick fog. I could remember all the places I ended up, but the details were sketchy. I do remember stepping out of the Five Star and looking back at the bar through the enormous front window; the place was a fishbowl. I'd put my drunken, desperate morning on display, for all of James North to see. Shameful, but somehow necessary.

The sun was still shining. I'd lost track of time, and had no desire to find it again. It was an unseasonably warm day for late December. Whatever snow had accumulated was now forming shallow puddles on the road. Without making any conscious decision, I let the Beast pull me. I started walking further north, toward the relatively new Harbour West Go Station. It was only three or four blocks from The Five Star, and I wouldn't be the only drunk looking to take a nap there. The station was an appropriate bunkie – and I'd be able to catch the train home, after a wee rest.

By the time I reached Harbour West, the eight or nine pints I'd consumed were hitting me full force. A bench offered itself up and I accepted with gratitude. Curled up like a kid after a big turkey dinner, I drifted off.

The thing about unseasonably warm December days in Southern Ontario is that they quickly become seasonably cold December nights, usually right around 5:00 PM. By the time I was rudely shaken from my blissful slumber, I was borderline cryogenic… and feeling considerably less intoxicated than I had been.

"Al. wake up. What the hell is wrong with you?"

Shake shake shake.

The voice was familiar. When I opened the one eye that felt like it might cooperate, it was promptly blinded by a bike helmet light. Which helped me figure out why the voice sounded familiar – it was the other Al, from Miller Shoes. He cycled in to work most days of the year – not bad for a fellow in his mid-60s. There had been two of us Als at the store since I started there, a few days after I sobered up in 2010. The first Al had assumed the role of mentor to me, taking me under his wing – but that tends to be a pretty stinky place when things heat up. Pain in the ass though he was, I did consider him a friend.

"Aller! How the fuck did you find me?"

"Your friend – Marvin or whatever his name is – came into the store and told me you were passed out on a fucking bench down here. What's going on?"

Marvin. He must have been keeping an eye on me. I would have to remember to thank him for that.

"Just a little slip up. Not to worry. I'll nip it in the bud. I am capable."

"So you say." Ah, Al. Ever the pedant. "You'd better get on that train – it's the last one. And where are your shoes?"

"Fuck. No wonder my feet are so bloody cold."

My shoes were gone. There was a significant homeless contingent hanging around James North, and a sleeping dude wearing five-hundred-dollar Allen Edmonds was a pretty easy target.

"Here. Marvin said you might need these."

Other Al reached into his backpack and pulled out a pair of my shoes. I usually kept several pairs at the store, especially in the winter months.

"Thanks, Man, I appreciate it. Sorry about this."

"Don't apologize to me, just get on the train. See you tomorrow."

"God willing."

We both said it at the same time. It was kind of a regular joke that neither of us quite understood.

Other Al climbed back onto his bike and rode off. I managed to get my shoes tied, and boarded the last train with moments to spare. Although I had yet to decide where I would go, I knew the folks at home were expecting me.

I would be back at the Bronte Station at the same time I would have been, if I had worked. And it did make sense to head home – but I dreaded being there. The thought of a warm bed was the deciding factor.

Remembering the note Marvin had left me, I rifled through my coat pockets until I found the folded piece of paper. I unfolded it. It was short.

Al,

Remember, see what you are here to see, hear what you are here to hear. Then either figure out how to untrigger the jump, or learn to love it here. Be careful what you wish for. You will make ripples.

"Well. Isn't that comforting," I said, out loud to an otherwise empty train car.

Now that I was sobering up, Marvin's ramblings were starting to feel empty. I was more inclined to talk to Doctor Luke and his friends to see if we could figure my brain out.

"Shit. Maybe he called." Out loud again.

I hadn't looked at my phone in hours, and I was almost hoping it was dead. I could feel that it was still in my pocket. The shoe thief apparently had not been interested in anything but footwear.

It wasn't dead.

Bridget Reynolds

-Hey Babe. Got your note. Love you. Have a good day.

-How's your morning?

-Babe. I have a surprise for you when you get home.

-You ok?

-Babe. Please answer.

-Al??

-This isn't fair.

I had clearly pissed her off. The fact that I was losing my mind didn't seem terribly important.

Baby Tessa

-Daddy, u ok?

Bradley Boy

-Hope everything is okay Dad. We're a little worried.

Dennis Miller

-Ok. Feel better. Let me know about tomorrow.

Nick Rocher

-Hi Mr. Isaac. I hope you're okay. Lilly is worried. Please call her when you can? Thank you Sir.

Lilly Doll

-Daddy. Please??

-Hey Daddio. Call?

-Still waiting……

-☹

This was all way too much. Lilly and Nick? Maybe if I kept scrolling, I'd find one from Jesus? John Lennon? Genghis Khan? I couldn't bear to read any more, and was stuffing the phone back into my pocket when it rang. Bridget.

"Hey," I answered.

"Oh. Phew! Are you okay?

"Yeah. I'm okay."

"Did you lose your phone?"

"Uh. The day just turned out... weird," I answered, fumbling for an explanation.

"Okay. Are you on the train? Do you want me to pick you up?

"Yeah. Just at Burlington now."

"Ok. I'll leave now."

"Thanks, B."

It was an awkward call. There was a palpable detachment. I definitely reeked of beer, and had no idea how to explain that. And now that my clothes were thawing, it was becoming clear that I had pissed myself while I slept. Magnificent. I was a sight to behold.

I called Bridget back.

"Hey Babe. I'm thinking maybe I should walk. The fresh air will probably do me good." And hopefully dry my pants out.

"Okay. Are you sure? It's pretty cold."

"Yeah, I'll be fine.

"Okay, see you soon."

I needed some time to figure out my predicament. There was a little mall on the way home – maybe I could find some replacement pants. I still seemed to be alone on the train, and felt fortunate that most likely no one had noticed.

"Next Stop, Bronte."

Nearly home. I was wearing a long, dark-navy winter coat; if there was a piss spot, it might not be totally obvious. The train squealed to a stop, and I hustled off. Another lucky break – I was the only person disembarking at Bronte.

The air was now much colder than when I'd boarded.

I was wishing I'd just gone to work. Not had any beer. Not pissed myself. And maybe that only real people existed. I lowered my head, and started putting one foot in front of the other.

"Coffee. I should have a coffee." I was still thinking out loud.

The same Esso Timmie's I had visited that morning was thankfully still open. A black coffee would sober me up a little more, and maybe keep me warm for a few more minutes. The kid behind the counter looked at me with head tilted, in complete confusion. His expression looked like he could puke at any second. Apparently, I wasn't as debonair as I'd hoped.

The walk to the mall took an eternity, but the coffee helped. And the first thing I noticed was the liquor store. Everything about booze was suddenly becoming much more attractive. The liquor store might as well have been wearing a cute little skirt with heels… and red lipstick. The temptation was real.

The blast of hot air at the mall entrance made me realize it was only the cold keeping me sober. Inside, I was still tipsy. Worse. Other than the Metro and the LCBO, the mall was just shitty little stores selling absolutely nothing useful. After wandering nearly the entire length of it, I found a Mom and Pop store that might sell pants that would fit me. I was greeted by the Mom half of the partnership – a very angry Eastern European lady.

"We close. Five minute," she barked.

"Ok. I'll be quick. Do you have pants?"

"Five minute," she barked again, pointing to the back of the store.

I did my best speed wobble toward a little "MEN" sign hanging from the ceiling and immediately spotted three-packs of underwear. SCORE! The selection of casual dress pants was not quite so helpful. A choice between plaid flannel pajamas or grey elastic-bottom sweatpants. Deciding that green and blue plaid PJ pants were the dressier option, I picked up the last pair of mediums and headed for the cash.

"Thanks for your patience. I work in retail too. I hate last minute shoppers…"

I was trying to make a new friend.

"Me too. $18.50," she interrupted, without a hint of a smile.

I always keep my wallet in my coat pocket in the winter. But it was not there. The shoe thief must have pilfered that too.

"AYTEENFIFTY!" She was glaring now.

Checking my pants, I found the wallet in the left, front pocket. Phew. The thief really was only interested in quality footwear.

Dragon Lady was growing impatient. And I quickly discovered that my wallet was soaked… in piss. Trying my best to wipe it off, I pulled it free from its watery grave. I could have tapped a credit card to pay. But perhaps this kind lady deserved a tip. I handed her the only bill I had – a twenty.

"Keep the change, sweetheart," I offered with a wink. The bill was dripping on the counter as she took it from my hand.

I walked out of the store.

"Pig! You are PIG!"

"You're welcome!" I waved back.

There is no feeling quite so gratifying as that special smugness only a drinker knows.

I needed something to put my wet pants in, and a bathroom in which to change. Thankfully, Metro was open later than the rest of the mall. I bought a small box of garbage bags and headed to the bathroom. As I removed my pants and underwear, my previous smugness began giving way to drunken shame. I used the sink and paper towel to clean myself up as much as possible. Then a new pair of underwear, and the plaid PJ pants to complete the ensemble.

I hadn't noticed while I was shopping for garbage bags, but it was now apparent that folks were noticing me. And I was clearly something to behold. I tried my best to smile at my admirers, but that did nothing to curb their curiosity. I hadn't bothered to look at my reflection while I was changing, so I snuck a peek at myself in the store window.

Blood. The left side of my face was covered in blood. I could not determine the source, but odds were, it was somewhere on my cranium. I was already late, and there was no time to get back into the bathroom to tidy up. I needed to make my way home. But, maybe… there was time to stop at that sexy little liquor store.

I could see no reason to hide the fact that I'd been drinking. It would be far more embarrassing to look and smell the way I did without an excuse. Plus, there was no better way to apologize to Bridget for my actions than with a bottle of her favourite wine. And fortunately, the liquor store was not busy. The only other two fellows in there didn't look much better than I did. When I grabbed a bottle of Shiraz for Bridget, and a six pack of Keith's for myself, the nice gentleman behind the counter looked at me with sympathy.

"Tough day, Mate?"

"Well. It hasn't been one of my best."

"A drink to ease the pain, eh?"

"That is the plan, Brother. That is the plan."

He didn't seem to notice or care that I stank. I could smell myself by now, and it definitely wasn't pretty. Maybe it was my bag of piss clothes. I'd have to leave that outside when I got home. I would try to explain the day to Bridget, and then take the filth to the laundry room.

Three more blocks to Bridget's house. If the kids were home, they'd be getting high in their caves. I'd only be facing Bridget's judgement. Although she was generally a pretty understanding partner, she had not had to deal with my drunkenness since we were in college. This was uncharted territory.

As I neared home, I could feel the eyes on me. Drunks are paranoid and I was no exception. Eyes. Everywhere. Beady little buggers, peering out from behind pulled back curtains, or pushed open blinds. I was on display and headed to the gallows. Dead Man Walkin'.

I didn't see any point in hesitating when I reached the house. Might as well just barge in and announce myself. Maybe even demand some lovin'.

Steeling myself against the potential barrage, I walked up the driveway, dropped my bag of stink, and opened the front door.

"I'm ho…" I could not finish.

Eyes. More eyes. Six sets of them, staring at me. Six jaws, dropped. The whole family was waiting for me. Aiden was the first to speak.

"What the fuck happened to YOU? Haaaa." At least he saw some humour in the situation.

"Baby. Al! Oh god. What have you done?" Bridget was tearing up.

"I brod you some wine, my love," I offered, cheerfully.

Tessa was crying. Brad looked disgusted. I could see that Sierra was biting her tongue. Pam looked baked.

"What happened to your face? Oh my God, Al. You STINK." Bridget was panicking. "Let's get you cleaned up."

"Why don't we have a drink?" I suggested, hopefully.

Aiden was cracking up. "You're hammered! Oh my god. This is awesome."

"We are getting you cleaned up," Bridget insisted.

"I have some clothes in a bag outside. One sec."

I went outside and grabbed my bag of stink, and brought it into the house.

"These… will need to be washed."

"Holy FUCK. Oh my fucking GOD. You pissed yourself. Haaaaa." Aiden was nearly convulsing with laughter.

"Jesus Christ, Al. What is WRONG with you?"

Bridget was even more pissed than my pants. She grabbed me by the hand and dragged me through the kitchen to the stairs. Snatching my stink bag out of my hand, she pulled me down to the basement.

"Now, strip down. Get in the fucking shower and clean yourself up. Where are you cut?" She asked.

"I dunno, Babe. I didn't even know I was bleeding."

"Let me see."

I removed my cap and tilted my head down.

"Oh my God. How did this happen?"

"What?"

"There's a huge gash over your ear, Al! For God's sake!"

"I honestly don't know."

"Get in the shower. We are having a Zoom call with your daughter," she informed me.

"My daughter is here. What?"

"With Lilly, you idiot. Jesus, Al."

"Oh. Christ. I don't think that's a good idea."

Bridget was shaking her head as she threw all my stuff into the washing machine. Even my new undies and pants. I navigated my way through the storage stuff to the bathroom, which (like the rec room) was tucked off in a corner. I turned the shower on and had a quick look in the mirror while it heated up. There was indeed a large, deep gash over my left ear.

"Hmm? No clue. No fucking idea." I was still muttering to myself as I stepped into the shower.

I let the warm water pour over me. It felt so good, even with the red swirling around the drain. Gingerly running my fingers along the area where the cut was, I could feel it had apparently stopped bleeding. Meaning the blood going down the drain was probably just dried stuff from around the wound. Still, there was an awful lot of it, and I couldn't figure out where the cut had come from.

"Maybe that happened in some other fucking dimension."

Watching the red water disappear down the drain, I felt the pull. The Beast was having none of this. There was no way, no matter how drunk I could get myself, that it would allow me to consider that MY truth, MY memory, MY recollection of the last twenty odd years was incorrect. I could not lose my grip. Maybe there was something to what Marvin had said.

Bridget came into the bathroom.

"I brought you some clean clothes."

"K. Thanks, Babe."

"Are you still bleeding?"

"I don't think so. It is pretty deep though."

"You're going to need stitches."

"You think so?"

"I know so. I'll just do it."

Bridget was a nurse by trade. And either she trusted that I was numb enough to not need freezing, or she was fixing to inflict some punishment on my sorry ass.

I got out of the shower feeling way better, but far more sober than I wanted to be. I got dressed in the clothes Bridget had laid out and headed back upstairs where she was waiting at the dining room table, all prepped for my surgery. The kids were all still sitting in the living room. Poor Tessa still looked upset.

"Are you ok, Chick?" I asked her.

"I just… don't understand, Dad."

"I'm sorry T. I've been having a really hard time the last few days."

Bridget was already into the wine, so I grabbed myself a beer from the kitchen. It would be the first time in a very long while that the kids had seen me drink.

"Jesus, Dad. What are you doing?" Brad was not a happy boy.

"I'm already drunk, dude. One or two more won't make a difference now."

Sierra was bursting at the seams. "Are we still doing the Zoom call?"

"Yes. We absolutely are," Bridget answered.

"No. We absolutely are NOT." I was in no mood to argue, and certainly in no shape to meet an imaginary friend. "I am just not doing that. Not tonight."

"Babe, Lilly is really upset. She wants to see you."

"Bridget, my answer is NO. Not tonight. End of story. Why don't we all talk about what's going on? I would love to hear the kids' opinions. Are you going to stab me with that?"

She was holding the needle, ready to stitch me up.

"Just keep still."

I took a giant swig of my beer and held still. Bridget went to work on me.

"So, guys. Can you tell me what you remember about Christmas Eve?" I asked, almost expecting vindication.

It was Brad, as usual, who offered up the summary of the general consensus.

"We had a great dinner, and we exchanged gifts. Lilly couldn't be here, so you had her gifts to us all put together, and we made Cocoa. It was a really nice Christmas, Dad."

I watched my boy and waited for a punchline that didn't come. Everyone watched me get stitched up in silence, apparently wondering when I was going to snap out of whatever this was. I finally spoke up again.

"Yeah. Well, I do NOT remember it that way. Somebody get me another beer, please."

Aiden was only too happy to oblige. He was the only one finding my ordeal super-duper entertaining.

"What do you remember happening, Big Al?" He was laughing as he handed me the beer.

I downed it in one gulp, before Aiden even sat down.

"I don't remember it the same way."

He stood up to get me another beer.

"He's had enough, Aiden." Bridget fumed.

"No, he hasn't. This is fucking awesome!" Aiden passed me another cold one.

The buzz was setting in again, and I was not displeased.

Bridget finished mending my wound and stood up.

"I am calling Lilly."

"Fill yer boots, Baby. Jus don't ask me to talk."

I put my foot down.

She looked at me with the kind of disdain people normally reserved for serial killers or politicians.

"Do any of you have any clue what it feels like to have everyone around you telling you your memories are completely wrong?" I asked. "DO YOU? No. You don't. Id's fugged."

"Daddy, please just stop." My Tessa was so upset.

"I am not faking this, Chick. I don't wanna talk about this anymore. I am fugging DONE."

I stood up and made my way toward the bedroom.

"Don't piss yourself, Big Al. You want some Depends?" Aiden did not seem genuinely concerned.

"AIDEN REYNOLDS!" Bridget scolded him.

I slammed the bedroom door and dropped onto the bed. I'd been hammered all day, and I was a mess. Nothing had improved. Either I was crazy, or the rest of the world was crazy. And honestly, it was far more likely to be me.

Shit. I need to clarify something.

I got back up, opened the door and shouted down the hall.

"I fuggin' love you guys. Ogay? Dis family means errthing to me? I'm jus mezzed up. I'm SORRY."

Without waiting for a response, I slammed the door again. This time I crawled under the covers and closed my eyes, praying for sleep to come… permanently.

It did not.

Chapter 10:
This Won't Hurt a Bit

I did manage to fall asleep, but it was not a peaceful rest. At some point, Bridget joined me – I likely wouldn't have noticed, but she made a point of waking me up to tell me that I reeked of beer. Also, that Luke had called.

"You have appointments tomorrow, Al. I wrote them down." Her tone was decidedly cool.

"Where did you write them down?"

"Piece of paper in the kitchen."

I got up and went to the kitchen to find the note, and Bridget followed me.

Brain scan, OTMH 8:45 AM

Dr. Ogilvy OTMH, 3:20 PM

Dec. 28

"These appointments are for tomorrow?" I was confused that she hadn't told me earlier.

"I guess so. Sorry about that." She was not sorry.

"I won't be able to work. Maybe not such a bad thing."

I really didn't want to work. There was no way I could concentrate on shoe fitting.

"I won't be able to take you. Pam needs the car," Bridget explained.

"Okay. I can walk or take the bus."

OTMH was short for the Oakville Trafalgar Memorial Hospital, just a few kilometres north of Bridget's house. I was familiar with the facility, and with many of the good folks who worked there.

Miller Shoes had a contract with a good portion of the OTMH staff to fulfil their insured footwear allotment. That put me at the hospital once a week, all year round. We also ran huge shoe clearance sales there. Twice a year, for three or four days at a time, I spent twelve hours each day managing these events. And every single person who worked in the hospital would attend these sales. There was a very real probability that I would know the brain scan people. I most definitely knew Dr. Ogilvy. That was Luke's psych friend. We had played golf together.

"Nice. OTMH. You may as well just parade me around the town with a sign that says 'Look at me! I'm crazy!'" I was not exaggerating.

"They're medical professionals, Babe. You'll be in good hands. And Mark is excellent."

Bridget seemed a little too enthusiastic with that comment. She was on a first name basis with Dr. Ogilvy. I was fairly certain they had known each other on a naked basis as well. There was an unmistakable twinkle in her eye whenever his name came up.

"Right. Good hands with Mark. Perfect."

"Relax."

"Yeah. 'Relax, Al. You are losing your mind – and my former lover Doctor Goodhands is going to help you find it!'" I imitated, in my best Smug Bridget voice.

"Go back to sleep, Al. We can talk in the morning."

I must have fallen asleep again, but I was agitated that Bridget still seemed to have the hots for the good doctor. Or at the very least, she wanted me to think she did. I wouldn't really blame her. He was rich, handsome… and decidedly not crazy.

In the middle of the night, I awoke sweating and short of breath. This was my body's low fuel warning system, and not an unusual occurrence when I was drinking. In the past I might have topped up with a shot of whiskey, but on this occasion, I resisted that temptation. I didn't want to dive back into full on alcoholism. Whatever I needed booze to do, it had already done earlier that day.

I dozed fitfully for the rest of the night. At some point it occurred to me that somewhere, in some other reality, there was another poor sod named Al. A guy with a daughter named Lilly who everyone was now telling him was just a sketch, and to stop imagining shit. Suddenly, his emergency was my emergency. Did I trigger the jump? Or wait – what if he triggered the jump, and was happy as a clam in my fucking reality? Then I am stuck? What if Mark Doctor-Good-Hands Ogilvy sends me to the loony bin? What if the scan shows a gigantic tumour? What if I only have six months to live?

A crazy brain is a busy brain, it would seem.

My alarm went off at 6:00 AM. I was hungover, with another headache – although nowhere near as severe as the one I had endured on Christmas day. I decided to shower off the beer stink that was oozing out my pores. It would be frowned upon by the folks at the hospital. Bridget was in the kitchen when I came back up to get dressed. She had made coffee.

"Yours is on the table."

"Yeah. Thanks."

We sat together in the dining room, in darkness, waiting for the sun to come up.

"How are you feeling? How's the cut?"

"I'm hangin'. Head hurts."

"No surprise there. Are you proud of yourself?"

"What the fuck B? This is not easy stuff."

Bridget rolled her eyes.

"Seriously! Do you think I am making this shit up? It sure feels like you do." I was winding myself up.

"I don't think you are making it up, Al. I do think something's happened, and I think you need help."

"Yeah. Which is why I'm going to see Good Hands."

She cracked a little smile. "Will you just stop? Christ, Al."

"Well, you're awfully grinny."

"I am not grinny. I'm worried about you. I'm worried about what Lilly might think, if she ever gets word of this," she sighed, her grin evaporating.

"I'm worried about me too."

Bridget reached over and took my hand. She was clearly overwhelmed… but she was a lot more concerned about how this might affect Lilly than she was about me.

"I love you, Al."

"I love you too. I'm so sorry."

"You don't have to be sorry. But – I don't understand why you drank. It's the opposite of what you always say – that it only makes things harder." She had a point.

"Well. Yeah. Except drinking never made things this hard. It's just too much. Crazy, untested waters. I feel so messed up."

Pam appeared, exiting her cave to greet the day.

"It lives!" I exclaimed. She was never up this early.

"Morning. Is there coffee?"

"I'll make some more," Bridget offered.

"How are you feeling, Al?" Pam turned her attention to me.

"I don't know, kiddo. I am getting my brain zapped and seeing a shrink today."

"Yeah. Mom said. I can drive you up there if you want – except you'd be pretty early."

"Okay, thanks Pam. That would be great. I appreciate it."

I was relieved. I was far too hungover to walk, and the idea of taking the bus with a bunch of strangers gawking at me just felt gross. But I was also surprised. Pam was not one to interact with me voluntarily. Ever, really. She hadn't said a single word throughout this entire ordeal.

"Will wonders never cease," I whispered to Bridget.

She raised her eyebrows in agreement. "Awfully nice of you, Pammy."

"I am driving right by. No biggie."

"I'll go get dressed – just let me know when you're ready. Cool?" I asked.

"Five minutes."

I went back to the bedroom to find some everyday clothes, and threw them on. I picked up my phone to text Henry Miller. His Dad was en route to Europe so the young fellow would be at the helm for the next couple weeks. I'd have to let them know I wouldn't be in today either.

-Hey. I have doc appointments today. Can't be there. Sorry. Will keep you posted.

-K

His response came immediately, and felt pointed. The Millers took none-too-kindly to worker bees missing workdays for any reason, let alone simple medical appointments. They could happen on days off, or perhaps in the middle of the night. Never during work hours.

Whatever. Fuck him.

I checked for other messages.

Doc Luke

-Left messages with Bridge. Hope the appointments go well, brother. Let me know.

Baby Tessa

-Hi Daddy. Pls lmk how appointments go.

Sierra Cell

-Brad and I are thinking of you. Please don't drink again. He's worried. Let us know how the appointments go?

Lilly Doll

-Daddio, I don't know if you are mad at me about something, or what's going on. But it's not fair that you are just completely ignoring me. PLEASE call. Please, Dad. I am begging. Begging sucks. I love you. L

Damn. She seemed like such a nice kid. But... she wasn't even REAL. So, what the fuck?

"I'm ready Al," Pam hollered from the front door.

"One sec."

I laced up my runners and met her at the door, where Bridget was waiting too.

"Good luck, Babe. Love you. Keep me posted." We kissed... a friendly kiss.

"I will. Love you too."

I wasn't even sure about that anymore. When a brain spirals into madness, love is almost always the first castoff. Extra baggage. Unnecessary weight. But still, it did feel like I had to say it.

Pam was a new driver. I'd taught her in the weeks leading up to her test. She and her Mom had too tense a relationship to foster a mentor/protege sort of understanding. And she was good. The family car was a stick shift, and Pam seemed to relish the control that gave the driver. On this day though, she was hesitant to take the wheel.

"Maybe – do you want to drive?" she asked.

"I'd rather not, Kiddo. Honestly, I'm probably still tipsy."

"Okay." She climbed in the driver's side.

Once I'd joined her in the car, it became obvious that there was an agenda.

"Ok, Al. What the fuck is actually going on?"

"I think you know, don't you?"

She backed out of the driveway, shifted into first, and started in the direction of the hospital. For a moment, she just stared straight ahead, like a good little driver person. Then she laid it on me.

"Are you... crazy? Is that what all... THIS... is about?" The words were stumbling out of her mouth.

"It sure feels like I am. But I don't get it. Any of it. At all."

"Well, neither do we, Al. Lilly is going to find out, you know. Aiden is such a dick."

"What do you mean?" I knew Aiden was a dick, but I wasn't sure how that related to my current situation.

"He thinks this is fucking hilarious. And he doesn't give a shit if it would break Lilly's heart that her own Dad is denying that she even exists."

"Jesus." Nothing like a guilt trip to straighten an insane person out.

"You have to talk to her, Al. Before Aiden does. You just... have to."

"I can't, Kiddo. I think it would melt my brain," I answered, not daring to mention the Beast.

"But why? She is your daughter. She's my sister. You've always been so proud of her. And she loves you."

I couldn't respond. This conversation was making my head spin, and the more Pam talked, the tighter the Beast's grip became. I could not accept any other reality than the one I knew.

By the time we arrived at the East Entrance of OTMH, it was foggy, and getting worse by the second – the gigantic, grey building was barely visible, even from only a few feet away.

"Be careful out there, Kiddo," I warned her.

"Just think about what I said, Al. It's super important."

"I will. Just, please be careful."

"I will, I promise. We all love you too, Al."

"Love you, Kiddo."

Well, that was a first. My kids barely ever said they loved me. Bridget's kids never said it to anyone. Apparently, all I had to do to earn the privilege was completely lose my mind, get hammered, and piss myself. Whatever the reason, I was grateful. It was reassuring.

I felt eyes on me as I entered the hospital. There was a baby grand piano in the lobby, usually manned by one of several volunteer maestros. On this day, it lay blanketed and asleep, with a "DO NOT TOUCH" sign on top. I was tempted to peel the blanket off and tickle the ivories, but that would likely get me tossed into the bin even faster than a visit with Dr. Goodhands. I took a chair beside the piano instead.

I was still about an hour early for my brain zap. Sitting back, it occurred to me that I still had unheard voice messages from Christmas day. With a sense of dread, I dialed 1.

Dun dun "Who's calling please. Enter your password, then press pound."

9879

Da da "You have… two… new messages. To listen, press 1 now.

1

"First new message"

"You give me THAT bullshit and then you hang up on me? Jesus, you can be an ass. Call me whenever. Hope you are ok."

It was Nadene. I guess she called right after I hung up on her.

"To Delete the message, press 7. to save, press 9"

7

"Message deleted. Next message."

"Hey Allan. It's your big sister. Merry Christmas. Just checking in on you, bro. Call when you get a chance. Love you, Al. It's Lana."

"To delete th"…

7

Damn. She sounded good. It was hit and miss with Lana. Sometimes her schizophrenia got the better of her and she made little sense. This message was lucid, clear headed. More normal than I could remember hearing her in a very long time. At least one of us sounded sane. I would call her back between appointments.

The Maestro of the day appeared and set himself up at the piano. At least there would be some entertainment while I waited to learn if I had two brains. This particular piano man was also a singer. He was the only one who brought along a mic and a little P.A. He typically would sing 50s boogie woogie far too loudly and this day was no exception. Rock Around the Clock led into a few Chuck Berry tunes, followed by some surprise Beatles. I Wanna Hold Your Hand, Here Comes the Sun.

And then, the Great Mind Fuck of the Century launched full force. Maestro broke into a song that sounded far more familiar than it should have.

"You can't stop the merry-go-round, there's nothin' good between up and down."

It was my tune. Classic Allan Isaac. But it wasn't even finished. I had started writing it a decade earlier, and there were bits of it stored in my phone. But I'd never performed it live, let alone recorded it. I had one verse, a chorus intro, and a chorus written. Where did this insipid turd even hear this song?

"Hey! Where did you get that song, Man?" I had to yell over his stupid P.A.

"And if the world's so simple, why am I, then, so confused, and I feel I'm being used. I just can't seem to choose." He ignored me and kept singing.

I continued it for him. *"Between the broken-hearted people and those who have no heart, and it's tearing me apart, I just don't know where to start."*

He winked at me, and kept going.

"Where the FUCK did you hear this?" This was making no sense.

He stopped mid-song, just for a second. "Watch your language, Buddy. Jeez. Everyone knows this song."

I sat back down, in disbelief, and listened quietly until he'd finished. The lyrics were no longer registering in my spinning brain, but a very nice little bridge caught my ear. When he finally finished, I approached him again.

"Seriously, Man. That song isn't even finished. How could you possibly know it?" I asked.

He looked at me like I was as crazy as I felt. "My friend, I'm afraid I don't understand?"

"Dude, that is MY song. Mine. I haven't ever even played it. It's not finished."

"Ha. You wish. It's Blue Rodeo, Buddy. Get a life."

"What? No, it's not, Man. Seriously."

"Listen, Asshole. Look it up. Leave me alone." He waved me off and went back to playing.

I was pulling out my phone with every intention of googling it, but noticed that it was time for my brain zap. I had to walk past the song thief toward Information, to find out where the brain zap department was. He scowled at me.

"I'll show you, you window licking dick wad. I have it saved in MY fucking phone. Loser." Said under my breath.

The nice lady behind the information counter knew me well. She often would validate my parking pass, so I wouldn't have to pay.

"Hi, Al. You need a stamp?" she asked.

"Hey. No, not here for shoes this time. I'm having a brain scan. The docs seem to think I have a whole community of chipmunks running around in there. Where do I go?"

"Ha! You're funny. Third Floor. South wing."

"Thanks, Linda."

I knew where that was, so I headed to the appropriate elevator. The Imaging Department was easy to find. Everyone I passed smiled like they knew me – because they did know me. Eyes were on me, everywhere. People stealing my freaking songs. I wanted to crawl into the machine and die there.

"Hey! Shoe guy! I thought that was your name on the docket." Another familiar face greeted me. I could see she was wearing Miller's shoes.

"Hey."

"Grab a gown. The change room is just down there. You can put your valuables in one of the lockers across the hall."

"Thanks."

"Smile, Handsome! It's not that scary."

She had no idea how scary it was. And, I was most definitely not feeling handsome that day.

I changed into the hospital robe and stuffed my clothes into a locker. Another nurse led me to the imaging room.

"We are just doing your brain today, Mr. Isaac. Can you just lie down on the table for me, on your back? Oh – WOW, what happened here?" She pointed to the cut behind my ear.

I said nothing, and did what I was told. Obviously, I had cut myself. I didn't think it needed an explanation. I had endured several MRIs for my back over the years. This felt the same, except they were only sticking me into the tube cranium deep. The rest of me was exposed to the elements, and the eyes. The robe was completely unnecessary, but they were in the business of humiliation. The scan was over in ten minutes.

"When will we know the results?" I asked.

"Dr. Daniel requested immediate access to the images, so you will probably hear from him today. That nasty cut may have implications."

"Okay. Thank you. Can I change now?"

"Absolutely. Have a great day."

"Yeah. Right."

People who are having brain scans typically do not have great days. I grabbed my clothes from the locker and took a minute in the change room to contemplate the day's options. There were several hours to kill before my appointment with Goodhands, and I was dreading that stretch of time. Where would I go? If I had to sit listening to some idiot play my unfinished songs, I would lose it. The temptation to get smashed again was gnawing at me.

I'd planned to call Lana back, but struggling with my own crazy felt like more than enough. I didn't have it in me to deal with hers as well.

Gnaw gnaw gnaw.

Jesus. A beer or five would definitely fix this hangover.

And that was how I became a drunk in the first place. Once you learn that a couple of drinks can cure a hangover, the thought of just sitting through that nasty feeling for a day or two becomes way less appealing.

Gnaw Gnaw Gnaw.

Damn it. I did not want to dive back into drunky Al. He was not pretty. But the thought of this appointment with Dr. Goodhands was beginning to irritate me. What if he was in cahoots with Bridget? How convenient would it be for him to just lock me up, so he could shag my lady?

These are exactly the kind of thoughts that will get you locked up, Asshole.

Gnaw Gnaw Gnaw

Needing something to occupy my brain, I decided to find out how many songs Blue Rodeo had stolen from me. But I needed earbuds. Certain that the hospital gift shop would have them, I rode the elevator down to the main floor. When two doctors joined me on the second floor, my paranoia began snowballing. The feeling that they were staring at me, judging me, was intense. I was crawling out of my skin to escape the elevator and needed air, so I stepped outside into the soupy fog for a breath of... mist.

This fog was making the entire situation even more surreal. There was a sense that at any moment, The Grim Reaper himself could emerge from the murk to pluck me up. And it was not an unappealing thought, given the currently undeniable lapse in my sanity.

Gnaw Gnaw Gnaw

Alas, the good horseman failed to manifest. I turned back into the hospital to find the gift shop and some headphones. Only $27.95 for two little plastic balls I could stick in my ears. And they definitely sold this exact same set at the gas station for three bucks. But money was no object. I had a dream-like memory that the bank had recently increased my credit card limit. I forked over the asking price without any attempt to bargain.

The hospital was huge, with a food court that could make most shopping malls blush with envy. Finding a relatively quiet, private place to listen to music was going to be next to impossible. It was still early enough in the day that there were empty tables in the corners of the eating area. The perimeter of the space was floor to ceiling windows – but on this day they could just as easily have been concrete walls. Zero visibility. I managed to find a table near the recycling bins; these didn't usually attract a crowd.

Sitting down to face the window, I plugged the earbuds into my phone and searched "Blue Rodeo songs." Most of the tunes listed were familiar. The very first song, though, was titled "Merry-Go-Round". What was left of my heart… sank. It was the only song that looked out of place. It was my song. Why was it first on the list?

I was shocked, but not surprised, to see that it had its own Wikipedia page.

Merry-Go-Round is a song by Canadian band, Blue Rodeo. Released in 2011, the song is credited giving the band the international following it has today.

BLA BLA BLA

Gnaw Gnaw Gnaw

I'd read enough. Clicking on the YouTube link, I suffered through an ad for Viagra and then hit play.

It. Was. Exactly. The. Fucking. Same. The same C F pattern for the verse, the same C G Am D chorus intro, and back to C F for the chorus. Shit, Jim Cuddy even sounded like me. How was this possible? I couldn't wait to hear the second verse, and to see if idiot piano boy had nailed the bridge.

"The time it takes to make mistakes, you just don't have to spend

No chance to make amends

Just how this story ends"

"What the fuck? Is he singing AT me?" I asked out loud.

GNAW GNAW GNAW

"The faces that you see 'round here, they're looking back at you

Does your story ring out true?

Are you payin' up your dues?

You can't just lay back, and hope that, no one's gonna knock you down off your track"

Jesus Christ.

GNAW GNAW GNAW

The second verse felt like it was clearly aimed at me. It didn't feel or sound like something I would write. It was my melody, my song overall, but it had been hijacked. Pirated. And now it was flat out yelling at me.

I hated this cryptic shit. The Beast communicated in riddles, and I couldn't stand the prick.

The second chorus repeated the first – just as I would have done. When the bridge fell to the relative minor (just like an Al song) it seemed the piano guy had done it correctly. I had to listen to it a few times for the lyrics to sink in.

"Get you back where you belong

You gotta undo what you've done

We won't miss you when you're gone"

It may as well have said "Get ye the fuck out of Dodge, Al! This ain't your playground. This ain't your sandbox."

GNAW GNAW GNAW. CRUNCH

Fuck it. The Beast was digging its claws into me. There was no escape. I had to get out of this insanity. And the shortest route was a good, old-fashioned piss up. Dr. Goodhands be damned. He would have to deal with drunky Al. No two ways about it. I set out into the fog to find a watering hole.

The intersection at Third Line and Dundas is six lanes across, both ways. There were little strip malls on both southwest and southeast corners. My untrustworthy memory was telling me that there was at least one bar in there somewhere. My instinct was to search the southeast mall first, but that meant crossing both ways in this treacherous fog. The stoplights were a mirage, just a hint of colour if you tilted your head, squinted at just the right angle.

As I approached the corner, I made out what seemed to be a green light through the mist. But when I stepped onto the road, the side mirror of a car brushed up against my coat as it passed. It probably wasn't moving fast enough to knock me down, but it meant the drivers had no better idea than I had. Headlights were no match for this soup. Still, I was more than happy to take my chances. I trudged on.

I nearly tripped over the southwest curb when I reached it. A large vehicle (probably a truck) zoomed right behind me. Blind luck. Damn it. The crossing to the east side might not end quite as well, so I decided to explore the little mall on the west corner.

I knew the closest two buildings were a Bank of Montreal and a fast-food joint. Not appropriate saloons. The first door in the mall turned out to be a Mediterranean restaurant, but they did not open until dinner time. I passed a hardware store, then a sporting goods shop. About five stores in, I spotted a flashing OPEN sign. The door was open, just a crack and there was a sign on it.

Ralph's Sports Bar

I had found my home for the next few hours.

"Good morning!" A wise-looking fellow about my age was drying a glass behind the bar.

"Good morning. You can fill that up with a Keith's if you have it. Are you Ralph?"

"I do indeed have it, and sure. Ralph was my Dad. I'm Tom."

"Hey Tom. I'm Al. Your Dad couldn't have owned this place?"

"Nah. He always wanted to own a bar. So, when I got one, I named it after the old bugger. Think he would have liked this place."

Tom poured a perfect pint and handed it to me.

"I think so too, Man. Very cool spot. You've done a nice job."

The bar was richer looking than most of the sports dives I'd seen. Typical deep red decor, two dart boards, seven or eight TVs hanging from the ceiling, a few booths, five or six tables. But it was sparkling clean. That was the difference. The floor looked freshly refinished, the walls cleanly painted, and there was no residual stench of smoke from the days when bars had as many full ashtrays as they had drunken patrons.

"Thank you, Sir. What brings you outside on a shitbox day like this?" Tom asked.

"Well, Thomas, that's a very long story. Let's just say that a few pints right now might just save my life."

"Don't they always? Right up until they kill you."

"Ain't that the truth."

We shared an understanding laugh over that. Tom seemed to know the ins and outs of alcoholism. How it gets into your blood. How it is both the solution to, and the cause of all your problems.

"Will you join me in a pint, Brother?" I asked. The times when a barkeep would drink with a barfly were few and far between. But this day might be an exception. Mine would likely be the only face he'd see all day.

"You know, Al, I just might. Nothin' doin' anyway."

He pulled himself a pint of Guinness and raised it in my direction

"Cheers."

"Slainte."

We clinked glasses, and each took a deep pull on our pints. Again, I could feel the first swallow in my fingertips. It was still the best calmer of nerves I had ever experienced. Despite all I'd said against it over the previous six years.

"You drink much?" I was curious.

"Used to. Not so much anymore. You?" Tom answered.

"Same. Quit six years ago; never ever thought I would go back to it. But then, I never thought I'd ever be in the situation I'm in now."

"What situation is that? What could possibly claw you back in after that long? It's a woman, isn't it?" An assumption most drunks would make.

"Ha. Not so much. It's complicated. I don't think you'd understand."

"You underestimate the talent and experience of a pourer of pints!"

"Indeed. True. Pour me another, and I might try to explain."

"Fair enough, my Man. Fair enough."

Tom was becoming the best friend I'd ever had. He pulled and handed me another pint without judgement. Without hesitation. Without question.

"Thank you, Sir."

"So. What could knock a six-year man off the wagon?"

"You want the abridged version?"

"Whatever version you want to give me, my Man."

I decided this strange new friend would not get every detail. I explained that I seemed to have landed in an unfamiliar place, where people existed who never had before. Where songs I had written were huge hits for other performers. Where everyone was staring at me, judging me. I told him I was scared, and that I desperately needed to get back.

"Well. That is some seriously fucked up shit, Al. You seem like a pretty straight shooter. I would never have guessed. What do the Docs say?"

"That is another story entirely, Brother. I am going to get myself a little sauced before I go see the Psych dude… who used to shag my girlfriend. How's that for fucked up?"

"Sweet Jesus, Al. That doesn't sound like a good idea." Tom was genuinely concerned.

"If I go in straight, I won't be able to handle what this guy says. I just won't. Better pour me another."

"I got you, Man. Here you go. Is this bastard still into your wife?"

"We're not married – and I really have no clue. I wouldn't be surprised, though."

"No shit. Well, I hope he puts that stuff aside and helps you get to the bottom of this."

"Me too. But I don't have a good feeling about it. At all."

"How tanked do you want to be when you see this guy?"

"Pour me another, Tom."

This little pattern continued, interspersed with occasional pissings, until the clock on the wall told me it was time to head back to the hospital to see Dr. Goodhands. It was 3:00 PM. I was at least eleven pints in, maybe more.

"Very good da meed you, Tom. Thangs zo mush for errthing, Man. Seerzly."

"Good to meet you too, Al. Hey, drop in any time you like. Let me know how things go. I'm rootin' for you, my Man!"

I nodded, and stumbled toward the door. The fog had finally lifted, and the sun was shining, but I was no more confident in my ability to cross the street than I had been totally blind. Still, I steadied myself somewhat, and made the crossing unscathed.

There was still time to buy a coffee, which I hoped might hide my drunkenness a little. One for Goodhands too, as an olive branch. I knew where his office was, after bringing a pair of shoes up to him during the last sale; he was far too important to come down among the peasants. Jumping onto the elevator again, I hit the 5th floor button.

Hospitals are busy places, making it nearly impossible to ride the elevators alone. The stairs, hallways and elevators were always bustling. A comely lady doctor entered the lift with me on the second floor.

Well, SHE's not staring at me.

"Hello, Dog der," I used my best sober guy voice.

She looked at me like she had just thrown up a little in her mouth.

"Ad leez the fog's lifded."

"It has. Nice day now," she responded! I was doing well.

Ha. No one can even tell that I am wasted!

"Maybe get yourself into detox when you're finished playing on the elevator." This, thrown over her shoulder as she exited the lift on the 4th floor.

"You too," I responded, like a drunken moron. It took a minute for her comment to register.

Shit. IDIOT!

When the doors opened onto the 5th floor, I realized I had completely forgotten where I was going. Luckily, an orderly was passing.

"Skuze me. D'you know where Dogder Goodhands' offiz is?" I was swaying, but trying to look very serious.

"Goodhands? No. I don't know that name."

"Shit. OGlevee. Dogder Ogilvy."

"Oh, yes. Dr. Ogilvy's office is just down that hall, on the right."

"Thang you. Have a nize day."

"Are you okay, Sir?"

I nodded and speed wobbled in the direction he had indicated. Turning left at the hallway and four doors down, I found Dr. Goodhands' door wide open on the right side. I could hear him on the phone.

"Ha! Well, good to hear from you, Luke. I will, I will. Talk soon. Oh, Al just arrived. Take care. Yeah. Bye now." He hung up the phone and extended a good hand to greet me.

"Al! How the hell are you, Man? Good to see you. Have a seat."

We shook hands.

"I brod you gawvee." I put his coffee on his desk, and sat in the chair he offered, with a clumsy thud.

"Thanks, Al. So, how are things? How's Bridge? The kids? Luke tells me you are having some trouble?"

"Ah, Bridge. Good Ol' Bridge. She's good. Kids are good. Idz me. I'm fugged, Man."

"Tell me what's going on? What happened there?" He pointed to my cut.

"Fer fug sakes. It is a cud, I got a cud. It has fug all to do wid anything."

"Uh. Okay, Al."

"Bridge, you know Bridge, she stidged me ub. I am good ta go," I explained.

"Fair enough. So. Tell me what's going on?"

"Well, Dogder Goodhands, why don't you tell ME whadz goin' on? Are you still fugging good ol' Bridge?"

Shit, I let that slip out.

"Al. Come on, Man."

"She cerdnlee has a LOD of smiley faces when she tawgs aboud you, Goodhands. LODs of 'em."

"Jesus Christ, Al, you are completely hammered. What the hell is going on?"

"Lemme zee those hands. How good are they? Good ol Bridge, she juz LOVES em."

"That's enough, Al. I can help you, but you'll have to stop this business, okay?

"NO, YOU have to stop, Goodhands. Maybe keeb yer dig in yer panz, fer fug saygs."

It seemed I couldn't keep any of this to myself.

"Alright, Buddy. I'm calling security and you can spend the night in the round room."

"Woah, woah, woah, Big Fella. I'm juz jozshin ya. Haaa. Got you there, Mark!"

I could see, quite clearly, that the good Doctor was not amused. I was one stupid remark away from the bin.

"I promiz…I PROMISE TO CO OPERADE!" I was trying my damnedest to enunciate.

"I'm not sure we can accomplish much here, Al. You are intoxicated."

"I AM INOXI… (Hiccup)… INTOXICATED. I'm sorry, Mark. Idz really the ONLY way I could tawg to you. I will straighten up, Brother. I'm sorry."

"Can you even tell me what is happening to you, Al?"

"Yes. I think so."

"Alright, we can try. Luke told me you are having trouble with your perception of reality?"

"Is that all he tole you?" I asked.

"Basically, yes. He didn't get into detail. That is for you and me to work out. Can you give me some details?"

"Sure. Lilly. Lilly is the detail. And some other shit."

"Bridge's daughter, Lilly?"

"Seerzly? Are you THAT fuggin' insensitive?"

"I'm sorry, Al. She's your daughter too. I just knew Bridge way before I met you."

"Listen, Big Fella. If we are gonna tawg aboud this for real, you gotta call Bridget 'Bridget'. Cool? When you call her Bridge, it makes me wanna punch yer face."

"Ok, Al. I wasn't aware. Bridge-et will be Bridge-et. So, with Lilly, are you guys having problems with her? I thought she was doing really well?"

"I's egspegting you to say that. I went to bed Christmas Eve after drawing a skedge of a fictional kid, called her Lilly. Christmas morning comes, and all you bazdurds are telling me this kid has actually existed for more than twenty years! And my memory is combleedly fugging differnt? Those are the details, Doc. Thad's why I'm here."

It was the best I could do. That was all the detail he was going to get.

"Okay. That is a lot. It's pretty unusual to have one reality replaced with a different one."

"You think? Overnight, Mark? Over fugging night? It makes zero sense."

"I agree. I don't know what to make of it. What is Bridge-et saying?" He was saying her full name like someone had shoved a turd in his mouth.

"Err one spects me to juz embraze the fact that this kid is alive and well and living in Kingston."

"Well, Al. That's because she is."

How dismissive could he be?

"EXCEPT this version of me, of Allan Isaac, does NOT know this kid. Do you have any idea what that feels like? When people are telling you that your entire perception of reality is wrong?"

"You have schizophrenia in your family, is that right?"

"I knew you were going to go there. Are you gonna lock me up?"

I was almost hoping that he would lock me up. It felt like it might be safer than being out in this unrecognizable world. Taking a sip of my black coffee, I waited for his response.

"Does Bridge-et know about your drinking?"

"She knew aboud id yezerday."

The coffee wasn't sitting well. After six years of sobriety, I had forgotten that (for me, sometimes) beer and coffee did not mix.

"Not today?"

The coffee-beer-stew was brewing up a rumbly bumbly in my tumbly. I shook my head.

"No. Nod doday."

I was going to lose the contents of my gut.

"You ok, Al? You look green."

I motioned to his wastepaper basket. He did not understand my gesture, with a most unfortunate result. I did attempt to lift myself out of the chair to get to said basket, but I did not make it. Beer and coffee, and tiny, soggy bits of morning muffin, now adorned two walls, most of his desk, and a good portion of the carpet. Not to mention Dr. Goodhands' shoes. The same ones I had delivered to his office. There was a good part of me that was tickled neon pink with my redecorating effort.

"Jesus Christ, Al. For God's sake."

He picked up the phone and called hospital maintenance for cleanup. I was on my hands and knees, failing to stifle hysterical laughter.

"I'm sorry, Mark. Didn't see that coming!"

I could not hold back. I laughed so hard that the remaining contents of my stomach violently escaped their bodily prison. At least by this time I was perfectly positioned over the basket.

"Nothin' but net! SWISH!"

I could not control my laughter and fell over into a pool of puke. Which made me giggle even harder.

"Lez zee if your good hands can clean THIS up!" Ha.

"Ok, Buddy. We don't want Bridge seeing you like this. Let's get you checked in and cleaned up. You can stay here for the night, and I'll tell her we are keeping you for observation. For a concussion."

"Ogay."

"Can you hear me, AL? Do you understand?"

"I do. Thang you, Mark. I am sorry. I appreeshade thad."

"You are going through something incomprehensible. I do want to help."

Maybe Goodhands wasn't so bad after all. But he was locking me up. Probably going to shag good ol' Bridge. I didn't even care. I just wanted to sleep.

The cleaning crew turned up before my hysterical laughter had completely abated. There were thousands of them, it seemed. Working at lightning speed. Chemicals and deodorizers with magical capabilities. They were still hard at work when the porter, whom Goodhands had summoned, arrived. The hulking young fellow pushed a stretcher into the room for me, hauled me up onto it, and rolled me away.

"Where are you tayging me, big guy?" I asked.

"We've got a room for you. We'll get you cleaned up, and probably give you something to help sleep it off."

"My dream come true."

I would not have to face a soul. I would not have to answer any more questions. I could escape for a little while. I had a reprieve. The day began to feel much better.

Once I'd been wheeled into my private room, the (apparently) identical cleaning crew from Goodhands' office came in to give me a similar treatment. My pukey clothes were stripped off, bagged, and taken away. They sponged me down, outfitted me in a stylish blue robe, and laid me flat out on the bed.

A few minutes later, a nurse arrived, IV in tow.

"How are you feeling, Mr. Isaac?"

"Not too bad, actually."

"I'm going to give you something that will help you sleep. Okay?"

"Okay."

"It'll keep you more comfortable when you wake up, too. Give me your arm, Mr. Isaac? This won't hurt a bit."

I presented my left arm and felt a needle prick, but it was painless.

"You are an angel sent by God," I said, with eternal gratitude.

"Aren't you a charmer? Have a good rest, Sir. Sweet dreams."

Chapter 11:
Road Trip

Whatever that lovely angel had given me, it worked instantly. I was out, quickly and deeply. If I did in fact dream, I had no recollection of it. When the sound of conversation finally woke me, it was only because I recognized the voices. Dr. Goodhands, Dr. Luke, and Good Ol' Bridge. I kept my eyes closed, feigning sleep, and did my best to listen. They were speaking in hushed whispers, but I could make out most of it.

"Do you think meds might help?" Bridget was asking.

Dr. Luke replied. "Absolutely. They'll help. He might not feel completely settled… but at least he might not feel compelled to escape. Would you agree, Mark?"

"We'd have to try a couple different approaches, but we can definitely find the right combination," Goodhands agreed.

"What do you mean – escape?" That was Bridget again.

I'd had just about enough of these three people – none of whom were me – deciding what to do with ME. I opened my eyes and spoke.

"Do I get a say in any of this?" I asked the brain trust.

"Oh, hey Sweetie! You're awake." Bridget leaned in and gave me a kiss.

I felt momentarily self-conscious, assuming my breath would be all beer-pukey. But somehow, I was minty fresh. *These people are magic!*

"How long was I… not awake?" I had no idea if I'd been sleeping for an hour or a month, and I was definitely confused by the lack of hangover and stink.

"About 24 hours, Al. We thought it best to keep you resting." Goodhands was doing me a solid. Good Ol' Bridge didn't look the slightest bit angry. She would have been, had she heard about my second consecutive day of debauchery.

"Thanks, Mark. I do feel better. What's the plan?"

"We thought we should talk about how you want to tackle this," Luke answered for him.

"Well, Buddy. I would like to tackle it by getting my life back."

"Oh, Sweetie. That's all we want too. I promise. I just need you home. I need my Al."

Bridget was squeezing my hand. She was starting to seem as desperate as I felt. Maybe she wasn't shaggin' Goodhands after all. No guarantee it would stay that way though, and I knew I wasn't winning any points by being crazy. That tends to lose its charm about as fast as a fart on a first date.

"But you need your Al to buy into this notion that, overnight, his brain completely dumped a whole bunch of data and replaced it with other data. Yes?" I asked.

"I guess that's about right. Yeah," she answered, like that shouldn't be such a tough thing for me.

Goodhands continued: "Al, we do believe that with the right meds, and some consistent therapy, we can gradually re-introduce you to your memory."

"RE-introduce? RE-INTRODUCE?? What you are proposing is a first meeting!" I barked. "You can't RE-introduce something that has never been introduced in the first place! You'd need to purge the last 20-odd YEARS, and then somehow dump new information into it! You can't look me in the eye and tell me you think that's possible??"

Mic Drop. I'd left them speechless. Good Ol' Bridge started crying again.

"Damn it. I'm sorry, Babe. I don't want to upset you. I'll try. I will try, okay?"

I was trying to sound reassuring. After all, I was probably the only one in the room who felt the strength of the Beast, pulling, pulling, and dragging. But there was no way in hell I was going to try – I just didn't want Bridget to know that.

"We don't have to jump on the first option that comes to mind, Buddy. Mark and I will do some digging to see if there have been similar cases, and we can go from there. Sound good?"

Luke was calm and reasonable. I felt lucky to have my friend as my doctor. And I trusted him a lot more than I trusted Goodhands – although he seemed to be on Team AL too, for the most part.

"Alright, Luke. I trust you guys," I answered, half-truthfully.

"In the meantime, I think it would be a good idea for you to stay here another night. Your brain scan showed nothing abnormal, but there was some trauma around that cut. I'd like to monitor it for a bit, if you don't mind."

"If Bridget can live without me for another night," I joked.

She was still squeezing my hand, and her eyes were still fixed on mine.

"I'll try. Just get better, okay? Please?" She was pleading.

"Okay Docs. That settles it. I'll get settled back in. Are you going to get me all drugged up again?"

"Ha! Not quite the same tonight – but we can give you an oral sleep aid," Goodhands offered.

Oddly, I was still very tired and felt like I could sleep again without any help. But I wasn't about to refuse.

"I'll take it. Also, I'm starving. Any chance I could get something to eat?"

"Dinner is on its way. Pretty sure they're making their rounds now."

"Thanks, Mark."

"No problem, Buddy. Luke, why don't we leave these kids alone for a bit. I'll buy you some dinner."

Goodhands and Luke having dinner, discussing their crazy friend. Yay. Not awkward at all. They said their goodbyes, then each gave Bridget a peck on the cheek. I was a little surprised that Luke lingered a bit longer than Goodhands. Maybe I had to worry about him, too?

And then I was finally alone with Bridget, for the first time in what felt like weeks. In reality, only two days – but I was hammered for one of them, and asleep for the other.

She looked exhausted.

"You okay, Babe?" I asked.

"Am I okay? No. I am not okay, Al."

"I did say I'll try?"

"I know, sweetie. I know. It's just been a hard few days. Pam was in a little accident after she dropped you off. That fog was crazy."

"Oh shit! I'm so sorry, babe. Is she okay?"

"She's fine. The car… not so much. The airbags deployed and shattered the windshield. She said she was going super slow. Pain in the ass, more than anything."

"I was really worried. The fog rolled in stupid fast, like a movie. It was wild."

"She said you told her to be careful, so she was being careful. But she couldn't even see the road. She hit a light pole on Dundas."

"I'll bet. Where did she go? It was tough to see just walking down the sidewalk."

"Yeah, for sure. I guess some lady heard the crash and came out of her house with a flashlight. Pam stayed with her until the fog lifted."

"Where's the car now?" I was curious how Bridget was getting around.

"It's at the dealer – we had it towed. I'm driving a rental. Insurance is covering it."

"That's good. I'm just glad she's okay. You look tired, B. Why don't you go home and get some rest."

"Yeah. I think I will."

As she stood up to go, the food cart was wheeled in with my dinner. Watery mashed potatoes and chicken, with a little plastic container of applesauce, and an orange juice. And another tiny paper cup with three pills inside.

"Perfect timing. My lady was just leaving." I was talking to the expressionless guy pushing the cart, but he did not appear to notice.

"Take the pills with the food." And he was gone.

Bridget leaned in and gave me a big kiss, like she really wanted me to feel the love. I did. But I wasn't sad she was leaving; the less I interacted with people, the easier the time went by.

"I love you, Al. I always have. And I will, no matter what." She squeezed my hand again.

"I love you too, Babe. See you tomorrow?"

"Of course. I'll be by around lunch."

Another quick kiss, and she was gone. I'd lied to her – I had absolutely no intention of taking the pills. Something Marvin told me had stuck. I couldn't cloud my thinking with meds until I could figure out where the hell I was.

I did not believe in a magic combination of pills that could do what they'd proposed. All I could hope for was a numbing to this reality, or rather, this surreality. And numbness was more easily achieved through pints. And pints at least offered an excuse to puke on Goodhands' shoes.

I was alone with my shitty dinner and the pills. If I took them, they'd likely knock me out. I decided to tuck them away, but it occurred to me that I didn't know what they'd done with my clothes. Opening the little cupboard beside my bed, lo and behold I found my duds. All laundered up and folded like nothing bad had ever happened to them. Which gave me an idea.

I would wait until everyone was asleep, get dressed… and escape. I didn't know where I'd go, but I had to get out of there. They'd tie me down and force meds back down my throat if I stayed. And Bridget would help them. As much as I wanted to sleep, it wasn't going to happen in that bed.

I needed fuel, and the dinner (as unappealing as it was) would have to suffice. Something so utterly flavourless would probably also be devoid of any nutritional value, but it would fill my empty gut, which would have to be enough. I ate every bite.

I needed a plan. Hidden in the back of my untrustworthy brain, there was something that I absolutely had to do, but I didn't know what. I was being pulled, but not in the direction of beer – which was a very good thing. The last place I wanted to wind up was back in the hospital, and that was exactly where another piss up would land me.

So, the details of my plan so far: Eat. Wait. Dress. Walk out.

It was a start. I'd already crossed off the first task, and hunkered down to complete the second. I had time to consider my options while I waited.

I could get a hotel room for the night, which would satisfy the need for sleep. I could go home, but that would mean dealing with people. Neither option seemed to satisfy the Beast.

"Where the fuck do you want me to go, you prick?" I was muttering, but it heard me.

I noticed a magazine face down on my bedside table that had not been there before. On the back cover was an ad for VIA Rail. It was as though someone, or something, had just placed it there, that very second.

Then, it hit me.

"Kingston. I'm going to Kingston. Holy shit."

In that instant, I knew I needed to go to Queen's University. I had to at least see Lilly. Not for a second did I think I'd be able to actually converse with her. But if I could just see her, just get a look at the "Sketch who became a Girl," I felt that would somehow satisfy the Beast.

With no idea how late the trains and buses ran, I rummaged around for my phone under the pile of clothes. And of course it was dead; I hadn't thought to buy a charger when I picked up the earbuds earlier. The clock on the wall indicated nearly 5:00 PM. I had time, but I needed to act fast, and suddenly I didn't care if anybody saw me leave.

I got myself dressed, pocketed my phone and headed for the gift shop, which luckily was still open. I bought myself a charger and asked the kid behind the counter to call me a cab.

"There are always cabs waiting outside that entrance over there." She was pointing in the general direction of the East entrance.

After paying roughly seven million dollars for the charger, I bolted for the cab stand. I'd never noticed them there before, but she was quite right. There were four shiny Oakville taxi cabs lined up just outside the entrance. I hopped in the first one.

"How much to get me to Union Station?" I asked the driver.

"I can do flat rate. Eighty?" The cabby answered.

"Perfect. Do you take Visa?"

"Prefer cash, if you can."

"No problem, we'll just have to stop at a machine. Let's go to that BMO?" I pointed to the Bank of Montreal, in the same little plaza as Ralph's Sports Bar. With relief, I realized I felt zero temptation to visit my friend Tom.

"Okay." He drove us across the street to the bank.

"I'll be just a minute." I exited the cab and found the bank closed. But the two ATMs were accessible 24/7, and inside I found Tom the bartender at the far machine.

"My Man! How'd your meeting go?"

"Much better than I'd hoped. I'll fill you in next time I see you, Brother. Thanks again."

"No problem, Al. Listen, all the best, eh? Take care of yourself."

"You too, Tom."

I was strangely glad to have seen him after all. For whatever reason, I wanted him to remember me in a kinder light. I couldn't remember if I'd even paid my tab the day before, but had the feeling that Tom wouldn't have cared either way. I could feel that there was something of great significance in my drunken conversation with him. No idea what it was… but it was in there.

When I climbed back into the cab, the driver had turned the radio on. And of course, that beautiful Blue Rodeo classic, Merry-Go-Round, was playing.

"You like Classic Rock?" he asked.

"Maybe no music for this drive, Buddy. If that's okay?"

"Sure, sure." He switched it off.

My ears didn't mind hearing the song, but my brain couldn't wrap itself around any of it. Silence was better.

"We have very different music back home. I just play the radio for passengers."

"Where is home?" I asked. From his accent I was guessing India, and I was right.

"Mumbai, in India."

"Very cool. I'm Al. Good to meet you."

"I am Vishal. Where are you going from Union?"

"Kingston – I'm visiting someone." There was no way the Beast would allow me to say, "my daughter."

"Oh, Kingston is beautiful. I almost went there when I came to Canada, but my wife liked Oakville."

"I haven't been there in a long time." Not that I could remember, at least.

"Are you visiting family?"

"You could say that, I suppose."

If his curiosity went any further, I might have to kill him and steal the cab.

"You suppose? What does that mean? You don't know your family?" He was pushing his luck.

"Exactly. I don't know my family."

There was a long silence. I hoped it would stay that way until we arrived at Union Station.

It did not.

"Mr. Al. Forgive me. I didn't mean to upset you, Sir."

"That's okay, Brother. I'm just sensitive about this stuff."

"See? You DO know your family. I am your brother! You know me. A little bit, now. Hahahaha."

He looked back at me in the rearview mirror, hoping I would laugh at his joke. I smiled. That was all he was getting.

"Mr. Al. Has anyone ever told you about your aura?"

"What? Why do all you aura people call me Mr. Al?"

"So, you HAVE been told? Your aura is not like anything I have ever seen. You are very, very special, Mr. Al."

"Special, yeah. That's me. Special fucking Al. Going to Kingston to visit family I don't even know."

"Seriously, Mister. Al. You are doing something beautiful. You will see what you need to see. You will."

That made me laugh. How could this dude know anything? It felt like the Beast was dropping these strangers in my lap, offering clues to find my way home. Somehow, I found a little comfort in his encouragement.

We didn't speak again until he pulled up to the station. I had taken $400 from the machine, and now I counted out $100 of it for Vishal.

"Here you go. Thank you, my friend."

"Oh, you are welcome, Mr. Al. Something good is going to happen. I know it! You should take flowers. Maybe lilies. Everyone likes lilies."

He winked at me as I closed the door.

Some of these fuckers KNOW. I can feel it.

I rushed into the station to find a train or bus heading for Kingston – and found a VIA train scheduled to leave at 6:30. I had twenty minutes to figure out where to go. I bought a ticket and was directed to the tracks and the waiting train. I climbed aboard and made my way to the back of the car. There would be some privacy there, and probably an outlet for my phone. I knew I had to check it, but at that moment I had no desire to see who was mad at me.

What I needed most was sleep. I'd been out for 24 hours at the hospital, but that had been an artificial, drug-and-booze-induced unconsciousness. It hadn't felt like rest, and I was exhausted. The train was quiet enough, with only a few other passengers seated in my car. I plugged my phone into the outlet, tilted the seat way back, and shut my eyes.

The ride from Toronto to Kingston was direct – no stops, and travel time was just over two and a half hours. That was likely not enough time for my phone (or myself) to recharge, but it was better than nothing.

I passed out instantly, and was jarred awake by the slowing of the train and the announcement that we were already arriving at Kingston. It felt like there'd been exactly zero time between closing my eyes and re-opening them. My phone was fully charged, thanks to the seven-million-dollar charger. I wished there was something similar I could use to plug myself in for a recharge.

I still had no idea where I was going. I'd thought the University might be my destination, but my brain had not even considered the possibility that "Lilly" might still be in Montreal, with "Nick." And what would I do if I did see her? I was confident I'd recognize her, BECAUSE I DREW HER. And I'd seen photographs. But there was no way I'd be able to talk with her.

Disembarking, I wandered into the station and found a place to sit. I didn't know the city, so I would have to Google student hot spots. First things first, though. It was time to power up my phone. Or maybe it was time to throw my stupid phone into the St. Lawrence River. The latter did feel like the sexier choice, but I knew it wouldn't be fair to people. Like, oh you know, work. Or Bridget.

When the phone came to life, I discovered surprisingly little in the way of message overload. A few, but nowhere near as many as I'd expected.

Bridget Reynolds

-My darling Al. Thank you for being willing to try. I love you. See you tomorrow. Goodnight.   XO

Lilly Doll

-Daddio. I talked to Mom. I'm so sorry for coming down on you. I didn't know you were hanging   out at the hospital. No fun at all. Nick and I are thinking of you Dad. Love you. Get better soon.

Henry Miller

-Hey Buddy. Bridget called to let us know you're in the hospital. Don't worry about it at all. It's super slow anyway, and your health is the

most important thing. Take care of yourself. We'll see you when we see you.

He really was a great guy, and it was a very solid place to work. I was often too harsh with them.

Bradley Boy

-Hey Dad. Just checking in. Hope you feel better soon.

The phone showed that I had two voice messages as well. I was psyching myself up to listen to them when I heard a familiar voice.

"Mr. I? What the heck are you doing here?"

It was Colby, son of Dr. Luke. He must have ridden into town on the same train. I'd known this kid since before he was born. Athletic, with dark, wavy hair, and a smile that made everyone love him. He looked like a walking Harlequin Romance book cover.

"Hey Buddy. How are you?" I was very much taken aback, and felt super awkward. Like I was caught red-handed thieving a pack of gum from the corner store.

"I'm good, I'm good. Surprised to see you here, though! Lilly is still in Montreal. I was just talking with her and Nick."

Shit. Maybe this trip had been a waste of time after all. Or maybe some time with Colby could shine a light on… something. I still didn't have any clue what I was looking for.

"Oh. Okay, I wasn't sure. I just kinda hopped on the train on a whim, and here I am. Want to grab a coffee?" I was hoping he might be able to guide me around town a little.

"Absolutely. There's a cool place on campus, The Cogro. We can take an Uber?"

"Sounds good."

Colby ordered up an Uber on his phone, and it arrived immediately. We stayed dead quiet for the entire ten-minute drive – until we arrived on campus, when Colby started giving directions to the coffee shop. The driver already knew the way of course, but like most fourth-year students, Colby was certain that the world would be a giant spinning ball of chaos without his input. I wondered if this Lilly character was like that, too. Perhaps knowledge like that was not mine to know. I felt nervous.

I excused myself to use the men's room when we entered the Cogro; it had been hours since I'd gone. I didn't feel desperate to relieve myself, but figured I must be. Colby was on his phone when I came looking for our table, and my throat closed up. Was he on the phone with Lilly? My first instinct was to run, but Colby waved me over to where he was sitting. We were the only patrons in the place.

"Yeah, yeah. He's here with me right now – I ran into him at the train station. We must've been on the same train!"

Fuck fuck fuck. Who is he talking to? Oh My God. I have to run.

"Yeah. Cool. Okay, give me a sec," Colby said to the mystery guest on the other end of the call.

He reached the phone out to hand it to me.

"It's my Dad."

I nearly fell to my knees in relief. But I was not without fear of talking to my doctor friend guy. I shook a little as I took the phone from Colby.

"Hey, Luke!"

"Al?! What in God's name are you doing there, Buddy?" He sounded bewildered.

"I had to get out, Man. You guys were kinda suffocating me."

"Okay – but Kingston? Kind of extreme, isn't it?"

"I don't know, Luke. Something was telling me I had to come here. Maybe I needed to see Colby." I was trying to make light of the situation, but Luke was not amused.

"Al, listen to me. You're playing with fire here, Buddy. You don't even know how you'd react emotionally if you ran into Lilly. Or, even physically, for that matter."

"I had to come here, Luke. It doesn't even feel like I have a choice sometimes. You know? There is something, some BEAST pulling me. Does that make any sense?" Suddenly I wanted an honest answer.

"I get it, Al. And I don't blame you. I just want you to be careful. Do you want me to talk to Bridget?"

"Shit, Man. 'Careful' doesn't even come into play. I am fucking desperate. This is the most brutal feeling. And, yeah. Can you come up with something to say to her? I'm planning to come back with the first train in the morning."

Actually, I didn't have any plan to return. Or to stay. I was utterly plan-free. But I did want to allay the Doc's concerns.

"Ok, Buddy. I'll come up with something. Just... be safe? I give a shit. So does Mark. And you know damned well Bridget loves you."

"You've got my word, Brother. I'm doing my best – and thanks, Man. You want Colby again?"

"Yeah. Thanks, Al."

I handed the phone back to Colby, who did not appear to have been listening to my conversation with his Dad. At least, I couldn't see any surprise or concern on his face. Just that same old winning smile.

"Hey Dad. Yeah. I'm good. Lookin' forward to New Years. Okay, you too. Ha! Yeah, I'll take care of him. Talk soon. Yeah, bye."

He ended the call and turned his attention to me.

"So... my Dad says I've gotta take care of you. Get you back safely. Ha!"

"Ok, Buddy. I guess I'm at your mercy."

"Do you want me to let Lilly know you're here? I think she said they were driving back tonight."

"NO!" Too loud. I tried to compose myself. "Colby – please don't do that? If I can stay long enough, I want to surprise her."

I had to say something that could sound plausible, but I didn't want to surprise her. I was, in fact, absolutely terrified to see her – and I was second guessing this decision to come to Kingston in the first place. The Beast was rag-dolling me around the coffee shop. Something I had done was clearly not according to his plan. I was way out of my lane.

"Ok, Mister I. But I know she'd be so freakin' happy to see you. She'll want to show off her diamond. They're super excited!"

Colby's enthusiasm was unwavering, but most definitely not contagious.

"Thanks, Colby."

"No problem. Hey, what's your plan? I'm supposed to be meeting Vicki in a bit."

Vicki? A girlfriend? Colby always had several on the go, but I'd never met any of them.

"You go ahead, Buddy. I can keep myself busy for a bit."

"Ok, Mister I. You sure you don't need me to hold your hand? I don't wanna piss my Dad off…"

"I'm good. Promise. Great to see you, Colbs."

"Really great to see you, too! What an awesome surprise."

Colby downed the last of his java in one giant gulp as we got up from our seats to share a hug. And he walked out, leaving me the last man standing at the Common Ground Coffee Shop. I paid our tab and stuffed the receipt into my back pocket. I now had some time to collect my thoughts and get my bearings. Somehow, I needed to establish just what the hell I was doing in Kingston.

Voice messages. The first one was from Tessa, just letting me know she loved me. My poor little girl sounded scared for her Dad, and it broke my heart. I should have gone to see her – at least I knew she was real. I could remember her entire life.

The next one was the kick in the nuts.

"Hey Daddio? It's Lilly. I guess you're sleeping. Nick and I are just driving back to school. We're both thinking of you. I don't know what kind of sick you have. Mom says it's pretty nasty. Anyway, we should be back in Kingston around 10:30. Give us a call if you wake up bored? Hospitals suck. Love you, Daddio. Hope you are okay! MMMMWAHH."

She sounded like a nice kid, and I needed to see her. My brain, or the Beast, had to satisfy that requirement before I could move on to whatever came next. My phone read 10:15, so they should be back any minute. I had no idea what their destination would be. I froze, with no sense of what to do next.

COLBY... He'd know where they'd be going. I gave him a call.

"Hey, Mister, I. Did you get lost?"

"A little. Hey Colby – any idea where they'd be going when they get back?"

"You mean Nick and Lilly? Probably straight home?"

"Yeah. Makes sense. Uh, could you remind me where that is again?"

"They've been in that same apartment for three years – we moved them in together!"

"Yeah. I know. My memory isn't what it used to be, Buddy."

"That's crazy, Mister I. One sec."

As I waited for Colby to check their address, I felt a sudden desperate urge to get out of the coffee shop. So, I pulled my coat back on, pushed through the door, and started walking in the direction from which we'd come. If I had to sleep at the train station, I could live with it. At least it wasn't likely to be a place someone arriving by car would wind up.

"K, Mister I. You there?"

"I'm here. Just outside freezing."

"Yeah. It's super cold tonight. They live at 123 King Street East. Remember now?"

"Ah, shit, yes of course. Stupid-easy to remember. I'll find it from here."

"Ten minute walk, max."

"Thanks, Colbs. Talk soon."

"Bye, Mister I."

I punched the address into Google Maps and confirmed Colby's estimate – a ten minute walk that looked like a pretty straight shot. Pointing myself in the direction the map suggested, I began to follow where the Beast was pulling, trudging toward their address, despite an uneasy feeling in every molecule of my being.

My tentative plan was to see, but remain unseen. Lilly could not know that I was in Kingston. Damn. I would have to let Colby know, in no uncertain terms, that he could not mention our meeting.

I got to about half way (the ETA thing on the map said 4 minutes) when, suddenly, a car drove past. It screeched to an abrupt halt, about 100 yards in front of me. The passenger door flew open, and a young woman leapt out.

"DADDY!? DADDY?" She was nearly hysterical.

I was between streetlights and relatively hidden in the shadows, but this girl was lit up like an angel in a moonbeam. And she was beautiful. Fire red hair, huge smile. Looking directly into her wild, green eyes, I knew instantly that this was Lilly – my sketch, come to life.

She started walking toward me, but then broke into a near sprint. Which was when the Beast whipped me around and yanked me back in the direction from whence I came. Although I couldn't feel myself running, I was moving faster than I'd ever managed, even as a fit teenager. This force was irresistible. I felt like a paperclip on a desktop, manipulated by a giant magnet from below.

"Daddio? What the FUCK, DAD?? Don't run! WAIT. DADDY WAIT!"

Her voice was growing quieter every second, and I was moving far too quickly for her to catch up. The Beast pulled me into an alley, where it finally slowed me down. A huge part of me had wanted to run into her arms, but the familiarity had been overpowered by utter fear. She was not mine to know. She was not mine to hold. She was not mine to talk to. She was not mine. Period. The Beast had laid any doubt to rest. I could not live here. I could not be this version of Allan Isaac. I had to find a way out, a way home.

I broke into tears, grateful that beer wasn't commanding me to consume it. In a daze, I started walking again. I could smell and then hear the St. Lawrence River. That was where the Beast was guiding me.

Weaving my way through parking lots and back yards, I found my way out onto Maitland Street. With all that commotion, I wasn't able to recall the make of her car, or even the colour. So, I kept looking over my shoulder, ready to hit the deck with any sign of headlights. When the river came into clear view, I noticed tiny icebergs clumping together; little white mountains of snow and ice lined the banks. The river was trying to flow between them, fighting a deep freeze. I started following the edge, letting the Beast and the River guide me until I found... something.

After walking for 20 minutes or so, I came upon a wharf with a sign that read "Gord Downie Memorial Pier."

"What the fuck? He isn't even dead yet and we already have a memorial fucking pier?"

I was talking to the Beast by now, fully expecting an answer. Gordon Downie was the lead singer of The Tragically Hip, a band native to Kingston and a full-on Canadian institution. Just a few months ago they'd played their final concert at the Kingston Rogers K-Rock Centre. With Gord's brain cancer diagnosis, the band was completing a cross-country goodbye tour, and Canada was a nation in mourning.

Except the dude wasn't dead. He was dying, but he was not dead. And yet somehow, here I was, standing at a pier named in his memory.

So… I was now in a world where I had a previously non-existent daughter. Where Blue Rodeo had an international hit with my unfinished song. And where Gord Downie had a memorial pier – before he became a memory. Dorothy, we were not in Kansas anymore. What the hell; I clicked my heels together.

"I wish I was in my world. I WISH I WAS IN MY WORLD!"

Nothing happened. I was still at Gord's Pier, and it was cold enough to freeze the balls off the Devil himself. My coat was thin and on my head was a light Gatsby cap. I should have been hypothermic, but I felt nothing. I was impervious.

To honour Mr. Downie, I made my way down to the water. When I found a little bare spot between the snow mountains, I laid myself down and started acting out the lyrics to The Hip's smash hit, New Orleans is Sinking.

"I put my hands in the river, with my feet back up on the banks, looked up to the Gord above and said 'Hey Man. Thanks'."

I performed the actions while I sang the words. Except I changed "Lord" to "Gord," which seemed to work better for this situation – and I actually believed in Gord.

Now, that kind of cold, my hands could feel; the river was next-level frigid. Which gave me an idea, a feeling I hadn't known since I was a full-time drunk. Instead of just throwing my phone into the river, I could throw my entire self in. I would be dead within minutes. A sense of calm washed over me as I realized I could end this unfathomable pain... by ending my life.

Simple. Tidy, even.

But what would doing such a thing mean in this godforsaken reality? Lilly – and all the rest of the kids – would lose their Daddio. Although to be fair, they didn't really have one. I couldn't be a father here; I was a complete lunatic. Good Ol' Bridge would be without a partner. But again – unless she was indeed shagging Goodhands, she didn't have one anyway. They could be happy together, with Crazy Al well out of their hair. Goodhands' shoes would probably never get puked on again.

Not to mention my life insurance policy. My loved ones would all be a little richer. The more I thought about it, the more sense it made.

Who knows? Maybe if I die here, I end up where I belong?

Yes. It had to work. I couldn't think of a single drawback. With my mind made up, I stood up and began walking to the end of the Gord Downie Memorial Pier, prepared to introduce myself to the depths of the frigid St. Lawrence River. I wasn't even sad. In fact, this was the first time since Christmas Eve I'd felt any sort of peace. I started weeping out of sheer relief. This was my way out.

It occurred to me that idiots love to cry "SELFISH" when someone offs themself.

"Selfish? You want to trade spots? Dickhead."

Again, I was talking to the Beast. But I felt released from his grip – released from everything. At the end of the pier, I turned back to look at the city behind me. This was a beautiful place to die. Maybe I'd end up jamming with Gord Downie! Cool.

"THANK YOU, KINGSTON! I LOVE YOU!" I shouted like I was exiting the stage, half expecting to be called back for an encore.

Shit. Maybe I should have a beer or six before I jump.

I was considering that option when I felt my phone buzzing in my pocket. I had no reason to look, but I was curious. And of course it was Bridget. Lilly had probably called to tell her she'd seen me. I didn't answer. I didn't care.

I took a moment to text Colby; he needed to understand that under no circumstances should he let Lilly know he'd seen me. At this point, I didn't want her to think Colby could have done something to prevent what I was about to do. I was protecting him now.

And I didn't need beer – that was just stalling. I looked up at the crescent shaped moon and found it surrounded by stars. There was enough light pollution in Kingston to hide most of the diamonds in the sky – and yet, there they were. Gazillions of sparkling gems reflecting off the black water. It was a spectacular panoramic experience, and I was grateful.

Something, maybe the Beast's last gasp, gave me pause for a moment. I pulled Marvin's note out of my pocket, clean and intact – it had somehow avoided disaster when I pissed myself.

Al,

Remember, see what you are here to see, hear what you are here to hear.

Then either figure out how to untrigger the jump, or learn to love it here.

Be careful what you wish for. You will make ripples.

Gibberish. Abject bullshit. Ramblings of a crazy man.

"I'll tell you what happened. I went nuts."

Was I talking to the Beast, or the sky, or myself? It didn't matter. At some point over the last couple weeks, I'd lost my mind. Nothing was triggered; I just went mad. And now I was stuck in a world where I could not exist. I certainly couldn't learn to love it here. Rather than "untrigger the jump," I'd jump into the icy water. It was the only option that made any sense. The reality I remembered, the one where I thought I belonged, probably didn't even exist. It had likely never existed. And I was not going to find my way back to a place that had never been there in the first place.

Decision made, all I had to do was muster the will to jump.

But what if it doesn't kill me? What if some prick comes along and scoops me out?

My mind was tricking me, still stalling. No more. I was ready.

"Peace out, bitches!" I stepped up to the edge of the structure.

Again, my stupid phone buzzed. It was a notification that I had a voicemail. Didn't care. I readied myself again.

"Peace out again, You miserable shithole!"

Damnit, I should go out in style, though.

If anyone was watching, including the Beast, I wanted to put on a show. Maybe do a somersault off the Gord Downie Memorial Pier, right into the nearly frozen St. Lawrence River. I took about twenty steps back to make a run for it. I was having way more fun than a fellow in this situation should be having.

"One, two, THR…."

The asshole phone buzzed again. This time, I was getting a call. Perhaps God was calling to tell me I was committing a sin. That I would be banished to the fires of Hades for all eternity. He wouldn't be in my contacts though, so I wouldn't recognize the number. I checked anyway.

It was not God. It wasn't even Gord. It was my friend and bandmate, Darren. Damn it, really shitty timing – because I had to answer it. If there was any single thing worth interrupting my glorious event, it was my band, Chip Wagon.

"Hey Darren."

"Hi Al. How's it going?"

"Uh. Strange few days, Brother. Looking forward to taking the leap into my next chapter."

I was trying to be subtle, but I wasn't making any sense.

"Ha. Well, I'm looking forward to tomorrow! Do you need a ride?"

"Tomorrow? What's happening tomorrow?" I had no idea what he was talking about.

"Dude! Seriously. It's New Year's Eve. We're playing This Ain't Hollywood. It's gonna be awesome, Man. I can't believe you forgot!"

Well, shit. I couldn't let my band down. So much for the plan.

"Neither can I – and I was so close to committing to… something else."

"Well, I'm glad I caught you! Terri's doing up the set list. Anything special you want to do?"

"Um – I can't remember if we've ever played Merry-Go-Round?"

"That Blue Rodeo tune? Years ago, I think. I'm not sure I could remember it all."

So, this world's Al had been covering a song that I was still writing. I was obviously insane.

Still...

"Let's see if we can do it? Ask everybody if they can refresh their memories? It's an easy tune."

"Yeah, okay Buddy. I'll let Terri know, and I'll send you the list as soon as she gets it to me."

"Thanks, Darren. See you tomorrow."

The Beast was toying with me. He had been, the entire time. He knew exactly how to prevent my jump.

My phone was showing 11:20, which meant that in the span of roughly sixty minutes I'd gone from trying to catch a glimpse of someone who shouldn't exist, to deciding to end my life, to working on a set list for tomorrow's gig. An exhausting hour. I'd have to find a place to sleep.

I had to catch the first train back home, so I found my way back to the train station, surprised to find the doors unlocked. It was warm inside, and I doubted that Lilly and Nick would be out trying to find me. Honestly, I really didn't care anymore. If they found me, they found me. I'd either find another place to jump, or I'd do what Marvin said. Learn to love it here.

The seats in the station were lined up in such a way that four or five of them made a half decent bed, with my coat for a blanket and my cap for a pillow. My eyes were almost closed when the phone buzzed. Again. A text from Colby.

-Okay Mister I. That's super weird. I don't get it. But I won't say anything. I hope everything is okay.

I felt reassured. Another day was over. I was no closer to figuring things out, but I was still alive – or something like it. And tomorrow, I was going to ring in a brand new year with Chip Wagon. I was almost looking forward to it.

What could go wrong?

Chapter 12:

She's Come Undone

The chairs provided a surprisingly comfortable bed, and the station was bustling with commuters and travelers by the time I opened my eyes. No one seemed to notice, or care, that a man was sleeping there. It was likely not uncommon for someone to catch a little cat nap before the trains came.

I sat up to check the schedule and saw that the first train was to arrive at 7:34. It could get me all the way to Bronte by 11:00. It was now 7:08, which meant I could theoretically get my ass back to the hospital by lunchtime – before Bridget would arrive. It might even look as though I'd never left. My last order of business was to make sure my room hadn't been given to someone else. I didn't have Goodhands' personal cell number, so I texted Luke.

-Hey Brother. Just hopping on the train home. Any chance we could make sure that room is still mine?

He responded immediately.

-Hey Al. No problem. Even if it's been taken, we can just say you were transferred to another room. It happens all the time.

-Cool. I should be at Bronte by 11:00.

-Perfect. I'll pick you up. North entrance.

-Thanks Man.

The westbound train pulled in right on time. I climbed aboard and found a quiet place for my journey. While no one else seemed to like sitting at the back of a train car, it felt very much like home to me. I was settled in my seat and staring out the window by the time the train pulled out of the station.

What a night. Reliving it all in my brain, I knew the image of Lilly standing in a shower of light would stick with me forever. And I was glad to have that, at least – even if this strong pull to see her was still a mystery to me. If anything, seeing her live and in person was making it more difficult for me to continue denying her existence. The Beast worked in strange and mysterious ways.

I felt compelled to read Marvin's note one more time. It might have a different meaning, here on the other side of my recent, unsuccessful bid to end my existence.

See what you are here to see. Hear what you are here to hear.

I reread that bit several times. Yes, I had heard something completely unexpected – my song. Which was somehow not my song here... and I'd seen Lilly. The Beast had dragged me all the way to Kingston and demanded I lay eyes on her. So, I had ticked the boxes. If the Beast wasn't pleased, he must have at least been placated.

I still had no idea how to "untrigger the jump" – or what that even meant. Marvin's words sometimes seemed like mumbo jumbo, and yet, at other times they were absolute Gospel. If I had indeed done something to shift myself from one reality to another, what was it? Had I been dreaming something, when that headache landed in the wee hours of Christmas morning? How could I undream what I couldn't remember having dreamt? And how could I control my dreams anyway? That made zero sense.

I thought it through. Before I could undo anything, I first had to determine what it was that I had done in the first place. Maybe I should finally finish my own second verse and bridge to Merry-Go-Round? I'd never even called it that. In my world, it was called All the Way – but Merry-Go-Round was a way better song name. I wondered why I hadn't chosen that.

Maybe that's why I was brought here? Because I chose the wrong song name? That didn't make sense either. Nothing made sense. Trying to make sense out of chaos was making my mind spin. Chaos does not like change; it really loves being chaos.

It would be more productive to consider the Chip Wagon show that night – what if I didn't know any of the songs here? I mean, if Blue Rodeo had my song, maybe we had a Blue Rodeo song? I needed to know what I was expected to know. I texted Darren.

-Any word on the set list?

After staring at the phone in anticipation of a response for a few minutes, I gave up. Sending the same message to Terri (our bass player) would probably be more fruitful. Her partner Rob was our drummer. When you can find a rhythm section that is a couple, you should hire that rhythm section immediately. These two were completely in sync. They played together like a Swiss-made clock, keeping the rest of the band firmly in the pocket.

Also, they tended to respond to texts in a timely Manner.

-Here it is Big Al! Can't wait.

10,000 Tires

Lock Me Up

Seeds and Sockets

Merry-Go-Round

I'm Not Concerned

Violet and Red

Rock Salt

I'm Alright Now

Maybe it's Me

Big Yellow Moon

Appalachian Man

Good Mornin' Mr. Coffee

This Ain't Hollywood

BBB

Shake Hands

Brother Down

-Got it. Thanks. See you there.

I was relieved. I knew all those songs. All Chip Wagon standards, except one.

-Um, except, what the hell is Appalachian Man??

-Huh??

-I don't know that one.

-Uh, What? You wrote it Buddy

I wasn't surprised anymore. Of course I wrote it. How the hell was I supposed to get out of this?

-Oh. Right. Forgot. Not really feeling that one for tonight though. Can we switch it out?

-Ok. Sure. Too bad though, love that tune.

-Let's do Pearls instead?

-Ok. Cool. Done. I'll make that change and print off some copies.

-Thanks, Terri

Was I learning to navigate this place? I pulled off that escape pretty well.

But then Darren texted back.

-Hey Al. Terri says no Appalachian Man? Wtf? That won't go over well.

-Just not feeling it brother.

Disaster averted. I was curious about this Appalachian Man song. Dan and Terri made it seem like it was a favourite. It rang exactly zero bells with me, though. I had no clue. The rest of the set, I could pull off in my sleep, or in an alternate universe. I hoped.

Now that the set list was confirmed, my mind returned to my predicament. Was there a way back to my own reality, to a place where I only had to consider people who actually existed? Or should I just accept this life and learn to live in it? As soon as that thought popped into my head… BOOM, a gut punch. The Beast would not allow me to even consider that option. I felt winded, like I'd been physically assaulted. If there was a way back… clearly, I needed to find it.

"So, what do you want me to do, Asshole?" I asked the Beast, flat out. "Just tell me, for fuck's sakes."

Whatever this thing was, I was tired of it pushing me around without a fight. If he was going to gut punch me for having a thought, I was calling him out. He had a strange way of responding. Signs had been popping up. The VIA Rail ad had been the most obvious – but there had been other, more subtle ones. Strangers winking at me, Marvin showing up with all the answers. Definitely signs. So, I waited for another one. And I waited. Nothing – or at least, nothing obvious. I tried to find answers in the shapes of tree branches we hurtled past. On billboards. In the clouds. Still, nothing.

"You hit me like that, and you don't even give me a clue? Fucking bully," I goaded him.

We were already in Toronto, which meant I had about an hour before landing at Bronte to meet Luke. Pulling out my phone to relay my ETA to the good Doctor, I found it open to my original sketch of Lilly. *Strange.* Now that I had seen her in person, my mind was twisted up like a balloon at a clown show. No matter where I ended up, one thing was certain, I was nuts. Certifiable. You don't come out of this kind of thing with a full bag of marbles.

Luke and I had agreed to meet at the North parking lot of the Bronte GO station at around 11:00 AM. There was a minor delay before the train pulled out of Union Station, but that wouldn't affect our timing. Not another soul joined me in my private car. I now had enough quiet time to think. To try to figure this thing out.

Something – the Beast maybe – made me pull my phone out again. Why? My phone seemed to bring me nothing but trouble, save for this gig – which I was actually looking forward to. I texted Bridget to make sure she wasn't coming early.

-Still on for lunch, babe?

-Yep. Did you get my message? Running a bit late. 1:00 ok?

I had forgotten that she had called while I was on the Pier, contemplating the big jump, and I was relieved that it wasn't about Lilly seeing me.

-Sounds good B. See you soon.

After I closed the text, the Lilly sketch popped up again. *Very strange.* I knew I hadn't opened it since Christmas day.

Then it hit me. The Beast was talking. Suddenly, his signs were becoming dead clear.

He must think I'm an idiot.

In the song, Merry-Go-Round: "Undo what you've done." In Marvin's note: "untrigger the jump". What if I deleted the sketch from my phone? Was that what the Beast was looking for? Is that what triggered everything? A SKETCH? Why didn't I jump into another dimension when I drew a monster? Or a leprechaun? What was it about this particular collection of lines and curves that had shifted time and space? Or that had just made me crazy?

UNDO WHAT YOU'VE DONE

The answer to my dilemma was staring me right in the face. The sketch was open in the drawing app on my phone, in edit mode. In the top left corner of the screen there was a little reverse arrow – the UNDO button. I hit that button, and a swath of Lilly's red hair vanished. I hit it again. More hair disappeared. I hit it again and again. With each hit, more of the sketch was undone.

All of her red curls were gone, leaving just a dark outline of hair. Her mouth disappeared next. Then her nose, and her eyes. Her left cheek vanished, came back, and vanished again. Within five minutes, the entire sketch of Lilly was erased. And to be absolutely sure I couldn't open the sketch again, I hit the delete button.

I could feel the Beast loosening its grip. Maybe I had fed it what it wanted? Maybe that had been the thing I was supposed to undo? I didn't know, but at least it was something. I felt a little more at ease for having done it, but there was also a palpable… emptiness in my core.

Nothing was simple anymore. Absolutely nothing.

"Next Stop, Bronte. Bronte next stop."

The hour from Union to Bronte had gone by in a flash. Shaking the train-ride-induced cobwebs from my brain as we pulled into the station, I hopped off and made my way through the tunnel. About half way, I could smell cigarette smoke. And not surprisingly, I found Ally Oddly tucked into a corner by the elevator. Was she another sign from the Beast?

"You shouldn't be smoking in here, Ally." I'd caught her red handed.

"Hey! Mr. Al! Happy New Year."

"Happy New Year, Kid."

"See you tonight!" I heard her yell out as I walked away.

Hmm. I guess she's coming to the show. Cool.

Making my way to the north entrance of the station, I found Luke waiting in his car. I jumped into the passenger side and fastened my seatbelt.

"Thanks for grabbing me, Buddy."

"No problem, Al. Everything go okay?"

"I don't know. I really don't. But... I think I'm glad I went."

"Good. I'm glad to hear it. Colby told me you'd asked him not to mention he saw you?"

"Yeah. I did."

"That's a big ask. They're best friends. And he's a shitty liar."

"I saw her, Luke. And I'm certain she saw me," I confessed.

"What did you do?!"

"I ran the fuck away. At breakneck speed. Faster than I thought I could ever move."

"Jesus Christ, Al! Did you ever consider how this stuff is going to affect HER?"

"She's a movie character to me, Luke. And besides, if she'd thought it was me, she would've un-thought it when she saw me run like that. Seriously, Man – I wasn't moving myself! I was picked up and carried away. It wasn't human speed." I still couldn't fathom that I'd moved like that.

"I doubt that, Buddy. We'll see if she says anything. In the meantime, let's get you back to your room. It's still yours, by the way."

"Thanks, Man. Did you talk to Bridget?"

"Not yet. I wanted to make sure it was necessary before I stirred up any more shit."

"Perfect. So, as far as she's concerned, I slept in that same bed last night."

"Yep. And probably better that way. I hate deceiving her, but we don't want to freak her out anymore, either."

It seemed we agreed that an impromptu train ride to Kingston and back in the middle of the night would most likely freak her all the way out. It freaked me out too, of course. But I was nuts.

Luke was an on-call physician at the hospital, which meant he had a parking pass. His designated spot was a short walk into the building. As we approached the lobby, I could hear Piano Boy playing Merry-Go-Round again. Luckily the elevator doors came before the piano, so I didn't have to face him. Small mercies. Luke managed to hustle me through fast enough that nobody recognized me. When we reached my room, there was a clean robe waiting.

"Get changed. If you throw those clothes back into the cupboard, we should be all good. I'm so glad you didn't get drunk and do something stupid there, Buddy."

"Me too. Thanks, Luke. Any plans for New Years?"

"Yeah, we're coming to the show – looking forward to it," he said, like I should've known.

"Cool. See you there, Brother."

As I stripped my clothes off, I saw that they were muddy, which was to be expected. After all, I had "had my hands in the river, my feet back up on the bank." The memory brought a smile to my face – it had been a surprisingly fun experience. Folding up the clothes the best I could, I pulled on my sexy, blue, bum-showin' robe and slid back under the covers. It wasn't even noon, I was home and dry, and there was even time for a nap. I took immediate advantage of that.

A loving hand lightly shook me awake.

"Hey, Sleepy Head." Bridget leaned down and kissed my forehead.

"Hey B. How are you?"

"Good. More importantly, how are you? Did you get a good sleep?"

"Not bad, I guess. A little restless." An understatement.

"Luke says I can take you home? You have a gig tonight – are you up for that?" It sounded like she was hoping I might cancel. I couldn't do that to my mates.

"Yeah. I was already talking about the set list with Darren and Terri."

"Oh good. I'm so glad. Then let's get you dressed and home."

Except she didn't sound sincere.

"My clothes are over in that cupboard." I pointed, as if there were a thousand options to choose from.

Bridget opened the lone cupboard and pulled out my clothes.

"What the heck? Why are your pants muddy?"

She held up my jeans to show me the filth. They were pretty bad.

"I thought they cleaned them for you?" She looked disappointed.

As she handed them over, the receipt for the Cogro fell out of the back pocket. She picked it up.

"Common Grounds? Isn't that at Queen's" Her look was turning from disappointment to something else entirely.

"Is it? I don't know Babe." I was a shitty liar, too. I couldn't even look at her.

"Weird."

"Very. I don't get it. No clue."

"I can't read the date on it. I don't remember us ever going there." She seemed very confused, so I pretended to be, too.

"Makes no sense. But then, nothing makes any sense."

"It's just strange. Especially since…. Ah, never mind."

"Especially since what?" Actually, maybe I didn't want to know.

"Don't worry about it, Al. Let's just get you home and ready for the show."

I was happy to leave it at that. For whatever reason, I was feeling more at peace than I had in days. Tonight's gig would be my focus for now. And the songs – were they the same as I remembered them? I would find out soon enough.

With nothing to pack once I got my muddy clothes back on, we were on our way.

"Do you want this?" Bridget held up the tell-tale receipt.

"I have no idea what the hell it even is. No, I don't need it."

She crumpled it up and tossed it into the trash by the door of my room. But on the way to the car, she became very quiet – like she was in a different reality herself.

"Where did you park?" I couldn't see her car in the parking lot.

"Right there. It's a rental, remember?"

"Oh, right. Totally forgot. Nice ride!"

The cool, metallic burgundy Acura rental was a big step up the food chain from her little Mazda. She continued the silent treatment.

"Is something wrong, Babe?"

It was never a good idea to ask that question, but she didn't answer. Instead, she lowered herself into the driver's seat, let her head fall to the steering wheel, and started sobbing.

"Hey, B! What's wrong?" I reached over and attempted to console her with a little back rub.

"This is all just... too much. It's too much."

"I know it is. Trust me."

"No. You don't know. You can't know what it's like to watch your partner lose his fucking mind. And now you are lying to me? Jesus, Al. How much of this am I supposed to take?"

"Lying to you? What do you mean?"

"Al. Come ON. I talked to Lilly."

"What is that supposed to mean?" I was stalling.

"For fuck's sakes, Al. Your pants are muddy. I know they cleaned them. I put them away for you in the first place. And you have a fucking receipt in your pocket? Lilly saw you, Al. She saw you run away. You ran away from your own fucking daughter?! What IS that?"

Shit. Shit shit fucking shit. I had nothing. And why did I even have to answer? I was the guy whose life was turned upside down, inside out, and twisted to shit.

"I don't know what you are talking about." I shouldn't have said that. So transparent.

"Stop it! Just stop, Al. You went to fucking Kingston. You never intended to fix any of this, did you? You aren't going to take any meds, are you?"

Now it was my turn to be silent. I could not think of a single clever word to say. I wanted to blurt out the truth, but I knew that wouldn't help. I managed to keep quiet the entire drive back to the house, but then words just started falling out of my idiot mouth.

"Baby. What if, to get you your Al back, I have to get my Al back to where he belongs? Maybe your Al is stuck where I am supposed to be?"

It did not help. I should have kept my mouth shut.

"Jesus, Al! Listen to yourself! Can you hear yourself? I've got news for you. THERE IS ONLY ONE REALITY! You're in it. So am I. So is our daughter. So is the rest of this family. It isn't fair that you aren't even willing to try to accept that. It just... isn't fair, Al."

She had a point, but maybe cut a fella some slack? I mean, I was the one who'd woken up in a completely new reality. Hello?

"You think this is easy, Bridge? You think I'm having fun here? I just about offed myself last night, for fuck's sakes!"

Goddammit. I was my own worst enemy. I couldn't keep my own secret. Plus, I never called her Bridge. Ever. This was such a messed up place.

"WHAAAT are you talking about, Al?"

I didn't know how to answer, so she continued.

"You're planning to kill yourself? Nice. That's real nice, Al. So considerate of you. Where the fuck does that leave us?"

"So now I'm selfish? Is that what you're saying? I'm the guy who has his whole life pulled out from under him, and I AM FUCKING SELFISH?" My last nerve had been hit, dead on.

"You tell me." She was flatly accusing me.

"I will tell you. Fuck you. Fuck Lilly. Fuck everything. I am out."

We didn't fight much – barely at all, really. It felt like hell. It was hell. I was in a fiery pit of brimstone and shit. So much for mundane. I couldn't take any more. I went to the bedroom to change into gig-worthy clothes. I packed up my guitar, got my rock star boots on, and headed for the door.

"You manipulative prick," she growled. An ugly 50/50 blend of devastated and angry.

"Manipulative?! MANIPULATIVE? Right. Why don't we trade places? Any time, B. Give me a fucking break."

"Just go play your show, Mr. Crazy Rockstar! I'm sure you can find a sympathetic hussy who'll believe your bullshit."

She had to change her panties any time Goodhands was even mentioned, but she was accusing ME of stepping out?

"Nice. You know what? Don't bother coming. I won't be coming home." I meant it.

"Happy New Year, Asshole." I was pretty sure she meant that, too.

I didn't respond. She was livid, but that was not a good way to talk to Allan Isaac at any time, let alone when his world had been twisted. There were only a few deal breakers in my rule book, but that was one of them. Actually, it may as well have been the title:

THOU SHALT NOT SHIT ON AL WHEN AL IS THE VICTIM

It had a certain charm to it. Truth be told, it would have been easier for me to walk in on Good Ol' Bridge shaggin' Dr. Goodhands in our bed than it was to hear her say I was manipulative. When all I wanted to do was stop the insanity. I was done. I was gone. And I was not going back.

Chapter 13:
The Great Gig in the Mind

I wasn't sure where I was heading, but it was most definitely not home. Walking toward Third Line, I decided to either call a cab or catch the bus. I knew I needed to be out of sight. If I stayed out on the sidewalk, Bridget would easily find me – if she decided to follow. And I was lucky. Perfect timing. I got to the first bus stop fifteen seconds before the bus arrived. The bus could get me to the train, which would get me to Hamilton. Then I'd just have to figure out where to hang my hat until This Ain't Hollywood.

The Saint was a flagship venue for the Hamilton music community. We'd played there dozens of times, in various incarnations. Solo, three-piece, full band, duo. The whole enchilada. That night's show was the full-on Chip Wagon experience, with me on acoustic guitar and vocals, Darren on electric guitar and vocals, Mick on pedal steel and vocals, Terri on bass, Rob on drums, and Cam on fiddle. Darren and I shared the bulk of the songwriting duties, but we did a few of Mick's songs as well. I had to admit we were a pretty special band. Almost a little super group.

I made it to the train station just in time. Maybe the Beast was pulling strings, manipulating schedules to get me to do his bidding. I could almost sense his satisfaction. He probably wanted Bridget to dump my sorry ass, anyway. If things hadn't fallen apart, she and I would be riding into Hamilton together right now. Ah well. A time to live, a time to die.

Nice not to wait for the train, at least. I had it to myself again, but I was almost hoping to see Ally Oddly. A happy-ish conversation would have been extremely welcome, and I needed to get out of my head. But sadly, no Ally as far as I could see. My head would have to suffice. Where the hell was I going anyway? None of my bandmates lived anywhere near the venue – plus, it was way too early to head there. I shot Darren a text.

-Hey Buddy. What're you up to?

-Hey Al! Just getting ready. Are you SURE you don't want to do A-Man?

Assuming he meant Appalachian Man, and assuming I could find footage of the band performing the thing on YouTube or something, there was still no way I could learn it and commit it to memory in time for tonight's show. I'd have to be honest with the guy.

-It's hard to explain, Man. I've been having some cognitive issues lately. Honestly, I don't know the song. At all.

That was as close to the truth I was going to get, without divulging my full-on insanity.

-Holy shit brother! That's scary stuff. We've been playing it for years! Everyone freaking loves it!

Even if Darren stopped pressuring me, it sounded like the audience would still expect us to play it. But it was scary enough wondering if all the other songs – the ones I knew – would be the same as I knew them.

-Yeah, I get it. But…. no can do. Right now, I need to find a place to hang out until the show.

Darren hadn't responded by the time the train pulled into Aldershot. I made my way to the bus for the final leg of my journey to The Hammer, but I still didn't know where I was going. This Ain't Hollywood was just a few blocks north of Miller Shoes, and a half block north of The Five Star (the scene of my first piss up, where I'd run into Marvin).

I got off the bus at City Hall and started walking toward the venue. Someone might be there early, and it wouldn't be such a bad place to hang around until show time. Approaching Miller Shoes, I could see they were just closing up – always an early shutdown on Christmas Eve and New Years Eve. Even from the opposite side of the street, young Henry Miller noticed me.

"Al! What are you doing? I thought you were in the hospital," he hollered, loping across the street to greet me.

"They let me out for the gig."

"But what's going on? Are you sick?"

"I'm not sure you really want to know, Buddy."

"Well – I kinda have to know. My Dad is super pissed."

I was not even remotely surprised, but it was disappointing to hear.

"Pissed that I've been in the hospital? Nice." I was getting sick of people shitting on me.

"But we don't even know why! All we know is that Bridget said you were in there."

"Fair enough. I won't be surprised if I end up back in there, to be honest."

"But – you don't look sick?"

"It's not that kind of sick, Dude. I'm nuts. Like, lock-me-up kinda nuts. Really weird shit has been going on."

"Can't you be nuts and work?" I could see he was only half joking.

"Jesus Christ, Buddy. NO. I can't be nuts and work."

"Okay! Sawwrrry! When do you think you'll be back?"

"Seriously? Dude!"

He was a good kid, but not the most sensitive fellow. I felt like telling him I was never coming back, but I couldn't leave the Al who belonged in this particular reality without employment. I was becoming deeply mindful of the mess I might leave for that Al to clean up, if I ever made it back to where I belonged. I changed the subject.

"Are you coming to the show?" I asked.

"Yeah! Love me some Chip Wagon! Especially with Big Al Isaac! I'm bringing a bunch of friends too."

Henry had seen our band a number of times. We often played under the Chip Wagon banner, even when one or more members were unavailable. I was flattered that he preferred the band with me in it – and it was good that he was coming, considering I had no idea what sort of crowd we'd draw. New Years could be tough, with something cool going on at every venue, and only so much audience to go around. So… the more, the merrier. I knew Bridget and her kids would be no-shows. The prospect of a very tiny audience was real.

"Cool – see you there, Henry."

He waved, and we headed off in opposite directions. The faces I passed on the sidewalk were not looking familiar to me. I'd spent the last six years on James St. North – even if I didn't know everyone, I'd recognize many of the regulars. But I felt like a stranger. I did not belong.

I passed the Five Star without even looking inside. The lack of any sense of temptation was a relief; it would have been disastrous if I'd shown up to the gig shit faced.

My mind kept replaying the conversation with Bridget. Anger was a very uncomfortable feeling for me, but I could see her point. She just wanted to be kept in the loop. But she also wanted me to shut up and swallow the notion that my brain had just fried itself. She couldn't see how desperate I was, and she had no concept of how powerful the Beast was.

This Ain't Hollywood, very fondly nicknamed "The Saint," was named after an album by a legendary Hamilton band, The Forgotten Rebels. The venerable old gal had been a tavern for generations. It had been Copper John's before new owners turned it into a popular music venue in 2008. It was an honour to be asked to grace this stage at any time, but particularly on a special night like New Year's Eve.

The Saint sat at the southwest corner of James North and Murray Street, about fifty steps south of the Harbour West Go Station, where I had passed out and pissed myself. The marquee on the north wall of the building faced Murray Street. If I had any doubts that we were booked to play there that night, they were put to rest.

HAPPY NEW YEAR

RING IN 2017 WITH CHIP WAGON

And Marvin Carol

Holy shit – Marvin was on the bill with us! This was going to be a banger of a show. Marvin was one of my favourite local songwriters. It was a perfect fit, and it would be good to see him again. I was curious to hear his thoughts on what I had "undone," and if he thought any of it would make any difference, although I was putting about as much stock in his opinion as I had in Goodhands'. Everything anyone said now sounded completely crazy. Because it was. Because I was.

I shouldn't have been surprised that the door was open. This was a bar, and it was New Year's Eve. Of course it was open.

Walking through the door at This Ain't Hollywood was like stepping into the ultimate cooldom. It was shaped a bit like an hourglass, with the stage at the top, to the left of the door. The room thinned out to barely enough space for a human body in the middle, with a bar on one side, and the sound booth on the other. The right, or bottom half was dappled with tables, and punctuated with a giant black and white rendering of Johnny Cash over a stone fireplace. It was perfect.

My search for a place to chill was over. Between the bar and the stage, on the opposite side of the room from the main door, there was a passage to the "Green Room," and I knew I'd be welcome to use it. It was a huge space – nearly half as big as the bar itself – and the walls were covered with signed pictures of the famous and almost famous artists who had graced the stage, including Chip Wagon. And there was a couch. If I needed a nap, this was as good a spot as any, so I lay down.

My thoughts kept returning to the conversation with Bridget. I knew she was right; secrets suck. But I was right, too. I was not fit to be in any kind of romantic relationship. How could I be? Either I was insane, or everyone else was, which does not make for happy couplehood. Bridget seemed incapable of seeing how implausible and brutal my situation was. To her, it was simply a matter of me taking some pills, and all would be well. But that was not possible, not even remotely, and I resented it. I didn't want to be involved with anyone who belittled my suffering.

Good fucking riddance.

I hadn't checked my phone since getting off off the train, and I was dreading it. Undoubtedly, I'd find a thousand scathing texts from Bridget, maybe from her kids, maybe mine. But it was gig night – I did need to check. There may have been questions from bandmates. Anything was possible. I pulled my phone out of my pocket.

Bridget Reynolds

-Sweetie. I'm so sorry. I've been an insensitive bitch. I just need you to be honest with me. I love you.

Right. Except that if I had been honest and told her I was going to Kingston, she would have insisted on coming with me, and she would have set up a dinner date with Lilly and Nick. She wouldn't have understood that I could not, under any circumstances, interact with a person whose very existence was unfathomable to me.

She'd sent another message previously, with a distinctly different tone.

-Wow. You are a piece of work, Mr. Isaac. Part of me thinks you are just making all this shit up to get away from me so you can fuck whoever you want. Go ahead. I don't care. Just don't you dare show your face in this house again.

Ahh. There it was, the truth, the Bridget I knew existed. Every other part of her seemed at best dismissive, and at worst completely phony.

Surprisingly there were no other messages, which was a huge relief. Bridget's first message had been enough to piss me off, though. Maybe a pint – or 30 – would be the tonic I needed. Pushing myself up off the couch, I headed out to the bar. I wasn't feeling a pull, but it did feel like I didn't have much to stay sober for. Except for myself, of course – but I didn't know if I'd ever see that guy again.

I found my friend Carl behind the bar. More of an acquaintance than a friend, I suppose. Carl was a rock star bartender, and the ladies loved him. When he was pouring, he was the real main attraction.

"Hey, Buddy. Are we getting drink tickets?" I asked. It was customary for performers to get 2 or 3 drinks each.

"Hey, Al. Yeah. Gimme a sec."

He produced a string of twelve tickets and handed it over. It had been many shows since I had used one for myself, but that was about to change.

"Thanks, Man. May as well use one of mine now – Keith's please."

"Back on the horse, Brother?" He looked surprised.

"Don't ask. Just pour."

From the satisfied grin on his face, it seemed Carl didn't much like Sober Al. I wasn't convinced he liked Drunk Al either, but he considered himself superior to that version. He pulled a perfect pint and slid it over to me across the shiny bar.

"Very happy to pour you one, Big Guy."

He turned his attention back to the blonde gal he had been chatting up when I walked in and left me alone with my pint.

I hesitated to gulp it down. Something, maybe the Beast, was forcing a strange restraint. I started a staring contest with a frothy beer.

Win or lose, it would be going down my gullet forthwith. I was clasping the handle and pulling the jug to my lips when I heard a familiar voice.

"You really wanna do THAT again?" It was Marvin.

The chat I'd had with Tom the bartender in Oakville suddenly came back: *Every pint saves your life, right up until it kills you.* Beer was of no use to me now, or ever. It would only make whatever I had to do far more difficult. I wouldn't be drinking tonight. I handed the pint over to Marvin.

"It's for you, Buddy. I'm glad you're playing with us."

"I thought so. I'll take it. You don't need this shit, Al."

He was right, and I knew it. The night, the gig, my struggle – all of these would be impossible to navigate smashed. If I started drinking now, it was unlikely I'd ever stop. And if I wanted to die, there were faster and more efficient ways to get there. Marvin, on the other hand, seemed able to drink constantly and still function normally. He seemed perfectly sober when I handed him the pint.

"I came early hoping to find you here. Wanted to ask how you're doing? Still not so good?" Nice of him to ask.

"Honest truth? I'm fucked, Man. Doctors want to pump me full of pills so I'll believe all this shit is normal. I can't do it, Man. I just can't."

"I can see that. Have you tried anything else?"

"I went to Kingston. I saw her, Brother. It was so messed up."

"YOU SAW HER?? Jesus Al. WHY? Did she see you?" He was incredulous.

"I just... had to. There's this force, pulling me, dragging me. I didn't have a choice, Man. I've been calling it the Beast."

Marvin's eyes turned a deeper kind of strange.

"I know that force, Man. I do. I get it. It fucking grabs you, and takes you wherever it wants you to go."

"Exactly. I had to see her. I had to know that in some version of some reality, she was a genuine human being, not just an idea. You know?" It was such a relief to talk with someone who seemed to understand.

"If your Beast wanted you to see her, you had to see her. For real, Man. For real."

I was fully aware that if anyone else was listening in to this conversation, the men in white suits would be along any minute. Luckily, we still had some privacy. Carl was enamoured with Blondie, and she was enthusiastically reciprocating. We were still at risk of being overheard though, so I suggested we move the conversation back to the Green Room. Marvin agreed. Once we got situated, he wanted to dig deeper.

"So, did she see you? Did you talk to her?"

"She saw me. But I ran the fuck away. More like the Beast picked me up and threw me away. I mean, I practically flew."

"Shit Man. That can't be good. You are making ripples, my friend. I told you. I TOLD you. Shit."

He slammed the pint glass down, hard onto the table, spilling at least three valuable gulps. He was concerned… and frustrated.

"I still don't know what that means, Brother."

"You will know, Al. I promise you."

"I think I'm stuck here. I'll probably just have to get to know her. Or something."

Marvin looked into my eyes like he was trying to watch my thoughts form.

"Nah. You aren't stuck here, Al. Have you tried to figure out what triggered the jump?"

"I thought maybe it was the sketch, so I undid it. I didn't just delete it, I hit the undo button over and over again until there was no sketch left. Then I deleted the file – but I'm still here. I'm starting to think I really am just plain nuts."

"Of course you're still here. And you aren't nuts. It doesn't just happen immediately. I mean, when did you draw that sketch? It was weeks before the jump, wasn't it?"

"Yeah. A few weeks before. So wait – I have to undo everything I did between the time I drew her and the time I landed here?"

It felt like I was making a thousand times more headway than I'd made with actual doctors. By talking with a poet. An artist. A Man supposedly as crazy as I was.

"No, Man. If the sketch was the thing, it should work eventually. It'll happen without warning though, Brother. No fucking warning at all."

That made me pause. The idea that I could just one day, out of the blue, end up back home – back where I belonged – gave me some hope.

"What if the Beast just throws me into another crazy place where I don't belong?" That could not happen.

"Ha! First of all, don't piss him off, Man. Because he just might do that. But from my experience, it doesn't work that way. Have you noticed anything else completely out of place?"

I was glad he asked, because I still was wondering about the songs.

"I have. You know Merry-Go-Round? The Blue Rodeo tune?"

"Of course. Why?"

"That's my fucking tune, Man. And it wasn't even finished. Now I'm hearing somebody else sing a song I've been trying to finish for years. What is that? AND now my band tells me I have a song called Appalachian Man that we should have in our set. I have zero clue what that song even is!"

"Right. That makes sense. It really does." He leaned back and nodded, running his hand through his beard. He looked like he was making some major discovery.

"Makes sense? No, it does NOT make fucking sense. It makes me insane, Marvin!"

"Al, I told you. You kinda have one foot (or maybe one ear) here sometimes. You probably heard that tune in your dreams or something. To you, it fell out of the sky, but you heard it. Now you can take it back there, all finished. Maybe you'll have a huge hit, too. HA! Appalachian Man is my favourite Chip Wagon tune. Totally sucks that you don't know it."

I didn't have a chance to respond because another voice entered the conversation.

"I agree! We have to do A Man, Al. What do you mean you don't know it? I bet if we start, it'll come to you." It was Darren.

The rest of the band would be arriving any minute now, too, for soundcheck.

Darren greeted both Marvin and me with a hug. He seemed exactly the same as always. I guess some folks remained themselves, regardless of what reality one might happen to find them in.

"Buddy, I don't want to freak you out, but I swear to God I have never heard that song. It would be impossible for me to play it."

Darren was a good enough friend that I felt comfortable telling him that much. The confused look on his face turned into laughter.

"Ha. You're hilarious, Buddy. Let's just play it by ear. See how it goes." He thought I was joking.

Our other bandmates started trickling in. First, Terri and Rob, then Cam, then Mick. It had been months, in my reality at least, since we'd played together. It felt good to be with my friends, but my brain was spinning. There were so many things that had stayed exactly the same. My job, my band, my girlfriend. Why were there so Many similarities, but the differences so great? The thoughts wanted to take over my brain, but I had to try to focus on the show.

Typically, the closing act does their soundcheck first. The sound guys get all the levels saved. Then the opening act does their check, right before their performance. After that, and right before the closing act goes on, levels can be reset for their show.

When Chip Wagon took the stage for our check, we quickly set levels for each instrument. Only the drums took forever; there are so bloody many of them, and each one is like a separate instrument unto itself. Once all the instruments and vocal mic levels were set, we ran through a couple songs. One of mine, Pearls. And one of Darren's, 10,000 Tires. We sounded fantastic, better than I could ever remember us sounding. Almost too good.

Dougie was our sound Man that night, and he was very excited for the show.

"Sounds really great, Al. Really great!" He approached the stage while we were putting our instruments back on stands, where they'd rest during Marvin's performance. "How are the stage levels?"

There had been times at The Saint when it was very difficult to hear my own voice on stage. The result was that I would push too hard, and blow my voice out by the third song. I'd expressed that concern to Dougie in the past, and he wanted to be sure he had fully addressed it. He had.

"Levels are perfect, Dougie. Thanks, Man. Really nice up there, for sure."

Marvin took the stage for his check, and our crew reconvened in the Green Room. That's when the wolves came out. My band mates were all over me about Appalachian Man. I was surrounded.

"Dude, we have to do it! The people will go nuts if we don't," Terri reasoned.

"Yeeah, Mate. There'll be a mutiny." Mick's Australian drawl.

"Guys, you have to believe me here, ok? I've been having some really serious cognitive issues lately. I've been in the hospital and it's really bad. I don't remember that song, like at all. I can't do it."

It finally clicked with Darren.

"You're not joking, are you?"

"No! I am dead fucking serious. I'm really sorry."

Rob had an idea.

"Do you know the words, Darren? The rest of us could play it for sure. Al could just follow along."

That wasn't a bad idea. Except I was the only one who sang the other guys' songs if they weren't around. No one else seemed to know the lyrics to any songs but the ones they were expected to sing.

"Nah, I don't. Fuck. We have a problem," Darren summed up the situation.

"Guys, what the fuck? It's one song. We've left out songs that we like lots of times. It shouldn't be such a big deal!"

I couldn't understand what the fuss was all about, but Cam finally made it a little clearer.

"Yeah – but you don't generally leave out the tune that got you a record deal. You kind of have to play the song that's going to fill this place tonight."

"A RECORD DEAL? What record deal?" This was news to me.

"Jesus, Al. You are messed up. It's one night. We can just forget about it. Everyone is going to be hammered, anyway." Darren was finally a voice of reason.

So, it was settled. We could play through the tunes on our set list, and call it a night. I was not going to allow myself to worry about where I'd go afterwards, or about the next day. I'd just do my best to play well and enjoy the show with my friends.

We could hear Marvin's check through our conversation, and then he joined us in the Green Room. He was sounding great as usual – it was remarkable how entertaining he was. Just a dude and his guitar.

Once my band stopped the pressure to play a song I didn't know, we all started chatting normally. I asked them how their kids were, they asked about mine. Polite banter mostly, not genuine interest. We were killing time.

Soon we could hear the crowd starting to come in. I was curious to see how full this place would get. In my reality, I would have expected about one third capacity, but it was already sounding like we'd comfortably surpassed that. The seriousness of my issue started drifting away. If there was a way I could hide in my music and not worry about family, or work, or any other real-life shit, I might be able to handle this. And – we had a record contract? I would need to find out more about that.

The sound of the crowd became loud enough to pique my curiosity, so I decided to go out and take a look. It was closing in on eight o'clock and Marvin was meant to take the stage at 9:00. Shockingly, the place was already packed. Wall to wall people an hour before the music? On New Year's Eve? This was not what I expected. And everyone was greeting me with huge smiles, handshakes, hugs, and the occasional peck on the cheek.

A familiar voice cut through the din.

"Mr. Al!" It was Ally Oddly, and she was beaming. "Hey, this is my Mom, Tricia."

"Hey, Ally. Great to see you. Thanks so much for coming. I know YOU!"

I gave them both a hug. Tricia seemed to want to hang on a little longer than most. I'd seen her before at our shows, and Ally was not wrong – she was quiet. I couldn't recall ever having spoken a single word with her.

"I've wanted to say hello for a long time," she said. "I'm a big fan. You guys are great! I'm glad I have such an extroverted kid!" She seemed lovely – a holdover from the hippy days – and I was genuinely glad to see them both.

"Thanks so much, I'm really glad you came! Nice to finally meet you."

"Ally said your aura was all messed up. But I think you look great!"

"Ha! Thanks." I couldn't tell if she was an aura person, or if she was flirting with me. She definitely wasn't the sympathetic hussy type. I didn't really feel like flirting though, so I moved on just in case.

I made my way to the very back of the room for my customary hello to Johnny Cash. I greeted him every time I played there, for good luck – although it never seemed to make much of a difference. There were good nights, and there were bad nights. Johnny didn't give a shit. I said hello anyway.

People were still coming in, which never happened. I was in shock. It meant that most of the other shows that night would be poorly attended. We all relied on the same core audience, and the entirety of that group was at The Saint to see Chip Wagon... to see Chip Wagon perform a song that I didn't know.

Henry Miller and his two friends were the last ones allowed to enter; we were well beyond capacity. I'd never seen the place this full. It was exhilarating. Marvin was preparing to take the stage by the time I'd made my way back through the crowd, still shaking hands and hugging people along the way. 9:00 PM on the button. Usually, we waited for stragglers to fill the room as much as possible before the first act started, but clearly there was no need. We were all raring to go.

The crowd was chanting. "MARVIN, MARVIN, MARVIN." There was no room left for doubt in my mind. This was most certainly another reality. In my world, Hamilton crowds were grumpy. This crew was over the moon to see my friend play, and their enthusiasm was contagious. My brain was reveling in it. I wasn't thinking about Bridget or Lilly. I wasn't drowning in my own insanity. I was in the moment, and it was a very good place to be.

When Marvin ambled out of the Green Room and started climbing the stairs to the stage, the crowd went wild.

"Happy Fuckin' New Year Hamilton!"

He greeted the howling mob, and then broke into a set of relentlessly cool, rocky folk. Stuff that would have made Nick Cave green with envy – Dylanesque, but somehow even cooler. He was on his game and the crowd was eating it up. Song after song with the audience singing along, and swaying back and forth to music that defied sway. After twelve tunes, he thanked the good people for being such a great audience and told them to stay tuned for some delicious Chip Wagon.

My band was already in the Green Room by the time Marvin made his way back there from the stage. He was elated. Drunk on the love the crowd had poured onto him. I was so happy for him.

"Killer fucking show, Marvin!" I gave him a big hug.

"Thanks, Man. For real. I'm so glad you asked me to play. Soak it up, my friend. This is as good as it gets."

I wasn't sure what he meant by that, but I wasn't concerned. I was just happy to be there, and I couldn't remember the last time I'd felt that way.

The crowd started calling for us. Chip Wa Gon, Chip Wa Gon. That was a first – I'd never heard our band name chanted. Not even once. Not even as a joke. I couldn't help getting a little puffy chested. Every second it seemed to get more intense. It was earlier than we'd planned, but the crowd was deManding Chip Wagon – obviously we didn't have a choice. Who were we to deny them?

After a quick group hug, we started for the stage. It occurred to me that I hadn't checked my phone in a while. I pulled it out for a quick peek as I walked and was relieved to see no new messages. Darren was the first to leave the Green Room. The roar of the crowd was stadium loud. When Cam followed him, it seemed to get even louder. Terri and Rob were next, then Mick. And then me – Allan Isaac of the other, weird reality was making his way to the stage.

Something very strange happened then. The Beast was clearly dicking around again. Somehow, for a moment, I felt like I was floating above the crowd, watching the band, watching myself walk up the stairs to the stage. Everything was in slow motion.

Is this what people see when they die?

Then, BOOM, I was walking up the stairs again. I felt a hand grab my left arm – Tricia, mother of Ally Oddly. She pulled me down one step, and kissed my cheek.

"Sorry. I just HAD to. I'm drunk!" She smiled.

I didn't say anything, but now I knew that she'd been flirting. No good could come of that, so I just smiled back, and made my way up to the stage. It felt like home.

"Hey! How's everybody doing tonight?"

I loved the way it felt to speak into a microphone. I could feel my voice coming out of my core. The crowd responded more loudly than I'd ever experienced as a performer. Although the lights made it difficult to see them, and even though my mind knew there could be a maximum of 200 souls in the place, my ears were telling me the crowd was thousands strong.

"Happy New Year, guys! Let's hear it for Marvin Carol. What an amazing set!" Darren offered.

The roar continued. Darren and I shared front person duties. I usually took centre stage, with Darren to my right. Cam was positioned between Darren and me, a few steps back. Mick was to my left, his pedal steel angled in such a way that he was as much facing the rest of the band as he was the audience. Terri was parked by the drum kit, between Mick and Rob.

When Darren broke into the opening riff of 10,000 Tires, the crowd somehow got even louder. The Beast grabbed me again and pulled me high above the room. Surely this place was way over capacity. Hundreds of heads bobbing up and down, fists punching the air.

God, we looked good up there. And we sounded fantastic. Then, BOOM, I was back on the stage looking out at the lights, just in time for my harmonies on the first chorus. My voice had never felt stronger. Our harmonies were historically a little lazy. Mick and I would sometimes double each other. But that night, we were perfect. Chip Wagon was a force.

The switching pattern continued, moving me from the stage to watching from above and back again. I was starting to think I'd died back on Christmas morning, and everything since had been some kind of weird afterlife. This part at least – being able to watch myself playing the gig of a lifetime – this was heavenly.

From both perspectives, this was definitely the best Chip Wagon had ever sounded. No wonder we filled the room. We were fantastic. When we got to the spot in the set where we were to play Merry-Go-Round, Darren announced that I had insisted we do this song instead of Appalachian Man. There was a quick gasp of disbelief, but once we broke into it, the crowd loved it. It was far superior to Blue Rodeo's version…OF MY SONG! As we finished Darren's Big Yellow Moon, he noticed we were fast approaching midnight.

"Okay guys! In a couple minutes, we're gonna count down to 2017. Who wants to lead the count?" Darren asked.

Every single hand in the joint went up. The atmosphere was electric. I was likely the only sober person in the entire room. Everybody wanted to be a star, even if only for ten seconds. But one set of hands seemed to reach higher. One voice rang louder. It was Henry Miller, and he had no intention of not being the chosen one. He was a big fellow, 6' 4". He bulldozed his way through the front third of the crowd and hopped right up on the stage – forgoing the stairs altogether.

"I'm gonna count this mofo DOWN!" He grabbed my mic stand and took hold of the situation.

"That's Henry Miller, folks. Let's hear it for our New Year's MC!" Darren introduced him.

"Okay! What time is it?" Henry asked. He didn't have a watch, or his phone. I pulled my phone out to use as the official clock for the countdown to the new year, and saw a text from Bridget.

-Happy New Year Sweetie. I love you. I am so sorry. I should be there.

Well shit. Now I felt guilty for telling her not to come. But there was no time to dwell on that. The clock now read 11:58:39 – just over a minute away. I closed the text message and prepared to give Henry the go ahead to start counting. The crowd started chanting his name. HENRY, HENRY, HENRY.

Shit. I guess they'd cheer for ANYBODY. I kept that to myself.

"Okay, Buddy. 20 seconds!" I made the clock as big as possible and handed the phone to him.

"Are You Ready Hamilton?" He was relishing this. "10-9-8" The crowd was counting along. "7-6..."

I noticed some movement to my left; Tricia was climbing up the stairs.

"5-4-3..." It was clear that she was heading directly for me. I was trapped. "2-1"

"HAPPY NEW YEAR!!" Henry was in his glory, and Tricia was planting a big, sloppy, drunken kiss, right on my lips. Henry passed my phone back to me.

"You looked like you needed that." She was looking up at me, making her about 5' 6".

"You look like you need this too!" She kissed me again, then faded back into the crowd.

No one seemed to notice, or care. Everyone was kissing everyone. Everyone was kissing Henry.

"Happy New Year, Mr. Al!" Ally Oddly yelled up from the floor.

"Happy New Year, Kiddo."

The band and the audience broke out in a stellar version of Auld Lang Syne, led by Mick. God, his voice was perfect. The Beast threw me up above the crowd again, but this time he had a purpose. I spotted Bridget standing by the sound booth, and I could see that she was crying. I could not go to her; I was not a physical being. Just a floating, sentient, apparently invisible dude who was somehow simultaneously up on the stage. It was clear that she'd seen the Tricia kiss. I looked up at the stage. That Al seemed oblivious to what Floating Al was seeing. I felt helpless. Bridget shook her head and walked out the door.

BOOM, back on stage, mid Auld Lang Syne. Now fully aware that Bridget had seen something that she would undoubtedly extrapolate into something else entirely. I could not just leave the situation like that, so I hung my guitar on its stand and jumped off the stage. Shouldering my way through the crowd, I ran out the door to find Bridget. I spent a few minutes searching, but I was too late – and the crowd was anxious for the set to continue. They started chanting my name.

Allan, Allan, Allan.

I needed to tell her that I had not solicited that kiss. I could have pushed Tricia away I suppose, but I'd been startled. I pulled my phone out to text Bridget, but she'd beaten me to the punch.

-Very nice, Al. I show up just in time to watch you make out with a hippy. In front of the whole city. Don't bother responding. And DO NOT bother coming home. Happy fucking new year, asshole.

Well, there goes that idea. Oh well. I really hadn't done anything wrong; I had my band to back me up on that. I was sure I could smooth all this over, if I wanted to. Except, I was not at all sure that I wanted to.

Allan. ALLAN. ALLAN. ALLAN.

I had to get back. A riot was about to ignite. Hurrying back through the door, I somehow navigated the human maze and leapt back up onto the stage. The crowd went berserk, and another chant erupted. The entire audience was singing a song, one that I did not know. When the chorus came, it culminated with a very loud, very clear "APPALACHIAN MAN." The band even joined in. Before I knew it, Darren was playing what were apparently the opening chords to the song. It was a cool sounding tune, though. B minor, G, D – but I was still bewildered. The band started playing along.

"Al's been having some trouble remembering the words to this one, folks. Why don't you help him along?" Darren announced through the mic.

BOOM. I was floating again. This should be interesting.

I was watching myself again – only now, from what I could see, I didn't look uncomfortable at all. After we'd played through the pattern a couple of times, Stage Al stepped up to the mic.

You been lovin' someone all night long

I could tell because your lights were on

The red ones, like you used to shine with me

The crowd knew every word. So did Stage Al. It was obvious that I was something like... dead.

BOOM. I was back on stage. What the fuck am I supposed to do now?

I felt the Beast move me up to the mic... and the words just started to fall out of my mouth, without conscious effort.

Shadows fall across the window wall

A different meaning for a curtain call

Please forgive me, I'm all apologies

Yeah, this one's all on me

I guess I shouldn'a moved in across the road

If I didn't wanna know things that ain't mine to know

It might be an aberration

But in my educated estimation

I'm the revelation of an Appalachian Man

BOOM. I was floating again. The back and forth, up and down thing was making me dizzy. I was loving this tune. Stage Al could write! I/he looked like a star up there. I was almost feeling like the Beast would have to plop me back on stage for the next verse, but I kept floating. I wanted to go back on stage. If the Beast was just going to feed me the lyrics anyway, then why the hell not? Stage Al moved back toward the mic. I was curious to see where he was going with these lyrics.

Then, I noticed Tricia, about three rows back from the stage. She was turned around with her back to the band, and she was looking directly at me. I felt absolutely invisible, so how could she see me? I was on the stage. I could see myself there. I turned my head around to see if she was looking beyond me, but there was nothing there. Not even a ceiling, just an indescribable void, a black nothingness. No stars, no clouds. Just… nothing. She was still looking at ME! Our eyes met, and it put me in a trance, completely oblivious to the song, lost in an impossible telepathic connection. But then she winked at me, and turned her attention back to the band.

BOOM, back up with the band, just in time for a cool pedal steel solo by Mick. The way my songs normally went, that meant that I would likely just repeat the chorus one or two more times after the solo and the song would be done. If any of my bandmates had any idea that I was popping in and out of consciousness on the stage, they were not letting on. They seemed to be having the time of their lives.

Mick finished his solo, and I inched toward the mic, fully expecting the Beast to take over. But I was on my own, so I took my cue from the band. I could feel the song breaking down. I did that a lot – start the last chorus quietly, then build it up. And sure enough, that was happening.

I guess I shouldn't'a moved in across the road

If I didn't wanna know things that ain't mine to know

Rob started building up the intensity on the toms, and the Beast stepped in with the finishing lyrics.

The audience was as loud as the band, and I was overwhelmed.

"And THAT's how you do THAT! WOOOOHHHHH!" I couldn't help myself; I was in full-on party mode.

"You folks are the best audience EVER!" I was not exaggerating.

The remainder of the set went by in a blink. The Beast was kind enough to leave me on the stage for the duration. We finished with Brother I'm Coming Down, a song written by our brother and former bandmate, Mike Andrews. It was a rockin' way to end a set. But the good people would have none of it. They demanded an encore, so we gave them a couple crowd pleasers. Sweet Caroline and The Weight. We had them eating out of our hands. They cheered for more, but we were spent. I, personally, was well beyond spent. I was still fairly certain that I was dead, floating in a kind of purgatory, still waiting to learn my final destination.

The Chip-Wagon-Mania made it difficult to get back to the Green Room. I'd never felt more like a rock star, out of body experiences be damned. It was a wonderful feeling. I was even confident that I could sort out the situation with Bridget. I didn't know if forgiveness was in the cards, or even if I wanted it, but I was willing to entertain the possibility.

Two large fellows were acting as bouncers. I couldn't recall The Saint ever requiring bouncers. A number of fans were becoming dangerously enthusiastic about seeing us backstage, but the bouncer boys were doing a nice job of keeping them at bay. They did allow the spouses in, and they seemed to know who everyone was. With one little exception – they let Ally Oddly and her mom pass the barricade. Apparently. the on-stage kiss was enough to confuse even the sharpest minds. But I didn't mind.

"Hey there! How'd you like the show?" I greeted them.

"OH MY GOD, Mr. Al! That was incredible!" Ally gushed.

"It really, really was, Al. So good," Tricia concurred.

I hugged them both and thanked them profusely. I was grateful to feel appreciated.

"Can we ask a favour?"

I expected Tricia wanted a selfie, or an autograph, but I was flattering myself.

"Sure. What do you need?"

"We're both hammered, and I don't wanna leave the car here. Ally tells me you're a train guy. So, if you need a ride, why don't you drive us back to Oakville? I can pay for a cab from my place."

My first thought was: no fucking way. But it was a way home – if I had a home. I really didn't know, but I agreed anyway.

"Sure. I can do that. I can be ready whenever. Just let me know when you want to leave."

"We're ready now. That was exhausting. So so good." Ally was a fan.

I packed my guitar up, and said my goodbyes to my band, and to Marvin.

"Great job on A-Man, Brother," Darren congratulated me. The band all agreed.

Marvin took me aside for a second.

"Fantastic night, Al. Thanks so much for having me on the bill. It was an honour."

"Dude, you were fantastic! Just a great night."

"By the way, I think that lady knows. She can see you." Marvin was pointing at Tricia.

That confirmed what I'd thought. Whatever ability Marvin possessed to see me, to see what I was going through, Tricia had it too. She'd seen me hanging from the void like a bat. She had seen the out-of-body Al. And that was crazy. The whole thing was just impossible. At that moment, I just... let go. Let the chips fall wherever they would fall.

"Ladies, take me to your rocketship." I don't know why I said that. I blamed the Beast. I was probably trying to be charming.

Ally and Tricia were both drunk. New Year's Eve drunk. They could still walk okay, but I was glad they'd asked me to drive. They led the way to Tricia's 2010 black Dodge Caravan. Tricia hit the unlock button, handed me the keys, and climbed into the passenger seat. Ally made a bed out of the back seat and fell asleep immediately. There was lots of room for my guitar in the back cargo area.

"So where are we going?" I asked. I still had no idea where they lived.

"Just off Postmaster, up by the hospital."

I knew the area; it was about a 25-minute drive. Enough time for some awkward silence before Tricia couldn't hold it in any longer.

"So… What the actual fuck was that, Mr. Al?"

"You're calling me Mr. Al now too?" I tried, unsuccessfully, to change the subject.

"You know I saw you. That is some fucked up shit."

"I thought you did. And yes, it is some fucked up shit." I wasn't planning to offer any more detail.

"I'm sorry I kissed you." She sounded sincere, but then her curiosity got the better of her. "Are you sorry I kissed you?"

"Well. I would say it was harmless, but I'm pretty sure Bridget saw us."

"Bridget? Is that your wife?"

"We aren't married. She's… was my girlfriend."

"Was your girlfriend? She probably still is your girlfriend somewhere."

"Do you understand what is happening to me?" Now my curiosity was piqued.

"I know that you aren't supposed to be here. I felt it the second I saw you tonight. I know something else, too."

"What might that be?"

"I know that we've been together. Somewhere. In some other reality we are – or were – together."

"How do you know that?" I wanted to dismiss her thoughts as wishful thinking. Once again, I was flattering myself.

"Al. I saw you floating in the air, for Christ's sake. I know SOME things. And I know that somewhere, you are my fella. I was kind of hoping it was this reality. That's why I took advantage of you."

I believed her. Although by this point, I might have believed anyone.

"Well. I'm flattered. But, honestly, you don't want anything to do with me. I'm a fucking mess." I hoped that would put an end to it.

"I know you are. Obviously. But I'm here, Al. If this is where you end up, I will still be here. Okay?"

It was a sweet offer, but I didn't answer. I wasn't sure I was even attracted to her. A hippy? She probably smoked a lot of weed, and I hated the smell of that shit. But there was something intriguing about her. She knew exactly what was happening to me, and it didn't seem to faze her. That, from my new perspective, was an extremely attractive quality.

"Turn right on Postmaster."

She guided me the rest of the way to her home. It was a townhouse in a row of other, nearly identical four-story townhouses. These neighbourhoods were how I'd always pictured Hell. Row upon row of mindless sameness.

"I hate this place, but it's all I can afford right now," she apologized.

"Ally. We're home. Wake up, Sweetie." Then, she turned her attention to me.

"You're welcome to crash here, if you want, Al. I promise I'll behave – unless you don't want me to."

It was a friendly offer, and I had nowhere else to go.

"Do you have a spare room?" I asked.

"I wish. It's a two bedroom. I do have a huge couch though, and it's yours if you want it."

"You know what? I think I'll take you up on that. Are you sure?"

"Absolutely no problem. I'll get you some blankets."

Just inside the front entrance there was a gigantic stairway leading to the living room. It was decorated just as I'd expected. Tapestries covered every flat surface, and at least two lava lamps glowed and bubbled. It smelled of incense, but not weed, which surprised me. Ally disappeared to her bedroom, wherever that was.

"Do you smoke weed?" I thought I would just come out and ask.

"No, I hate the stuff. Ally does though, if you want some. She always has a stash."

"Cool. Nope, I hate it too." I was relieved.

"I'll get you some blankets so you can get settled."

"Thanks so much, Tricia. That's really kind of you. I appreciate it."

"Happy to help."

She vanished up another gigantic stairway to fetch some bedding. She had not exaggerated; her couch was enormous. I lowered myself into a rocking chair directly across from it, drained of anything that might give me the energy to stay awake. The night started running back through my mind.

I was floating in mid fucking air and watching myself.

The enormity of that little tidbit was suddenly overwhelming. Tricia arrived with a pink duvet and a fluffy pillow.

"Here you go, Sir. You sure you don't want to join me upstairs?" She was flirting again.

"I do appreciate the offer, believe me. But I think I'm good here."

I was in no position to be of any use to anyone in that way. The last time I'd even thought about it, I had still been madly in love with

Bridget. An entire world of bat shit crazy had fallen on me, but that didn't mean I was free to love somebody else. It was just out of the question.

"That's fair. Probably wise. I might not let you go if you did come up. I am going to hug you though."

Tricia gave me a warm, genuine hug, and a peck on the cheek. I broke down a little bit. It was the closest thing I'd felt to friendship in some time. And she believed me.

"Thank you, Tricia. I mean it."

"Goodnight, Handsome."

"Goodnight."

Tricia disappeared back up the stairs, but I stayed on the couch. I hadn't checked my phone since just past midnight. It was now 2:40 AM January 1st, 2017. There were 17 missed calls. Holy shit. Something huge had happened. Every missed call was from Lilly. There were no text messages, but my voicemail inbox was full. I was shaking when I called for messages.

Your voice mailbox is full. Why don't you go ahead and delete the messages you don't need right away. You can dial 611 for assistance. You have... three new messages. To listen to your messages, press 1 now.

1

"Daddy. Please call me. Oh my god. I can't believe this. Please please please call me, Dad. Okay? It's Lill."

My heart dropped. She was sobbing. Uncontrollably.

"Dad. What the fuck? This can't be true. Colby told me you were here. Then Aiden told me everything. Dad. Please tell me this is a joke. Oh my god. Dad. Daddy. No. Please."

Now I was sobbing too. I had no choice but to admit that this kid was real. She loved and needed her Dad. I had to at least call her. I would kick the Beast in the nuts if it tried to stop me.

"That's it Dad. I am coming home. I can't believe this shit. You are my DAD. I'm coming home right fucking now."

Well, that was that. I would have to face her. Her last call came at 1:45 AM If she left then, she would be in Oakville by 4:00 AM or so. I mustered up the courage to try to call her, but my call went to voicemail after a couple rings. She was probably on the phone with Bridget, which would give her more reasons to hate me. Not only had I forgotten that she existed, but now I was fucking around on her Mom. Not exactly saintly stuff. I turned my phone ringer on, just in case she tried to call again, and I closed my eyes.

I must have fallen asleep within seconds. I have no more memories of reliving the show, or of thinking of Bridget, or Lilly. I just crashed.

Then, at 5:17 AM, I was startled awake by my ringtone. It was Bridget. I answered.

"Hello?" I squeezed the greeting out of still-sleeping vocal cords.

"Al! Can you come home? Please, Baby."

She was crying uncontrollably, and her words were barely discernible. It seemed I had that effect on everyone who loved me.

"B. It was not what it looked like. I promise."

"I don't care about that. Please just come home now. I need you, Al. Please?"

"I'll be right there."

I ordered an Uber on my phone. I had time to leave a note to thank Tricia and Ally before my ride arrived.

Tricia and Ally Oddly

Thank you both so much for coming to the show and for your hospitality.

I got called home. It sounds like everyone is very upset with me.

Thank you for the reprieve.

XOXO Mr. AL

The notification that my ride had arrived pinged through, so I found the downward stairs, locked the door behind me, and jumped into the car.

I was not prepared for what lay ahead.

Chapter 14:
While You Were Singing

My Dad… he has always been a little crazy, but this stuff was out there. Even for him. I hadn't heard a word from him since I announced my engagement to Nick, which was just weird. Normally he texted me every day, but now that I was heading into the hugest thing in my life, EVER… crickets. Mom told me he'd really been struggling, that he had even been in the hospital. So, I tried to cut him some slack.

Before Christmas, Nick insisted that we spend the holidays with his family in Montreal. His parents were super nice, but kind of intimidating. Mr. Rocher was a retired police chief. "Once you've been a cop, you are NEVER off duty," he would always say. He still carried his gun every freakin' where. From time to time, he acted as a Private Detective for his rich friends. That was his excuse for the gun, and the only legal way he could get away with it. He was a funny guy, but that was scary shit. Mrs. Rocher was a retired High School Principal. She didn't even need a gun. She could just shoot you with her eyeballs if you pissed her off.

I really wanted to be home with my brothers and sisters, to celebrate our first Christmas as a family. But Nick was super adamant. I knew he was going to propose, so I went along with it. I sent Daddio very specific instructions on what to get everyone for me. I also asked him to sketch me so Mom could finally have something hanging on a wall. She was crazy terrified to make even one nail hole... because, paint? Whatever.

Everyone else in the family sent me Merry Christmas wishes. But nothing from Big Al. They loved my gifts. I knew they would. I hand painted lilies on jars. It was so cool. I just knew that if they got to know each other, my brothers and sisters could be an awesome family. Mom and Dad were both really special people. My heart was bursting into happy bits, that we were all going to be one unit.

But since Christmas morning, Daddio had been AWOL. Zilch. It was like he didn't even exist. And I didn't like it at all. I mean, I was his pride and joy. Was he mad that I didn't come home for the Holidays? I knew he really liked Nick, so that shouldn't have been a problem. I couldn't figure it out. Even if he was really sick, normally I was his go-to. I was always the first person he would call. But, Mom said he was really having a hard time mentally, which scared me. I was as patient as I could be, but I just wanted to go home and give him a big hug. That would always make him feel better – and it would make me feel better, too. So, Nick and I planned to head back to Kingston for a big New Year's party. And after that, I figured we could go home to show off my ring.

We left Montreal on the 30th of December for the three hour drive to our apartment in Kingston. We lived five minutes from Queen's. It wasn't a great place, but convenience was important. Dad had helped move us in a couple years before. Even with his bad back, he was always more than willing to help.

I couldn't keep my eyes open on the drive back. It was pretty late, and I was so tired. I could never sleep much at Nick's parents' place with his Dad snoring so loud. I was zonked the whole drive home. Nick woke me up when we were nearly there.

"Hey, Fiancée. We're almost home."

"Holy shit. How long was I out?" I yawned and stretched.

"The entire trip, Babe."

I was still trying to get my bearings. I had to wake up; there was a bunch of stuff we'd have to carry in. That's when I saw someone walking down the sidewalk.

"Was that my Dad? Hey STOP!" I yelled at Nick.

"It was just some homeless guy, Lill. I'm pretty sure I've seen him before."

"STOP THE FUCKING CAR!" I was positive it was my Dad. I would know that goofy walk anywhere.

Nick slammed on the brakes and pulled off to the side of the road, right under a streetlight. I jumped out of the car and yelled out to my Dad. He was standing in shadow so I couldn't really see him, but I knew he could see me. I started running toward him. I just wanted to hug him sooooo bad. But after a second, he turned and ran the other way. I'd never seen him run... ever. I couldn't believe how fast he was. Maybe it's not him? I thought. There was no way I was going to catch him, so I just gave up and walked back to the car.

"Did you see that?" I asked Nick.

"That was NOT your Dad, Lill. He can't move like that. That dude was Olympics fast. I mean, holy shit!"

"Maybe you're right. I don't know. I'm probably just not awake yet."

I pretended to agree with him, but I knew my Dad. That was a very strange thing. But why would he run away? AND, if he was so sick, how could he run like that? He was supposed to be in the hospital. I was so confused. It hurt my heart. A lot.

When we got to our apartment, we unloaded all the Christmas presents and took them inside. The plan was to just go to bed right away, but I had to call my Mom to tell her what just happened. She picked up, first ring, like always.

"Hey Lill. Did you make it home ok?"

"Hi Mamma. Yeah, we're fine. But you won't believe what I just saw."

"Oh?"

"Nick woke me up just before we got to our place. And I swear to God, the first thing I see is Daddio walking down the sidewalk. No shit."

"Whhhaat? No. That's impossible, Sweetie. He's still in the hospital. I saw him earlier – and I'm going back in the morning."

"I know. It doesn't make any sense. Maybe just wishful thinking. He still hasn't responded to me. At all."

"Well, unless he can be in two places at once, I don't know?"

"So weird. I'm gonna try to go back to sleep Ma."

"Okay Sweetie. Me too. Try not to let it upset you. Your Dad loves you more than anything. Even me."

"Ha! Right. Anyway, let me know how he's doing when you see him, okay?"

"Okay, Sweetie. Goodnight. Love you."

"Love you too Mom. Goodnight."

Nick and I were both so tired, we fell asleep as soon as our heads hit the pillows. But my dreams were filled with my Dad, all night. I kept seeing him standing there, then running away. When I would try to chase after him, my feet wouldn't move. I hate those dreams. But, it wasn't far off from what actually happened, and I couldn't seem to let it go. So much of me was absolutely positive that the guy was my Dad.

We got up just before noon, after a pretty lousy sleep. But adrenaline gave me all the energy I needed. I was super excited for New Year's. Our friends, Colby and Vicki, were throwing a big party for us at The Grad Club, a cool bar on campus. This was our last year at Queen's, and we wanted to go out with a bang. AND we wanted to announce to the world that we would be Man and Wife! Nick and Lill forever. All that good stuff. I could barely contain myself.

Nick was making us brunch when my phone rang. It was my bratty little brother, Aiden.

"Hey Brat," I answered.

"Hey, Sis. I'm coming to your shindig. On my way there now actually."

"Oh my GOD. Wow. Thank you, Bro! That's so nice."

He was a brat, but it would be great to see him. He always made us laugh.

"I am stopping at my buddy's first. Cool if I get there around dinnertime?" He asked.

"That's perfect, Aiden. Can't wait to see you."

I let Nick know that Aiden would be joining us for New Year's celebrations. He was even more excited than I was. They pretended to get on each other's nerves, but they laughed nonstop when they were together, usually at my expense. They both liked to tease me about... well, about everything, really.

It would have been nice if my other siblings could've made it. I hadn't seen Brad or Tessa in way too long. They never lived with Dad full time, so seeing them was always hit and miss. Now that Brad had Sierra, I barely ever got to see him. And Pam was always so quiet with me – I didn't really expect her to come. Tessa was the one I wanted to see most. My baby sister. She was adorable. Smart. Just super cool. I decided to shoot her a text.

-Hey Baby Sis. Wish I could see you for New Year's. I MISS YOU.

-Miss you too Big Red. SO MUCH. Soon? I want to see your ring!

She had always called me Big Red. My hair had been a fascination to her from the time she was a baby.

It felt good to connect with her. She was growing up so fast, but still too young to be at our New Year's Eve party. There were a few minor preparations we still had to address. Like figuring out what to wear. Nick's Mom was determined to make me fat, and it was working. I had stuffed my face in Montreal, and it showed. Nothing fit me. And even if it did, it made me look fat. Nick refused to be honest with me. He just kept saying everything looked good, but that wasn't true. I could see for myself that nothing looked good. Not at all. If I had to, I'd wait for Aiden. I knew he'd be honest at least. He'd tell me which outfit made him want to puke the least.

In the meantime, I'd have to try to convince Nick to dress up a little. This was going to be our big night, and people would be taking pictures. I was going to wear something pretty, so he should too.

"What about your navy dress pants and a nice shirt?" I suggested.

"What's wrong with what I'm wearing?"

"You're joking, right? You can't wear a Habs jersey to a New Year's party. Seriously, Nick."

"Whatever. Do I even have a nice shirt?"

"Oh my God. YES, you have a nice shirt. Stop being an idiot. How about the light blue one? The shiny one?"

"It's all wrinkly."

"Just get it. I'll iron it. You're pathetic, you know?"

His whole act was just a ploy to get me to iron his clothes. I hated ironing, but he hated it more. And he also sucked at it. He went to get his shirt, and his pants. He knew I was going above and beyond, so he had the good sense to set up the ironing board, and the iron.

Once I got Nick dressed, I re-focused my efforts on choosing my own outfit. I had it down to three choices. First option was a sexy, silky red dress. Backless. It was shimmery and came down to just below the knee. I thought it was the most forgiving, but Nick thought it was too revealing. The second choice was a black, form fitting, knitted turtleneck number. It landed just above the knee. To me, it was at least as revealing as the red one, but Nick wasn't bothered by that kind of revealing. He didn't mind if you could see every curve, nook, and cranny, as long as it was covered up. The red one showed too much skin. My third option was a pair of very sexy black pants (they made my ass look great, even if there was three times the ass there used to be), with a shiny red top. Nick was no help at all. Thankfully Aiden was showing up shortly.

We ordered pizza for dinner – who would want to cook on New Year's Eve? The problem with ordering food on December 31 is the delivery time – we waited nearly two full hours for it to show up. But being the sucker I am, I still tipped 20%. I felt bad that anybody would have to work. By the time the pizza showed up, Aiden had arrived. Nick teased him about being short. Aiden teased Nick about being a Habs fan. They both teased me about the weight I'd gained. Nothing had changed. We inhaled the pizza, and I made Aiden suffer through my modelling session.

"I like the black one. It looks really nice on you."

He actually said something nice. I couldn't believe it. But – the Aiden giveth, the Aiden taketh away.

"You can't even tell that you're fat."

"Nice. Thank you. Brat."

It was a good enough endorsement for me. The black knit turtleneck dress was the choice. Once I had it on, I agreed. You couldn't really see that I had put on much weight. Black is slimming, they say. One nice thing about adding a few extra pounds is that some of those pounds end up in the boobs. That might take focus away from other lumps and bumps.

I never wore much makeup. My Dad always said that my freckles were too pretty to cover up, and that my green eyes were way better than fake rosy cheeks. So, I went with that. I put some lipstick on, and some mascara, but that was it. I pulled my hair up into a loose, messy bun and called it done.

Aiden was decidedly under dressed, but that was ok. He was not the guest of honour. Jeans and a hoodie were good enough. Nick, on the other hand, looked fabulous. He seemed to be able to eat anything he wanted to and never gain any weight. It probably helped that he was in the gym every day. And, his shoes! Daddio spoiled us both with the very best footwear. When I met Nick, he was strictly a Nike guy. Now, he had all the coolest shoes. All different styles and colours, he had a pair for every occasion. For this outfit, he chose a dark chili, double monk strap. And he

231

always had a matching belt. He looked perfect. Daddio would have been proud, but I wasn't even going to send him a pic. He wouldn't look at it anyway – or at least, that's how it felt.

The only thing left to do before heading out was to get a drink or two into ourselves. Nick had picked up a nice bottle of champagne for the occasion, and I was even happy to let Aiden have a glass. When Nick popped the top off the bottle, he made no attempt to stifle the explosion. Most of the good stuff ended up all over the table and floor, which seemed fitting. It wasn't champagne unless there was spillage.

Still, I didn't drink much. Dad had kind of scared me away from booze. I saw what it did to him, the effect it had on his ability to function. And my Gramps was like that too. I just didn't want to go down that road. I'd only been drunk twice before, neither time pretty. A glass or two of wine was no big deal, but I never drank more than that. Nick was another story entirely. He wasn't a lush, but no arm twisting was necessary for him to "enjoy himself." I'd only seen Aiden drink once. He didn't have the same drunky gene, so I wasn't worried as much about him. We were only a ten minute walk from the bar anyway; there was no need for anyone to be a Designated Driver.

We finished our champagne and started over to the bar. I put on runners for the walk, but I brought along my super cool John Fluevogs, packed up in a bag. They were comfy enough, but not walk-ten-minutes-in-the-cold comfy. And it was cold. Absolutely frigid. Nick was the only man under thirty that I'd ever seen wearing overshoes, but he rocked them.

Dad had given him a cool, orange pair of SWIMS. We made the walk in record time, mostly by trying to keep warm.

It was just after 9:00 PM when we walked into The Grad Club. Colby and Vicki had invited just a few other friends to help us ring in the New Year, and we were the last of the group to arrive. Our friends greeted us like we were the stars of the show. Most of them had met Aiden at some point, as he'd been a fairly regular visitor during my student days at Queen's, so introductions weren't necessary.

Colby forbade us to pay for anything, because the group had pooled resources to ensure we "could have a good time." Of course, Nick took that to mean "get wasted." He drank mostly beer – and nothing fancy, just Molson Export. I shit you not. He was only 23 years old, and already a seriously old fart. So he started with an Ex, and I asked for a glass of white wine. On top of the champagne we'd had earlier, that was likely more than enough for me.

From the corner of my eye, I could see that Aiden was clumsily trying to pick up my friend Sarah. That wasn't going to work – not in his wildest dreams, or in any conceivable alternate reality. His success with the ladies was limited to those of the canine persuasion. Although, I think the odd cat tolerated him too. He started with an Export as well. It didn't take much to get him to Sloppy Town.

We were not the only party at The Grad Club; it was full of students, with their friends and families. After a few drinks, the lines between the groups began to blur. Aiden was trying to pick up every girl in the place.

"Hey, Brat. The more you drink, the less likely it's going to be. Maybe lay off the pints for a hot minute?"

I was his Big Sis. I was allowed to offer him advice on girls. He wasn't going to be successful, regardless of how drunk or sober he was. I just didn't want him to make a complete ass of himself.

When 11:00 PM rolled around, Nick was well into his cups. He was a wonderful storyteller, even when he was wasted. A crowd was always sure to gather around him, once he got going. And he was getting going.

"So, then, on Christmas Eve, we're at my parents in Montreal. My brother and his girlfriend are there. That's it. Me and Lill, my parents, and my brother and his chick. I tell Lill I am going out to meet some friends. She's like 'What the fuck, Nick?'. I'm like 'I never see them, Babe. It will only be for a few hours.' She is SO PISSED. Like I would actually leave her all alone with my family. But she bought it. My Dad played along perfect. He's like, 'It'll be fun Lill, we can play Trivial Pursuit!' HHHAAAA. TRIVIAL FUCKING PURSUIT. Oh my God. He actually gets the game out. He sets up the board and everything. Lill is just sitting there in pure disbelief. I say 'Ok, I'm off. I'll see you guys in a few hours. Love you Lill.' She wouldn't even LOOK at me. So fucking pissed. I get in the car, drive around the block a few times, and come back into the house. She looks up, confused as shit. I go 'I changed my mind. I don't even like my friends. Why don't we just get married instead?' I got down on one knee. The WHOLE shit, you know? And she's like 'You asshole.

Yes. I will marry you. Jerk'. Isn't that nice? Calls me an asshole right after I propose."

Ahh, the story of how he proposed. Only slightly embellished. He had them rolling in the aisles. The entire place was in the palm of his hand.

"You ARE an asshole. But I love you anyway!" I said.

I gave him a huge hug and a big sloppy kiss. Everyone cheered like we were freaking rock stars. That's when things started to get really weird. Nick kept going with stories. Then he got to the one when we were just getting back to Kingston from Montreal.

"So, the whole fucking drive, I am by myself. She is snoring her ASS off. I have the tunes cranked and everything, but I can't hear shit 'cause she's snoring. Finally, we're like, two blocks from home when I wake her up. 'Hey Fiancée. Wake UP.' She's like 'Where the fuck are we?'. HOME, for fuck's sakes. We're home. Anyway, she sees some homeless guy on the sidewalk, but she thinks it's her DAD. HHHHAAA. Seriously! She makes me stop the car so she can get out. She yells out to the poor dude. 'Hey DAD!' She scares the living SHIT outta the guy, and he bolts. He turns and fuckin' runs faster than I have ever seen anyone go. Especially a homeless dude. It was hilarious. But she STILL thinks it was her old Man. He's in the HOSPITAL in Oakville. Not breaking the speed of freakin' sound in Kingston."

He had the whole place, even the bartender, in stitches. Everyone except Colby, who was standing right beside me. He went white as a ghost.

"You saw your Dad?" He asked me. He was shaking.

"Nah. It was just some super speedy homeless guy," Nick interrupted.

"Nick. Stop. It sure looked like my Dad. I mean, his walk, and everything."

Colby fell into a chair that was only partially under his ass. Like he was fainting, or something.

"Dude. What's wrong?" I asked him. I was really concerned. "You look grey, Colbs."

"Shit, Lill. Shit shit shit."

"Colby, what's going on?" Something seemed weird.

"I promised him I wouldn't tell you. I promised, Lill."

He looked like he might cry. He was clearly keeping something to himself that he did not want to keep to himself.

"Well, you kinda have to tell me now, Buddy. What's going on?"

Poor Colby was really upset – and he wasn't even that drunk. This was not like him. I put my arm around him. Vicki did too. She was concerned. Even Nick was freaked out.

"Colbs, Man, I didn't mean to trip you, Brother. I'm so sorry."

"Ah, fuck, guys. I can't keep this shit from you. I saw him, Lill. He came in on the same train as me. I saw him in the station. We had coffee at CoGro. He had to ask me where you lived. I was like 'what the fuck, Al. You helped them move in?' I didn't get it. He made me promise, like

PROMISE not to tell you I saw him. I didn't think he'd let *you* see him. I thought he just didn't want to disappoint you. Why would he run from you like that?"

Now, it was my turn to fall into a chair, but there was no chair. I was glad for the extra ass I'd grown, because it landed, full force, on the floor. I was numb. That was my Dad. What the actual F? Why was he here? How was he here? How could he possibly run that fast? Why would he run from me?

"Are you sure, Colbs?" Nick wasn't buying any of it.

"Dude, he's my Uncle Al. I've known him my entire life. We had coffee, then I left to meet Vick." Colby was telling the truth. I just knew it. He had never ever lied to me.

It was getting very close to midnight. I was going to try to just focus on having a good time, and ringing in the New Year with my fiancé. But Aiden didn't seem to be aware of – or even concerned with – the time.

"Oh my God, Lill. Your Dad is fucking nuts. He's gone crazy. Like, absolutely fucking insane."

"What are you talking about Aiden?" Apparently, there was way more to this than just a surprise sighting of Dad.

"Lill. He doesn't even think you exist! He thinks he made you up with that sketch! He doesn't believe you're even real. We've all been afraid to tell you. But you should know. I think you should know. And now he's stalking you? He's nuts, Lill. Like Bloody Crazy."

A hush came over the bar. I wanted to crawl into a hole. I couldn't wrap my head around what Aiden was telling me. But it made sense – it would explain why he refused to respond to anything. But, WHAT THE FUCK??? He was MY DAD. I was his baby girl. How could he not know THAT was true? I was spinning; it was way too much. Did the whole family know? Why didn't anyone tell me? I would have been home in two seconds if I'd known. If I could just hug my Dad, everything would be ok. I knew that, for sure. I needed to hug him, like right fucking NOW.

"It's almost midnight, folks!" The bartender wanted to keep the party going. He started the countdown.

"10-9-8..."

"I am soooo sorry Lill," Colby said. "I should have told you. I didn't know the other stuff though. I just had coffee with him. I promise." He wasn't paying attention to the count.

"7-6-5-4..."

"It's okay, Buddy. I get it. I'm just gutted, you know?" I was crying.

"3-2-1, HAPPY NEW YEAR!"

Nick kissed me, which brought me back to reality for a moment.

"Are you okay, Lill?" He asked.

"NO. I am not okay, Nick."

Aiden couldn't hold anything back.

"Lill, seriously, Mom showed him pictures of us growing up. He was acting like he'd never seen you. He had no clue. It was so messed up. He's a joke."

"Aiden, will you shut the fuck up? She doesn't need to hear any more, Man. It's hard enough." Nick was trying to minimize the damage, but it was way too late. I could see that he was hurting too. If I didn't exist to Dad, neither did he.

"It's ok, Babe. I need to know." I did need to know. He was my Dad, after all. I knew him better than anyone.

"What else, Aiden?"

"He came home absolutely hammered the other day. He pissed himself. So gross. He was all covered in blood and piss."

"For fuck sakes, Aiden. Shut UP!" Nick had heard enough. "Lill, you do not need this shit."

"My Dad got drunk?" I couldn't believe anything I was hearing. I needed to hear this stuff from the source. The more I thought about him not even knowing that I existed, the more upset I got. I was spiraling. I needed to call my Dad.

I took my purse into the bathroom. I wanted to try to regain some composure before I called, but the spiral quickened its pace. I called anyway. I knew Dad was playing a show, but I left a message. I wanted him to know that I knew what was going on now.

I went back to join Nick, but I was a basket case. I wasn't normally a drama queen, but this situation warranted a few histrionics.

"Why don't we go home, Lill. We don't need to stay."

Nick tried to comfort me. He was right. It made no sense to stay. I couldn't speak, so I nodded. He found our coats and helped me to pull mine on. We didn't even say goodbye to anyone – even Aiden had no idea that we were leaving. He'd be able to find his way back by himself, or maybe end up staying with the girl he was hitting on. She looked strangely impressed with him. We crept quietly out the door and started for home.

While we walked, I tried calling again. I figured Dad's show would have to be over by then. But he still didn't answer. I left another long sobby message, imploring him to call me back. Nick said nothing. He just kept his arm around me to comfort me and tried to keep me warm. I could tell he was really hurting too. This whole mess was enough to completely fry anyone's brain.

My dad doesn't think I exist. My dad doesn't think I exist. My dad doesn't think I exist.

I repeated it over and over in my mind. But those words, together in one sentence, they just didn't work. No one has ever had to say that sentence. Like… ever. I tried to call again. And again, and again, and again. Why won't he just answer? I was not going to give up. He needed to hear my voice, as much as possible. I decided I should call my Mom. She picked up, first ring of course.

"Lilly?" It sounded like she was crying.

"Mom? What's wrong?" I knew I sounded like I was crying too.

"Your father. Oh, God, Lill. I can't take any more."

"Mom. What happened? Aiden told me everything, by the way."

I was trying not to be angry with her. I just wished that she'd told me. It was hard to forgive that. But she sounded really upset.

"What? Nooo. I'm so sorry Lill. I didn't want you to find out. I just wanted to fix him. But he is too far gone. He was making out with some whore on the fucking stage."

Now, that was something I could not accept. He loved my Mom. He always had.

"Mom. I am so sorry. Are you okay? Why would he do that?"

"He tried to kill himself in Kingston, Sweetie. He's not himself. I don't even know this man."

This was all too much. Way too much. My evening started out as a beautiful celebration, and now it was turning into a steaming pile of shit.

"I'm so sorry Mom. I'm coming home."

My poor mother couldn't respond. She just hung up the phone.

"Nick, we have to go," I demanded.

"Ok Babe. First thing in the morning."

"I'm leaving right now. You don't have to come."

"Lill, you're too upset. I'm drunk. Let's leave it 'til morning."

I didn't respond to him. I called my Dad one more time and left him a message that I was coming home. Nick heard me, and did not protest. When we got back to our apartment, Nick opened a beer. I changed into my sweats. I dialed my Dad's number a few more times, but still nothing, and then his inbox was full. If Mom was right, he was probably somewhere with that woman. I didn't want to believe that, though. I still thought if I could just hug him, everything would be ok. My Dad needed Lilly hugs. He always said that.

I started lacing up my runners. I had every intention to leave that very moment.

"You seriously want to drive to Oakville tonight?" Nick was not enthusiastic.

"I would like my father to know I exist. Yes. As soon as possible."

"Okay. Right. That's fair. Then let me get changed too."

Nick went to get his casual stuff back on while I tried to call my Dad again. No answer. I was oscillating between calm and panicked. I took a gulp of Nick's beer to keep me more on the calm side, but it was no use.

I texted my mom that we were on our way, and tried my Dad one last time, to no avail. I was relieved that Nick was coming. He had a way with Daddio, and I thought maybe his charm could help.

"Are you sure you're okay to drive, Babe?" Nick's last-ditch attempt to change my mind.

"I'm fine. We're leaving. Let's just go. You can sleep on the way."

We climbed into the car and hit the road. It was 2:05 AM on the first day of 2017. It had not been the best start to a year, but we were on our way home. To my home. So that I might introduce myself to my own father – the man I had known for my entire life.

Chapter 15:
The Messenger Came Today

It was a relief that the Uber driver wasn't chatty. I was working on a couple of hours' sleep, at best. And while I'd been grateful for a place to crash, I'd done so with one eye open, in case Tricia had any designs on waking me. It had not been a peaceful rest.

My hope was that Bridget had seen the light, maybe even recognized that I wasn't the philandering pig she'd made me out to be. She had said she didn't care about any of that now, which I took as a good sign. She'd been very upset, but that was understandable. This entire situation was enough to break the strongest and most resolute of souls. It had certainly broken me – not that I was strong. I felt like a weak ass bitch, actually. I had let the stupid Beast push me around as though I'd had no other option.

Well, I was done with that.

I would tell Bridget that I was willing to do whatever it would take – pills or therapy (not with Goodhands though, too awkward). I would try to explain that I'd been so convinced the world was trying to trick me, that I hadn't been able to accept I was just sick and needed help.

And the most helpful thing (in my opinion, as ignorant as it was) would be for me to meet Lilly. To see her up close. To hug her. In her messages, she sounded like she loved her Dad so much. I couldn't dismiss that. And damn it… I deeply regretted running away (not that it was actually Allan Isaac doing that running bit). There had to be a way I could stand up to the Beast. Although, I noticed that I couldn't feel his presence anymore. If he did show up, I was going to figure out where his balls were, and kick them straight back into whatever godforsaken place he'd come from.

That was it. I was going to tell Bridget I wanted to go to Kingston to meet our daughter. She did say she needed me to come home, so I hoped I wasn't assuming too much. I would reassure her I truly did want to get our life back. Only now, we would have a beautiful, sweet daughter together. I realized I was excited to meet Lilly – maybe memories would start flooding back when I hugged her? Wow. I couldn't feel the Beast anymore, but I sure did want to hug my Baby Girl. That pull was as strong as anything the Beast had ever thrown at me.

It was still the very early hours of the first day of the year. The sun hadn't even considered popping up yet. As we approached Bridget's house – our home – I could see that she was standing on the front porch in her nightgown. The only light was coming from inside the house.

Once in the driveway I thanked the Uber guy, and climbed out of the car. I could now see that Bridget was shaking, and weeping.

"Baby, you must be freezing!"

I rushed toward her – I needed to get her back inside. But before I reached her, she somehow mustered up the strength to speak.

"It's Lilly. She's DEAD."

Her words hit my gut like a battering ram. THUD. I was stopped in my tracks. I had to snap out of it to take care of my Bridget, so I resumed my stride and made it to her. I'd already instinctively removed my coat, so I could wrap it around her.

"She's gone, Al. Our baby is gone. I'm so sorry."

I couldn't speak. I guided Bridget back into the house, where Pam was sitting on the couch, also bawling. I was normally a pretty resourceful guy. I could always find the right words to say in any situation. But in that moment, I had no words. None. Did I even have the right to be upset? Just a day earlier, I'd refused to acknowledge that Lilly even existed. Was I allowed to mourn? Was this the Beast at work again? Was he laughing at me? Had this been his Maniacal plan the entire time?

"What happened?" It was all I could squeak out.

"She. Was. Coming. Home." Bridget's words were broken. Frayed.

"Tonight? She was coming home tonight?" I still didn't understand.

"To see you. She wanted to see her Dad. Aiden told her everything, Al. She was so hurt."

"My God. Oh my God." My head was a tornado.

There was not a single thing I could do to help Bridget. Or to make Pam feel better. Or to feel better myself. But in those situations, the need to do something, anything, is formidable. I was pacing. That was all I could do. Pace. Mutter. Pace. Mutter some more.

"I left a message for Aiden to call me. You are going to have to let your kids know, Al." Bridget seemed to be calming down, just as I started spinning into full on panic.

"Ripples. Fucking ripples," I muttered.

"What is that supposed to mean?" Bridget asked.

Had I done this? Did deleting the sketch mean that Lilly would have to die? I was crawling out of my skin. I felt completely responsible for the death of a girl who – to me – didn't even exist.

"It means I feel responsible, B."

"You aren't responsible, Al. Someone ran a red. That's who's responsible. You need to call your kids, Sweetie. I know it's going to be hard."

I couldn't call my kids. What the hell would I say? *"Hey, you know that girl I sketched at Christmas, and said she was your sister and stuff? Yeah. She died."* It would sound ridiculous. Nothing I could say to my kids, or anyone else, would do any good at all.

Before I had a chance to express these thoughts, Bridget's phone rang.

"Aiden?"

"Hey Ma. Got your message. What's up? Everything okay? I had the most amazing night."

"Aiden. Are you sober?"

"Ish. I stopped drinking hours ago. Lilly told me to go easy. It worked! I met someone, Ma!"

"Oh, Sweetie. We need to get you home."

"Ma? Why? I left my car at Colby's. What's going on? Is it Al again?"

Bridget choked up and couldn't find any more words, but I was close enough to hear the entire conversation. I had to make a tough call — grab the phone and tell Aiden that his sister is gone? Tell him to get his car, or catch the first train home? It wasn't fair to let him think all was well whilst he rode home. But it also wasn't fair to put the boy on the road by himself with the crippling knowledge that his sister was dead. I grabbed the phone before I'd made my mind up.

"Aiden, It's Al."

"Oh. Good. I was worried. Hey Al."

"Are you sitting down?"

"What the fuck is going on, guys? Where'd Ma go?"

"Buddy, Lilly… your sister was in an accident."

"What the fuck? I literally JUST saw them. What kind of accident? Are they ok?"

I put my big boy pants on, and just let him have it.

"Aiden. Your sister is dead. I'm so sorry."

There was silence on the other end of the line. Then, I could hear Aiden was crying.

"Can you get yourself home? Aiden?"

"Does. Colby. Know?"

Bridget could hear his question. She shook her head indicating that Colby did not know.

"No. Family first, Buddy. Can you come home? I can send you some money if you need."

"Uhh. Ok. I gotta figure it out. I will call you guys back. FUCK. This SUCKS. Can I talk to Mom again?"

I handed the phone back to Bridget. She still couldn't speak.

"Mom? I am so sorry. I'm coming home. As soon as I can. OK? I'm coming home."

"Be. Careful. Aiden." Bridget managed to make her plea for her son's safety before they hung up. "Those were the last words I ever heard from Lill, too. I never said anything back. I didn't know I would never see my baby again."

"Bridget. I'm so sorry. I want to take it away. I want to make it all better."

I couldn't come up with anything better than that. At least it was honest. I really did wish I could make everything ok. I knew I couldn't, but I wanted to.

"Just call your kids. You have to, Al – you don't want them finding out from anyone else."

She was right, I had to call. Lilly was their sister, and it didn't matter in the least whether I could accept her or not. This version of Brad and Tessa had grown up with Lilly pouring love on them. That was clear. I was their Dad, and Lilly was their sister. She was gone, and I was the link.

It was just about 7:00 AM now, so I called Brad first. He was an early riser and would likely be up and at 'em. He picked up after a couple rings.

"Hi Dad."

"Hey Buddy. What do you have planned today?"

God. I sounded like I was going to invite him to go on a hike with me. I was not prepared to make this call.

"Not much, really. Why? What did you have in mind?"

"I need you and Tessa to come here, as soon as you can. It's very important. Okay?"

"Sure, I'll see if I can get her up. What's going on?"

"We just need you here. For sure. Please, Buddy?"

"Okay, Dad. I hope everything's okay?"

"Just promise me that you're on your way?"

"I'll get her up and head over there right now."

"Thanks, Brad. Love you, Buddy."

"Love you too Dad."

Tessa was very much a sleeper-inner, but I knew she was capable of early morning activity if the occasion called for it. I hoped that my urgency was evident enough to inspire Brad to convey the same to Tessa. If he did that, I knew they would arrive within the hour.

Bridget was keeping busy in the kitchen, trying to numb her emotions. Pam was still on the couch, sitting in utter disbelief. My own emotions were completely unfamiliar. I just didn't know how to respond to this messy blend of guilt, sadness, empathy, and indifference. Top off that stew with pure exhaustion, and I was left sitting motionless, staring at the table.

Bridget carried coffees in for both of us, and placed mine on the table beside me.

"Your kids are coming now?" she asked.

"Yeah. I think so. Brad was going to try to get T up. I didn't tell them. I thought it would be better in person."

"I agree , I hope Aiden doesn't text them though."

That hadn't occurred to me. Aiden and tact had never been formally introduced – and honestly, I wouldn't have put it past him to announce Lilly's death on Instagram. I decided to text him.

-Hey Buddy. Please keep quiet about this. Brad and Tessa are on their way. I wanted to tell them in person.

-OK, Al. No problem. I told Colby though. He's picking me up and we're driving home.

-OK. I'll let your Mom know. Be safe, Kiddo.

I relayed the update, and then realized that I had no idea what had actually happened. I hadn't even asked Bridget how she found out.

"Do we know how it happened, Babe?" I asked.

"The cops said Lilly was driving and Nick was in the passenger seat. Some drunk ran a red. They were still in Kingston."

"The cops came here? They woke you up?"

"I answered the door. I was awake, but I got Mom up to talk to them," Pam answered, speaking up for the first time in a long while.

"I just knew something terrible had happened," added Bridget. "Cops don't show up at your door in the middle of the night with good news. But... I thought it was going to be about you."

"You're right, they don't. I probably would have thought that too. Do we know if Nick's okay?"

It was becoming easier to talk about them now, as though Lilly's death had made them more real, somehow.

"He broke his arm. That's it. And his heart."

Bridget's answer hit me with anchor-like weight. My heart broke for Nick. That poor kid had just taken a huge step, only to have his life plans pulled out from under him. But still, it felt like I was reading the story in a newspaper. It made me very sad that this happened to anyone. It made me sad that the people I loved would have a gigantic hole in their lives. But it didn't feel like my loss.

"Has anyone talked to him yet?" I asked. I even considered offering to be the one to reach out to him.

"He's still in the hospital. They're making sure there aren't more injuries. He's just not ready yet."

I was relieved. I wanted to keep our circle as small as possible until my kids knew, and until I could get some more sleep. Maybe until I'd found a way to wrap my head around the whole thing. I was still willing to talk with Nick, but I wanted to be much more prepared than I currently was.

My phone buzzed with a text from Tessa.

-Hi Daddy, we're on our way. Is everything okay?

I couldn't lie to her, but obviously I couldn't break the news via text. So, I just didn't respond. If they were on their way, they'd be here in twenty minutes. I'd have to tell them then.

Bridget started losing it again, and grabbed my hand.

"Oh, Sweetie. What are we going to do? What are we going to do without our Lilly Doll?"

I could feel her heartbreak, and it broke mine. I felt useless, but I moved my chair closer to Bridget and put my arms around her. It was all I had to offer. It wasn't enough, but I offered it anyway.

No one said a word until Brad and Tessa showed up. This time, they didn't knock; they just walked right in through the front door, like family. The air in the room reeked with sadness, and my beautiful kids could immediately see that all was not as it should have been.

"Hey. Is everything okay? What's going on?" Brad looked nervous.

The question was obviously directed at me, but I was hoping Pam or Bridget would respond. They didn't. All eyes turned to Al. So, I allowed the words to leak from my mouth.

"There has been an accident, guys. Lilly and Nick were on their way here, late last night. They were hit, and your sister didn't make it. I am so sorry, guys… Lilly's gone."

Brad stayed standing, stoic and resolute, but my baby Tessa could not comprehend what she'd been told. Tears filled her big blue eyes, and she shook her head without speaking. She looked up at her brother, then back at me. She was asking one of us to fix this. I stood up to hug her, all I seemed able to do. But she pushed me away, dropped onto the couch, and curled up into a ball.

"No. No no no no no no no." Talking to no one in particular, Tessa started rocking herself back and forth. It seemed more of a self-soothing exercise – if she denied the news hard enough, maybe it would become untrue.

Brad sat down beside her and put his giant arm around her shoulders. For several minutes, he didn't speak. When he did, it was calm and calculated.

"Dad. Are you okay? This must be pretty overwhelming for you?"

He seemed to understand the unique dynamic of my situation. And while I appreciated the empathy, there was something pointed in his tone. Almost accusatory.

"I'm really trying to understand my emotions right now, Bud." It was the best response I could come up with.

"Yeah, I bet you are."

There was sarcasm in the statement. I hadn't thought he'd be angry with me, but it was apparent that – to him at least – this session of mourning might best be left to members of the family who hadn't disputed Lilly's very existence.

"Would you rather I wasn't here, Brad?" I asked him, straight up.

"No. You need to be here. I would just rather you weren't so messed up, Dad."

Tessa elbowed his arm off of her.

"It's not Daddy's fault, Brad. Don't be so stupid." I had an ally.

"I get it, Guys. I do. But, I'm here – for you guys, and for Bridget. I will do whatever I can to soften this for you," I reassured, poorly.

"You know what I think, Dad? I think maybe if you had 'been there' for Lilly, this wouldn't have happened." Brad's emotions were breaking free.

"Bradly Isaac. That is enough! This is probably harder on your Dad than anyone." Bridget was standing up for me.

"No. It is not, Bridget. It's harder on you. It's harder on Tessa. It's harder on Pam and me, and Aiden. And it is by far the hardest on Lilly. Dad doesn't give a crap about anyone but himself. You know that."

Brad got up from beside Tessa and left through the front door, slamming it behind him. Hard enough to knock pictures off the walls, if there'd been any. He was hurting, and I knew sadness was not something he could easily express. With him, it would often manifest in bursts of anger. I knew he didn't mean what he said – not entirely, at least. There was some truth in it. I had been a selfish Dad. My kids' feelings were rarely considered when I'd made life choices. I'd been oblivious to how my actions might affect them. I'd always thought I was mildly entertaining to them, at the very worst. But the truth was that I was distant, at best. At worst, absent and neglectful. Brad probably felt that if I was capable of obliterating Lilly from my mind, it wouldn't be too great a stretch for me to erase him, too.

I got up to follow him. If I could find him, I might be able to let him take his sadness out on me, in a more private manner. I wasn't sure if I deserved what he was throwing at me. But if he needed to throw it, I wanted to be there to catch it. His car was still in the driveway, so I knew he couldn't have gone far. In his place, I'd have walked toward the lake, so that was the direction I followed.

By making my way toward Third Line and heading south, it wasn't long before I could see Brad's giant frame ahead of me. He was ambling slowly along the sidewalk, head down. My poor dude; I could see that he was crushed. Stooped shoulders, dragging feet – he would stop every few steps to look up at the heavens. I quickened my pace, hoping to catch him. He might have thought he needed to be far away from his Dad, but Dad knew better. At that moment at least, the last thing my boy needed was to be alone.

"Brad. Wait up."

He didn't look back.

"Bud, please. Give me a chance? Please just talk to me?"

That worked. Brad stopped to wait, and I caught up with him, offering a hug. We hadn't hugged much since he got to be so big, but it was clear that he needed one. He had to lean down to hug me back, which felt strange. I wasn't used to feeling small. His weight on my shoulders clearly showed he was carrying too much. It was the most sincere embrace we'd shared since he'd been a wee fellow. It felt so good to be needed, even just a little.

"I'm so, so sorry, Big Guy. I really am."

"I know you are Dad. I'm sorry too. I didn't mean that stuff. I just… can't believe this. I don't know how I'm supposed to tell Sierra."

He had a real concern there. Other than Grandparents, this was the first significant loss any of the kids had suffered. I was feeling far enough removed from the situation that I was confident I could act as a pillar of support for everyone. The optics might not sparkle, but better than pretending otherwise. There would be no void in my life, only empathy for my loved ones.

"Where is she now, Bud?" I asked.

Sierra was very much a part of our family by now, and should have been here – even if only to hold Brad's hand through his grief.

"She's probably still sleeping. I texted her to call me as soon as possible."

We continued toward the water, Brad quiet and introspective. I respected that, and just wanted him to know that I was there with him. At the lake, it started to feel like something was nagging at my boy's insides.

"Brad. You can say whatever you need to say. I won't fight you."

It took a minute or two for him to gather his thoughts enough to speak.

"Dad. Have you ever thought about what it does to us when you leave a relationship and then jump right into another one?"

It was a fair question, and it had never occurred to me to ask it of myself.

"I can't honestly say that I thought it had any effect on you guys. I'm so sorry, Brad."

"Yeah. Well, it does. You know, we're part of a family, and we get to know everyone. New aunts and uncles, sometimes even brothers and sisters. And then, you break up and POOF. They're gone. Just like that, they aren't family anymore. And then before you know it, you throw a brand new family at us. And you expect us to jump right in, just like nothing happened. It's kinda gross. And, impossible. It's fucking impossible."

I knew what he was going to say, but I didn't interrupt him. I didn't finish his sentences. I didn't want to belittle what he was saying. He had a very good point, and I let him continue.

"And, that's the thing about Lilly. She was your biggest fan. She was your champion. If it wasn't for her... I don't know what our relationship would look like, Dad. I really don't. She had so much faith in you."

Ouch. Maybe this was the thing that Marvin was referring to in his note – the thing that I was here to hear? I thought it was probably that Merry-Go-Round tune, but this little nugget from my boy carried an awful lot more weight.

"I hear you, Bud. I will try to do better."

"You forgot about your own daughter, Dad. Better? You'll TRY to do better than that? Jeez. I would hope so."

I felt myself wishing – with everything in me – that the Beast would come back and shove me into a hole. Why the fuck had I answered the phone on that Pier in Kingston? If I'd just jumped in the water, Lilly would never have felt like she had to rush home to see me, and she would likely still be alive in this twilight zone. And it sounded like I wouldn't even have been missed.

"You can hate me all you need to, Brad. I get it. I'll just shut up. I'm glad you could get that off your chest."

He didn't respond, but I could see tears welling up in his eyes. Aiden and Colby would likely be showing up any time, so I suggested we head back to the house. I felt like I needed to be there for my family, Brad agreed. We said nothing to each other as we walked. About half way home, Sierra called. Brad asked if she could get herself to Oakville, said it was really important. She immediately agreed to get a ride with her Mom. I was glad that he would have her there.

Back home, I could see that Aiden and Colby had also arrived. Aiden's car was in the driveway, and there was another one parked on the road in front of the house. I didn't recognize it and couldn't think of who it might belong to. But it was fancy. We didn't see too many Porsches around our place.

We were greeted like it was a surprise party. Tessa was sitting with Pam, on the wall side of the L shaped couch, and they were laughing about their big sister. Aiden was tipped back in the rocking chair, and Colby was on the other leg of the couch with his Dad, Dr. Luke. Bridget had disappeared. There were so many tears; we'd all soon be drowning in them, if it kept going like that.

"I'm so sorry, Al. Truly, I am." It was Luke, standing up to greet me.

I wasn't sure what he was sorry about, because he knew full well where my head was. He knew that Lilly's death was not likely to clear up my ongoing confusion.

"Do you think I am responsible for this, Brother?" I was almost afraid to ask him.

"It's not your fault that your brain did this to you, Al. But Colby tells me she found out, and that would have been devastating to her, for sure. And he confirmed that she did see you, which was unfortunate."

"If you're trying to make me feel better, Buddy, that ain't workin'. Where's Bridget? Have you seen her?"

"I'm sorry, Al. Just being straight with you. Bridget's in the kitchen."

I thought I should check on my Gal; this version of her had just lost a daughter and I had to keep that top of mind. *My people have lost a person. My people have lost a person.* I headed over to the kitchen. Everyone's head turned in that direction, slightly panicked eyes following my every step.

In the kitchen doorway, I could see why. Good ol' Dr. Goodhands was standing there, with my Bridget in his arms. He was doing such a good job of consoling her that he was kissing the top of her head. Nice touch.

"Hey, Mark. Is that your ride out front? Pretty sweet," I announced.

Bridget looked startled, but Goodhands looked smug. In his defence, though, that was his resting face – Smug Prick. He always looked like the foremost thing on his mind was his utter superiority to everyone else in any room.

"Al! Don't be such an ass," Bridget instructed.

"I was just complimenting our friend on his choice of vehicles! Obviously only a very important man could afford something like that. Super impressive."

"Come on, Al. I came here with Luke to offer our condolences. And to offer help to you, if you think you need it." Goodhands was rising above my pettiness. I couldn't even get the jerk to bite. Damn it.

"I'm all good, here, Mark. But thanks."

Luke could sense my upset and came to my rescue – or so I thought.

"Okay, Al. Why don't the three of us go downstairs for a little chat – you, me and Mark?"

Great. Either they were ganging up on me, or Luke and I were going to show Goodhands some Old Time Hockey moves. Give him what for. The former ended up being closer to what was about to happen. We went to the basement and tunneled our way through the storage debris, finding our way to the little rec room.

"Al. Aiden has Colby convinced that you did this. There is a growing sentiment here that you are responsible." Luke got right to the point.

"Brad indicated the same. Does everyone think I did this to myself? On purpose?"

"Come on, Al," Goodhands chimed in. "With grief, often folks try to find something, or someone to blame. You're a very convenient scapegoat here. Of course it isn't all your fault, but that isn't the point. You're the pariah here, my friend. Luke and I are getting worried that the feeling might snowball." He was also doing his level best to appear genuinely concerned for me, but I didn't buy it.

"Seems to me you're looking for an opening here, Big Guy." I was cold sober, but somehow the jealous asshole in me was winning out anyway.

"Jesus, Al! Mark is a professional. So am I. And we are concerned here, Brother. For real. We just want you to be prepared," Luke responded, frustrated.

"Do you guys honestly feel like I'm incapable of shouldering some blame, and still being there for my family?"

I was asking them both, but Luke answered.

"Al. You know this is a unique situation. I don't think there's a man in history who could handle what you're facing. If you act like you didn't know Lilly, you'll be perceived as the coldest person who ever lived. But if you pretend to be gutted, everyone will see you as a phony."

"No shit, Luke! I'm fully aware. So, what would you experts suggest I do here?" I asked.

Nothing. Neither of my Doctor pals had a single suggestion. Apparently, they both just wanted to add their voices to the growing chorus of finger pointers. There were no pills, no therapies, no anything that could help me. I was in a very large, ugly pickle.

And it was only going to get uglier.

Chapter 16:

Through the Eyes of a Flower

Yeah. So… that happened. Kinda put the kibosh on all the plans. Maybe Nick was right – maybe I wasn't ok to drive after all. I was really upset, and it would seem that's just as bad as being drunk. I don't know, but the drive did not go as planned, and here we were. My body was down there, looking like a pot of mashed potatoes, and I was up here, somehow already free from the all-over pain of nearly being dissected. The perspective was certainly different from up here. I could see… almost everything. One thing was clear; my poor Dad was going through Hell.

When Colby confirmed that it was my Dad I saw on the sidewalk, and Aiden told me that Dad didn't believe that I existed, well… it sent my head spinning. I blamed Daddio. He had done something to mess up his mind, and I wanted so badly to unmess it. Mostly because, as far as I could tell, I did exist. I was existing the shit out of life. I was in my fourth year at Queen's. I had my career all planned out. I was newly engaged to the sweetest guy on the planet. How much more existing could one person do?

It seemed to me that it should be easy enough to illustrate that to my Dad. *"Here I am. Here's my fiancé. Here's a hug. Yay. I EXIST!! Can we just be normal again?"* That's why I insisted that Nick and I get in the car and drive to Oakville, just after ringing in the new year. Until I could put my freckled mug in front of Daddio, I felt like I wasn't really here. Like I needed to see myself reflected in his eyes to know I was real. I needed some validation in the worst way.

After I tried to call Dad a thousand times, and left a bunch of messages, I managed to convince Nick to get in the car. It was right around 2:00 AM New Year's Day. We were on the road for only ten minutes when I realized we had virtually zero gas. It was at the very same time that I also realized that I had literally zero purse. So, we had to go back to the apartment. Nick waited in the car while I went in to look for my bag. I could have made Nick pay for the gas, but I really didn't want to drive all that way without my license.

Normally, I put my keys, and my purse, in the exact same place at home, every night. But that night, everything was all asunder. Absolutely nothing was as it should have been. It took me a few minutes to find what I was looking for and that got me even more flustered.

By the time I got back to the car, Nick was fast asleep. Until I needed his chatter to keep me awake, I thought it might be easier to let him just sleep off his drunk. But I didn't feel the least bit tired. There was definitely enough adrenaline rushing through me to get us to Oakville.

I was sure the Shell station near the corner of Bath Road and Portsmouth Avenue would be open, it never seemed to close. Plus, it was only a few blocks out of the way. The streets were quiet, particularly considering it was New Year's. With free buses running, only the occasional taxi or unmistakable Uber dotted the road, handling most of the night's traffic.

I headed down King Street to Sir John A. Macdonald, turning north toward the 401. Halfway to the highway, I veered left onto Bath. The familiar glow of the open sign at the Shell station was a relief. I turned right, pulling in just before Portsmouth.

Gas prices had gone completely insane. $1.55 per litre? Yikes. But, with a three-hour drive ahead, I had no choice but to fill up. My bank account could handle it, though. Mom and Dad had sent me $1000 just before Christmas. How could Dad go from sending me that kind of money, to thinking I wasn't even real? And in such a short time?

The fill up cost me sixty-five buckaroos. It was bloody cold out and I wasn't wearing mittens, so my hands nearly froze to the nozzle. Stupid Nick was still sawing logs. After I finished pumping, I climbed back into the car and, in my hurry to get warm, I slammed the door loudly enough to stir the Snoring Fiancé.

"Huh? Where are we, Babe?" he slurred.

"Still in K town, Nicky. I just stopped for gas."

He looked up and saw the price sign.

"A dollar fifty-five? Holy shit, eh?"

"No kidding. I put $65 in. Crazy," I agreed.

Since the car was facing Portsmouth, it was easier just to exit that way and make a left to get to the stoplight at Bath. It was 2:39 AM. Damn. We wouldn't be getting to Oakville until around 5:45. But I still had lots of energy. Nicky was awake now, so I wasn't worried about falling asleep. The light was red. I was facing south, needing to turn left to get back to Sir John A MacDonald. From there, we would turn left to head north to the 401. Easy peasy.

When the light turned green, I eased my way into the intersection. And right at that very moment... Ring. It was my Daddio calling me back, finally! I grabbed my phone out of the cup holder.

"Nicky, it's Dad!" I was so excited. I couldn't wait to hear his voice.

But instead of hearing Dad's voice, I heard Nick's.

"LILL, NOOO!" His eyes were as big as saucers and he was frantically reaching over to grab me.

In that split second, I sensed the glare of headlights bearing down. I didn't even have time to turn my head to see where they were coming from. James Carmichael hadn't noticed his light had turned red. He was speeding west on Bath, too fast to stop. Just as my car inched into the intersection, his Dodge Journey came barreling through, slamming into the driver's side of my Honda Civic. Beyond the initial millisecond, I didn't feel a thing. Poor Nicky, reaching over in a desperate attempt to shield me, could do nothing to stop what was happening.

I was gone on impact, before our car even came to a stop. We ended up gently nudged up against the big concrete pole holding up the stoplight. Mr. Carmichael's vehicle was still firmly smushed into ours, its nose encroaching a full two feet into the interior.

Bang. Just like that... no more Lilly. Daddio was right. Now, I really didn't exist. My poor Nicky's right arm was snapped; even his considerable strength was no match for a speeding SUV. He was drowning in both physical and emotional pain, whispering my name, hoping for a miracle that he knew wasn't coming. I was gone. Parts of my insides were now very much on my outside, even on Nick's pants.

I wanted so much to tell him that I still felt his love, even stronger now. I ached to tell him that I loved him that much too. But it turns out, it's not easy for a newly not-alive person to communicate with a still-very-much-alive loved one. They don't hand you a manual when you leave your body.

Nick needed to let go of my lifeless body and get out of the car. When it finally crashed against the pole, the impact had been back far enough that he could still open his door. Through his shock, he thought he could smell gas.

"Oh, my Lilly. I'm so sorry. God. Lill. Nooo. I can't..." He pressed a kiss to my forehead.

I was watching him, hovering over the scene somehow, willing him to leave. He needed to get out.

"Please, Nicky. Get out of the car. That isn't me anymore. Please, just get out."

I couldn't hear my own voice. It was more like thinking the words, but somehow, he seemed to feel them. Nicky whispered, "Okay," three times under his breath, kissed my head once more, then reached over to the door with his left hand. His badly broken arm was in the way, but he managed to hit the unlock button. Miraculously, it still worked, even with the car crushed around us. He pulled the handle, and the door popped open.

The pain in his arm was unbearable, but I could feel that his heart hurt even more.

Once Nick got out of the car, the smell of gas was even stronger. He looked over to the other vehicle, needing to get a glimpse of the monster who was responsible for this. Mr. Carmichael was slumped over his steering wheel, blood leaking from his bald head.

"Go to him, Nicky." I was still experimenting with this communication business.

Nick made his way to the driver door of the Dodge, which opened without any resistance. Mr. Carmichael was unconscious but still breathing. Alive. He was a short, heavyset man, and even with only one good arm, Nick's strength hadn't faltered. He tried to rouse Mr. Carmichael, but the Man was unresponsive. With the stench of gasoline now thick in the air, Nick knew he had to get Mr. Carmichael out of, and away from, the vehicles.

Ignoring his pain, Nick reached around Mr. Carmichael's substantial belly, unfastened the seatbelt, and with all the strength he could gather in his uninjured arm, was able to pull him from the driver's seat. He dragged Mr. Carmichael about ten feet from the vehicles. It wasn't as far as he would've liked, but it was all he could manage. Once they were clear, he fumbled for his phone and dialed 911.

"911, what's your emergency?"

"There has been an accident. My fiancée… my fiancée is dead. And the man who hit us is unconscious." Nick's voice cracked as he struggled to get the words out. Then he saw a flicker of flame coming from under the crumpled hood of Mr. Carmichael's truck. "Oh my God. The car is on fire. Lilly is still in there. Oh my fucking God."

"Sir, where are you?" The dispatcher's voice softened, sensing his despair.

"Bath and Portsmouth. Please hurry. Please. She's still in the car. Oh my God."

"Emergency services are on their way to you now, Sir. Stay on the line with me."

The little flame quickly turned into a much bigger flame. Nick couldn't bear to watch as the fire threatened to consume my body. He turned to Mr. Carmichael and slapped his face – a last-ditch effort to wake him. The man stirred, groggy and disoriented, clearly concussed.

"What…what happened?" He mumbled.

"What happened?" Nick's voice shook with rage. "You killed my fiancée, you motherfucker. That's what happened. She's still in that car. LOOK!"

He grabbed Mr. Carmichael and twisted him toward the burning vehicles. The flames weren't getting any smaller. Nicky, practically losing his mind, left Mr. Carmichael and raced back to the passenger side of our car. The fire was still mostly confined to Mr. Carmichael's truck, but with the smell of gas now overpowering, an explosion seemed inevitable.

I wanted to scream for him to stay away, but Nick was bent on getting my body out of the car. He flung open the door and began pulling on me, his face a mixture of desperation and sorrow.

"Please, God. Please. Oh God, she can't burn. Lilly, please help me. Please, Baby." He was pleading with God – and a lifeless body. He kept begging, pulling, sobbing, oblivious to the sirens and the flashing lights.

Suddenly, a voice cut through the chaos.

"Get away from the vehicle, Sir. Right NOW. GET AWAY!" A very large fireman grabbed Nicky by his broken arm.

"AHHHHHH, my fucking ARM."

"I am sorry Sir, but you need to get away from the car. NOW!"

The pain snapped Nick back to reality. He realized he wasn't going to be able to get my body out; his efforts had been for naught. He didn't want my body to burn, but he was very much risking his life trying to free it from a ticking time bomb. The firefighter spoke again, more gently.

"We've got this, Sir. Let us handle the fire. Okay?"

As he reassured Nick, the rest of the crew began hosing down the vehicles. Within two minutes, they had the fire completely extinguished. Other than my crushed midsection and lacerations on my abdomen, I looked strangely untouched. Aside from a small bump on the left side of my head, from my chest up, I was without a scrape. One of the firemen checked for signs of life and confirmed what was already painfully obvious. I was gone.

Not long after they got the fire out, the tow trucks arrived. They managed to pull Mr. Carmichael's Dodge away from our vehicle. The firefighters used a special tool to pry my door open and once they did, they could see that most of the damage was below my chest. It wasn't a pretty sight. My Nicky was clamouring to reach me, and despite the firefighters' attempts to hold him back, he broke free, collapsing to his knees beside my body.

"NOOOOOO. No. Lill. Please. Please. PLEASE LILLY. I love you. Oh God."

"Sir. Please… let us get her out of there," a fireman urged, as gently as possible.

"I can't. I can't leave her. Oh my God. Lill." My poor Nicky was so distraught that he'd forgotten about his own injuries.

"Sir, we need to get you to the hospital. I think your arm is broken."

As if on cue, the pain in Nick's arm flared up again. His forearm was going East and North at the same time. The fireman beside him was the same one who had yanked Nick away from the burning car. He knew the arm was broken.

"What's your name?"

"Nick. I'm Nick. That's Lilly… we just got engaged at Christmas."

"Okay, Nick. I'm Phil. I am so sorry. The police are here, and they're getting a statement from the other driver. They'll probably want one from you too, but right now, let's focus on getting you to the hospital and taking care of that arm. Alright, Nick?"

Nicky reluctantly agreed with Fireman Phil and walked with him to the ambulance. Only then did he fully notice the swarm of emergency vehicles – fire trucks, police cars, paramedics, ambulances – all flashing their lights in the night. As the medical crew guided Nick into the back of his ambulance, he glanced over and saw Mr. Carmichael receiving the same treatment. He also caught sight of the firefighters carefully extracting my very lifeless body from the car.

"Where are they taking Lilly?" He asked the paramedic.

"We're all going to the same place, Nick. We're going to the hospital. I am going to give you something for the pain, okay?"

The nice paramedic lady gave Nicky a needle in his good arm. That, combined with his alcohol consumption from earlier in the evening, was enough to settle him down. I wished I could physically be in the back of that ambulance with him. I mean… I was with him, but I couldn't hold his hand. I couldn't whisper in his ear that I loved him, and that everything was going to be ok.

The funny thing about not being alive anymore was that I could also tune into the conversation Mr. Carmichael was having with the cops and the medics. It was obvious that he had no recollection of the crash. It was also very clear that he was hammered. Either that, or his ability to speak clearly was knocked out of him when he hit his head. The medics had dressed his wound, so he wasn't leaking blood anymore.

"How much have you had to drink tonight, James?" A policeman asked.

"Guilty as charged, officer."

"I haven't charged you with anything yet, James. Do you remember what happened?"

"I do not. I just woke up to a young fellow slapping me and yelling."

"Do you know what he was yelling at you about, James?"

"My truck was on fire. I think he saved my life?" Poor Mr. Carmichael had already forgotten the little part about the dead fiancée.

"He did save your life, James. With only one good arm. He saved your life, alright."

"I'll have to thank him for that."

"I doubt he will be interested in your gratitude, Mr. Carmichael."

That was an understatement. Nicky was in the other ambulance wondering why he'd bothered to help the little, fat man. He wouldn't have minded watching him burn at all. In his mind, that was likely how the little shit was going to spend eternity anyway.

After a short pause, Mr. Carmichael's curiosity got the better of him.

"Why would a man not want my gratitude? That doesn't make any sense," he asked the medic.

"James, do you see that third ambulance over there?"

"Yes. I see it," he answered, confused.

"Well, Jimmy, my partners just loaded the body of that young man's fiancée into that vehicle. Her name was Lilly Isaac. She was 22 years old. Now she's gone. That might be why he doesn't want your thanks. Just maybe."

There was a longer pause this time. Long enough for Mr. Carmichael to cobble together a few little snapshots from his drunken memory. He was reminded that, perhaps, he had done a very bad thing.

"No… I don't suppose he would want my thanks."

From my new vantage point – that neat little spot where I could see virtually everything – I was able to have a look back and piece together how Mr. Carmichael's Dodge Journey came to be hurtling through a red light at the very second my car was entering the intersection.

It would seem that he was not a happily married Man. His wife always nagged him about his weight, about his baldness… about everything. He wasn't a heavy drinker, but on that New Year's Eve, he and his wife, Audrey, had an unusually intense argument. Poor James had had enough. He drove to the liquor store and bought himself a 20 ouncer of cheap vodka. Then he parked his Dodge Journey in the lot at the Gardiners Town Centre Shopping Mall. Not wanting to be noticed, he waited until all the stores were all closed and the parking lot emptied, then he drank the entire bottle. He mixed it with Tropicana Orange Juice from a carton he'd taken from the fridge at home. With each sip, he grew angrier and angrier. He was going to tell her, alright. Enough was enough. He was going to tell that bitch that he wanted a divorce.

Once he finished the vodka, he wasted no time. He was going to rush home and tell Audrey he was done. If he got caught at a RIDE program, so be it. If it was meant to be, he would make it home unbeknownst to anyone, and finally escape his awful marriage.

He didn't stop to consider, not even for a fraction of a second, that someone else might get in the way. Sadly, for me – and mostly for my Nicky – my car was in the way. The result was that Mr. Carmichael, Nicky, and my very busted up body were all headed to Hotel Dieu Hospital in separate medical vehicles. I would never make it back to Oakville to hug my poor Daddio. Nicky and I would never be married. And Mr. Carmichael would have much bigger problems to contend with than a bitchy wife.

Chapter 17:
The Aftermath

The Hospital was only a seven-minute drive from the accident, and all three ambulances arrived within moments of each other. My situation was apparently the least urgent. All they needed to do for me was get my body to the morgue – and maybe get me cleaned up a little. Nick, on the other hand, had a badly broken arm, so they got him checked in first. To avoid any scene, they waited until Nick was out of sight before they brought Mr. Carmichael in. He would need to have his brain checked, seeing as he had hit his head badly enough to split it open. There very well could have been some greater damage.

In the meantime, the Kingston Police notified the Halton Police of my untimely passing, leaving them with the unenviable task (in the wee hours of New Year's Day) of informing my family. Officer Don Robertson and his partner, Amber Andersen, were the team given that responsibility.

Pammy was still up when the police knocked. She woke Mom, and then they were given the news. Instantly, all my Mom's anger toward Daddio evaporated – she needed him. Poor Momma could feel herself sinking. I so wanted to ease her pain, to reach her somehow, but it quickly became apparent that the only "superpower" I possessed was a sort of universal awareness. And it sucked. I could see and feel how much everyone was hurting, but I couldn't do anything to help them. I tried with all my might to let her know that I was there, that I loved her so much, but I didn't know if she could feel it.

This stuff was hard work for someone in my position. I didn't even know how to be a dead person yet – I was just winging it. There was so much information to take in, so many rules I didn't understand. As my family started finding out about the accident, I felt this need to be with each of them, to somehow let them know I loved them. I did my best, newbie that I was, to reach them.

Poor Nicky was left to cope with the physical pain of his busted arm and all the emotional torture on top of it. He had so many questions, circling like angry wasps. Why did we have to go to that gas station? Why did Lilly insist on leaving so suddenly? Why the FUCK did Aiden have to open his giant mouth? Why did Lilly's Dad have to be a nutbar? And most of all – why would God take Lilly away? No matter how hard I tried, I couldn't seem to soften his anger.

Mom was just… heartbroken. So were Pam and Aiden, and Brad and Tessa. They were drowning in sadness and loss. I hoped, somehow, that I could console them, that they could sense me with them.

Then there was Daddio. His emotional state was pure chaos, tangled up in guilt. He felt completely responsible for my demise, but he didn't experience the same sense of loss as the rest of my crew. He truly did not know me. So, here I was – a newly dead ghost-type thing – still trying to show my Dad that I existed.

I was curious enough to keep tabs on Mr. Carmichael too. He was still in the hospital, still very much out cold. The lovely Mrs. Carmichael had been notified and was on her way to visit him. Now that would be interesting.

Meanwhile, Mom had made arrangements with Smith's Funeral Home in Burlington to have my body transported over the next day or two. But where I wished I could be was at Mom's house. The wolves were coming for my Dad, and that just wasn't right. He needed an ally… or nine.

Aiden had never really liked Dad. I had hoped the Christmas gifts I gave would help everyone in my family see past their respective prejudices. Each of them was so cool in their own way, but as soon as Dad's mental health issues became apparent, Aiden wrote him off. He was completely convinced that Daddio was responsible for my accident. He spent the entire drive back to Oakville convincing Colby of it too – and it worked.

So, now, the team against my Dad included Aiden, Colby, probably Big Brad, and maybe even my Nicky. And even though he so desperately wanted to appear professional, Dr. Mark Ogilvy still had the hots for my Mom. Sure, he seemed like he was trying to help, but he'd have no problem seeing my Dad shamed and ostracized. Even Mom herself wasn't convinced that Daddio was blameless.

Team Allan Isaac consisted of far fewer players. I knew this wasn't his fault, but here I was on the sidelines, watching the whole thing with a career ending lower body injury. Tessa, my baby sis, loved our Dad so much and knew that he would never hurt anyone. Pammy was trying to be understanding, so I counted her among Dad's supporters. On paper, it was a lopsided contest. I wasn't able to see the future, but it didn't look good for Daddio.

Everyone started gathering at the house. My siblings, Mom and Dad, Colby, Dr. Luke, and Dr. Mark were all there. Brad was doing his best to remain strong, but he knew that I'd been the glue holding this weird family together. In the basement, the two Doctors were telling Dad he needed to brace himself – that he might be facing a family turning against him.

The moment Daddio, Dr. Mark, and Dr. Luke rejoined the group in the living room, things started to get pretty tense. Sierra had arrived and was helping to keep Brad from completely losing it. Her feelings were abundantly evident; she wouldn't even look at Dad. She expressed sincere condolences to Mom and Tessa, but her focus was on Brad.

Aiden was more abrupt.

"Are you happy now, Al?" He yelled at Dad.

"Aiden Reynolds. That is enough!" Mom shot him down.

But Sierra chimed in. "He has a point. All Mr. Isaac had to do was be willing to accept Lilly. I think it's kind of pathetic."

Dad shook his head, his face tightening. "Maybe it's best if I get out of here and let everyone grieve the way they need to."

He couldn't take any more, and I was helpless to stop the barrage of blame. All I wanted was to comfort my Dad. The emotional stew he was wrestling with was likely more confusing than any of the others could even imagine. I focused everything I had on him. *Stay calm Daddio. Stay calm Daddio. Get out of there. Just leave.*

It seemed to help; he walked out. Mom begged him to stay, but he couldn't. He needed to find someone who might still be on his side. I sure wished that someone could've been me, but there seemed to be pretty strict rules in place – obstacles really – against fraternizing with the living folk.

After Dad left, the talk at the house only grew more heated. Aiden was screaming that it was "all Al's fault". Mom was screaming at Aiden to stop screaming. Brad was very excitedly ordering people to not be so excited. In short, chaos. Poor Tessa and Pammy just held each other and cried, while Colby stayed silent, looking completely lost. Dr. Mark, ever the opportunist, went right back to "comforting" Mom. What a creep. Meanwhile, Dr. Luke walked with my Dad.

"Is there anyone you want to call, Al?" Dr. Luke asked, thinking a friendly voice might help.

"I don't know, Man. Maybe Nadene? Not many people know how fucked up all this shit is."

Dad tried to call Nadene, but there was no answer. It was still very early, and she and Mario were known to party on New Year's.

"Shit. No answer," Dad muttered, then thought for a second. "You know what? Maybe I should try my niece."

Peggy, his sister Fran's youngest, and my cousin, was more like a cousin to him. Just a few years apart in age, they had been close since childhood. With four kids of her own, she would likely be up with the dawn, and she loved Dad unconditionally. He could be honest with her and know that she'd still be on Team Al. He found her in his contacts and called her up. She answered on the second ring.

"Hey Unc! Happy New Year!"

"Hey Niecey. How are you guys doing?" He hadn't even considered the fact that he would have to break the bad news to anyone.

"Really good. You know, livin' the dream. In bed at ten on New Year's Eve. Gotta love it, eh? How are you guys? Did you play?"

"Uh. Yeah. We had a really nice gig. But, I have some terrible news, Peg. That's why I called."

"What's wrong, Unc? You and Bridget ok?"

"Well, it's bigger than that, Peg. There was an accident last night. Lilly… Lilly was killed."

There was a pause on the line, then things went a little strange. It seemed Peg had a sense that something was amok, not sitting right. When she spoke again, her tone was anchor heavy.

"Oh my GOD, Unc. I am so sorry. Are you… are you holding up ok?" she asked.

"Not really, Peg. Some weird shit has been going on. Impossible to explain. And now… this."

"I think I get it, for real. You've been feeling off, haven't you? Like, you don't belong anywhere?" That was an understatement.

"You could say that."

"Unc. I had this dream. You were lost. You didn't recognize anything, or anyone. I was trying to help you, but I couldn't reach you. It was so real, ya know?"

Peg had hit the nail on the head. Hers was the only voice in the world that sounded truly sympathetic. So, I focused all my energy on Daddio, sending every ghosty vibe I had: *GO TO PEG!*

"Wow, Niecey, that's… it's bang on, really. The scary thing is, everyone here, and I mean every-fucking-one, is pointing the finger at me. Like I killed her, or something. It was a car accident in Kingston, for Chrissakes".

"What the heck? How the hell could they be blaming you?"

"Long story. I'll fill you in later."

"Oh, Unc, I am so sorry. That's awful. Can you come here? No one will blame you here. I promise. This is a safe place. You know that."

"Thanks, Peg. I think I just might take you up on that. I'll find a way there."

After Dad and Peg said their goodbyes, Dr. Luke offered to drive Dad wherever he needed to go. Peg and her family lived in St. Catharines, close to Niagara Falls. From Oakville, that was about a forty minute trip on the QEW. It was far enough for Daddio to escape the wrath of the angry mob, but close enough to be available if anyone needed him.

They headed back to the house so Dad could explain his plan. By the time they got there, the mood there had quieted to a somber acceptance.

Creepy Dr. Mark thankfully had the good sense to leave my family to their grief and had gone home.

Dad headed to the bedroom and packed a small bag, before returning to make his announcement.

"Listen, guys. I can appreciate why you're upset with me. But, please, please know this: I love you guys. All of you. I am deeply sorry that this has happened. I'm hopelessly regretful for any role I may have played. I'm going to go to Peggy's place for a few days. I think my being here would just add fuel to the fire. Luke's going to give me a lift. You know how to reach me. I love you, ok? I'm sorry."

He walked over to where Mom was sitting at the dining room table, hugged her, and kissed her forehead.

"Goodbye, my love. Brad, Aiden, even you Colby – you guys can help Bridget with any arrangements that need to be made. Please find me if you need my help."

No one even looked up. The boys understood that they'd need to be there for Mom. Sierra even offered to help where needed. She was a good sister-in-law.

Dr. Luke led Dad to his house, where their family Land Rover was parked. They walked in silence, and barely spoke on the way to St. Catharines. Dr. Luke talked a little bit about how hard this would be on Colby. Dad listened, lost in his thoughts.

When they got to Peg's, Dad stepped out of the truck to meet her on the front porch. She didn't say a word, just pulled him into a big, sympathetic hug. He held on, letting out a breath he didn't realize he'd been holding. Dr. Luke introduced himself to Peg, and reminded Dad that he was just a text or a phone call away.

Once inside, Daddio laid it all out for Peg – the secret stuff. How he remembered sketching me, creating an identity for me, giving everyone gifts in my name, only to find out the next day that I, Lilly, was the real deal. He explained how he'd come to Kingston, and that we had seen each other. Peg listened, jaw dropped, as he unraveled the entire story.

Even for me, it was still hard to wrap my head around it. When I say that I was all-seeing, that only pertains to my reality at this point. I didn't know yet, if I'd ever be able to look into other realities or other histories. But one thing I did know was that this Daddio came from a place where I didn't even exist, yet he still thought of me. He still knew me enough to draw an eerily accurate sketch of me. How cool is that?

"And she died in a car crash on her way home to see you?" Peg asked, eyes wide.

"Yeah. That is basically what went down. Unfuckingbelievable, really. Isn't it?"

"Jesus, Unc. I'm so sorry. I have to tell you, it makes the dream I had that much creepier. Holy shit!"

It was the second time Peg had touched on this dream that she had. Dad was curious, and wondered if there might be some kind of connection.

"It's just weird that you dreamt about me at all, Niecey. What was it all about?"

"I was actually dreaming of my kids, then all of a sudden, the dream camera jumps to you. You're out there alone on a road, just in your tighty whities, and it's pouring rain. I can see you're freezing, but I can't get to you to help. Then, you won't fucking believe this – LILLY comes up to you with a blanket, but you don't even see her. She keeps waving the stupid blanket in front of you, screaming for you to notice her, but you never see her. You end up just cowering in a ditch. I can't get to you. No one can get to you. Then I wake up. Can you believe that?"

"Well, I don't wear tighty whities, but that just about sums it up. It's such a shit show."

Dad was just grateful to have someone – anyone – who had a modicum of empathy for what he was going through.

"But now, this poor girl is dead. And I still haven't acknowledged her. I wish I could have. You understand why I couldn't, though, right?" He looked at her, hoping she would get it.

"Absolutely, Unc. Totally. It's just… so strange that it happened though. It makes no sense."

"No… No, it doesn't make any fucking sense, Peg. None at all."

Dad and Peg sat quietly together for hours after that. Just being in each other's space, sharing the same air, was comforting for both of them. I was glad that Daddio had gone there. He was safely away from all the blaming.

My focus, however, was split three ways, really. I had to be there with Dad, at home with Mom and my brothers and sisters, and with my

Nicky in the hospital. And that's where I felt I was needed the most. Nick had managed to fall asleep after they reset his arm and got him in a cast, thanks to a heavy dose of pain meds. But they only dulled his physical pain. His mind was plagued by nightmares. He kept reliving the accident. The smell of gasoline. Mr. Carmichael's fat, little face. And worst of all, my lifeless body beside him.

He jolted awake, hoping for an instant that it had just been a bad dream. But the cast on his arm and the sterile hospital room told him otherwise. He broke down, sobbing, just as his parents walked in.

"Oh, my Nicky. I am so sorry, Son." His mom, Mrs. Rocher, rushed to clasp his good hand, both of them in tears.

Mr. Rocher's voice trembled. "I'm just glad you're ok, Nicky."

"I'm NOT ok. Fuck sakes Dad. Lilly is gone. She is actually gone. She's not coming back. I am NOT going to be ok."

All three of them were crying now. Bawling. Mr. Rocher, who'd always been fond of me, was devastated too. He would always joke with Nick about how beautiful his grandchildren would be someday.

"I know, Nicky. I know. I'm sorry." Mr. Rocher paused, wiping a tear away. "Do you know how her Mom and Dad are holding up?"

"Jesus. No. I haven't talked to them. I'm too upset. You wouldn't believe what was going on with her Dad, though. That's why we were driving to fucking Oakville in the middle of the night."

Nicky went on to explain, in as much detail as he could, what the situation was. How Colby had coffee with Dad. How we saw him on the sidewalk. He got stuck when he was trying to explain how Aiden spilled the beans.

"Then, her brother, Aiden, the little shit, he tells her everything. Every last detail. She didn't need to know that. Of course that would upset her. Why couldn't he just keep his fucking mouth shut? I swear to God, I could kill him."

"Now, Nicky. Don't say that," his Mom said, gripping his hand a little tighter. "Aiden didn't do this. That other driver did this, Son. That's who you should be mad at, if you have to be mad at someone. It's him."

Nick's eyes narrowed. "That guy. I saved his fucking life, Mom. I could have just left him there to die. I should have. Where is he? Is he here?" He shifted, trying to push himself up. "He probably is. I'm going to go kick his fat, ugly ass."

My poor Nicky, my brave hero, was overwhelmed with grief. He needed someone to blame and couldn't shake the fury building in him, channeling it at Aiden and Mr. Carmichael. Maybe he was on Team Al after all.

"You will do no such thing, my boy," his Dad said firmly, placing a hand on Nick's shoulder. "Just rest. God will take care of everything else." Mr. Rocher's religion was showing, but Nick found some comfort in the sound of his voice.

The three of them sat in silence for a long time after that. I allowed myself to check in on Mr. Carmichael and his wife. Sure enough, there he was, fast asleep (or passed out), with a content little smile on his face.

Every third or fourth breath, his lips would burst open with a fart of snorey, vodka-stink air. Mrs. Carmichael sat by his bedside in a dingy, pink tracksuit. Her black coat with a faux fur hood was draped over Mr. Carmichael's feet. She looked half interested at best, but every time her husband puffed out another noisy snore, she shook her unwashed head and muttered "Pig."

"Look what you've done now, Pig," she hissed with venom. "Ha. Divorce. You want to divorce ME? You are gonna be locked up, Pig. Jail. That's where you'll be. You killed a kid. Real nice, Asshole." She spoke as though he might actually be listening. "You know what, James? Fuck you. You can go through this without me. Goodbye. Pig."

She grabbed her coat, threw it on, and turned to look back at him, one last time, from the doorway. "Fucking Pig."

Once he sensed that she was gone, Mr. Carmichael cracked open one eye and flipped the bird in her general direction. "Bitch." He'd heard her rant but didn't want to engage. He knew his plight, and did not need her reminding him of the shitstorm he'd created.

My curiosity was as satisfied as I needed it to be. I harboured no ill will toward Mr. Carmichael, but I had more important things to focus on. If I could help Nicky, or Daddio, or Mom, or my brothers and sisters, it would be worth so much more than watching the Carmichael train wreck from the bleachers.

New Year's Day was coming to a close now. It hadn't gone the way anyone had hoped or expected. Back at Mom's house, everyone was still there. I was glad for that. They all needed each other, and maybe, just maybe, I could still be the thing that would bring them closer together. My siblings decided to spend the night at Mom's so that they could help with arrangements. Dr. Luke had stopped by on his way home to pick up Colby, so now it was just the family at the house, minus Daddio.

Peg had set up one of her kids' bedrooms for Dad. She offered him a huge dinner, but his appetite wouldn't let him eat much. The poor guy had barely slept. He excused himself from the dinner table and went to bed before eight o'clock, and luckily, sleep came fast. I tried to send him comfort, and I think it reached him.

Peg took it upon herself to notify Dad's people – our aunts, uncles and cousins, even ones I barely knew. They were all heartbroken when they heard the news. She left a message at Miller Shoes, letting them know that Dad had lost a child, and not to expect him in for a while. The only person Peg confided in about Dad's confusion was her husband, Tony. The others didn't need to know.

Nicky's Mom and Dad stayed with him for a few hours before they went home. He was left alone in the hospital. The doctors wanted to keep him one more night for observation, which was probably a good thing. I didn't want him to have to go to our place by himself. They had him drugged up enough that he, too, fell asleep quickly. I sent him all the love I could, hoping he'd dream of happy times we had. That is what I wished for him, and I think it came true. He slept peacefully.

By the day's end, my body had been prepared for the journey to the funeral home in Burlington. They had planned the trip for the following morning. I was zipped up in a bag, hidden from view, so no one could see how gross I looked. But I could see, Zip Lock Hefty Bags were no match for my ghosty X-ray vision. I felt sorry for that girl in the bag. Until just a few hours ago, she was beautiful and had a wonderful life ahead of her. Now, all she had to look forward to was a bumpy ride to a funeral home… and a hope they could make her pretty enough for an open casket.

She was going to be the life of the party.

Chapter 18:
The Hardest Thing

For my family, the next few days were a whirlwind. Even though she was shouldering her own grief, and unsure how to approach the future with Dad, Mom was a rock. Brad and Colby did what they could, but she managed nearly all the heavy lifting when it came to arranging my funeral. She only let Dad help with one thing: the wording for the obituary. It was all Mom was willing to accept from him. From the look of things, they might not be a couple much longer, and that was a shame.

The plan was to hold the service at Smith's Funeral Home (turns out I was pretty enough that everyone would be able to look at me, after all). From there, they would bury my body at Trafalgar Lawn Cemetery on Dundas Street, in Oakville. After that, everyone was invited back to the house for a celebration of life. With Mom's Irish family, it would likely be more like a wake. Without doubt, there would be a good deal of imbibing. Tessa and Pam worked super hard getting the place cleaned up and ready for guests. Aiden's sole contribution was to hang some pictures, including Daddio's now-famous sketch and that photo of Dad and me, on the living room wall. Finally!

Nick's parents had stayed in Kingston, picking him up from the hospital after his discharge and driving him straight to Oakville so that he could be with my family. But he didn't want to talk much and mostly kept to the hotel. Mr. and Mrs. Rocher did their best to let him grieve. Their family had almost more money than they knew what to do with, so they offered to cover some of the funeral expenses. Mom was reluctant at first, but she eventually accepted. She had no choice – she needed the help.

There was a disturbing rumble growing louder at Mom's, though. "Team Al" was shrinking… and fast. Aiden would not stop with his criticism of Dad. At first, Mom defended him, but even she was wearing thin. Brad was not much help either – he and Sierra chimed in with their own complaints about Dad not being there to help. The truth was, though, that if he had been there, he would have been torn to pieces. Only Tessa spoke up to remind everyone that a mental illness isn't something you can fault someone for, but it fell on deaf ears.

Dad, meanwhile, stayed holed up at Peg's the entire time, not going anywhere. He spent hours obsessively searching online, googling every term he could think of relating to alternate realities. Most of what he found was bullshit, but there were a few helpful tidbits down that rabbit hole. He truly wanted to understand what had happened. He tortured himself wondering if deleting the sketch from his phone was what caused my fate. I did my best to reassure him it wasn't his fault; something else makes these decisions. I was likely going to die whether Dad erased me or not. Would he have come to this place if he hadn't sketched me? From everything I could see, that would be a hard no. Something in the way that he drew me, at exactly the time he did it, with exactly those lines and curves and colours, must have been enough to confuse or convince the decision makers to bring Daddio to me, and I was grateful. I had always loved my Dad, but the idea that he could love me over two realities, one in which I didn't even exist… well, that was pretty special.

As the day of the funeral approached, Mom was leaning on Dr. Mark a lot more than I would have liked. She convinced herself that he was "helping her with grief," but it was obvious to everyone – living or otherwise – that he was prowling. It was kind of gross. I could see where this was heading, and I didn't like it one bit. He drove Mom to the funeral home to make arrangements, even offered to sit in on the meeting with the director. Thankfully, she handled that part on her own.

My biggest worry was Nicky. He was floundering, barely talking to anyone now. He seemed to be stuck in angry mode, which wasn't like him at all. He'd always been so happy and hopeful, so strong and sure of himself. Now, it was like the accident ripped all of that away from him. He hadn't cracked a smile since that night. I tried and tried sending him comfort and calm, over and over, but it either wasn't reaching him or just wasn't enough. His Mom and Dad were doing their best to keep his spirits up too, but he was completely mired in his misery.

The morning of the funeral – Friday, January 6, 2017 – dawned beautifully, almost like spring. The warm sun had melted away the last bit of snow, and it turned out to be exactly the kind of day I'd been hoping for. Maybe I had a little sway in that? Doubtful, but I was testing the waters. Spreading my dead girl wings.

The service was set for two o'clock in the afternoon. Considering the perfect weather, I was expecting a fabulous turnout. I was only 22, but everyone I knew (even the ones my age) wondered about watching their own funerals. And honestly? I was no different. I was going to be front row, with a giant bag of popcorn for this particular show.

My family had opted to have no visitation on the days leading up to the main event. Anyone who wanted to say their goodbyes would have to show up that day. Mom and my siblings all arrived at the funeral home just after noon and gathered in the private room for family members. Peg drove Daddio in from St. Catharines, arriving about fifteen minutes after Mom. Her Mom (my Auntie Fran) came too, but no one else from that arm of the family could make it. Dad joined the rest of the family in the private room while Peg and Fran waited outside. As much as Peg wanted to be in there as a buffer for Dad, it would have been too awkward.

A few minutes later, Nick and his parents showed up. The funeral director offered to guide them to join my family, but Nick refused. He hadn't spoken with any of them – not even Mom – since the accident. I so wished he would sit with them, but his anger toward Aiden – and maybe even Daddio – was still white-hot. I kept sending him calm, and love, and peace, anything that might help. But it was like he had some sort of force field around him; nothing was getting through.

It was the first time it had occurred to me – was he mad at me, too? For dying? I mean, people do get angry with dead loved ones for being dead loved ones, instead of living loved ones. It made sense, and Nicky was only human. He had every right to be upset. After all, it was my decision to get into that car and drive in the middle of the night. My decision to go to that particular gas station. Maybe, in his mind, I was to blame… just a little.

Around 12:30, they opened the doors to the main parlour. The oak casket holding my body was surrounded by flowers at the front. Four rows of pews faced me, backed up by another hundred or so temporary folding chairs. Mine was the only funeral happening that afternoon, so overflow seating was set up in the adjacent rooms. They expected a mob! The funeral director led my family, and Nicky and his family, into the room where I lay. It was the first time any of them had seen me since I'd left. I looked pretty good, considering. They had done a nice job making me look like… me.

It was also the first time, since the big event, that Nicky had seen anyone from my family. Mom went straight to him, before even coming to the coffin to see my body. She wrapped him in a big hug, careful not to jostle his broken arm, and I could see his shoulders begin to shake – his first real tears in days. Mom held him tightly, as if her own strength could hold him together. Then Brad and Sierra, Tessa, and Pam took turns hugging him. Aiden approached him but he must have seen lasers coming from Nick's eyes or something, because he backed off without so much as a word.

Poor Daddio (this version of him), had only ever seen Nicky in pictures. I could see the awkwardness he felt, as he took in Nick's presence. But he gathered his courage, offering Nicky a little hug too. It was Aiden alone who stayed at arm's length, cast out into Nicky's bad books – or maybe I was in there too. It was impossible to tell.

Then, it was finally time for everyone to look at the dead chick in the box. The whole custom seemed kind of morbid, but I took it as a chance to send what little comfort I could. Maybe if they were looking at my face, they would be more receptive to whatever I was trying to send them. Mom was the first to approach. My poor Momma, carrying so much, finally letting the weight fall. She collapsed onto the coffin, her pale skin matching mine. The pain I felt coming from her was almost unbearable.

She sobbed. "No. NO. NO. NO. NO. Not my Lilly."

"Mom. I am right here. I love you. I am okay, Mommy." I mustered whatever presence I could, hoping she would feel me there beside her.

"I love you so much, my sweet baby girl. So much. Be my Angel now, okay? Ok Lil? Can you do that?" She leaned down to whisper to me, brushing my hair with her fingers.

"I can do that Mommy. I WILL do that."

She stood up straight, regathering her strength, pulling herself together. Maybe I'd reached her. She put on a brave smile, motioning for Nick to join her. He hesitated, but slowly stepped toward the casket. I could feel him now – maybe his anger toward me was softening, just a little. But, the sadness… it was weighing him down like an anchor. I wanted to make my body jump out of that stupid box and wrap my arms around him. He was my hero.

"My brave, brave Nicky. Thank you for loving me, Sweetheart. I love you. I love you. I love you." That seemed to bring a faint smile to his face.

"She looks so pretty. She looks like Lil." He seemed to be talking to me, but referring to me in third person. Mom agreed with him. They were both right. I did look pretty.

They turned to the flower arrangements, reading the notes. Pictures of us as kids were displayed nearby, that's where Dad was, looking them over with his head tilted in utter confusion. Nick's parents tried to say hello to him, but Dad had no clue who they were. All the poor guy could offer was his trademark shit eating grin. Luckily, Tessa jumped in to save the day.

"Did you see this one, Daddy?" she said, pointing to an absolutely adorable picture of her riding on my back, with me on all fours, pretending to be a horse. That gave everyone a chuckle and took the Rochers' attention away from Dad. She was such a smart cookie.

Aiden stood at my casket the longest, just looking down at my face. He didn't seem as sad as the others, but he was bewildered. Like he was trying to comprehend what he was seeing.

"Dude. It's going to be ok. You'll be ok. Just take care of Mom. I love you, Little A."

Brad, Sierra, Tessa, and Pam all stepped up to the casket together, side by side. I loved that Pammy was jumping right in there with Daddio's other spawn. Maybe they would become a happy family! I would just have to work a little magic to nudge Mom and Dad back onto good terms. That might not be so easy, though. My siblings were doing a real good job of supporting each other. I felt like they would be okay without too much more help from me.

Nick's parents, then Peg and Auntie Fran, approached to pay their respects. There was sadness there, but my talents, whatever they might have been, could be put to better use helping Mom and Nick.

It seemed to me that Daddio was trying to avoid the big walk to the box – he was kind of hovering at a distance. From what I could tell, his emotions were still in turmoil. I still, even now, just wanted to give him a hug, thank him for trying to call me back – even if it was horrible timing. Heck, even if it was a butt dial, I was still grateful. I needed him to come see me, though. Soon, the room would fill up. We were running out of time for a one on one.

Finally, Mom turned to him, her voice soft, but firm.

"Al. You need to go up there. Say goodbye to your daughter. You owe her that much."

She didn't need to be that harsh, but I was glad she spoke up. I'd never seen anyone walk as slowly as Dad was, making his way to my casket. It was the total and exact opposite of how he had bolted from me on the sidewalk in Kingston. Now, he was like the little engine that could.

"I think I can. I think I can. You can do it, Daddio!" I cheered him on. At last, he made it.

"Well. I guess I am supposed to say something. I am truly sorry, Lilly," he whispered, so softly that no one else would hear. But I heard him, and I could see that he was moved, that there was some connection after all. He started crying.

"I don't really know anything, Baby Girl. But I know you loved your Dad. You were a special girl. Your Daddio loved you too." His words, so quiet they would have only been audible to the dead girl in the box – but that girl was me, and I felt like I could still use her ears. He was speaking directly to me. And then, he said it.

"I love you, Lilly."

BOOM. All of a sudden, I could feel his presence. It wasn't like we were sitting together at the movies, but he was right beside me, up wherever I was, watching himself lean over my body. His body kept talking to my body, but his actual self was not in his body. He was with me.

"Dad?" I asked, to see if he could hear me. It felt more like thinking than speaking, as if sound didn't exist where we were – a vast, weightless void, a nothingness where normal physical parameters were non-existent.

"Lilly? Oh my God. Can you hear me?"

"I am right here, Daddio."

We could see each other – both down there in the funeral home – and up where we were talking now, in this otherworldly space.

"I need a hug. Can we do that?" he asked, like it might offer mercy.

"I need that too, Dad. I'm so sorry I died."

"I'm sorry I went nuts. This is crazy. I am crazy."

"No, you're not crazy, Dad."

We hugged. Well, our souls did something deeper than a hug. It was as if we were in each other's minds. I could feel his confusion, the beautiful, empathetic man that he was. And he could feel how much his daughter loved him.

"Can you communicate with the others?" He wondered.

"Not like this, I don't think. But it does seem like they can sense when I'm trying to comfort them."

Then, POOF, he vanished. He was back in his body, still standing at the coffin. Brad was coming up from the back of the room, ready to gently pull him away. In our enthusiasm for seeing each other in the realm of souls, we failed to notice that there was some unrest among the people watching him at my body's side. Aiden, in particular, was shaking his head in anger. Brad was just trying to save our Dad from embarrassment. But he was smiling wide, which may have seemed inappropriate, as he leaned down to kiss my forehead. Before Brad could reach him, I decided to test something. I wanted to check if I could still communicate with Body Dad, to see if he could still hear me. Just as Brad grabbed his arm, I spoke.

"Booga Booga Booga."

If he could hear me, I figured I may as well make him chuckle.

Dad jumped back, laughing out loud. It worked – I was in his ear! This was going to be so much fun.

"Jesus Christ, Al. You don't even belong here." Aiden was disgusted, clearly offended. I needed to settle him down, so I tried sending waves of calm, understanding – anything to soften his anger, but he was fuming.

"I'm sorry. I, uh, I just thought of something funny she said one time." Dad tried to explain.

"Tell them I am talking to you right now! Mess with their heads."

He laughed even louder, barely contained.

"I'm so sorry everyone. Really." He spoke through laughter – not very convincingly.

"Sorry, Daddio. This is just too much fun. I'll behave."

Mom was glaring at Dad. I couldn't help myself – I was overdoing it a little. But Daddio and I were just so excited to finally connect. It just really sucked that I was dead, and he was stuck in this weird reality – but at least we had each other now. He did manage to stifle his laughter long enough to sit with the rest of the family. Nicky looked over at him, curious.

"Everything ok, Mr. I?" Nick asked, speaking to this version of my Dad for the first time.

"Yeah. Yeah. I'm okay, Nick. Thanks for asking. How are you holding up, Buddy?"

"I'm okay too. I feel like she's here. Smiling down on us. It's comforting, ya know?" Nicky did feel what I was sending.

"Oh, Daddy, tell him I love him so much." Maybe I could communicate with Nick through my old Man.

"Nick. She is here. I never, ever would have said that before, but I know it. I absolutely believe that to be true. And she loves you so much, Buddy. She really does."

"Couldn't have said that any better myself, Daddio!" He really had nailed it right on the head.

 But Aiden was being so… Aiden.

"What the fuck do YOU know, Al? And stop fucking pretending that you even give a shit. Asshole." He was seething, and nothing that I could send was getting through to him. Aiden was completely convinced that Dad was responsible for my death. Nicky did not agree, and he wasn't afraid to let Aiden know it, in no uncertain terms.

"Aiden, you little shit, shut your mouth! Mr. I never would have done what you did. Just SHUT UP, for once."

Mr. Rocher stepped in to restore order.

"Boys. We're all upset. Let's just stop pointing fingers here. People are beginning to arrive now. Settle down." He was a large Man. He commanded respect, even from Aiden.

Mom's glare was fixed on Aiden, a look I'd never seen before. A weird mix of disappointment, disgust, sadness, anger, disbelief – it was all in there. Between that and what Mr. Rocher had said, Aiden got the point. His criticism of Dad, especially in the kind of language he was using, was not going to be tolerated. At least not at the funeral home.

The throngs of spectators began to arrive not long after my family had taken their seats and calmed down. My Uncle Will came with his family. I hadn't met his new lady friend yet, but she looked lovely on his arm. His two boys, Ray and David, stayed close by their Dad. The four of them went, en masse, to look at my beautiful face in the casket. I was dying (see what I did there?) to have some fun with them. They all looked so somber. I had to share my thoughts with Dad. He had been sitting quietly for long enough now.

"Yo, Daddio. I'm trying to get my body to stick her tongue out at Uncle Will, but they have my stupid mouth all stitched shut. Damn it!"

He tried not to laugh, but he couldn't help it. He snorted loudly, startling everyone in the place. Uncle Will snapped his head around to see what was going on. He and Dad had some sort of psychic connection. Uncle Will's first instinct, when he heard Dad laugh, was to laugh as well. If Daddio was laughing, something funny must have happened.

So, here we had the father and the uncle of the dead chick in the box, both laughing their faces off. Once they got going, Uncle Will's boys started laughing too. Not to be outdone, Peg and Auntie Fran caught the giggles. Brad tried to be stern, but the tickle monster had him too. Even little Tessa got it. Before long, every person with any Isaac blood in them was in on a joke that they didn't even understand. If only Dad could tell them.

Mom elbowed Dad in the ribs hard enough to knock the laugh (and the wind) clean out of him. Once Dad stopped laughing, so did everyone else. Mom had the look of a teacher walking back into a class to find the kids acting up. And I was the kid playing hooky, making faces from outside the window. I was the reason everyone was laughing, but they were the ones getting in trouble. I tried to send some fun vibes to Mom, but she was being a boss. There was no joking with the Boss.

Nick didn't seem to mind at all; he was taking it all in, but kept one eye on Aiden the whole time. Mr. and Mrs. Rocher watched all the Isaacs with a hint of curiosity, but no judgment. If people were laughing at a funeral, there was probably a good reason.

Uncle Will's family found seats next to Auntie Fran and Peg. Once the laughing calmed down, they were catching up. It was a shame I couldn't be down there with everyone. I hadn't seen these people in far too long. It sucked that I wouldn't be able to hang out with them anymore. The best I could do now was eavesdrop on their conversations.

"Thanks for letting us know, Peg. Al is messed up. He never even called." Will sounded concerned.

"I know. He is. Really bad, actually. He's been struggling. I'll fill you in later, if he doesn't. Were you able to get hold of everyone else to let them know?" Peg asked.

"I made a bunch of calls, sent some messages. I don't know if everyone got them though. Some people are hard to reach."

That was interesting. I didn't know how much of my Dad's side of the family would be there, but everyone else was starting to file in now. My aunts and uncles on Mom's side came, none of my cousins, though. That was weird, but lots and lots of other people were there. Friends from as far back as kindergarten. Nadene and Mario, Dr. Luke and of course Colby too. Poor dude seemed as sad as Mom and Nick, but then, he had been my best pal since we were little.

The place filled up quickly. The overflow rooms were at capacity. Then, right before the minister was about to start, Dr. Mark rushed in and wedged himself between Pammy and Mom.

"So sorry I'm late. I had an emergency patient. How are you guys holding up?" He asked, not-so-subtly flashing his Rolex.

Gross. What gave him the right to sit with the family? Then, I spotted Mom giving his hand a little squeeze. Ewwww.

"Thanks for being here, Mark. It means a lot."

"Barfffff. Mom! He is a creep. What the actual EFF!" She couldn't hear me. But Dad could. He looked up toward the ceiling and winked. I took that as a note of approval.

"Kick him in the balls, Daddio," I suggested. He did what he could.

"Ya, Mark. Thanks for sitting with the family. Mighty big of you."

Dad got that nice little dig in before the Minister started. Mom elbowed him again. Poor guy was going to be all bruised up by the time this was over.

I was glad that Mom had the good sense to ask Dad's friend, Chistopher Connor, to be the officiant. I didn't know him, but he was a musician too. He wasn't going to be stupid and drag the whole thing out for hours. No one that I knew would want to sit through a sermon at a funeral. He did say some nice things about God, whom I had yet to meet. Then he told some stories about me as a little girl. Specifically, the one about the time I hated my red hair so much, I took a can of Dad's spray paint, and gave myself a nice black dye job. It was a huge improvement, in my eyes.

Then he told the one about when I pulled pieces of foam out of the rec room couch cushions and shoved them up my nose. I got them far enough up there that Mom had to take me to emergency, so the nice doctor could pull them all out. That Doc was the person who convinced me that my red hair was pretty.

Mr. Connor must have heard these stories from Mom and Dad, over the years. It was a nice touch. He made them laugh, he made them cry, it was the feel-good funeral of the year. Even the people in the overflow rooms, who were watching him talk on TV screens, were laughing and crying on cue.

The hardest part for everyone was when Colby got up to deliver my eulogy. I could've smacked him – it's not nice to make a ghost cry.

"Lilly Isaac was... no IS – she still is my best friend. When we were little, our parents wanted us to marry each other. But... I was a boy, and boys were gross. The only boy she would ever marry was her Daddio. That was ok, because she was a girl, and let's face it, girls were gross too.

Lilly was honestly like that forever. Even in high school, she was more concerned about her marks than she was about boys. Then, we went to Queens. There were French dudes at Queens. French boys were not gross. One French boy in particular, was especially not gross. That French boy was Nick. Nicky Rocher. He won Lilly's heart. She couldn't wait to show him off to her Mom and Dad. To her brothers and sisters. To me, to MY Dad. Everyone loved him. Everyone loved Lilly and Nick together.

Damn. This was supposed to be the speech I gave at their wedding. Instead, I'm giving it… at our Lilly's funeral. But, just because she isn't here physically, that doesn't mean she shouldn't hear it.

Lilly, you are our favourite flower. You are my best friend. You and Nick are my favourite couple. I look up to you guys. You're supposed to be together forever. I'm so sorry Nick. I am so sorry Lill. I am so sorry to everyone here.

We all love you so much Lilly. We're going to miss you. I'm going to miss you. You aren't even gross, okay? There. I said it.

Here's to Lilly and Nick."

There wasn't a dry eye in the house. I didn't know Colby had it in him, but he was a pro up there. I wanted to hug him so bad. I think Nick could sense that, because he got up and gave Colbs the biggest one-armed hug ever.

After Colby's beautiful speech, Mr. Connor got back up and led the crowd in the "Yea, though I walk through the valley of the shadow of death" prayer. I had never really listened to it before. It really was nice – it even brought me some comfort. This guy was good. After the prayer, he instructed everyone to meet at the cemetery to watch my body get put in the ground. My fans were told that they were all welcome to join the family at Mom's house afterward, to celebrate how awesome I had been.

The pallbearers were called up next. Mom had asked Aiden and Brad, my cousins David and Ray, and Colby and Dr. Luke to finish the line up. It looked like a pretty solid squad to me. I wasn't a heavy girl, but that box looked pretty sturdy. As soon as the boys picked my body up, I felt a sense of comfort, like I was being cradled. But that was short lived. Something felt off. It was Nicky. His anger was coming to a boil again. Before I even had a chance to send him some calm, he jumped up and tried to push Aiden from his post.

"You have no right to carry her. Just get out of the way, Aiden."

"Jesus, Nick. Back off. She's my sister." Aiden wouldn't budge.

"I swear to God I'll punch you in the throat if you don't get away from her."

My poor Nicky was losing it. Dr. Luke had a suggestion.

"Nick, if you want to help carry, you can have my spot."

"I don't care who carries her, as long as it's not him!" Nick pointed to Aiden.

"Whatever, Asshole. Do what you want." Aiden acquiesced.

But it wasn't done without some testosteronical posturing. They stood chest to chest, glaring at each other. They looked like morons. This was my funeral, and they were making it all about their pettiness.

Nick had to switch sides with Colby so his good arm was in position to hold the lift bar on the casket. The whole thing was just so awkward. My fans were all staring at the boys, jaws dropped. I was embarrassed for them, and I wasn't even alive to be embarrassed. Aiden slumped back into his chair beside Pam, crossing his arms and huffing like a petulant brat.

Although Nick got his way, his anger was back – one hundred percent. They lugged me to the hearse, and slid me into the back like they had rehearsed a thousand times. Smooth as silk. They were pros. But the mood was flat out wrong. Funerals were supposed to be somber, reflective times. There was a hint of that, but there were too many bristling tempers now. That was so not cool. I was trying to send calm and cool to everyone, but that amount of nastiness was too much for my limited ghosty abilities to overcome.

The drive to the cemetery was silent. The mood was just wrong in every car, and there was way too much anger in the air. Aiden was mad at Dad. Nick was mad at Aiden. Dad was mad at Dr. Mark. Mom was mad at everyone. I wasn't mad at anyone. This was my show, though. I was the star, and everyone better get their heads right pretty quickly, or they would face the wrath of the Lillster.

In the twenty minutes it took to get from the funeral home to the cemetery, I was hoping some of the madness would subside, but the opposite happened. Nick's Dad convinced him that Aiden deserved to carry his sister from the hearse to the gravesite. Nick relented, but only with the same grumpiness that Aiden had when he gave up his spot earlier.

The lineup of cars was formidable. I was impressed. There must have been at least 200 people who came to see my show. Daddio should have been proud; that was a good crowd for any kind of performance. It took another half hour or so for all the cars to get parked, and for the people to gather 'round the big hole. They had my box propped up just above the void. God, I wanted to mess with everyone and make the casket fall or, better yet, jump out of it and yell at them all for being so grumpy.

My family had the front row. Once again, Dr. Mark had weaseled his way in there too. Right next to Mom. Nick and his family were right up front as well. Daddio was kind of… off to the side. Brad and Sierra stayed close to him, but Mom's preference for masculine support clearly lay with Dr. Mark. I was desperately trying to turn in my grave, but I wasn't quite in it just yet. Even if Mom couldn't be with Dad, she was way too good for that self-centred creep.

Mr. Connor welcomed everyone to the interment, which was kind of strange – but I liked it. Then he started talking about how God was going to welcome me as a new angel or something. I wasn't sure I was up to the task, but whatever the boss wanted, I guess I owed him that. It still freaked me out that I could watch everything like this. I was so grateful to see Daddio. And, if I could always communicate with him, I would consider myself the luckiest girl ever.

Mr. Connor continued to pray.

"And we ask, Oh Lord, that you look after Lilly's parents, Allan and Bridget, as we offer them our condolences and our love."

BOOM. Daddio was up beside me again.

"Woah! I didn't expect that. This is fun!" I greeted him.

"Jesus Christ. I am never going to get used to this. Ah, Lill, I sure wish I could just hang out up here with you. Everyone is so intense. And I am beginning to hate Goodhands."

The weirdest thing is that I knew exactly who he meant. Dr. Mark was Goodhands!

"Oh my God! Dad! I don't know why you call him that, but I love it! Goodhands it shall be!"

"Your Mom told me I would be in good hands with him. I guess she knows something about that," he explained.

We did that soul hug thing again. What an amazing feeling. Hugs are even more important when you're dead.

"Hey look. You're putting a lily on my casket!" I pointed Dad out to himself.

"So strange. I don't even know what I am thinking down there. How am I doing that?"

"No clue, Daddio. I am just glad you're here."

"Me too, Lilly. Me too."

This was a longer visit. We watched as people walked up to place yellow lilies on my casket. It was a beautiful thing to see. There was one woman who stood away from the crowd, though – she didn't go up to place a flower anywhere. She was dressed all in black, and looking super somber. She looked like the Queen of Somber. I didn't know who she was.

"Dad, who's that woman? Do you know her?" I pointed to where she was standing.

"WOW! That is Ally Oddly's Mom. I can't believe she's here."

"Ally Oddly? Who's that?" I was curious.

"Just a kid I met on the train. Strange that her Mom is here."

I was about to ask for more info, but... he was gone again. Back down on the ground with all the angry people. Mr. Connor was wrapping things up, and inviting all my fans back to Mom's, when a terribly inconvenient idea occurred to him.

"Al, why don't you lead us all in a chorus of Lilly's Song?"

Oh boy. This was not good. Daddio clearly had no idea that there even was a Lilly's Song. I wanted to sing it to him, so he would at least have a clue, but I am no singer. Also, while I loved the song, I had no idea how it went unless he was singing it to me. The problem was, everyone else seemed to love the idea. They applauded, modestly but with a good deal of enthusiasm.

"That would be so nice, Al. Lilly would love that."

"Beautiful idea."

"Hear Hear!"

There was a chorus of encouragement, not a single dissenting voice in the crowd. Then, Goodhands showed his true, hideous colours.

"Yes, Al. Why don't you sing your daughter's song? We would all love to hear it."

I half-hoped my Mother would kick him in the shin or something, but she joined in with a nod and sinister grin. I couldn't believe what I was seeing.

"Shit, Dad. I will try to sing it, but I can't sing." I hoped he could still hear me. Poor Daddio looked completely lost, eying the six foot hole for possible refuge.

There was a hush over the crowd now, all ears bent toward Dad, in anticipation of what promised to be the most heart wrenching performance in history: my Dad, singing a song he wrote for me when I was a baby, while standing at my graveside, with the giant group of mourners joining in. A picture-perfect send-off. Except... DADDIO DIDN'T KNOW THE SONG.

I could see that Dr. Luke was trying to come up with a solution to relieve Dad of this little task, but even he was at a loss. Dad looked up toward... the sky? Me? God? I wasn't sure, but I took it as my cue to try to feed him the song through our secret channel.

"Any time now, Lill. Help your old Man out?" He asked, out loud, for everyone to hear.

Aiden snickered in doubtful glee – the little twerp. I tried to sing the first line, pretty sure I had it right.

When you wake up in the morning to painted flowers on your wall

I hope you always know you're the prettiest flower of them all

No other flower has a smile like you do

No other flower ever made our dreams come true

I thought I was nailing it, but Daddio hadn't started singing yet. Not a note. He was panicking. I was stuck, struggling to remember where it went from there. Songs were his thing, not mine.

"Come on, Al. We'll join in," Mr. Connor encouraged.

"Uh. I'm, I'm, uh, just trying to remember, uh, the tune… How it goes, you know." Poor Daddio was in the weeds. He tried:

"When you wake up and see flowers painted on your wall…"

Then, the most awkward pause. All the people were giving Dad the doggy-head-tilt. Whatever tune he was following was more Palmolive commercial than Lullaby. Maybe this version of Daddio was a shite singer? I honestly didn't know.

"No other flower can answer my prayers."

He was croaking out sounds more like volcanic rumble than song.

"Ok , Dad, now you're just making shit up." I wanted him to stop digging, but it was too late. Aiden seized the opportunity to throw Dad completely under the bus.

"You don't even know the song, do you?" He hissed, barely suppressing his disgust. He couldn't help himself. "He doesn't even know the SONG!" He blurted out to the whole crowd. "This isn't even Lilly's

Dad. He refused to even admit that she existed until she died. Now he's trying to play Super-Dad, but he can't. You're pathetic, Al. Just give it up."

The crowd was divided into two camps. One small group was made up of folks who already knew about Dad's little predicament. The second, much larger group was composed of all the other kind folks who thought the only thing wrong with the entire picture was that there was a young girl in a box. Every head among that camp turned, neck-craned to catch a glimpse of the father who didn't know his own daughter. There were gasps of disbelief and grunts of disapproval, with questions coming at my Dad from all angles. It was practically a witch hunt.

"Is that true, Al?"

"Are you drinking again, Al?"

"Oh, your poor baby girl. You should be ashamed of yourself, Allan Isaac."

The questions and accusations ballooned into a din as the circle around my father grew smaller… and smaller. He looked up toward me again, for some kind of sign.

"Get the heck out of there, Daddio." That was the best I could do.

He was crying, likely unable to speak, but then he saw it – a small crack in the crowd. An opening. He made the decision to bolt. It was his only option. Like a running back, he split the defense, and busted through, with no idea where to run. But there, in the clearing, he spotted his getaway. Ally Oddly's mom stood by her van, the side door wide open.

She had been standing close enough to the melee to hear what was going on, and knew Dad might need help to escape. He jumped right in. She slammed the door behind him, ran around to the driver side, hopped in and hit the gas.

The mob chased them on foot. I couldn't believe what I was seeing.

"You people should be ashamed of yourselves!" I screamed at the top of my lungs, or thoughts, or whatever – but no one could hear me. Just my Dad.

"It's okay Lill. It's okay. Just take care of your brothers and sisters, and your Mom. I'll be fine," he said, holding strong.

"Okay Daddio. I will do my best. I'm only a thought away. You know that?"

"Okay, Kiddo."

Mrs. Oddly – or whatever her name was – seemed to know that Dad was talking with me.

"I saw you two. I saw you up there." Her eyes looked toward me, like she could totally see me. "I can still see her. Are you able to communicate with her?" She asked my Dad.

"Yeah. I met her today. We hugged. I wish I could tell everyone, but those assholes wouldn't believe me."

"Daddio. This is so cool. You have a friend! What's her name?"

"Her name is Tricia, Kiddo."

Mrs. Oddly, Tricia, looked up at me again and waved. I waved back. "Thank you, Mrs., Oddly, for taking care of Daddio."

"Lilly says thank you." Dad passed my gratitude along.

Tricia's van managed to get far enough away that, by the time the mob reached their cars, it was too late.

Daddio was safe from the torches and pitchforks – for now.

Chapter 19:
Celebration Time, Come on

So much for my party. Cars peeled off in all directions, barely a handful heading toward Mom's house. When the dust finally settled, the only ones left at my wake were my immediate family, Dr. Luke and Colby, Nadene and Mario, Uncle Will and his crew – and (of course) Goodhands. Nicky and his parents showed up about half an hour later. That was it. Two hundred people turned out for my party, but barely a dozen stuck around for the celebration. Hey, I didn't mind. I could keep an eye on everyone from my new vantage point.

Once again, the mood was the exact opposite of what I wanted it to be. No one was celebrating a damned thing. Tessa and Pammy had spent hours making the place look perfect, and Mom had brought in enough sandwiches to feed the entire planet, plus enough booze to keep this tiny crowd hammered for two years straight. By the looks of it, that was the plan. Nicky went straight for the beer when he walked in. Aiden too. Colby found the whiskey, and Mom and Goodhands opened the wine. Drinks in one hand, sandwiches in the other. The only ones who weren't double fisting were Uncle Will, Brad, and Sierra. Even Tessa had a cooler.

The awkward silence dragged on for ages before Tessa, finally, couldn't take it anymore.

"I hope you're happy, Aiden. Daddy should be here," she said, her voice shaking as she fought back tears.

"Sorry, T. Your dad's a loser." Aiden was sticking to his guns.

And all I wanted was for someone to think about me for one second – to think about what I might want, if they could ask me. I was supposed to be the star of this show, damn it. There was a supposed "professional" in the room – Dr. Goodhands. But, instead of helping, he clearly had his mind up Mom's skirt. Creep.

"Will everyone please just try to get along? For Lilly's sake?" Mom pleaded. Maybe she heard me on some level. Thanks, Mama.

That was enough to keep everyone quiet for a little while, but I could feel the tension brewing. Anger simmered under the surface. Everyone seemed to be mad at someone. Nick was quiet... too quiet. He looked like he was ready to jump out of his own skin. I was worried about him.

The weirdest part was that everyone was divided into sections. Dad's side huddled together, Mom's side – plus the two doctors and Colby – had their own thing going on, and Nick's family was chatting with Nadene and Mario. The only time they mixed was at the booze cooler, which became a more frequent meeting point as the night dragged on.

Dr. Luke and my pal Colby were the first to leave. They lived close enough to walk, and Colby was just too drained to stick around. Dr. Luke said his goodbyes, offered condolences from his whole family to ours, then he and Colby each gave Mom a big hug before heading out. In that moment, an entire lifetime of little Lilly and Colby memories flashed before me. I sent them all the love I could muster. I could feel Colby's hurt.

Their exit didn't exactly spark conversation. Nadene looked around the room, tired of the small talk – or, really, the lack of any talk at all.

"Okay. I'll bring it up. There is a pretty giant elephant in this room, right? What the actual fuck is up with Al?" She didn't hesitate. "And I DO NOT want to hear it from YOU, Aiden."

Uncle Will joined in, adding, "Indeed. Will someone please fill us in?"

Side-eyes darted around the room, everyone avoiding the question – except Aiden, who looked more than ready to jump in. Thank God Nadene had already ruled him out, because that could have been ugly. Finally, someone stepped up. Of course, it was Goodhands.

"I think I might be the most qualified to explain."

As much as I hated to admit it, he probably was.

"It seems that Al had a huge swath of his memory replaced with a completely different set of memories for the same time period. It wasn't just that he didn't remember Lilly as his daughter, but he had somehow conjured up a memory. A memory that was very real to him, that he had imagined Lilly, and created a sketch of her. In his mind, he did this as a means to bring the sides of the family closer together. My opinion is that this was a reactive mechanism. I believe he knew the family was never going to be a cohesive unit. He saw himself as the hero. And creating this common relative, a daughter, a sister, would be the solution. But, as we know, in reality, Lilly already did exist, and the family was still drifting apart. It was enough to send him over the edge."

Well… what a load of shit that was. Unless he was already shagging Mom, there was nothing wrong with our family. Mom loved Dad very much; I think she always had. Maybe that was what pissed Goodhands off. Thankfully, Tessa was on my side.

"Doesn't this make anyone else want to puke? God, Dr. Whoever, you are sooo transparent." She didn't hold back.

"I beg your pardon, young lady." Goodhands looked insulted.

"You will never be as cool as my Dad, and you don't know anything. All Dad ever does is try to make everyone happy. Maybe he just takes on a little too much. We're lucky to have him. Right, guys?" She looked to our siblings for backup, but got nothing. Crickets.

"Brad? We're lucky to have him as our dad, right? Pam? You like him, don't you?" She kept pushing, desperate for someone to agree. But still, nothing. My baby sis was standing there, all alone, against a room of bullies. She was right, and she knew it.

"Seriously? You guys are too much. I've had enough. Take me home right now. This is just so gross, and Lilly would be ashamed of all of you." She grabbed her coat and stormed out.

Nadene was livid. She yanked Mario up by his collar. "We're leaving. We'll drive that poor girl home. You're all a disgrace. Tessa is right. If I know Lilly at all – and believe me, she told me more than she told any of you – I know she's looking down and crying right now. Wake the fuck up, Bridge. You have a good man, a very good man, and you're pushing him away."

She was spot on. I was looking down, and I was crying. I was getting used to being dead, but I would never, ever get used to my family sucking this bad. Nadene and Mario grabbed their coats and went outside, where they found Tessa pacing back and forth on the road.

"Come on, Tessy. We'll take you home. I've had enough of these assholes for one night."

"Are you sure? Are you okay to drive?" Tessa asked.

"Mario only had one drink, Kiddo. We're good. Your Mom's in Hamilton, right?"

"Yeah. Is that okay?"

"Absolutely. Hop in. Give your mom a call and let her know we're on our way."

Tessa called her Mom and, through tears, told her she was coming home before Brad and Sierra. Nadene and Mario were heroes for her. I tried my best to send them gratitude, but I think Nadene already knew. She could sense me.

Back in the house, things were heating up. Aiden was officially drunk, and far less able to keep his mouth shut. Nick's parents decided they'd had enough drama for one night and announced they were leaving. Mr. Rocher asked Nick if he wanted to come along.

"There's more booze here than at the hotel," Nick replied. "They've got a bed set up for me, Dad. You guys go ahead. I'll call you in the morning."

"Alright, Nicky. Maybe you can be a voice of reason for the family. Everyone's been through way too much." Mr. Rocher offered some solid advice.

After the Rochers left, Uncle Will and his people weren't far behind. Normally, he was a man of all the words, but he was empty that night. His brother, my Daddio, had lost a daughter… and apparently his mind. Difficult times lay ahead, and Uncle Will was wise enough to see that. They left without much of a goodbye.

Mom sat at the dining room table throughout the entire conversation. She was numb from grief… and the wine. Goodhands had kept her glass full, edging closer and closer with each pour. He was so obviously angling to score – with my mom – on the day of my funeral? What a CREEP.

The party had now dwindled down to a few stragglers: Mom and Goodhands, who were practically sitting on each other now, Brad and Sierra, Pam, Aiden, Nicky. Only Brad and Sierra were anywhere near the same postal code as sober. Nicky had been quiet all night, but that was about to change – because Aiden had wound himself as tight as a drum, and he was one hair trigger pull away from the big uncoil.

And…POP.

"You know WHA?? I hade da say dis aboud yer sizder, Brad, bud she is fugged. Your zo-called DAD is the ONLY reason Lilly died. Period. Enn of story. Finido. Goobye."

The difference in size between Brad and Aiden was like comparing the Earth to the moon. Aiden's words were way too big for his tiny self.

"That's about enough of that, Aiden," Brad warned, trying to keep his cool, but Aiden was still unwinding.

"I'm nod kidding. Thing aboud id."

Brad stood, towering over Aiden, who was slouched in his chair.

"I said that's enough, Aiden." His presence was intimidating, but Aiden was still visibly itching to say more.

Pammy tried to break the tension. "Hey, Tessy and I baked a cake! Why don't we all have some for Lill? It's a lily cake for Lilly!" She went to the kitchen.

"Mom, where's the big knife?"

"In the second drawer, Sweetie." Mom spoke for the first time in hours.

Pammy returned with the cake, placing it on the dining room table, near where Mom and Goodhands were sitting. It was a beautiful cake – white and yellow with lilies, and the words "We will miss you, Sweet Lilly." Ohh… I loved my sisters so much.

"Who wants a piece?" She asked, as she started cutting huge slabs. The cake was made to feed fifty people or so. There were only seven left at the party, so it looked like everyone was going to have to dig in.

"I'll have two pieces!" Brad's eyes always lit up when it came to dessert.

"Anyone else?" Pam asked.

"You know whad? Why don't we save the BIGGESS peez fer AL! Everbody LOVES AL. Led AL Eat Cake! Ha. Led him ead cake. Cake for the murderer! Hhhaa." Aiden had lost it now.

That's when shit got real. Nick – My Nicky – sprang from the couch and lunged at my brother. I had never seen him move like that. Mid lunge, he reached behind his back and pulled a pistol out of his belt. Where did THAT come from? It must have been his Dad's, but what the fuck? I couldn't believe that he was packing heat at my funeral. What the hell was he planning to do with a GUN?

He pressed the barrel to Aiden's temple.

"You know who the fucking murderer is, you little piece of shit?" He shouted in my brother's face.

"Whad the FUG, Man. Whad are you DOING?" Aiden shook in disbelief.

"Nicky, Put that gun down right this minute." Mom jumped up, asserting herself, only to fall back into her chair in wine-induced dizziness.

Nick had always known about gun safety. His dad taught him to shoot as a kid, and they kept several guns at home. But I never expected to see my Nicky using one to scare another person, let alone my baby brother. I tried to send him calm and reason, but he was completely closed off from me.

"Nick, come on, Man, you're scaring everyone," Brad urged, stepping toward him.

Nicky pivoted and fired past Brad's head, the bullet missing him by a whisker, hitting the wall behind him. Brad sat down, white as a ghost. Actually, way whiter than me. He looked really white, okay?

"I am NOT trying to scare anyone!" Nicky roared, turning back to Aiden. "I want this little fuck to admit who killed my Lilly." He shoved the gun back to Aiden's temple.

Goodhands jumped out of his chair, attempting to look like he hadn't been drinking wine for hours, and stretched to grab the gun from Nick's hand. He got his ear buzzed by a bullet too. Another hole in Mom's precious wall. Nick wasn't done.

"Everyone will SIT THE FUCK DOWN! Just sit down. Aiden has a story to tell us. He likes to tell stories. DON'T YOU AIDEN? You had to tell YOUR FUCKING SISTER that her Dad didn't know her, DIDN'T YOU?" Nicky was beet red, and boiling mad.

"He DIDN'T know her, Nick. Jeez. Whad wuz I spoza do, Man? Come ON!" Aiden was crying now.

"You could've kept your mouth shut! There was a reason people were protecting her until her dad could figure it out. BUT YOU HAD TO

SPILL, DIDN'T YOU?" Nick was in his face, spit flying with every word. Aiden's face was wet with his own tears and Nick's fury.

"You murdered Lilly, and you're going to say it!"

"Whad da fug, Nick. No. Don't make me say that, Nick. Please."

"SAAAAY IT. 'I MURDERED MY SISTER, LILLY.' Say it or I will blow your fucking head off, Aiden. You know I am crazy enough to do it. SAY IT!"

"Nick, Please." Mom begged.

"SHUT UP, BRIDGET. Your little boy has something he wants to tell you. Don't you Aiden?"

Sierra curled up into Brad. They were both shaking in silence, faces pale. Across the room, Goodhands hadn't fully made it back to his chair. He was kind of frozen in time, but had obviously pissed himself. Classy.

"I can't, Nick," Aiden sobbed.

Nick leveled the gun at Aiden's temple.

"SAY IT OR I PULL THIS TRIGGER, ASSHOLE."

"I....MURDERed...My..." Aiden's voice cracked "AH, fuck, Nick. I can't. I can't fucking say it."

Without hesitation, Nick shifted the barrel just enough, and pulled the trigger. The sound exploded in the room, leaving Aiden screaming in pain and terror. My heart broke, watching the man I loved. He was unrecognizable, transformed into some kind of raging monster. Someone had to stop him – before he did the unthinkable.

"YOU WILL SAY IT OR YOU WILL DI……"

And then… IT happened. Before Nick could get all of those murderous words out, my baby sister – my little Pammy Lou – moved behind him in a blur. The cake knife, still coated in white and yellow icing, sank deep between Nick's ribs. He staggered, his gaze searching for forgiveness, before he fell onto Aiden.

"I'm sorry," he managed to whisper before his body collapsed, lifeless, to the floor.

My Nicky… my fiancé was dead. My ghost heart was shattered. I'd wanted him to live a long and happy life. Now, I could only hope that he might join me, wherever I was.

Goodhands managed to snap out of his scared-shitless deep-freeze long enough to declare, "I can't possibly be associated with this madness." Then he and his piss-soaked scaredy-pants turned tail and ran out the door, further proving his pitiful nature by driving his drunk ass home… from the funeral of a girl who had been killed by a drunk driver.

The ensuing silence was broken by a buzzing sound from the end table near where Nick had been sitting. Brad picked up Nick's phone. "It's from Mr. Rocher," he said, and read aloud.

"Nicky. I left my gun in the glove box. Didn't want to have it at the funeral. It's not there now. You didn't grab it, did you? Let me know, son. Love you, Bud."

Well, that explained where Nicky got the stupid gun. His poor Dad – always so careful.

Mom stared at Pam, her voice trembling. "Pam. Oh, Pammy. What have you done?" She repeated the question over and over again.

Nick's blood was still dripping from the knife in her hand. Pam looked down, head tilted, at her victim. Aiden had very nearly shit himself with fear. He dragged himself to his feet and ran to the loo. Brad and Sierra were still wrapped up in each other, but noticeably less terrified. Brad had the wherewithal to answer Mom's question.

"She saved Aiden's life. That is what she did. Maybe mine, too."

"You're a hero, Pam," Sierra whispered.

That was enough to snap both Mom and Pam out of their shock. Pam dropped the knife, and fell to the floor in tears, rocking herself back and forth for comfort. Mom knelt beside her, wrapping her arms around her.

"We love you, Pammy. You did the right thing. It'll be ok. I promise, it will be ok, Baby Girl."

Mom held Pam like that for a very long time. I wished I could join them in that hug. I loved my Nicky, but he had gone crazy there for a minute. He was very capable of doing serious damage. Pammy did the only reasonable thing a girl with a knife in her hand could do. She eliminated a very real threat. As sad as I was for Nick – and especially for his family – I was proud of my sister.

I know Nicky didn't suffer very long: almost immediately, he was up beside me. I smacked his soul shoulder for almost killing my brother, and for scaring the living shit out of everyone in the room. And the dead shit out of me.

"I am so sorry, Lill. I… I don't know what happened to me. Wow, I've never sobered up so fast. What the fuck? Are we in Heaven? This is wild! I'm with YOU? Looking down at them, and ME. Can you forgive me?" His first words as a dead dude.

Forgiveness felt like a foregone conclusion in this place, wherever we were. I had no real anger or negative feelings at all in me. We shared our first hug in the ever after. It felt very much like this was how it was supposed to be – always together, forever young.

But looking down, we realized there was a very nasty mess left behind, one my family would have to clean up. And I knew what Brad was thinking even before he said it.

"Someone needs to call Dad."

Once again, Daddio would be called upon to make things as right as they could be.

Chapter 20:
The Deepest of Cover

I was a little shocked when my phone rang and I saw that Brad was the caller. I mean, I welcomed the distraction, but I was surprised. Tricia had been kind enough to have her van at the ready to accommodate my escape, but her incessant ramblings about how she could see things that no one else seemed to be able to see, made me question whether I'd made the right choice when I jumped in. Up until when my "confusion" began, I would never have had the time for anyone who wanted to talk about "alternative realities" or "life after death." To me, it was all a load of shit. Even after all I'd been through, I wasn't convinced that any of what I was experiencing was real.

So, when Brad told me that he needed me to come to the house ASAP, with more panic in his voice than I'd ever heard before, I was more than ready.

"I'll get there as soon as I can, Bud. Is everything ok?" I asked.

"No. Everything is most definitely not ok. Please hurry."

"I'm on my way."

I had to interrupt another Tricia story – this one was about how she had pretty much shagged a ghost behind the shed of a haunted house in Campbellville – to ask her to drive me to the house. Without missing a beat, she started the van and hit the road. She headed in the right direction while she finished the story.

"It was quite literally the best fuck I ever had. Kinda wrecked me for the living guys, though. You live near Third Line and Hixon, right?" She asked.

"Uh, ya. Right around there. How'd you know?"

"I told you. I see things. It's a fucking curse most of the time," she explained.

I offered her the final directions to get me home, but I don't think she even needed them. Either she could see things, or she had been stalking me. My curiosity made me ask how she knew about Lilly's funeral.

"Did you know I was going to be at the cemetery today?"

"The night you stayed on my couch, and left before dawn, I knew something was wrong. I could feel a huge shift. But I couldn't see any specifics. It was weird. Something felt blocked, ya know?" She asked, like I might know… I did not know. She continued. "I keep my eye on the obituaries and when I saw Lilly's announcement, it broke my heart. Probably more than it should have. So, I showed up. I didn't know what to expect, but something felt very heavy there. Crazy heavy. It was scary. I was glad to help you get out of there."

We were in front of the house now. I felt obligated to express just how grateful I was for everything she had done that day.

"Thanks so much for saving my ass. That was scary. I just don't get it. I'm still blown away with everything that's happened. Anyway, thank you for everything today, and thanks for the ride here. I appreciate it, Tricia."

"Really, it's nothing at all, Al. Do you want me to wait here for you?" She asked.

"I'm good. It sounds like I'll be a while here. Brad seemed really upset. Thanks though. You have a good night."

She smiled her goodbye and drove away. Through the gigantic, uncovered living room window, I could see some erratic arm flailing. Something definitely wasn't right. I made my way up to the house and opened the door. What I saw when I walked in is something that will be burned into my soul for eternity. Now that I actually believed that to be a thing, I was terrified at the thought.

Aiden was the source of the arm flailing. He was running around the room screaming.

"He was going to fucking KILL me? He was going to KILL ME!"

Nick lay face down in a huge pool of blood, pistol still in hand, just to the left of the chair that sat between the living and dining rooms. Pam sat on the floor, about two feet from Nick's body. Her Mom was right behind her, holding her like she might never let her go. Brad and Sierra were on the couch, clutching each other so tightly they appeared to have morphed into a single being. A huge knife, covered in blood and cake icing, lay next to Nick, looking like something from a scary clown flick. My brain couldn't make any sense of what my eyes were showing it.

"What… exactly happened here, guys?" I thought that was a good place to start. No one seemed capable of an answer, until Pam looked up at me, her eyes wide with panic.

"Am I going to go to jail, Al?" She whispered. "I can't go to jail. Mom, will I be going to jail?" Her voice cracked, as she dissolved into tears, clinging to her mom.

Bridget tried to console her, stroking her hair. "It'll be ok, Pammy. It will be ok. I promise."

Now I was really confused. Did this mean that PAM had killed Nick? PAM?!

"YOU did this, Pam?" I had to ask. She nodded, looking down, and I felt the floor tilt beneath me. "Brad, What the fuck is going on?"

"Basically… It was Aiden. He got hammered and wouldn't stop going off on how you were responsible for Lilly's death, what a loser you are. Tessa stuck up for you, but he kept going. He wouldn't stop."

Brad paused and looked at Aiden, who, by then, had calmed down and now sat staring into space. Aiden broke into tears.

"I am so, so sorry. I don't know why I can't keep my fucking mouth shut. Oh God. I did this too? I… killed them BOTH! Oh My God." Without even finding his mind, he was losing it again – but in a different place now.

"Will someone tell me who did this?" My question snapped Brad back to the moment, and he finished his explanation.

"Tessa went home. Aiden just kept going and going. Nick had enough, I guess. He jumped up and held a gun to Aiden's head. It was crazy." Brad was reliving the moment, shaking his head in disbelief. "I tried to stop him but he shot a bullet right by my head. Dr. Mark tried too.

Same thing. He shot another hole in the wall over there. He was screaming at Aiden to admit that he killed Lilly. Pam was cutting the cake, right by Aiden's chair." He paused, his voice thick. "She took the knife, and she did what she had to do. She's a hero, Dad. She really is."

Bridget nodded, confirming what Brad had told me. I was starting to think that if I was going to be stuck in this reality, it was going to be one unending shit show. I couldn't wrap my head around what I was seeing and hearing. There was a very dead young man on the floor. We had to do something … but what?

I excused myself, hoping that whatever force had pulled me into Lilly's realm earlier might do it again. Nothing happened, so I went downstairs and stared upward, willing my thoughts through the ceiling.

"Are you there, Lill?" I asked, feeling half-crazy as I spoke out loud.

Her voice came back, clear and calm. "I hear you, Daddio. I'm here with Nick. We're catching up a little." What a relief.

"Hey, Nick. So sorry this happened to you. We definitely have a situation down here," I said, not sure what I expected.

There was silence, and I wondered if the connection had cut out. Then Lilly spoke again.

"Daddio? Can't you hear him?"

"Hear who? Nick?"

"Yeah, he responded to you. Can't you hear him? He's still nattering."

"I guess I only get you, Kiddo. Weird. I don't understand these rules. We should file a complaint with management," I said, trying to find a sliver of humour.

Lilly laughed. "HA. Definitely. But you do have a situation down there."

Suddenly, an idea hit me – a crazy, reckless idea – that might just work.

"We do indeed," I said, "but I think I have a solution. Just had a thought. Did you send that?"

"I don't know what you mean, Daddio."

"Okay, Lill. You guys'll have to look after Nick's parents now. This is going to be brutal for them."

"Of course. What's your idea?"

I didn't answer because I wasn't even sure yet. All I knew was that I had come up with something. And whatever it was, I couldn't see a single flaw. I went back upstairs, ready to roll.

The scene was unchanged. Everyone remained where they'd been when I left, and Bridget looked at me, desperate.

"Who were you talking to, Al? What are we going to do?" she asked, her eyes wide with uncertainty.

"I was praying… I have an idea. Give me 20 minutes, then we'll call the police. Okay? Guys, did you hear that? We call in 20 minutes." My voice was firm, allowing no space for hesitation.

We needed to work fast. If we delayed too long, the story would unravel – sitting here with a dead body for hours, without calling the police, would definitely raise some eyebrows. I grabbed the knife, pressing my fingerprints into the blood and icing. The gooey mixture squished through my fingers, sticky and cold… and gross. There was no going back now. Taking a deep breath to steady myself, I gave them precise instructions.

"Here's what happened. I did this. I put the knife in Nick. There will be no argument. No second-guessing. That's how it's going to be," I said, looking each one of them in the eyes until they nodded, relief easing into their faces.

"We'll say I've been… losing it. Insane. Maybe I am," I said, forcing a dry chuckle. "But it makes more sense for me to take the fall than any of you. Understood?" More nods, more relief.

"We'll tell them about the whole Lilly thing – that I didn't know her, that people got upset with me at the burial. We'll have witnesses from the gravesite to back that up."

They looked at each other, then back at me, nodding in agreement. They were buying in.

"I came back here about an hour ago," I continued. "Got that? An hour ago, after most people had left. And I was drunk. Someone bring me the whiskey. It has to look like I was hammered."

Sierra passed me the whiskey, and I guzzled a throat-full. It burned like lava going down, but somehow felt right. A drunken wild man – that's what they'd need me to be.

"Alright, so I came home, drunk. Started yelling and waving the knife around. Screaming that everyone was against me. Threatening. Nick grabbed his gun to protect you guys. I tricked him into relaxing, long enough for me to snatch the gun. I started firing shots around the room, barely missing you guys."

Using my left hand, I grabbed the gun from Nick's very dead fingers. My right hand was occupied by the knife, and needed some more blood on it. I lay my right forearm across Nick's back. The scene still looked untouched, and there was now enough blood on me to make it look almost believable that I had done this.

I knew absolutely nothing about guns, but I had seen on TV that when you fire one, there is residue on your hand. I needed that residue. I took another glug from the whiskey bottle. A bullet had to come from the gun while it was in my hand. I fired one more shot into Bridget's precious wall. BANG. The sound cracked the air, but what a rush! Puffed up with adrenaline, my confidence swelled.

"Brad," I barked, "grab a wet paper towel, with some dish soap on it. Wipe down Nick's gun hand. Make sure it looks clean. That hand wasn't in the blood, so it shouldn't look like we changed anything."

Brad moved quickly, working with steady precision. I was grateful for my boy.

"Ok. Listen up. Here's what went down," I said, addressing my troops. "After I fired the gun, Nick and Brad jumped in to stop me. I reacted on instinct – stuck the knife in Nick's back, before my brain clued in. Brad, you grabbed me, threw me down into this chair, and held me there. Nick died a hero here tonight, defending you guys. Burn that into your brains. DO YOU ALL UNDERSTAND?"

They nodded in unison, their faces pale but obedient. I turned to Aiden, the weakest link. He reeked of whiskey and beer, and his eyes were glassy with confusion.

"Aiden, you were passed out in your room. Do you hear me? YOU SAW NOTHING."

"I understand, Al. I'm so sorry. I'm so fucking sorry," he slurred.

"Aiden!" I snapped, grabbing his face in both hands. "YOU ARE NOT SORRY. YOU WERE PASSED OUT. You saw NOTHING."

It took a moment, but a flicker of comprehension crossed his face.

"Got it. Copy that," he said, wobbling on his feet.

"Good. Now go lie down. Get under the covers. Get your booze stink all over the pillow. Go. Now."

He stumble-marched to his room like a good little soldier boy.

Then, I noticed the first flaw in my plan. Pam had blood on her, a substantial amount of blood. Her Mom did too, from holding her. There was no point in trying to clean that up. There wasn't time.

"Pam, I am so sorry, but I need you to do some fake CPR on Nick. Can you do that?" I asked. It was a necessity. Without that, Pam was guilty.

"What? NO. I can't touch him. MOM. PLEASE. PLEEEAASSE. NO," she pleaded.

It was too much to ask. The poor girl was still in shock, trapped in a living nightmare. Bridget had a suggestion.

"I'll do the CPR. I'm the nurse here. It would have been me doing it anyway. Then I can hold Pam again. That would explain the blood on her," she offered.

"That's perfect. Is that OK, Pam?" I asked. She nodded in agreement. We had our gameplan.

Pam went to wash the blood off her hands, and Bridget got to work doing fake CPR on a dead guy. The hollow thud of her hands against his chest almost made me lose the minimal contents of my gut. I took another swig of whiskey, to push everything back down, and turned back to the others.

"Brad, your job is to keep an eye on me. I'll be sitting right there, in shock, unable to comprehend what I've done. Okay, Sierra, you call 911 now. Do it NOW!" I laid out the last element of the plan.

Sierra took out her phone and dialed 911. She had it on speaker.

"911. What's your emergency?"

Sierra played the part perfectly. Her acting experience came in handy. She was frantic.

"There has been a MURDER. OH MY GOD. Our friend is DEAD. Please, please come right away."

The emergency operator took the rest of the information. Sierra was spot on. She had probably been waiting to make that call since the moment Nick was killed. It turned out that Brad was the one who convinced everybody else to wait for me to get there. My boy had some faith in me after all.

"You're a hero too, Dad," he said, quietly, his voice full of something close to pride.

Aiden had stumbled back into the room. "You are a hero, Al. I'm zo zorry. Aboud everthing."

Even Bridget softened. "Sweetie, this is a huge sacrifice. I can't thank you enough. I am so sorry it came to this."

I nodded, feeling the weight of their gratitude settle on my shoulders. Then one last detail struck me.

"Where's Goodhands now?" I asked.

Sideways glances from every set of eyes in the room did not answer my question. But then... a voice from beyond.

"Ohhh, forgot to mention that, Daddio! Goodhands couldn't run away fast enough. He tried to play the hero until Nicky nearly shot him. Then, he peed himself, and turned tail as soon as it was safe to move."

No one else could hear Lilly, but it looked like they all understood that I had pieced that little mystery together.

"Bridget. It's your job to call him. You tell him he left hours ago. He saw nothing. Okay? He saw not a single thing."

Bridget made her call. Within minutes, the driveway was lit up with relentless red and blue strobes, casting shifting shadows across the living room. When the police arrived, Bridget noted in a soft, disbelieving whisper that it was the same two officers who had come in the middle of the night to break the news about Lilly.

The officers wasted no time. They began asking questions, and Brad stepped forward, delivering the story I'd given him with a calm, steady confidence, making his old man proud.

"Is this true, Mr. Isaac?" the big one – Officer Robertson – asked, his voice stern and probing, like we'd better be telling the truth.

I nodded. The whiskey was hitting me harder now, dulling my edges, but not enough to make me forget my role in this act.

The lady officer, Andersen, turned to the others. "Did you all see this happen like Brad described?"

They nodded one by one, except for Aiden, who played his role perfectly.

"I was passed out the whole time," he said, his voice a little slurred but surprisingly convincing.

Other officers and detectives moved methodically through the house, collecting evidence. They bagged the knife and the gun. They snapped pictures of Nick, of the bullet holes, of everything. I watched as they bent down to retrieve the bullets, each one feeling like another nail in my coffin, but I was strangely glad to finally see some imperfections in these walls.

When the paramedics loaded Nick's lifeless body into the ambulance, they pronounced him dead at the scene. It was a heavy moment, but I was in an almost dream-like state… and getting drunker by the minute.

The detectives started taking individual statements in the kitchen, pulling each person aside for a semblance of privacy. I couldn't hear what they were saying, but I didn't need to. I knew they'd stick to the story.

Then Robertson and Andersen turned their attention to me.

"You're going to have to come with us, Sir," Robertson said, without judgment. "Please stand up and turn around."

Officer Andersen cuffed me loosely. It was a formality; she knew I was no flight risk. She took me by the elbow, guiding me to the cruiser, while Robertson followed close behind.

Outside, the flashing lights had drawn a crowd. Neighbours stood on their porches and lawns, their faces illuminated by the swirling red and blue glow. I felt their eyes boring into me, their silent judgments loud and clear. It wouldn't be long before the neighbourhood tongue waggers would let the world know about Crazy AL Isaac.

When we reached the car, Andersen pushed my head down and tucked me into the back seat.

"We're going to have to take you down to the station, Mr. Isaac," she said, her tone clipped but not unkind. "You shouldn't make any plans for a while. You won't be going anywhere anytime soon, my friend."

The door slammed shut, and for the first time since I walked into that living room, the weight of the whole situation settled on me. Strangely relieved, I leaned back against the seat, and closed my eyes.

It was done. I had, maybe, regained an ounce of respect from my family, and they were safe. That was all that mattered.

Chapter 21:

Shrink Wrap

Sixteen sessions with Dr. Redwood – five per week, give or take – had yielded virtually nothing. At least, not from my perspective. I would talk. She would listen, or pretend to listen, raising an eyebrow here, nodding there. Occasionally, she'd jot something down in her notepad. Or doodle. I couldn't tell from where I sat. Too far to peek, and I wasn't about to ask.

This morning's meeting would finally wrap up the story of how I landed at Juravinski. Maybe once I finished, she'd offer me… oh, I don't know, a suggestion? An explanation? A bullet?

Herman had already delivered my breakfast, like clockwork. He was machine-like in his punctuality. Like every other morning, I had just enough time to eat my breakfast before he reappeared to escort me on our near daily pilgrimage to Dr. Redwood's office. I knew the way perfectly well, but I think he enjoyed passing by his young lady friend behind the desk every chance he could get.

As usual, Dr. Redwood's office door was wide open, waiting for me. Herman made the exact same hand gesture every single time, as if I might forget where to go if he didn't. I had claimed the chair – I sat in it every day. It had an imprint of my scrawny ass right there on the seat.

The good doctor always liked to make an entrance. She'd usually keep me waiting about five minutes before strolling in with her folder and her calm, measured smile. But this morning was different. Five minutes passed, then six, then nine. I started to feel uncomfortably exposed in the silence of her office. Just as I was about to fidget my way into a full-blown panic, she walked in and greeted me.

"Good morning, Allan. How are you doing today?"

"I'm good. Looking forward to finishing my little story for you. Maybe we can discuss a plan after that?" I wasn't asking so much as pleading.

"Absolutely. I wanted to ask you something before we get started, though. Is that ok?" She asked. Maybe she was so enthralled by my captivating storytelling ability that she was going to ask me to tell her another one.

"Sure. I'm game. Ask away."

"Lilly. Have you been able to communicate with her at all since you've been with us?"

So much for my budding career as a storyteller. I wasn't surprised. I had been expecting that question since the first time I told her about the nature of my contact with Lilly.

"Not since I have been here, no. I figure she's been busy with Nick's family, or she's disowned me. Or… the meds have blocked our contact. I don't know. But I haven't been able to talk with her."

In my heart, I knew it was the meds. For the past few days, I'd been secretly flushing my pills. Whatever force field they were putting up between me and Lilly, I wanted it gone. If I was going to be stuck in this place, I at least wanted to be able to chat with her, now that I knew her a little bit.

Dr. Redwood took a little longer than normal to jot – or doodle – in her notebook.

"Ok. Perfect. How do you feel about that? Are you feeling a little more at peace not having to maintain a link with… another realm?" Wow. She was getting deep on me.

"Uh, I don't know about that," I replied. "Lilly was my closest ally there, for a bit. No one else has visited me either. I don't really have a link with any realm now."

"I understand. Contact is important. I'm sure you'll have visitors soon."

"I hope so, Sarah. You and Herman are nice and everything, but …"

She offered only the slightest, polite laugh.

"Fair enough. So, back to your story. The police had just picked you up. That's where we left off. What do you remember happening after that?"

I took a deep breath. "After they stuffed me into the back of the cruiser, the whiskey hit me like a freight train. I couldn't focus. I kept repeating in my head that I was the killer. That I stabbed Nick with one hand and fired the gun with the other. But the details… they started slipping away. Everything got hazy. Opaque hazy, like the morning Pam drove me to the hospital."

I paused, shaking my head. "I could barely hold my head up, let alone keep my story straight. But apparently, I did a good enough job convincing the cops that I was already drunk when I got home. They bought it. Said it made sense that my memory was fuzzy. Everyone else in the family told the same story, too. I guess I made a decent drill sergeant after all."

I looked at her, searching for a reaction. She just nodded, pen poised over her notepad.

"The police were satisfied with my confession," I continued. "So, as far as I can remember, that's how it went down. I spent a couple days in jail, then they sent me here. The first few days were a blur, and then I started coming to see you. That's how I got here."

"Wow. That is quite a story, Mr. Isaac. Truly amazing. All of it. How do you feel about it all, looking back now?" she asked.

Maybe we were getting somewhere.

"I feel like if I could go back to my normal life, that'd be good. But, I can't unsee what I've seen, ya know? I'm not sure I belong anywhere now. Maybe it's best that I'm here."

That was the crux of it. When my confusion first started, the pull of the Beast dictated my every move. By now, I had managed to banish that fucker from the workings of my mind, but without him, I was kind of rudderless. I had more or less accepted that this was reality, and that I had been saddled with a very serious mental health issue. But I didn't want their medication. It seemed I possessed some kind of superpower to talk with dead people and stuff. There was something to be said for that.

"I understand. That must be hard," she said, genuinely sympathetic. "I think what we're going to focus on is getting you to a point where you feel at home, where you can come to terms with your surroundings. Does that make sense?" She asked.

That seemed like a perfect plan, but the reality was that I would likely be locked up for a very long time. I wasn't about to feel all cozy at a psychiatric hospital. My best hope was for a moderately tolerable existence, until I could quietly go to sleep and never wake up. My family were doing the right thing by distancing themselves. It made our whole story that much more believable. Still, it made for a pretty lonely existence. I couldn't even get Herman to play Scrabble with me.

General gameplan established, Dr. Redwood sent me back to my room to ponder next steps. Herman was waiting for me when the door opened.

"Good session Mr. Isaac?" Same question, every time.

"I finished my story. Now, maybe we can get something done."

"That's good, Mr. Isaac."

He wasn't listening – he almost never listened – but I didn't mind. I felt like I had talked more in the last few weeks than one fellow should ever have to talk. I thought it might be nice if I could be the listener for once, but Herman was a very quiet dude. If I wanted to find someone to talk to me, I would have to look elsewhere.

When we got back to my room, I waved Herman off and closed my door. I wanted to give Lilly another try.

"Testing, testing. Paging Lilly Isaac. Lilly Isaac to the Psych Ward." I sent my call out into the ether.

Nothing. Nada.

"Oh, well. I'll keep trying," I mumbled under my breath.

It would be lunch time soon anyway. I didn't want to talk to my ghosty daughter with my mouth full. That would be rude.

Herman delivered my tray not long after. I'd grown to love the food here. Better than cooking and cleaning for myself, that was for sure. The salads, in particular, were excellent. Today's lunch was a turkey sandwich with cheddar, mustard, and pepper – just how I liked it – and a salad of spinach, arugula, apple, avocado, walnuts, and goat cheese. The dressing? Sinfully good. Honey mustard base with what I could only assume were some secret psychiatric herbs and spices. I couldn't quite place them, but they were delicious. And they made me very sleepy.

Shit. If they're drugging the food, I'll have to starve myself if I ever want to talk to Lilly again.

That was my last thought before I stretched out for my daily afternoon siesta. Most days after lunch at Juravinski, I crashed hard. There wasn't much else to do, and that salad dressing? Practically horse tranquilizer. Today was no exception. I was out – cold. I didn't know for how long, but I was gone.

My wake-up was usually a gradual process – blinking myself back into the world bit by bit. But this time? Different story.

BANG BANG BANG.

The knock on the door thundered through my head, jolting me from my peaceful nap.

"Mr. Isaac, you have company. Security just notified me." Herman's voice followed the knock, softer than the racket he'd just made.

"Company? What the fuck? I don't get company." I sat up, rubbing my eyes, more confused than ever.

"A fellow named Marvin is on his way. He just checked in at security. Okay? Are you good to see him?"

"Marvin? Marvin Carol? Holy shit. Absolutely. I'll see Marvin."

I shook the cobwebs from my sleepy brain. I was shocked that I had any visitors, but… Marvin? We had never been all that close, and HE was my first company in a month? Not that I was complaining – I would take what I could get. Besides, he was a great guy, and he clearly knew stuff. Every time I had talked with him, I felt like I walked away with a little more clarity.

Protocol dictated that visitors would check in with security, and then take the long walk to the inmate/patient's ward. It felt like only seconds had passed since Herman had knocked, and he was back.

"Mr. Isaac. Marvin is here."

I opened the door to let my friend in.

"Hey, Brother! Thanks so much for coming. How the fuck are you?" I gave him a bear hug, kind of like I hadn't seen a friendly face in a month.

"Al. I'm good. Better than you, Man. What the hell. Dude? What happened?"

I knew the question was coming, but I wanted him to talk, dammit. I needed updates, wisdom, the world beyond these walls. Still, I answered.

"What happened? Shit very firmly hit the fan, Brother. That's what happened." It was the best explanation I could offer.

"You made ripples, my friend. Fucking waves! Tsunamis, Dude. You made tsunamis. Jesus. People DIED Al." He laughed, like it was some kind of joke.

"I made them? ME?" My voice rose, defensive.

"I'm not saying you did it consciously but, dude, if you don't make the jump here, those kids are still alive and planning their wedding."

Ouch. Fuck. I knew he was right, but it hurt. It's not like I wanted to make this jump.

"That is true," I admitted, with a deep sigh. "But I am doing my penance here. That's the best I can do, I guess."

"You are. So, what's going on here? They got you all drugged up?" He knew how these places worked.

"They give me pills. I don't know what they are. I have been flushing them the last few days, but I think the food is laced too."

"Yeah, it probably is. Why have you been flushing? The pills aren't helping?" he asked.

"Well, you won't believe what's been happening. So strange."

"Oh, I would believe it, Brother," he smirked. "I'd believe anything. You jumped here from another reality, Man. What could be more 'out-there' than that?" He had a point.

What did I have to lose? Marvin might even be able to help me, somehow. So, I told him.

"It started the night of our show. The New Year's show. Just as we were going on stage – after you'd finished – we were walking up the stage stairs, and all of a sudden, I'm out of body, Man. I shit you not. I was floating above the room, watching myself on the stage. It was a trip."

"That IS pretty wild, Man. I get it, though. Were you in control after that?" He spoke like someone familiar with the concept.

"No fucking way. The Beast was just popping me up and down. One second I'm on stage, the next I'm watching myself on stage. It totally messed with my senses. I didn't know Appalachian Man. Not at all. I watched some other version of myself sing that. It was crazy."

"Interesting. Go on," he urged.

"Well, that was that. It didn't happen again until Lilly's funeral. One minute, I am standing at her coffin, apologizing to her dead body for not knowing her, the next I am up there again." I pointed to the ceiling. "Only this time, I'm not alone. Lilly is right there with me! I GOT TO MEET HER! What the fuck is that?" I was reliving the shock. "Not only that, but from that point on, Lilly could communicate with me. Like I had a fucking earpiece in. She could talk to me!"

"Holy shit, Al! That is cool. So, she was experiencing her own funeral? In real time?"

"She was right there. Making me laugh, She's hilarious, Man. A really funny kid."

"Wow, Brother. Seriously, that is pretty wild stuff. Are you still able to talk with her?"

"That's the problem. Not since I've been in here. I am convinced it's the meds. That's why I've been flushing them. If I'm stuck here, I'd at least like her company."

"Shit, Man. Brutal. That is fucking brutal. You have to be able to talk with her. I bet it is the meds. That stuff takes everything away. It's fucked."

He paused, his eyes narrowing like he was hatching a plan. "You know what? I know what to do. Here. Take this." He handed me a capsule.

"What is it?" I asked. I didn't want to make things worse for myself.

"Totally natural, Brother. Special mushroom. It opens your brain. Their shit closes you off. Trust me. It won't hurt you. It won't bite back."

I believed him. He had a wisdom that was beyond what the "professionals" had. I took the pill.

"Just see what happens. See if Lilly comes back. Even if they are drugging your food, this'll even the playing field."

It sounded promising. I was up for the experiment.

"Will it take a while to kick in?" I asked.

"Depends. Might make you sleepy though. But, what else do you have to do? Ha. You're just sitting around anyway, right?"

Everything made me sleepy. Whatever. Small price to pay if it worked.

We chatted a bit longer before the pill started to take hold. My eyelids grew heavier by the second.

"You're looking pretty tired, Man. I'd best be off. I'll check in soon. Do you have somewhere you can hide a few more of those capsules?" he asked.

"For sure. I can find somewhere in here. Thanks so much for visiting, Marvin. I really appreciate the help."

We said our goodbyes, and he was off. The thought of sleeping the day away was appealing. First things first, though – I had to find a good hiding place for the pills. They never inspected anything, but that might have been because I never had any visitors. I looked around the room and realized it wasn't exactly full of discreet nooks and crannies. I had some clothes in the closet, but that would be the first place they would look if they did inspect. AH! My shoes. I had an extra pair of shoes that I hadn't worn yet. They had a removable insole, so I just pulled one up, and stashed the three pills that Marvin had given me in there. I flattened the insole and – Voila! Done. Unless they sent a sniffer dog in, I was golden.

Satisfied, I crawled back into bed and drifted off almost immediately. This time, it wasn't a knock that woke me. It was Herman, shaking me frantically.

"Mr. Isaac, wake up! You've been asleep for hours! It's dinner time."

"Uhh, sorry Buddy. I'm just super sleepy," I mumbled, trying to force my eyes all the way open.

"No kidding! If I didn't know better, I'd think your friend slipped you something!" Herman joked.

"Ha. Very funny. I think maybe I am a bit under the weather," I said, hoping to allay any genuine suspicion.

"I thought maybe that was the case. You didn't even hear me knocking – I had to break in. Do you think you can eat? I can bring your dinner now, if you want."

I was starving. The shrooms made me sleepy, and the sleep made me hungry.

"Sure, Buddy. I can eat."

He wasn't gone more than a minute before he returned with my tray. I told him to hold the salad. If they were indeed lacing my food, I was certain that was where the drugs were. Dinner was meatloaf, mashed potatoes, and four carrot sticks, with an apple for dessert.

I ate like a man possessed. The plate was clean in a matter of seconds. The poor apple didn't stand a chance.

"Everything tasting ok Mr. Isaac?" Herman asked.

I couldn't answer with a mouth full of Granny Smith.

"Oh my God, you're finished already?" He was in disbelief.

"I am. It was good."

"You sure you don't want some salad, if you're that hungry?" He had a point, but I wasn't buying.

"I'm good, Buddy. Thanks. I think I'll just read for a bit."

"Alright Mr. Isaac. Enjoy!"

Herman had grabbed a book from the library for me – Moular, by Michelle Morra. He had read it and said it was fantastic. It was the story of a nasty British woman who had emigrated to Canada to be nasty here. It sounded far more believable than the shit that I'd been through. That was about the extent of the contraband that had been offered to me until Marvin came with his magic pills.

I hadn't started the book yet, so I figured now was the perfect time. But as I lay back down and cracked it open, I realized I should try reaching out to Lilly again. Maybe Marvin's pill had worked its magic and opened the channel.

"Paging Lilly Isaac. Lilly Isaac to the Crazy Dad Ward," I said out loud, hopeful.

I waited a minute or two and tried again.

"Come on, Lill. I hope you can hear me, and it's just my receptors that are blocked. I guess this is how you felt when I wouldn't call or text you back. I'm so sorry, Kiddo. I wish I could've just accepted things. I'm truly sorry, Lilly. Hugs. Daddio."

It was more like a prayer than a call up. If that was my only way to communicate with her, it would have to do. That's how billions of other people, throughout the ages, have communicated with their deceased loved ones. I never had, because I was positive no one was listening. Now, I wasn't so sure of that. As a matter of fact, I could almost sense that she could hear me, or at least get the message later.

I waited just a little while longer before I gave up and went back to the book. I didn't even get to page one before I was interrupted again by a knock on the door.

"Mr. Isaac?" Herman's voice carried a note of hesitation, like he wasn't sure if I'd be home.

"Yes, Herman. I'm here." Where else would I be?

"Mr. Isaac, you have more visitors. They've checked in at security."

"Seriously? Who's here now?" My curiosity spiked. Maybe my family had decided I'd been ostracized long enough.

"I'm not sure, Mr. Isaac. I didn't catch their names. They'll be here in a couple of minutes."

Who the hell could it be? So strange. I'd been in this place a month without a peep from the outside world, and now two separate visits in one day? Someone was trying to tell me something, but damned if I knew what.

The knock came sooner than expected.

Knock Knock

"Mr. Isaac, your friends are here," Herman politely announced, and opened the door.

I stood up to greet my visitors, but when I saw them… I fainted.

Blam. Flat out on the floor.

I awoke to the sharp stink of smelling salts, with Herman gently slapping my cheek.

"Mr. Isaac? Are you ok? He hasn't been feeling himself today," he explained to my guests.

"I'm ok, Herman. Thanks."

I brought myself to a seated position, and took a look at my guests again. If I could have fainted a second time, I likely would have.

"Hi, Allan." My sister, Lana, spoke to me, in a clearer voice than I had heard from her in decades. "Are you ok?"

I couldn't answer her. She was standing in front of me, dressed like she had just come from work. Her lush hair was salon worthy. Her skin was clear. She looked fit. In my reality, her schizophrenia had prevented her from working for the last thousand years and had robbed her of her natural beauty.

Even more confusing than Lana being there, was the fellow standing next to her. It was my brother, Rick.

IT. WAS. MY. BROTHER. RICK.

As I said, it was my brother, Rick. The thing is, if you recall… the thing is, my brother, Rick had been dead lo these twenty plus years. And yet… and YET, HE WAS STANDING RIGHT IN FRONT OF ME, his brown eyes still intense and clear. His full head of hair and his beard were mostly grey now. In my reality, he died before his hair had a chance to go grey. I'd never even imagined him older than 37.

"Bro. You good? You Ok?" His voice as sharp and familiar as ever.

I couldn't speak. I threw my arms around him like… well, like he was my dead brother, come back to life.

"Dude. What the hell? You look like you've seen a ghost, for fuck sakes. It hasn't been THAT long." He laughed.

Herman brought in an extra chair for Lana while Rick took a seat in the one by the desk. I sat on the edge of my bed, staring at my guests – still unable to speak.

"I'm so sorry about Lilly, Allan. Nick too. It's just so sad. What happened? Why didn't you call us about the funeral?" Lana asked.

I stared back. Then I got up and hugged Rick again. Then I hugged Lana. Then I hugged Rick. Then I hugged Lana. They both laughed. That was enough to allow me to speak.

"Uh, I don't know, Lan. Will was in charge of calling people. I've been struggling lately," I explained.

"I got Will's message a day late. I can be tough to get hold of. I'm so sorry I missed it, Bro. So sorry," Rick lamented.

"I did too," Lana added. "To be honest, I don't know if I could have made it anyway. I've been having trouble keeping staff lately. I have to work nonstop."

My brain was on overload. Was this a dream? Was this some weird, mushroom induced hallucination? I was pretty sure that a hallucination was not a huggable thing. Shit, if I had known Rick was alive in this reality, and that Lana had a normal life (with a JOB and everything), I likely would have figured out a way to stay weeks ago.

"Where are you working, Lan?" I asked. I was trying to remember the last time she had a job in my reality. I couldn't.

"What? You know where I work. I manage Giant Tiger on Upper Ottawa. I've been there forever. Jeez. You really aren't feeling well, are you?

Wow. Lana was managing a store. She was a boss? This was just too cool.

"Right. Shit. I'm sorry. And how about you, Man? What's… uh, what's new?" I asked Rick.

"Same shit, different day. Just trying my best to spend time with my family, like you. Business is good though. Lots of jobs."

He owned a business? In my reality, before he died, he was a dreamer – a schemer. Looking for an easy buck, without a stitch of work ethic in his entire being.

"That is very cool, Brother. It is so good to see you guys. Really. You've made my month." I was over-the-moon. I hadn't felt joy like this in…. well, ever.

"It's just such a shame about Lilly and Nick. So sad. They were so perfect," Lana said, tearing up.

I had to be mindful of the fact that, for Rick and Lana, this was a somber visit. For me – I got my brother and sister back. How was I supposed to be sad? But, they had no way of knowing that. They expected a father, mourning the loss of his little girl.

"What happened with Nick, Bro?" Rick asked. "I know that's why you're in here, but that doesn't sound like you."

"Everything is not as it seems. I can tell you that, for sure. I can't go into too much detail, but Lilly was worried about my mental health. The accident happened when they were rushing home to see me. The truth about Nick is… a little more complicated. Let's just say, I'm happy to take all the blame."

I thought that was a fair explanation. I wasn't abdicating responsibility, but I was letting them know that maybe I wasn't the monster that our story made me out to be.

Our conversation shifted, becoming more natural… more familiar. We reminisced about childhood, dredging up old stories that made us laugh until our sides hurt.

Like the time we were playing football on the cul-de-sac in front of our house. Rick, being the oldest, was quarterback. He instructed Will to "Run ten steps and turn around, the ball will be there!" Will took about 8 steps. Rick fired the football. After two more steps, Will turned around just in time to make the catch… with his face!

Lana recalled a prank I once played on her, when she was babysitting Will and me. I'd shoved a cardboard tube from a roll of toilet paper down the back of my pajama pants, convincing her I'd shit myself. She freaked out so badly, she called the restaurant where Mom and Dad were eating, begging them to come home.

For a little while, it was like old times. The best surprise I'd ever had. I didn't want them to leave, but visiting hours are limited for crazy murderers. After about an hour, Herman returned.

"I'm sorry, Mr. Isaac, but it's time for your guests to go."

I held back tears as I stood to hug them both again.

"This has been a wonderful visit, guys. I can't thank you enough for coming. I really hope we can do this again. Maybe I won't be stuck in here forever. Who knows, right?"

"You'll get out of here, Bro. For sure," Rick said, with his customary over-confidence.

"Yes, you will, Allan. We'll have a big Isaac party when you do. Just know that Mom and Lilly are looking down on you, Allan. They're proud of you. I am too." Lana sounded like… Lana. She had the sweetest heart.

We said our goodbyes with a family hug. It was all I could do to not cry. I failed – I cried anyway. It was so hard to see them go.

Just as they were walking out the door, Rick stopped.

"Oh, shit. I almost forgot. I owed you one of these!"

He reached deep into the pocket of his charcoal grey overcoat and pulled out a CD. The Drive By Truckers, Decoration Day. In my reality, Rick could never afford to buy Christmas or birthday gifts. I had a stack of handmade cards from him, from years and years of holidays, that all said the same thing – "I owe you one album of your choice." Until that very moment, he had never made good on that promise.

"That's the one you wanted, right?" he asked.

"You have no idea how much that means to me, Rick. No idea at all."

I hugged him again, tighter than ever. Like I hadn't seen him in a lifetime. Like I may never see him again.

I hoped with all of my being that our visit had been real. If Marvin's mushrooms were potent enough to pull that off, that was terrifying. It certainly felt real. It brought a certain peace to me that I hadn't felt since I had been on this side of reality – and it felt good.

Even after all the sleeping and fainting I did that day, I was still tired. I had finished my story with Dr. Redwood, and we had a loose plan on how to move forward. Marvin had surprised me with a visit, and had given me something that might help me reconnect with Lilly. And, my dead brother came, very much alive, to visit me with our schizophrenic sister who appeared to not be schizophrenic at all. Considering where I was, that counted as just about the most perfect day possible. It couldn't get much better. But, it did.

"Daddio? Can you hear me?" The voice of an angel in my ear.

"Lill? Is that you?" I asked.

"It's me. I've been watching. That was the most amazing visit. Nick and I just loved watching you with Uncle Rick and Auntie Lana. It was beautiful."

"Wow. You could see all that? They aren't quite the same, back where I come from. Not at all," I explained.

"I gathered that. Is Uncle Rick dead there, or something?"

"Yes he is. Not long after you would have been born, Lill. And Lana… she's schizophrenic. It was so amazing to see them like this."

"Wow. No wonder you were surprised. That IS amazing. I'm glad you can hear me now, Dad. I thought I had lost you… again!"

"I'm glad too, Kiddo. Could you hear me when I was calling out to you?"

"Absolutely, Daddio. I can hear everything. You throw it, I catch it. 'Take ten steps and turn around. The ball will be there!'" She burst into laughter. "Oh my God. I love that story."

"That makes me happy, Lilly. I'm going to go to sleep now, ok? Keep an eye on me. Don't let the monsters get me!"

"Goodnight, Daddio, sweet dreams. I love you."

"I love you too. Thanks, Lill, Goodnight to you and Nick."

I had my Lilly back. Wow. That was a very surreal thought. I knew now that I would be happier in this reality than in the other one. Even if I couldn't always be in contact with Lilly, I could be confident that she would be ok, and that she would hear me if I talked to her.

In my mind, I made a rough pros-and-cons list of hanging out in Reality #2. The cons were pretty heavy: I had a dead daughter, and I was in crazy jail for offing her fiancé. Also, my lady friend was likely shagging the dude who was supposed to be my shrink. They were big cons. But the pros? The pros were convincing.

1) Chip Wagon had a hit song? And a record deal?

2) I had made contact with said dead daughter, and we were better than good.

3) Lana was healthy!

4) RICK WAS ALIVE!

5) The food in here was pretty good.

6) Marvin's shrooms.

7)   My kids, and Bridget's kids, thought I was a hero.

Those were pretty sweet pros.

Right then, I made a decision: I would do whatever it would take to make the doctors feel like I was capable of being a normal human being again. I wanted to get out of there. Even if it took a few years, I was determined to at least try to embrace my new home, and maybe even enjoy it.

For the first time since Christmas Eve, despite all that had happened, I went to sleep with a sense of peace. Hope, even.

I allowed myself a hint of confidence that everything might turn out just swell.

Chapter 22:
Mama, I'm Comin' Home

Despite how tired I was, the excitement of my visits – and reconnecting with Lilly – made me too excited to fall asleep. I basked in the afterglow of the day for a long time before my joy finally allowed me to nod off. Once I did, I was out. Big time.

I don't know how long I had been asleep when something very strange happened: I was dreaming. In and of itself, for me, that was weird. I was markedly more aware of my dream than I had been for years. It was almost like I was actually conscious in my dream. I thought it might be Marvin's shrooms allowing this weird, subconscious cognizance.

At first, it was surreally pleasant. Dream Al was wandering around in some kind of fairytale land, where everything was brightly coloured and oversized. Trees stretched a thousand feet tall, and the moon looked as though it was orbiting dream Earth at a distance of maybe three miles. Massive boulders lined the path that I was on, and the giant leaves on the trees glowed with dazzlingly brilliant colours. A trillion stars lit the night sky almost as brightly as the midday sun.

I walked along the path, completely content and comfortable in my dream surroundings, until I nearly tripped on something. Looking down, I realized that I was standing on a railway track – a gigantic railway track, at least five times the size of a normal one. The ties were more than a yard thick, and the rails looked like giant, metal roads.

Then, I felt the ground rumble beneath my feet. A train was coming! What a sight this would be – a train the size of a cruise ship flying right by. This was the coolest dream ever! But I was on the tracks. How far away from the tracks would I have to be to avoid being smooshed by this thing?

I soon discovered that was an irrelevant question. I was stuck. It was like my feet were glued to the tracks; there was no way I could move. *Good thing this is a dream!*

The rumbling grew into an earthquake-like shake. Then I saw the light – a second moon, barreling toward my stuck ass. The train seemed to be traveling at light speed, almost too massive for even my dream brain to comprehend. I was as insignificant as an ant in its path.

I kept thinking I was going to wake up. I knew it was a dream, but the intensity of it had my heart pounding. Dream Me could not resist the need to move. I had to get off the tracks. The train was getting closer and closer. Despite its blistering speed, it felt almost like slow motion, like it was coming from another galaxy. But my feet wouldn't budge. I braced my dream self for the inevitable impact. It was imminent. The light grew larger, brighter – blinding. My heart pounded as though it would burst from my chest. I was drenched in sweat. The ground trembled beneath me, as if the earth itself were about to explode. The train whistle screamed, splitting the air, just before impact.

BOOM

The collision unfolded frozen flashes, frame by frame. I felt an unfathomable pain, like every bone in my body was shattered by a sledgehammer all at once. My vision filled with blinding light as my dream body splintered, fragments of me flying in every direction. Why couldn't I wake up? Then I heard a voice – scared, screaming.

"DADDY!"

And, just like that, I was awake. I felt like I had been hit by a train. My pj's were sticking to my chest, my head pounding, the pain practically paralyzing.

"Lilly? That was you, right?" I asked, still trying to catch my breath. "Lill? It's ok. I'm awake now."

Damn. If Marvin's shrooms would give me dreams like that, maybe I'd have to reconsider. But, the ache in my head would not let up. It was relentless, excruciating. It felt like it hurt too much to even hear Lilly if she responded. I pulled myself up, and walked out to the desk, hoping to find something that might ease the pain.

"Hi. I don't recognize you," I said to the girl behind the desk.

"I'm night staff, Mr. Isaac. Everyone is asleep when I work," she replied.

"Makes sense. I have a terrible headache. Is there something I can take? This is brutal." The pain was so intense I could hardly see.

"Absolutely. Give me just a minute."

She stepped into the office and returned with three pills that looked like Tylenol. If they were extra strength, that might be enough to make a dent. She handed them to me along with a little cup of water.

"Thank you so much. I appreciate this."

"You're welcome, Mr. Isaac. Hopefully you can get back to sleep. I see you have a big day tomorrow?"

"Thanks again."

I headed back to my room and crawled into bed. What did she mean by "big day tomorrow"? Maybe I was having another visitor? I was really hoping the kids would come by. I tried to focus on that – and on the wonderful day I'd had – to give the pills a chance to kick in.

"Goodnight, Lill. I am going to try to go back to sleep. I hope we can talk in the morning, Kiddo."

I waited for a response, but when none came, I closed my eyes and surrendered to the darkness. It worked. The pills did their magic, and I fell back asleep.

When I woke up in the morning, a strange thing occurred to me. I had walked right out of my room in the middle of the night to get the pills. Normally, I'd have to buzz, and Herman would come open my door for me. Maybe they'd loosened some restrictions because I was such a good little inmate.

I was hungry, waiting for Herman to bring my breakfast like he did every other morning, but he was later than usual. I thought I should let Lilly know I was awake.

"Paging Lilly Isaac. Lilly Isaac to the murderous father ward."

Nothing. Silence. Maybe the shrooms had worn off and the hospital drugs had reclaimed my brain? Should I take another one? I went into the closet and pulled out the shoe where I'd hidden the extra capsules. I pulled the insole up – nothing. Left shoe? I checked. Zilch.

Did these bastards KNOW? Did they sneak in here in the middle of the night to pilfer my stash? What the fuck is going on?

Then there was a knock at my door. Finally, my breakfast!

"Mr. Isaac. Aren't you joining us for breakfast? You aren't leaving yourself much time," came a very unfamiliar, nasally, female voice.

"Isn't Herman bringing it to me?" I asked, completely bewildered.

'Who?" Nose voice asked.

"Herman. He always brings my meals."

"You're funny Mr. Isaac. Just come for breakfast when you're ready. Your wife will be here soon."

My WIFE? What the fuck? I had a very uneasy feeling about what was happening. I dressed and, without buzzing, opened my door and headed to the desk. The same lady from the night before was still there.

"Good morning. Can I ask what the heck is happening today?"

"Ha. Good morning, Mr. Isaac! I hope you got back to sleep ok."

"I did, thank you. Where's Herman?"

"Who? Who's Herman? Your kid?"

Something was very, very wrong.

"Can you just tell me what's going on?" I was getting agitated.

"Today is your big day, Mr. Isaac. You're going home! But you should go down the hall and grab your breakfast. You don't want to leave on an empty stomach!"

HOME? Ok. Something was definitely, seriously messed up. But… going home? I wasn't going to argue.

I pointed down the hall to my right. "This way to breakfast?"

"You're funny, Mr. Isaac. Yes, that way," she laughed.

Trying to smile (certain my shit-eating grin was making another appearance), I walked down the hall until I caught the scent of food. Four other inmates sat around tables eating bacon and eggs, watched over by a single staff member. She was stuffed into a three-sizes-too-small, navy uniform, dandruff flakes covering the shoulders.

"Good morning, Sleepy Head!" She chirped. It was Nose Voice, the girl who had knocked on my door earlier.

"Good morning. Where do I sit?"

"You can sit wherever your little heart desires, Mr. Isaac. You are the Man of the hour. Mr. Isaac is going home today, everyone!" She announced to the others.

There were a few half-hearted grunts of congratulations, but mostly nobody gave a shit, save for Nose Voice.

"I'm proud of you, Mr. Isaac. We're going to miss your smiling face around here, but you belong at home with your lucky wife. Here. I gave you a extra piece of bacon. I know you like our bacon," she winked.

"Thanks."

"Namaste." She put her hands together like she was praying.

It sounded like she was flirting with me. That was enough to pretty much squash my appetite. I picked at my bacon, eggs, and toast for a while. Certain that some of the avalanche of dandruff coming from her scalp had found its way onto my plate, I decided to head back to my room. On my way, I stopped at the desk to get some answers.

"Hi again. So, what time am I being picked up?" I asked. "And is this a day trip, or am I going home for good?"

She chuckled. "There you go again, you joker. I think your wife is coming to get you in about an hour. Let me check." She looked at her computer. "Actually, she is supposed to be here in 45 minutes. Better get packed and showered. You want to be all pretty for your release!"

Bridget was coming to get me. These people kept referring to her as my wife? Clearly, they were misinformed. I did suspect that I had somehow landed either back in my own reality, or perhaps in a third? I would have to keep quiet until I could get the lay of the land.

Back in my room, I noticed the ensuite was in perfect working order, complete with a shower stall. I didn't remember seeing that before.

Razor and shaving cream by the sink, soap and shampoo in the shower, and a towel hanging on the door, all laid out as though I, or someone else, had been using this room for some time.

I quickly showered and shaved around my beard. I found a clean change of clothes laid out on the desk. I couldn't remember having done that, but I must have. I got dressed and started to pack my belongings into the gym bag I had been allowed to bring with me. I grabbed my clothes from the closet, my extra shoes, and the few scraps of paper and sketches I had on the desk.

When I moved the last piece of paper, I saw my new CD had been under it. Drive By Truckers, Decoration Day, still in its cellophane. My heart sank. I didn't know if Rick was alive where I was now, but the CD he had given me was still here. Suddenly, the joy of the previous day was replaced with devastating uncertainty. How was I going to find out if he was alive? Falling onto the bed, I looked toward the ceiling.

"Are you there, Lilly? Give me something if you can," I pleaded.

Silence. I had no idea if I would be able to contact her from where I was now. Then, a knock.

"Come on in," I said, expecting to see a staff member.

The door opened.

"Hi Sweetie."

Bridget greeted me with a giant smile, and an even bigger hug.

"Hey. It's good to see you," I replied, hugging her back as sincerely as I could.

"See me? I was just here yesterday. But today… I'm taking you home! Are you all ready?" She seemed thrilled.

But… yesterday? Positive I was in another reality now, I relied on my experience with this "jumping" thing to keep calm. I was getting out. There was a far greater likelihood that I'd be better able to understand things out in the real world than in this place.

"Uh, yeah. I think I have everything packed. It's just always nice to see you, Babe," I said.

"Let's get you home Sweetie." She kissed me, and took my hand.

I grabbed the bag that I had packed, and we walked out the door. Completely unfamiliar staff offered their heartfelt goodbyes as we walked by. Some of them even applauded. Dr. Redwood met us at the door.

"I'm proud of you, Allan. You've done so well. Thanks for being a great patient." She sounded sincere.

"Thanks, Doc. Couldn't have done it without you," I replied, though I had no clue what I'd done.

She gave me a very professional hug, and we were out the door. I couldn't remember the last time I had been outside. The day was almost impossibly beautiful. Too beautiful.

"What's the date today?" I asked Bridget as we walked to her car.

"It's the sixth," she answered.

"The sixth of what? I just want to keep the date burned into my brain, 'The Day I Got Out.'" I motioned like I was putting the title on an imaginary marquee.

"Ha. You're funny. It's April. April 6th, Sweetie."

April 6th. I didn't dare ask what year it was, but that was the anniversary of the day I originally quit drinking in 2010. Maybe there was something to that.

"Well. It certainly is a beautiful day. Isn't it?" I said.

"It sure is. It'll be so nice to have you home."

On our way back to Oakville, I needed to discreetly ask some questions – to ascertain what was what.

"I had a dream that Rick and Lana visited me last night."

"Rick? Your brother Rick?" She asked, confused.

"Yeah. My brother. And my sister."

"Ah, that would be so nice, wouldn't it? Oh, well, I guess a visit in your dreams is better than no visit at all, eh? We can visit Lana when she's feeling better. It's too bad you two were in different wards."

Well, shit. Not the response I was hoping for, but it gave me all the information I needed. Rick was obviously dead, and Lana was clearly still schizophrenic. I hadn't been able to reach Lilly. A profound sense of loss was building up in my belly. I was right back where I supposedly belonged... and it sucked ass.

The drive home was quiet. Bridget would occasionally look over at me, squeeze my hand, and smile. Once we got there, my kids and her kids stood to greet me. I had no idea, in this reality, why I would have been in the psych hospital, but everyone was treating me like a fragile doll, like I might break.

After an awkward hour or so, my kids left to go home, and Bridget's kids retreated to their bedrooms. The skunky smell of weed crept into my nostrils for the first time in a long time; I liked it even less now. There was no evidence that any bullets had ever been pumped into the walls. Nothing was hanging on those walls, either. I had to ask.

"Still no art hanging?"

"I just can't bring myself to put holes in this beautiful paint job. Still!" She laughed.

"Babe, I have a question," I said, not at all sure what I was going to ask.

"Of course, Al. Anything."

"Forgive me. I woke up with a wicked headache. I'm a little confused. What was I doing in there in the first place?"

I laid it all out there. Her answer would reveal the map to my existence.

"To be honest, I'm kind of glad you forgot, Sweetie. You just weren't yourself. You were imagining things. You believed people existed who just didn't. Stuff like that. Does that ring a bell? You weren't there very long before you snapped out of it, though. The doctors were good," she explained.

"Yeah. That makes sense. Who were these pretend friends of mine?" I needed details.

"You were convinced that we had an older daughter named Lilly. It was kind of adorable at first, but you went crazy trying to figure out why we were hiding her from you."

My suspicions were correct. I had switched places with that poor sod – Al from the other reality. Fuck my life. If he was back there now, he would have been stuck in psychiatric prison after admitting he killed his dead daughter's fiancé. God damn it. If we had just stayed where we were. I knew what I was dealing with there. I could communicate with Lilly. Could he? I doubted that very much. Could I communicate with her from here? I doubted that very much, too. At least his Rick was alive, and his Lana was healthy. But I got his CD, damn it, and I was glad I did. The guilt was overwhelming, though. That Al would just die from a broken heart if he went back to the mess I'd made in his place.

After Bridget explained why I was in the crazy hospital, she dove right back into her laptop, like I wasn't even there.

"Still working crazy hard?" I asked.

"Crazy hard for sure. Crazy enough that it should have been me in that hospital," she joked.

I felt myself shrinking into a deep nothingness. Here I was, back "home," for less than the time it takes to play a game of Trivial Pursuit, and I was alone. I was acutely alone. My kids could barely look at me when I got there. Bridget's kids hardly even tried to be polite. I was just a nutbar to all of them. Bridget was still deeply in love with her laptop. I was itching to crawl out of my own skin. This, whatever it was, was not home.

"I'm gonna go for a walk, Babe. Maybe enjoy the outside air for a bit. Is that ok?" I asked.

"Absolutely, Sweetie. I have this assignment due tonight. I'll be busy anyway. Oh, it's just about time for your meds, though. You should take them before you go, ok?"

Meds. I had meds I was supposed to take. Wonderful. "Sure. Where are they?"

"I put them in the medicine cabinet in the main bathroom."

"Ok, Babe. Thanks."

I found two bottles with my name on them. The instructions indicated that I needed to take one pill from each bottle, three times daily, after meals. I grabbed a pill from each and went to the front door.

"I'm supposed to take these with food. I'll grab some lunch on my walk," I said.

"Ok, Sweetie. Hey, don't I get a kiss?"

I gave her a kiss on the top of her head and made my way out the door. There was no way I was taking those pills, but I had to make it look like I would. Thinking I might head down to the lake, I walked toward Third Line. But, something made me turn north. It wasn't quite as strong as the pull of the Beast, but it was formidable. I wasn't at all sure why, but I was northbound.

Then it hit me – the cemetery. I'd just watched Lilly be buried there. If there was no sign of that – no hint or clue – then I might be able to convince myself that Other Reality Al went back home to a daughter who was still alive. Maybe time was all twisted up and he could get back before all this shit went down.

My cell phone had been confiscated when the cops took me in, and I'd been without it since. I didn't miss it, at all. I had no way of knowing if other Al had his phone or not, but it didn't matter. I was starting to believe that I didn't even need it anymore.

I hopped on a bus that took me up the road as far as I needed to go. I got off at Dundas, right by the Oakville Hospital. My memories of the place were now filled with bat-shit crazy stuff. Bartender Tom, just across the road. In the other reality, Goodhands was probably in his office right now calling Good Ol' Bridge. Here, Piano Idiot had likely never even heard Merry-Go-Round.

I headed east along Dundas to the cemetery, soaking in the almost summer-like weather. Maybe I could make peace with this place. After all, for most of the time I was gone, the pull to come back was like a vacuum. I should have been happy to be home, but instead, I was going to hang out with dead people.

When I arrived at the graveyard, it took me a moment to get my bearings. Once I did, I made my way back to where I'd just been, at Lilly's interment. As I walked, I reached out to her one more time.

"Are you there, Lill? Things have gone kind of haywire again. I'm just coming here, to your grave, to see if there is any sign from you. Some kind of sign that maybe you are ok, that maybe your real Daddio came back to find you still alive. That's what I'm praying for Kiddo. I love you. I just hope we can all come out of this... happy."

There was no response. I didn't expect one. I was thinking that maybe if I ran into Marvin, I might ask for some mushrooms to open the cosmic airwaves. But, if she was still alive over there, she might not have any memory of me, her second Daddio. And maybe that would be best for everyone.

As I approached where her grave would have been, I was shocked to see a relatively fresh mound – someone had definitely been buried there recently. Curious to see the name of the dead old bastard who got put in the ground in my Lilly's resting place, I walked around to the front of the brand-spanking-new headstone to read the epitaph.

Our Beloved Daughter

Gone too soon, but always in our hearts

Allsion (Ally) Summerville

July 16, 1993 – January 1, 2016

Forever Young

Ally Summerville? That's Ally ODDLY? Oh my GOD...

The dates… they were the same as Lilly's… the exact same!

"What the actual fuck? Ally ODDLY? Jesus Christ. What the hell is this supposed to mean?" I was pulling what little remained of my hair out.

I collapsed to the ground, only then noticing a bunch of yellow lilies on the stone. If I was looking for a sign, there it was. No one, in this reality or the other, was safe from my tsunami ripples. This was on me. Two kids dead in the other world, and now my weird, little friend with the crazy Mama was dead in this one.

I had to get back. I belonged in the other reality. That poor sod – the Al from over there – would be much happier here. He would be crazy, but oblivious to the mess I made. And I'd be happier back there, where things now made as much sense as they ever would. I had triggered one jump. I would have to find a way to trigger another.

There really was no other choice: I would devote the rest of my life to getting back. Something put me there for a reason. That was my place, my home, not here.

"I'm so sorry, Lilly. I'm coming home."

Chapter 23:
Do Not Go Gentle

Well, doesn't THAT just suck? It does. It sucks sooo bad. My Daddio – Daddios, I suppose – both of them were wrapped in a tornado of shit. There was absolutely nothing I could do for either of them. All I could do was watch and listen.

The night of the big switcheroo, Nick and I had been tending to the wounds of his parents' broken hearts, as best we could. Something told me to check in on my Dad. He was sleeping, but all was not well. His body was shaking, convulsing, caught in some sort of deep nightmare.

I couldn't see what he was dreaming, but his shaking got to the point where I was very worried. That's when the weird stuff started happening.

They still hadn't given me a handbook, so I didn't know what happened when people jumped from one reality to another. There was, all of a sudden, a crazy-bright, white light shining from Daddio – coming out from his insides, like his skin was full of bullet holes, and all his light was leaking out. In a matter of milliseconds, there was more hole than skin. He was becoming all light.

I screamed out to him, but he was gone. His bed was empty, for at least a minute.

Then, he was back. But something was very different. This was not the same Daddio. This was my Daddio. The one who could always see me. The one I grew up with. He looked beaten, withered even. Something else was different, too – I could feel that my abilities were growing. I had graduated from Dead Person Pre-School. If I tilted my head just right, and squinted a little, I could see New Daddio's reality too. It was super weird. I could watch two different realities at the same time. It was like split screen TV for the ever after.

My insight into New Daddio's reality was somewhat limited, though. I couldn't see beyond things and people that were directly connected to him. It was like I was looking through a portal that moved with him.

Old Daddio's reality – my reality – was fully accessible. My afterlife was tethered to it. It seemed like the decision makers were giving me some access, albeit limited, to New Daddio, because we had bonded.

My attempts to communicate with either of them were futile. I could hear what they were saying. I could hear what they were hearing. But, neither of them could hear me – not at all. That was super frustrating, because they were both talking to me, asking me questions and stuff. I would answer, but nothing could get through. I tried my best to send them both comfort and peace, but neither of their environments were particularly conducive to those things.

Old Daddio had the more difficult situation. He, too, suffered a terrible headache whilst in transition, and was shocked to discover he couldn't open his door to get something for his pain. When Herman knocked on his door in the morning, Old Daddio had no clue who he was.

Herman was very specific to New Daddio's psychiatric hospital experience.

It didn't take Old Daddio too long to figure out that he was in a different realm, but he had no idea what he could possibly have done to end up in the cuckoo's nest here too.

During his first visit with the Dr. Redwood from this reality, he learned that he was at Juravinski, in the criminal ward, because he confessed – up and down – to killing his dead daughter's fiancé.

That was enough to just about put him over the edge. To make things even less welcoming, Mom visited him that same day to tell him that she was sorry, but they were done. She was back with Dr. Mark

"Goodhands" Ogilvy. She did mention how grateful she was that Daddio took the rap for little Pammy's knife work, though.

Old Daddio cursed the sky. He cursed God. He cursed the Satanic bastard who kept throwing him from one place to another. He cursed whatever version of himself could even have it in him to KILL NICK. For fuck sakes.

He decided that, maybe, there wasn't much here for him. So, instead of swallowing the complicated stew of pills that the good doctors were shoving at him, he decided to stuff them in his cheek like a squirrel. Once the pill pushers were satisfied he'd ingested his meds, he would retrieve them from said cheek, and hide them in his shoe, under the insole, where he also found three mysterious capsules, of which he had zero recollection.

After a month or so of stashing all those pills in his shoes, and making excuses to not ever put them on, Old Daddio asked to take a large bottle of water to bed one night. He had been especially thirsty that day. He waited until the ward fell silent – certain everyone, staff and patients alike – was asleep. Then, he took all the pills from under the insole of his shoe, including Marvin's shroomy capsules, and swallowed the entire lot, in one go.

Within minutes, he was fast asleep. Not many minutes after that, his breathing stopped. By the time Herman found his lifeless body, still comfortably tucked into bed, Old Daddio was already up with me and Nick, watching New Daddio below.

Old Daddio had a far greater understanding and appreciation for New Daddio once he was up with us, and could see the much larger picture. The three of us – Nick, Old Daddio, and I – had front row seats for what would be the long and painful decline of New Daddio.

I no longer had to tilt my head and squint to see what was happening with New Daddio. It was a much clearer picture, now that we were watching on full screen. After he had been to my grave, only to find his Ally Oddly friend buried there instead, he was convinced that there was some connection between her and me. He was right. We shared a date of birth, and a date of death. She was a young lady whose own father had dismissed her, while I was a girl completely forgotten by mine.

It turns out that poor Ally Oddly was also killed in a car crash. She and her mom had been to a Chip Wagon show on New Year's Eve. They both had too much to drink, but Tricia insisted she was ok to drive anyway.

While the accident wasn't entirely her fault, her reaction time was likely compromised. She failed to notice another, even drunker driver barreling through a red light. Just like me, Ally was killed instantly. The other drunk driver, who just happened to be named James Carmichael, was charged. Tricia somehow managed to avoid having to take a breathalyzer.

Beyond avoiding drunky tests, Tricia had some very special powers. She could see things that even I couldn't see from way up where I existed now. She knew, somehow, that she and New Daddio, in some reality, God knows where, were lovers. Somewhere, Ally was New Daddio's daughter. Somewhere... Ally was Me.

New Daddio sensed this too. So, every day after visiting Ally's grave for the first time, he brought a single yellow lily to her headstone. Rain, snow, or scorching heat, he never missed a day. When fresh lilies weren't available, he brought dried ones he'd stashed away.

Brad and Tessa kind of gave up on New Daddio. They saw him less and less. He knew that, in my reality, Brad and Tessa thought he was the absolute BOMB for taking the blame for Nick's death. But here? He was just a crazy man, obsessed with an imaginary daughter.

I wasn't the only reason New Daddio wanted to return to my reality. He wanted to get back to where his other kids loved him, where Uncle Rick was alive – and Auntie Lana was healthy – and where Chip Wagon had a hit song.

So, every day, after he would lay the flower on the stone, he would talk to me. He somehow knew I could hear. He would tell me about his day, his memories, his regrets. He would also, from time to time, say hello to Ally. I had no idea if she could hear him, so I listened for her.

At the end of every one-sided conversation, he made the same promise.

"Lilly, I'm coming home."

Then he would take out his sketch pad and attempt to recreate the drawing that had brought me to life in his original reality. He never did replace his cell phone, so he couldn't sketch on an app, with his finger. Although he knew that was how he had done the original sketch, he hoped to duplicate the same magical properties, and the same result, with pencil crayons on paper. That would be more permanent – not quite so undoable.

Even on rainy days he would sketch, on wet paper. When the pencil crayons wouldn't work, he would switch to pen. When the wet paper would rip and tear, he would draw in the mud with his finger.

One very cold, blustery day, New Daddio placed a dried yellow lily on Ally's headstone, and broke the news to me – Mom had left him for Goodhands. He said she told him that he was still very sick, and obsessed with his imaginary daughter. Goodhands, ever the "comforter," had helped her through the trauma of watching her partner descend into madness. She just couldn't help but fall in love with him again.

After that day, New Daddio spent more and more time at the grave. Eventually, he stopped going to work. He stopped doing anything. He would come to the grave, lay his flower down, and talk… and talk… and TALK. Like I was talking back to him. And he would sketch. He sketched me, over and over again. At first, he was clearly trying to match his original sketch exactly, but when that wasn't working, he started sketching me from all angles. He did his best to remember all the photos Mom had shown him from when I was little. He sketched those too.

The day came when New Daddio just stopped leaving the graveside. He just stayed there. He slept there. He stopped bathing. Eventually he stopped talking, other than to tell me he was coming home, every night before he went to sleep. The less he spoke, the louder his thoughts were to me. I could hear his mind swirling. He would wake up and sketch me. And he would cry. And he would remember. Then he would sketch me some more.

After many days of that routine, one morning he left for long enough to sing on the corner – to earn enough money to buy a bottle of Wiser's Special Deluxe Rye Whiskey, and to get some more sketch pads. He brought that bottle back to the grave, and drank it. And he sketched, feverishly. Page after page. One red headed girl after another.

That became the daily drill until, one day, Ally's mom, Tricia, came to visit her daughter's grave. She found New Daddio there, drunk and filthy, empty bottles strewn around him, and a ratty old satchel with dozens of sketch books containing hundreds, or thousands, of sketches of the same red headed, green eyed girl. She bundled him up, loaded him into her van, and drove him straight to Juravinski Psychiatric Hospital.

Dr. Sarah Redwood checked him in. They got him tidied up and gave him a clean change of clothes, and showed him to his new room:

B116 Willow Grove Unit 1.

All he asked for was a sketch book and some coloured pencil crayons.

He never went outside again. His only view of the sunshine was from a large glassed in room at the east end of his unit. He stopped even trying to walk. His mobility was limited to how far he could roll himself around in a wheelchair. He only sketched. All day, every day. He would finish one sketch, flip the page, and start another. As time went by, the sketches looked less and less like me, until, eventually, they were just scribbles on the page.

He was sick. Alzheimer's, they said. Lines blurred between the real and the imagined. He thought he heard the doctors talking about him having been there for decades. DECADES? He was certain he heard them say "schizophrenia" too. They must have been talking about Lana. No?

The only visitor he ever had was Tricia, Ally Oddly's mom. He did not speak to her, but she would sit with him while he sketched.

The days and weeks, the months and years flew by. Still, he would sketch. From time to time he would look up and say, "I'm sorry Lill. I am coming home. I just have to get this right."

One day, while he was sketching in the glassed-in room, the pencil crayon fell from his hand. He gulped a giant breath, and then, he just stopped.

A young fellow named Herman – who had just recently started working there, and had become rather fond of New Daddio – found him like that, when he brought supper.

By that point, New Daddio was already sitting up with us – me and Nick, and Old Daddio. I had them both with me. Finally, some peace.

They really seemed to like each other. They had an awful lot in common.

Am I Real?

I am the little voice inside your head

The monster underneath your bed

I am the twinkle in your eye

The star you wish upon, in the sky

I am the face you see in a summer cloud

The image of Jesus in a tattered shroud

I am the God you pray to when you feel alone

The joy you feel from an ice cream cone

What if you are just like me?

A fleeting thought in someone's story?

You will never know, you will never see.

Am I real? You read the book.

You tell me

Dave Pomfret is a songwriter and storyteller whose creative journey took an unexpected turn with Lilly, his debut novel. Known for crafting music that captures life's raw emotions, Dave discovered Lilly as a fully formed idea that deManded to be brought to life on the page.

Drawing inspiration from his own family's struggles with addiction, mental illness, and loss, Dave infused Lilly with heart, humour, and a touch of the surreal. His storytelling reflects his songwriter's sensibility – finding beauty in chaos and connection in even the most fractured realities.

When he's not writing with his lady, Michelle Morra, Dave is making music, spending time with his family, or chasing the next spark of inspiration. Lilly is a labour of love, dedicated to those who seek meaning in life's most challenging moments.